Upon A White Horse

Alison Payne

Illustrations by the author
Photographs by Emma-Louise Ogilvy

CANCELLED

'Ride a cock-horse to Banbury Cross
To see a Fiennes lady upon a white horse.'

Chatto & Windus
LONDON

For George, Bleeper, Puppy,
and especially for Catherine

Published in 1989 by
Chatto & Windus Ltd
30 Bedford Square
London WC1B 3SG

A CIP catalogue record for this book is available from the
British Library

ISBN 0 7011 3437 2

Photoset by Rowland Phototypesetting Ltd
Bury St Edmunds, Suffolk
Printed in Great Britain by Mackays of Chatham plc
Chatham, Kent

Contents

Broughton Castle

Foreword

Name two English ladies who made their names in time of yore and on horseback. Magnus Magnusson might pose such a query to an aspirant Mastermind, and I feel sure the most likely initial response would be Lady Godiva – the first of the 'streakers' who gadded about, so the old tales say, garmentless upon a white horse. But without a doubt the lady who really deserves her place in horse-borne history is Celia Fiennes, the greatest British travelling diarist and historian of her day.

Celia's ancestors included some interesting types. One was a signatory of the Magna Carta, one captured the French fleet at the Battle of Sluys and another donated his heart to the citizens of London along with a burial plot still known as Finsbury Square. Enguerrand Fiennes married the daughter of King Alexander of Scotland, and their direct descendants, responsible for the Wars of the Roses, included Edward IV, Richard III, Henry IV and Henry V.

Lord Thomas Fiennes was jailed for collusion with thieves in Kent, and his son, another lord, was hanged at Tyburn for poaching. James Fiennes, the Lord High Treasurer, was beheaded in 1450 by Jack Cade's mob. Twenty-one years later his son William fought for York at the Battle of Towton, in which his cousin Ranulph Fiennes was killed fighting for Lancaster.

A subsequent William Fiennes, the eighth Lord Saye and Sele, plotted with Hampden and Byrn against Charles I in an attic chamber at the Fiennes seat, Broughton Castle near Banbury.

Although this William was against regicide he was a prominent Roundhead activist, and his four sons raised a cavalry regiment against the Crown. Nonetheless 'Old Subtlety', as William is called by Shakespeare, was cunning enough in those mercurial times to retain the trust of both sides and, after the Restoration, was appointed Lord Privy Seal by Charles II.

In 1662 William's son Nathaniel, a Roundhead colonel, had a daughter named Cecilia, or Celia, who was to live through, and record for posterity, a period of social and political revolution which changed British society's ground rules for good.

Celia toured Britain on horseback, often accompanied by a single manservant. She moved easily between social spheres, lodging with aristocrats one night and merchants the next. She was fascinated by the fledgling world of industry, especially by mining, drainage and manufacturing projects. She had a great appetite for facts and small detail. Her journal, which records her travels, is full of minutiae which have proved of great worth to subsequent historians – and many a novelist.

The roads which Celia travelled are far more dangerous today than they were 300 years ago, but this does not lessen her bravery in facing the risks of vagabonds, highwaymen and disease, which were so much a reality in seventeenth-century Britain.

A fascinating aspect of *Upon a White Horse* is Alison Payne's colourful description of today's Britain when viewed side by side with Celia's own observations three centuries ago. Alison's quest in the hoofprints of my ancestress is all the more romantic due to the personal love story which unfolded en route.

The horseborne Alison had to cope with speed maniacs and spaghetti junctions, whereas her mentor travelled in times when wheeled vehicles were a rarity and a coach took six days to get from London to Newcastle. This is a book of wonderful comparisons, and, thanks to the lively and inquisitive eyes of two unique English ladies, *Upon a White Horse* is both an education and a fascinating read.

Ranulph Fiennes, 1989

UPON A WHITE HORSE

The Great Journey

North Sea

Irish Sea

English Channel

Carlisle
Newcastle
Lancaster
Leeds
Manchester
Liverpool
Derby
Shrewsbury
Norwich
Worcester
Banbury
Gloucester
Bristol
Bath
London
Exeter
Winchester
Plymouth

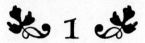

1

The Great Journey

'You bloody damn fool!' my father had exploded. 'Ride round England on a horse? You must be mad!'

Seven months later and I was almost beginning to agree with him.

Few landscapes can be painted in monochrome. Hadrian's Wall on that cold, bleak day was one of the exceptions. Beneath a leaden bank of cloud everything seemed drained of colour. Grey bare-backed hills reared up on either side, flecked with sheep and wreathed in mist. Dry-stone walls snaked away across the moor-land, dark and shiny beneath their varnish of rain. Grey, too, were the stunted bushes and the solitary trees. Greyest of all was the road, that relentless strip of straight tarmac stretching inexorably towards the horizon and beyond. It was 28 July 1988. For the third time that morning it began to rain.

Great quivering drops began to thrum a tattoo on my riding hat and plastic map case. Within seconds my horse was drenched. His mane was plastered to his neck and his white coat was so saturated that he too had turned to grey. Nor were clothes any protection. An almost constant trickle of water now fell from the brim of my hat, past my nose and onto the saddle, where it gradually seeped under my bottom, under my thighs and finally down into my boots. An icy gale was buffeting us with all the intensity of a Siberian wind scything across the Russian Steppes. Never in my life had I felt so cold, so wet or so miserable. Turning my collar up for the twentieth time, I wondered what the hell I was doing there.

*

It was during the Easter of 1987 that I first came across Celia Fiennes.

I was working as an Assistant Producer on 'Blue Peter' and writing freelance travel articles for the *Sunday Telegraph*, but was in something of a quandary about my future. Initially I had enjoyed the BBC, but four years of nine-to-fiving had left me disenchanted with television production. Besides, I wanted to write and travel, and the two were not compatible with 'Blue Peter'. But if I were to leave, what would I write, and where would I travel? Some friends had suggested South America, and it was with this in mind that I began reading Eric Newby's *A Book of Travellers' Tales*. I was just about to turn to the South American section when my attention was arrested by another extract.

It was taken from the journal of the daughter of a Cromwellian colonel, and was the account of a visit to Cornwall. Whether it was the charming, breathless, naiveté of her style, the tantalisingly brief biography, or simply a shared penchant for 'clouted creame' I could not say, but I was hooked. This was the stuff of adventure, and I determined to find out more about this Celia Fiennes. South America was soon forgotten.

The more I read, the more hooked I became. Here was a woman who, in a quarter of a century, had ridden well over three thousand miles. She had visited every county of England as well as Scotland and Wales, and at a time when few people – least of all women – ventured more than a couple of dozen miles beyond their own front door in a lifetime. During her Great Journey of 1698 alone, Celia Fiennes travelled as far north as Aitchison Bank in Scotland and as far south as Land's End in Cornwall – a total distance of 1600 miles. In any age her achievement would have been remarkable.

Why did she do it? What impelled her to spend her life riding round England? My questions seemed best answered by the woman herself. Addressing her readers, she begins her journal with the words:

'Now thus much without vanity may be asserted of the subject, that if all persons, both Ladies, much more Gentlemen, would spend some of their tyme in Journeys to visit their native Land, and be curious to inform themselves and

make observations of the pleasant prospects, good buildings, different produces and manufactures of each place,
with the variety of sports and recreations they are adapt to,
would be a souveraign remedy to cure or preserve from
these epidemick diseases of vapours, should I add Lazi-
ness? It would also form such an Idea of England, add much
to its Glory and Esteem in our minds and cure the evil itch of
over-valueing foreign parts'

I found myself beginning to share her views on this last point. I
too felt her love of England, its customs, its people, its landscape.
But was it the same England that we loved? And if Celia were to
come back, how different would she find it?

Visually, the country would have changed out of all recognition.
Seventeenth-century England was nothing like the landscape of
today with its hedged fields, networks of roads, and agglomera-
tions of cities. It was a rural nation of about five million inhabitants,
the greater part of the country a wilderness of forests, scrub and
moorland. Architecturally, too, the changes would be enormous.
Many of the great houses Celia visited would have been either
rebuilt or demolished. Gone would be the 'pretty neate market
towns' like Prescot, now all but submerged by the conurban sprawl
of Liverpool; and what was once a quiet track from Penrith to
Carlisle would now be the 70 m.p.h. fast lane of the M6.

My own knowledge of England, a country I professed to love,
barely extended beyond a passing acquaintance with a handful of
towns and the roads that linked them. Why not put that to rights?
Why not recreate one of Celia Fiennes' journeys? Why not the
Great Journey itself? One summer of my life would be a small
enough undertaking compared to Celia's twenty-five years. And
besides, what better way could there be to see this country than on
a horse? Slower than a car, faster than a man, the natural pace of a
horse would be the ideal speed at which to appreciate the country,
its sights, its sounds and its smells. From a saddle I would be able to
see beyond the hedges, and not only would I be in constant and
intimate contact with the rural landscape, on a horse I would
become a part of that landscape. There was just one problem. I
knew nothing about horses.

*

'You're joking,' declared Claudia, my only horsey friend, on being told of my plans, a sentiment that was to be echoed by many. Reactions to the ride varied from admiration, to amusement, to horror. Most people, however, simply did not believe me.

When I told my mother, who subscribes to the Are-you-taking-your-lozenges? school of parenthood, she was terrified. What if a car ran into the horse? What if the horse ran into a car? What if I fell from the horse? What if the horse fell on me? And where, in the first place, would I find the horse? For three days she made a concerted effort to dissuade me, until she realised that the strength of her protective instincts was matched only by the power of my resolve.

A somewhat different matter was my father, a retired army officer with a stentorian voice, volatile temper and an inexhaustible capacity for letter-writing. Whether they were tirades to his accountant, diatribes to the Post Office or *billets doux* to Mrs Thatcher, all were dispatched with the same prodigious ease and regularity.

On my resignation from the BBC in November he had written: 'Alison. You cannot bum around any more . . . You MUST get a PROPER JOB with a regular salary. Much Love Daddy xxxxx xxxx PS. Have you read the gas meter?'

It did not augur well for the disclosure of a year's projected penury. As I had expected, his reaction was one of scathing disbelief.

'But why the hell do you want to go and spend five months getting a sore arse?' he kept asking me.

'Because I want to see England,' I kept insisting. But I was scarcely being honest with him – still less with myself. Certainly my initial motivation had arisen out of a curiosity to see my own country. However, my desire to recreate one of Celia's journeys had been no more than a whim, a passing fancy that had appealed to the escapist in me. I enjoyed travelling, yes, but God knows I was not fired by any great *Wanderlust*.

In *Travels with a Donkey* Robert Louis Stevenson summed up what he believed to be the genuine traveller's credo:

'The great affair is to move; to feel the needs and hitches of our life more nearly; to come down off this featherbed of civilisation, and to find the globe granite underfoot and strewn with cutting flints.'

I could appreciate the attraction of such a philosophy. There was a Spartan purity about divesting oneself of the comforts of civilisation and pitting oneself against Nature; but if it came to the crunch and I was offered a choice between the featherbed and the granite underfoot, I was not so very sure that I wouldn't opt for the featherbed.

Had I sat down for five minutes and really considered just what I was taking on, I would probably never have undertaken the ride at all. But I didn't. Instead I handed in my resignation and, with scarcely a thought for the implications, publicly announced my intention of recreating Celia Fiennes' Great Journey. It was December 1987.

Only through the incredulity and horror of others did the sheer foolhardiness of the project really come home to me. People were all too eager to point out my lack of qualifications. I had never travelled outside Europe or for any length of time on my own. I had no experience of organising an expedition of any kind. I had no horse, nor any apparent means of acquiring one. More seriously, I knew nothing about the care and management of horses, nothing about saddlery and nothing about equitation. I didn't even know what equitation meant, and, to be frank, I wasn't sure that I really liked horses that much. If I had thought Celia naive, how much more naive was I? Suddenly, I felt terrified.

Encountering such opposition, most normal people would have abandoned the scheme there and then. With me it had the reverse effect. What had once been a mere spark of an idea was now fanned into a burning ambition: an ambition not so much to recreate Celia Fiennes' Great Journey as to prove everybody wrong. Such was the perverse reasoning that found me seven months later, sodden and dripping, beside Hadrian's Wall.

The rain continued. The only colours now visible in that muted landscape were my hands, a mottled combination of blue, purple and yellow. Apart from an occasional burning numbness, I could scarcely feel them. Nor could I feel the reins which, soft and wet, slid through my clasp like slippery chamois leather. It was now ten-thirty. Another seven hours' riding lay ahead of us. I turned my collar to the wind once more and felt an ice cold droplet of water slowly roll down my back.

Knightsbridge Barracks
to
Hyde Park

Twenty-nine weeks and five days earlier I was sitting on the floor of my flat in Pimlico in the grips of a slow but terrifying panic. It was the New Year. I had fixed my departure from London, appropriately enough, for April Fools' Day, and as yet it seemed I had achieved nothing.

I had never arranged a holiday in my life, let alone a five-month ride around England, and I hadn't the slightest idea where to begin. I knew that I needed sponsorship – both financial and in kind – otherwise the costs of the project would be prohibitive. That meant writing to big companies, famous people in the horse world, charitable trusts – anyone I could think of who might have the vaguest interest in such a journey. Then there was the question of stabling. As far as I knew, each night would find us in a different place, which would entail finding some 150 different stopovers. I had only a handful of acquaintances who lived on the route, and I was far from sure that any of them could accommodate a horse.

Before the stabling could be properly organised, there was the itinerary to work out, a day-by-day route plan which would follow as closely as possible the original Great Journey of 1698. This presented more difficulties. I had no knowledge of maps, still less of navigation. Each question I faced seemed instantly to throw up another six. I would have to write to the various police constabularies, parks authorities and the Forestry Commission, to ask for permission to ride through their areas. Someone had told me that every single local council would have to be informed as well. On top of everything else, I still had to find a horse, a groom, a horsebox, possibly a driver, and learn to ride – all in the space of three months.

It was impossible. Even I could see that. I stared round my flat in blank despair. Now would be the time to admit defeat, I thought. I certainly wouldn't be the first to do it, and I was sure people would understand. I had spent a miserable Christmas worrying about the trip, and now, at the mere thought of its cancellation, I felt as if a millstone were being lifted from my neck. Of course people would understand. They would simply dismiss the project as a temporary aberration and think of me as a foolish girl. How easy it would be for them to pat me on the back and, with a patronising voice, say, 'It's a woman's prerogative to change her mind.'

Well, I was damned if I was going to be treated like that. Besides, I knew that the chorus of 'I told you so's' would echo in my ears long after the decision had been made. And so it was that, out of a mixture of stubbornness and, as my father would have put it, 'rank bloody-mindedness', I put back the start of the Great Journey 1988 to 31 May and set about the colossal task of organising it, step by step.

No sooner had this new date been fixed than a bizarre series of coincidences began to occur. The first was on 4 January. I had written to the Fiennes family to ask their blessing for the trip, and received back not only that, but two rather extraordinary pieces of information. One was that the first ever exhibition about Celia Fiennes was going to be held by The Garden History Society at Broughton Castle that very summer, exactly coinciding with my proposed recreation of the Great Journey. The other was that a reprint of *The Illustrated Journeys of Celia Fiennes*, edited by Christopher Morris, was planned for the final week in May, just two days before I set off.

There was more. 1989, I learned, was the 300th anniversary of the accession to the British throne of William and Mary, and a Tercentenary Trust had been set up to co-ordinate a massive programme of commemorative events and celebrations throughout 1988 and 1989. Nothing could have been more fortuitous. 1988 was the centenary of the first publication of Celia's journal, under the title *Through England on Side Saddle in the time of William and*

8

Mary. Although I still had to finalise all my arrangements and, more pressingly, to find a horse, the Great Journey was quickly adopted as one of the forthcoming William and Mary Tercentenary attractions.

During my first visit to the Trust's office, I happened to mention my steedless plight to the chairman.

'Nothing could be simpler!' he cried, and proceeded to explain that he was an ex-chairman of Whitbread's. Of course I should have one of the famous dray horses. He would organise everything. Within days it was all arranged. My horse was to be Mighty, an eighteen-hand, twelve-year-old shire, good in traffic and as used to pulling the Lord Mayor's coach as a brewer's dray. As to his colour, in equestrian terms he was what is known as grey; in layman's terms he was white. What could be more appropriate for a would-be 'Fiennes lady upon a white horse'? It almost seemed as if the hand of destiny were at work.

I soon grew used to the smirking references to Lady Godiva, and to the snorts of derisory laughter from the more equine of my acquaintances; 'But my dear, a shire's so broad, you'll need a howdah!'

My feeling was that I was in no position to look a gift horse in the mouth, especially as Whitbread's were now promising to hire a horse-box or lorry for us as well. However, there was a problem. Mighty would not be free until the end of April, and I was planning to set out on 31 May. How could I learn to ride in a month?

By mid-February I had decided to ride in aid of a Westminster Hospital charity called START, the Skin Treatment And Research Trust, in which my brother, Christopher, was involved as a dermatologist. Quite apart from my brother's connection, I had been keen to choose START. The charity had only been in existence for a few months, and was pioneering new research into test-tube skin. Fire and accident victims would benefit enormously from the work, as would those with skin cancer, leg ulcers, birthmarks and psoriasis. Despite a £52,000 grant from the Medical Research Council, the charity desperately needed a further £1m to help keep the unit open. I couldn't think of a better cause in which to undertake the Great Journey.

Over supper one evening in February, I had intimated to one of the patrons of the charity that I was not altogether an expert on horses. Sensing that this might be a gross understatement, she quizzed me closely, and within seconds realised the full and awful extent of my ignorance. 'Don't worry,' she reassured me, 'we'll get Tom to sort you out.' One telephone call to her grandson later and Lieutenant Thomas Assheton of the Household Cavalry had been charged with the Herculean labour of teaching me to ride. I hoped to goodness that he was equal to it, for only twelve weeks now separated me from my self-imposed deadline.

Periodic military inspections of my flat by my father had not endeared the army to me, so it was with a mixture of trepidation and awkwardness that I arrived at Horseguards Parade and asked one of the guards on duty to direct me to Lieutenant Assheton's office. As a child I had ridden a few times, but had certainly never experienced the Thelwellian fanaticism that had gripped many of my contemporaries. It was fifteen years since I had been on a horse, and even then I had scarcely distinguished myself – at a pony trekking holiday gymkhana in west Wales I had carried off second prize in a consolation race between three competitors.

'The main thing,' said Tom in an avuncular way, 'is do you like horses?'

'Yes,' I lied.

Less than a week later I was presenting myself at Knightsbridge Barracks for the first of a daily series of 7 am training sessions with the Household Cavalry Regiment.

Much of the preliminary training is conducted in the Riding School, or 'sweat box'. With twenty black cavalry horses wheeling and weaving in formation at the canter the nickname was more than apposite. By 7.15, all the mirrors would be misted by condensation, and plumes of steam would be rising from horses and riders alike. Theory and practice were combined as instruction was conducted from the saddle.

''Ow do you use your seat, Plimmer?' Corporal Major Burns would bark.

'Don't know, sir.'

'Do you blow wind with it, Plimmer?'

'No, sir.'

'What then, Plimmer?'

Being the only girl amongst the troop of twenty men seemed at first to be an unfair advantage. For the most minor faults, the soldiers would be bombarded with invective.

'If you 'ad a sign above your 'ead, it would say "Idiot". What would it say?'

' "Idiot", sir.'

When it was I who made a minor fault, I would be encouraged with a kindly 'That's right, Alison, luv, that's right.' I realised later that this was not actually favouritism. Since my equitational faults were normally major ones, committing minor ones really did constitute an enormous improvement.

The worst part was the early mornings. In the beginning, I hardly needed an alarm clock. Sheer terror got me up in the first week; agonising muscle pains the second, and pleasurable anti-cipation the third. By the second day of the fourth week I was becoming quite blasé. The preceding evening I had even agreed to stay up for a late supper with a group of officers and their wives. Apparently Princess Michael of Kent was a regular rider at Knightsbridge. One Lieutenant Colonel recounted the story of how she had telephoned ten minutes late one morning to say she really didn't feel like coming in, and would he mind? 'Of course I bloody minded!' fumed the Lieutenant Colonel in a rush of remem-bered rage. 'Keeping my men hanging about like that! Damned cheek! I gave her a piece of my mind!'

That night I forgot to set my alarm. There is something about waking up in the dark that always fills me with a sense of forebod-ing. This was no exception. Sitting bolt upright, I forced my eyes to focus on the luminous hands of the clock by my bed. 6.50 am. I couldn't possibly reach Knightsbridge before 7.30.

For a few seconds I searched my mind frantically for an excuse, however flimsy. Then I crawled out of bed, crept to the telephone and rang the guard on duty to say that I was ill and didn't feel like coming in, and would they mind?

'Of course we don't mind, ma'am. You look after yourself, ma'am. I'll make sure the message gets through.' I felt like a real cad.

Whether because of my progress, or lack of it, after a few weeks I was out of the sweat box and riding in Hyde Park. Although I was still under supervision, cantering up Rotten Row was thrilling, especially when the acceleration in speed had been dictated by me and not by my horse, a wilful and cantankerous black mare called Angela. More often than not the initiative was Angela's. Also intoxicating was the camaraderie of the park. From dukes on horseback to tramps on benches, from policemen on duty to Rastas on speed, all were to be found in the park between seven and nine on a weekday morning. There was even a glamorous German baroness, admired from afar by my companions.

'We've all got the hots for her,' confided Corporal Major Burns.

It was now the middle of March. There is a theory, although it hasn't been proved, that Celia Fiennes rode sidesaddle. While I intended to ride the majority of the 1600 miles astride, I decided to try and master this alternative technique as far as I was able. Even if I only rode a little of the way sidesaddle, at least it would be a gesture towards authenticity. Thus one Saturday late in March I arrived at the Hampshire stables of Mrs Betty Skelton, President of the Side Saddle Association, a tiny seventy-nine-year-old with a wiry frame, simian features and a furze of cropped white hair tethered by a hairnet.

Kind, charming and witty, 'Mrs S', as she was universally known, was an absolute martinet with horses and people alike. Simply by clearing her throat she could command the most contumacious cobb to canter and reduce the stablest stable girl to jelly. Despite the long journey down to Andover every week, I loved going there; and while, as at Knightsbridge, my performance rarely did justice to the expertise of my teacher, I was really beginning to enjoy riding.

Another mentor was Irene Benjamin, *enfant terrible* of the Side Saddle Association. Permanently resident at Brown's Hotel, she possessed an ageless glamour and an endless collection of novelty spectacles. Like 'Mrs S' she was tiny and full of good advice.

'Beware of nesting meadowlarks and remember to take a step-ladder. Don't forget the wither pads either – that's for your bottom, not the horse, and take plenty of lavatory paper in your saddlebag. Oh yes – and most important of all, you must remember to stick your chest out and smile. "Teeth and tits," that's what I always say to my girls, "Teeth and tits"!'

With the riding thus taken care of, I felt considerable relief. While I was no great horsewoman, and would clearly never become one, at least I now had a fighting chance of completing the Great Journey. I tried not to dwell too much on my ignorance and inadequacies. With just eight weeks to go they were too horrifying even to contemplate.

Quite apart from the riding, the organisation of the journey was daunting. Lack of experience didn't help and as a result I wasted a great deal of time before locking into the appropriate equestrian, charitable and expeditionary networks. Since that moment of bleak despair back in January I had not stopped writing letters. I wrote to all the big banks, building societies and large companies like Ford, Avis, Trusthouse Forte and Spillers. I wrote to fifty chambers of commerce, the livery companies of the City of London, the Jockey Club, the Turf Club – I even wrote to people like Paul Getty Jnr and the Aga Khan. Most replied with discreetly photocopied standard letters. They were sorry that they could not help, but my project did not quite fit into their charitable brief . . .

I had discovered by this stage that BHS meant not only British Home Stores but also the British Horse Society, and had written to each of the relevant bridleways officers asking for advice about the route. A few did not reply; some excused themselves by saying they were too busy. The majority, however, sent back reams of suggestions and annotated photocopies of Ordnance Survey maps. Their forecasts for the journey were often far from optimistic.

'If I may be critical,' concluded one letter, 'if I were doing this ride I would have been at the planning stage six months ago.'

My letters to potential stablers fell on rather more fruitful ground. I had actually met no more than 2 per cent of the people I wrote to. All the other names I had come by through the most tortuous of connections. Whether they were descendants or successors of people with whom Celia stayed, owners of riding schools, organisers of pony clubs, members of The Garden History Society or friends of friends of friends mattered not in the least. All I cared was that they were based somewhere near the route of the

Great Journey. Amazingly, nearly everyone to whom I wrote replied, saying that they would be delighted to have us. The Earl of Carlisle even promised to have 'a glass of Whitbread ale' waiting for Mighty the moment we arrived. Only one person refused point-blank, adding the postscript: 'Your proposed route is a nightmare, but perhaps you don't mind that.'

Unlike Celia, I had no willing amanuensis to whom I might dictate all my letters. I simply had my Brother. Not Christopher, but an AX-10 portable on which I typed out about twenty-five letters a day, each one more mistake-ridden than the last. By the twenty-fifth my keyboard technique had become so erratic that I would find myself asking the Dike of Grafton for stabling, or thanking Whitbread's for their sipport.

Photocopying was another problem. To have typed out every letter would have been inconceivable, so it was suggested at the START office that I might discreetly make use of one of the hospital machines. The machine in question was situated in a corridor patrolled by terrifying secretaries, who operated a fierce system of paper rationing. The secret, I soon learned, was to locate various emergency paper caches about the hospital and then to time each bout of photocopying to coincide with a lunch, coffee or even loo break. Another means of slipping through the defences was to wear a white coat, but I used this gambit only once, for fear of being asked to deliver a baby or lance a boil. Most of the photocopying was done during clandestine nocturnal raids on the hospital, safe under cover of darkness.

Nor were my activities limited to riding and letter-writing. Whole days were taken up by visits to reference libraries, meetings with potential sponsors and endless conversations with anyone who might be able to offer advice on charitable fund-raising or expeditionary organisation.

By the beginning of April my whole life had undergone a massive change. Curious words like 'pommels', 'leaping-heads' and 'balance straps' were beginning to filter into my vocabulary, and what designer-label clothes I had in my wardrobe were now relegated to the back to make way for breeches, riding boots and hacking jackets. Noxious pink buttock-hardening gels cluttered up my bathroom cabinet, while *Horse and Hound* and *The British*

Equestrian Directory had become my bedside reading. Worse still, my postbag contained an increasingly alarming number of letters with hedgerow motifs and small furry animals crawling up the margins, and I had begun to hear horses' hoofs everywhere.

Any hope of earning my living evaporated. Every day, from nine in the morning until eight at night, was taken up with planning the journey. My one-room flat was littered with maps, books, files and notepads and endless lists of potential sponsors and stablers. Had I realised at the outset the donkey-work that this ride would require, I might never have carried on at all. By this stage, however, there was no turning back. For all the letters I was sending out, I received as many in return, every one of which needed an individual reply, and many of which resulted in prolonged correspondence. Like Frankenstein, I had unwittingly created a monster. After his first tentative steps, each day found him growing in confidence and strength. Now he seemed to be insolently grinning at me from the other side of the room, across a sea of paperwork.

A nervous twitch developed in my left thumb. I began to sleep fitfully, my dreams dogged by the recurring image of a tarpaulin flapping wildly in the wind despite all my desperate efforts to keep it down. One night I couldn't sleep at all, terrified into insomnia because I still didn't know what a fetlock was.

By the second week in April I was caught in a spiralling depression. I had so many letters to get through it felt as if I were writing to everyone in the telephone directory. And there were so many things left to organise: the costume; the groom; police permissions; the route out of London; the route around the rest of the country; 110 more stopovers. A thousand Damoclean swords seemed to be suspended over my head. Then, one Sunday as I was travelling by train to Andover, something happened.

I found myself sitting in the same compartment as three youths, who, sensing that I might provide some sport, began nudging each other, speculating loudly on my age and passing ribald comments on my riding clothes.

'Plenty of experience there,' said one, with mock knowingness. 'Rubber boots!'

''Ere, Tony,' said another, 'pass the paper over and let 'er give you a few tips on the three-thirty. I'll 'ave a fiver on Blue Boy.'

It was impossible to keep a straight face, and soon I was telling them all about sidesaddle riding, Celia Fiennes and the Great Journey.

'You'll 'ave a sore bum!' joked Tony, as we drew into Andover Station. As the train chugged off towards Exeter, I could hear their cries of 'Tally ho!' wafting back to me on the wind.

It seemed like a good omen.

It was now only five weeks until Mighty and I set off, and I knew now that I would never accomplish all the tasks I had set myself before 31 May. This worried me, but I took some comfort from the knowledge that I couldn't possibly be working any harder. Over the past two months I had detected a change in other people's attitudes towards the project. Outright dismissiveness had given way in most cases to at least tacit support. Friends, relations and sympathetic organisations would ring me with suggestions about potential stablers or sponsors, and the START office began to write some of the fund-raising letters. It was an enormous relief to be taken seriously at last, but I was increasingly aware of an added responsibility: if I were to fail now, I would be letting down not just myself but all these other people too. Even my father had grown used to the idea, and had begun to alternate his financial lectures with jocular pieces of advice: 'Hold tight to your chastity belt, my girl. And don't bring any wimps home.'

Bringing anyone home at all was the last thing on my mind. At least until October, the most important male in my life was going to be Mighty. Although Whitbread's had promised him in January, it was not until one afternoon late in April that I actually met him, at the Whitbread stables in the City. Until that moment Mighty had been just one piece of the jigsaw, a necessary component for the functioning of the ride, a concept. Now here he was standing in front of me, eighteen hands of grey shire, a ton of horse. This was no concept. This was a gigantic reality. I couldn't even mount him without a leg-up. I was terrified.

And then Catherine arrived.

'I heard about your trip through a friend,' she said, as we sat on the floor of my flat, surrounded by a mass of papers. The chairs and sofa had long since been submerged under a clutter of books, files and atlases.

'Is that the route?' she asked, indicating a map on the wall. I nodded.

'I'm in management consultancy, but I'm pretty bored. I've been looking for something different to do.'

'Do you think you might be interested then?' I asked, trying not to sound too keen.

'Mmm. Yes. When do we start?'

I telephoned Claudia immediately.

'She's terribly nice, very efficient and enthusiastic and her name is Catherine Bullen.'

'Catherine *Bullen*? Not one of the *Bullen* Bullens?'

'Presumably,' I replied blankly.

'But they're the most famous eventers! God, you're lucky to have her!'

I could almost hear her genuflecting down the telephone. I didn't like to admit that I had no idea what eventing meant, but Catherine sounded a more providential find than I could ever have expected, and I wasn't going to start arguing with Providence.

Nor, it seemed, did Providence have any argument with me. With the incalculable help of a bridleway expert and Celia Fiennes fanatic called Elizabeth Barrett, the entire route had now been planned and the mounted police had agreed to escort us out of London. Moreover, thanks to the Household Cavalry, Mighty was now stabled at Knightsbridge, which meant that I could ride him in the park every morning. During the afternoons Catherine attempted to fill at least some of the legion lacunae in my equine knowledge. By the beginning of May I knew the difference between hay and straw and could undo and clean the tack. Just one week later I knew how to put the tack back together again.

Reactions within the regiment to our outlandish trio varied enormously. One or two of the grander officers thought us quite mad, and whenever they were out riding in the park, they would keep their distance from the lolloping shire. The rest were rather amused by us. Without exception everyone was kind. Ours was a

curious, possibly unique, position within the Knightsbridge
hierarchy. One moment we might be chatting to the colonel in the
Officers' Mess; the next we might be brewing up tea with a trooper
in the tack room. We knew the men had really accepted us when
Corporal Bellringer from 2 Troop came up to us and said: 'D'jew
wanna come to the squadron party tonight? We thought as you'd
been knocking abaht the place so long, we'd ask yer.'

Mighty, on the other hand, had been accepted from the very
start, and soon acquired something of the status of a regimental
mascot. Brawny leather-apronned farriers would wander down
from the forge between shoeings to coo over him and canoodle

with him, while half the NCOs' Mess tried to seduce him into the ranks of the drum horses. He even numbered a general among his admirers.

All the Whitbread shires have stable names as well as official ones, and Mighty's was 'George'. It was agreed with Whitbread that we would use the official name for public appearances, but among ourselves he quickly became plain George.

As the date of our departure grew nearer, I gradually came to know my great companion, and to feel fond of him in the way that one becomes fond of an animal with whose welfare one is charged. I desperately wanted to like him more, but George was a self-sufficient animal, and very much his own horse. My affection met with no response. Nevertheless, from the outset my loyalty to him was total. This was a partnership, and I was determined to try and make it work.

Everything had been going so well that I should perhaps have expected a sudden run of bad luck. No sooner had Catherine appeared, the route been planned, and George been delivered, than my brother's bicycle was stolen from outside my flat, Austin Reed withdrew without explanation their offer to sponsor a costume, and George began to play up.

The bicycle had proved invaluable for travelling to and from Knightsbridge and the hospital, especially as I had no car. As for the costume, that was a disaster. Everyone had agreed that for the promotion of the charity a period sidesaddle costume would be essential for all press calls. George would always draw the crowds and cameras, but who would be interested in just another girl in a hard hat, Barbour and breeches?

George was the most worrying problem of all. One day in the park I suddenly found that I couldn't hold him at all. At first I thought he'd spooked at something; then I realised that he was just being bloody-minded. It took me two hours to get him back to the Barracks, with him snorting and in a muck sweat and me wondering how I was ever going to get him out of London, let alone ride him all the way round England.

Catherine's good sense prevailed.

'Don't worry. Just take him out again and make sure he knows you're the boss.'

I suspect it was more his exhaustion at being taken out again so soon than my horsemanship that calmed George down, but he completed a circuit of the park like a lamb, allowing me time to reflect on how best to solve the other two problems.

In the event, beyond the trauma of having to break the news to its owner, the loss of my brother's bicycle proved not to be so catastrophic after all. There was always the tube, the bus, or one's legs, and Catherine and I soon worked out a rota for using her bicycle to go and feed George when we weren't at Knightsbridge.

Two visits to the theatrical costumier Monty Berman, in Camden, and the sidesaddle costume had also been organised. A businessman with a hard nose and latex features, Monty Berman clearly had a soft spot for good causes, and for the girls.

'A hundred such requests I turn down each week. But to you I cannot say no. Go on! Take it before I cry or change my mind. You're too good a businesswoman!'

A quarter of an hour later I was sitting on the Number 24 bus bound for Pimlico, with a dashing seventeenth-century scarlet habit and an ostrich-plumed tricorn hat on the seat beside me.

Arriving home, I found a letter from my father on the doormat. 'Bugger the ride!' he wrote. 'You NEVER write and although asked REPEATEDLY about your GAS bill, you have NOT EVEN OBTAINED A READING. There is NO EXCUSE.'

Perhaps he was right. But what more could I do? All my waking hours were spent organising the ride and half my sleeping ones dreaming about it. After six months of hard work, patience and endless politeness, I felt I had reached breaking point. I sat down on my bed, and would have cried if I could. Instead, I read my gas meter.

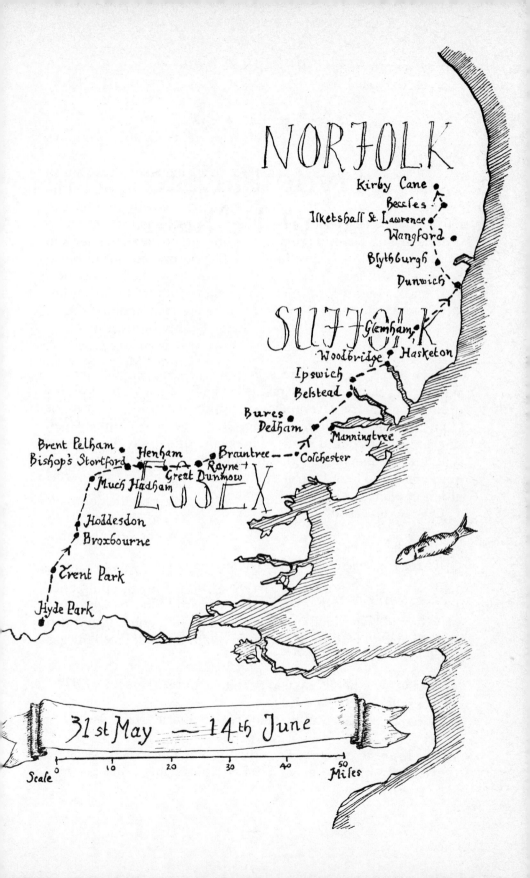

NORFOLK

Kirby Cane
Beccles
Ilketshall St. Lawrence
Wangford
Blythburgh
Dunwich

SUFFOLK
Glemham
Woodbridge   Hasketon
Ipswich
Belstead

Bures
Dedham   Manningtree
Brent Pelham   Henham   Braintree — — — Colchester
Bishop's Stortford   Rayne
Much Hadham   Great Dunmow
ESSEX
Hoddesdon
Broxbourne

Trent Park

Hyde Park

31st May — 14th June

Scale 0   10   20   30   40   50 Miles

'so difficult a way'

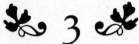

3

Hyde Park to Brent Pelham

A shock of red, a glint of brass, and the creaking, jangling procession swung slowly out of Knightsbridge Barracks to the beat of a drum and a fanfare of trumpets. As the procession advanced across the South Carriage Drive to Rotten Row, the oldest bridleway in England, the skid and spark of hoofs on tarmac gave way to the dull thud of hoofs on sand. An order was barked, the pace was quickened, and to the warm smell of horse was mingled the sweet aroma of plane trees. The ride had begun.

'Over here, Alison!'

'SMILE!'

Click, click, click.

'It's for *The Times*. What's his name?'

'A MIGHTY RIDE INTO HISTORY. The Household Cavalry played a fanfare yesterday as Miss Alison Payne, aged 27, set off from Hyde Park on a 1600-mile ride with Mighty, a one-ton Whitbread horse.'

'MIGHT-y! Over here! Can you get him to put his ears forward?'

Click, click, click.

'*Independent*, Alison. Who made the original journey? SMILE!'

'They are re-enacting The Great Journey in 1698 by Celia Fiennes, an ancestor of Sir Ranulph Fiennes, the polar explorer, and linked with the nursery rhyme "Ride a Cock Horse to Banbury Cross".'

'Over HERE! Over HERE! Big smile for the *Telegraph*. What's it all in aid of, Alison?'

'Miss Payne, a travel writer, is raising funds for the Skin Treatment And Research Trust and will return to London on 22 October via Newcastle upon Tyne and Land's End.'

Beyond the press of photographers and journalists, a cyclist in a pinstriped suit and horn-rimmed glasses had wobbled to a halt. A battered attaché case, precariously balanced on his bicycle basket, toppled to the ground, where it lay unheeded as its astonished owner gaped at the scene before him.

How strange indeed it must have seemed – the splendour and nobility of the Household Cavalry Regiment, plumed and magnificent beneath the trees, and the incongruity of the girl and the carthorse at their head.

And yet, perhaps there was something noble about the carthorse too – in the measured swing of the massive hindquarters; in the muscular power of the shoulders and the flying white mane; in the tossing great head and the huge, dark eyes.

How strange, too, the pantomime that followed, in which, with the photographers in close attendance, the girl was successively addressed by a Lord Mayor, congratulated by a general, kissed by Anthony Andrews, presented with a cheque, photographed holding an Ordnance Survey map, applauded by a group of hospital patients in pyjamas and fussed over by a tiny, glamorous figure in a bolero hat and novelty spectacles, who kept shouting, 'Teeth and tits! Teeth and tits!'

By the time we'd reached Trent Park Equestrian Centre, our first night's stabling, my facial muscles were exhausted by constant smiling, but I felt elated. Thanks to Chief Inspector Andrew Petter and two of his mounted police constables we had been provided with an escort for all seventeen miles of the route, and had negotiated narrow motorway bridges, rumbling underpasses, thundering juggernauts, hissing lorries and deafening roadworks – all without incident. And now, here we were at the northernmost tip of London, sipping tea and posing for the *Enfield Gazette* in front of George's stable, with the time only half-past four and the sun shining on a distant prospect of fields and woodland.

Catherine listened good-naturedly to my vainglorious account of the day's ride. Although she had managed to see something of the morning's spectacle, the lorry, and she with it, had soon been commandeered to taxi the patients back to St Stephen's Hospital in Fulham Road. The rest of the day she had spent leapfrogging us along the route to make sure that we were all right, finally meeting up with us for the night at Trent Park.

'Don't get too complacent,' she cautioned. 'We've still got one hundred and forty four days to go.'

That evening, the proprietress of the Equestrian Centre, Amanda Short, her daughter Gina and the head girl Rhian fêted us with German wine, melon and roast chicken. Exhaustion was gradually lowering my eyelids and my alcohol threshold, so I felt no small relief when the conversation shifted away from the ride and onto Wembley, eventing and the Bullen dynasty. I slept better that night than I had for a long time.

The first of June dawned fine, clear and warm. John Sparks, the groom who looked after George at Whitbread's and who lived in north London, had come to see us off, and by the time Catherine had hoisted me onto George's back quite a send-off committee had gathered.

'Goodbye! Good luck! Don't forget to send us a postcard.'

George was still very worked up from the day before, so I was rather relieved when Rhian said she would act as guide through the first three miles or so of woodland.

Apart from four days spent earlier that month at Betty Skelton's stables in Hampshire, this was the first time George had been in the country, and he rapidly gave the impression that he wished it to be his last. Heavy rainfall had reduced the paths to swampy mires, and George was soon floundering up to his fetlocks, mud-spattered and in a muck sweat. Rhian's horse remained unperturbed.

Once we were back on familiar, dependable tarmac, George calmed down somewhat, his exertions in the woods clearly having exhausted him. Rhian soon turned back, leaving us to continue on our way towards Hoddesdon and our lunchtime rendez-vous with Catherine.

Disaster soon struck. The route which I had so blithely arrowed on my Ordnance Survey map proved impassable at the first bridlepath, where an unhelpful farmer's wife and a cattle-grid barred our way. The only solution was to take a wide detour, past endless garden centres, mock-Tudor villas and pebbledash bungalows with sunburst gates and crazy-paved forecourts. It was horribly clear that we were still caught up in the sprawling tentacles of London. A solid welter of traffic cast noxious fumes in all directions, and the verges and hedgerows had lost their greenness beneath a greasy patina of clogging grey dust. Worse still, George had become desperately sluggish, and it was all I could do to get him to move at all. By the time we caught sight of the lorry in a pub carpark at Broxbourne, our spirits had sunk very low.

On hearing our approach, Catherine emerged from the lorry with a sour expression.

'What's the matter?'

'It's the ramp.'

Back in mid-May, when we had first set eyes on the lorry, neither of us could believe our eyes. Sleek and luxurious, here was the *ne plus ultra* in horse-box design, a seven-ton giant of E-reg Mercedes, a pleasure-dome on wheels. That the manufacturers, Banbury Boxes, should also be based near the Fiennes family seat in Oxfordshire seemed altogether too good to be true. Resplendent in the gold-and-brown Whitbread livery, a tall, dark and handsome exterior concealed a still more voluptuous interior, with soft-pile ceiling-to-ceiling carpeting, velour curtains and, over the cab, a double bed fit for a Turkish pasha. There were enough mod cons to tax even the most fulsome estate agent's powers of description: electric lights, a shower, a lavatory, a radio-cassette player, under-floor heating, a microwave oven, a fridge – everything, including the kitchen sink. There was even a television. And that wasn't all. Step through to the back and there was space enough for not one, not two, but three shires. 'Hampshire, Berkshire and Yorkshire,' as one person quipped; but the real *pièce de résistance*, and what made our horse-box the envy of all who saw it, was the hydraulic ramp. At the mere press of a button, one ton of reinforced steel would glide shut as easily and as silently as if it had been on casters.

'What's wrong with the ramp?'

'It's jammed.'

Catherine had been trying all morning to contact Banbury Boxes and ask them to send an engineer, but without success. To compli-cate matters, an electrical malfunction in the interior of the lorry, meant that the portable telephone couldn't be charged up through the lighter socket, and the batteries were running very low. Not even the sight of our pictures in *The Times* and the *Telegraph* boosted our morale, and lunch was passed in silence.

The afternoon was even worse. We had lost a great deal of time that morning, and by sticking to the main roads I hoped that we might make up at least an hour. But there was another reason for gloom. Any confidence I might have had in my navigational skills had now totally evaporated. At least if we followed major routes, I reasoned, frequent signposts would point us in the right direction.

And so they did, along with a tidal wave of commuting cars, sheer-sided pantechnicons, clanking skip lorries and rumbling cement mixers, each one shaving us that much closer than the last, squeezing us over and hemming us into the curb. More alarming still were the roundabouts. Had the hydraulic ramp been working, I would gladly have forfeited the glory of riding every single inch of the route to load George up and deposit him on the other side of each roundabout. Instead, at each intersection we were caught up in a deafening maelstrom, with Catherine close behind, trying in vain to steer us safely through the traffic from behind the wheel of seven tons of thirteen-foot high horse-box.

From the Charybdis of the roundabout we soon came face to face with the Scylla of a level-crossing. And face to face we remained. George had never been over one before and clearly did not intend to set a precedent now. After twenty minutes of trying to coax him over on foot, I was eventually rescued by Catherine, who had come back to find us. With no trouble at all and much to my shame, she led George across in seconds.

It was now 4 pm. George was exhausted and Catherine was fed up. She had never driven a lorry before, and negotiating it through rush-hour traffic had frayed even her steady nerves, as had her growing irritation at my ineptitude and her frustration at the non-functioning ramp. Above all she was very concerned about George. As for me, I was feeling totally demoralised and impotent. No one felt my inadequacies more keenly than I did, and I was beginning to hate myself for ever having conceived the project.

Eventually Catherine managed to locate Banbury Boxes. One of their engineers had just finished a job in Colchester, and it was arranged that he would meet us on his way back to Banbury, in the main street of Much Hadham.

In kinder circumstances the chequered brick and seventeenth-century gables of Much Hadham would have charmed us, as would the old tiebeams of the palace, birthplace of Edmund Tudor and for eight hundred years the country residence of the bishops of London. In our present predicament, with an exhausted horse sweating on the roadside and a perplexed engineer puzzling over a confusion of electrical circuits, we barely noticed them.

If Day Two was a foretaste of the months to come, how could we hope to complete even a fraction of the journey? Although I didn't give voice to my thoughts, I knew that Catherine shared my misgivings.

Eventually, the engineer rose to his feet. The ramp was now working, but the entire electrical system would need to be over-hauled within the next fortnight. Since we had been asked to appear on 'Blue Peter' the following week, it was arranged that the engineer would attend to the lorry at Television Centre, White City, while we were in the studio.

We were still three miles from Bishop's Stortford, our targeted destination for the day. It required little wrestling with our consciences to decide to load George up and set off immediately for our night's stabling. The extra three miles would have to be made up somewhere else. As we drove to Buntingford, I reflected how in her journal Celia Fiennes dismissed the ride to Bishop's Stortford in just fifteen words. That day it felt as though we had been on the road for fifteen years.

4

Brent Pelham to Woodbridge

A dramatic change in fortune was heralded by the elegant chimneys and pedimented façade of Brent Pelham Hall, and by our first glimpse of its current incumbent, Captain Charlie Barclay, Master of the Puckeridge Hunt, whose opening words to us as he emerged from the pilastered doorway were: 'Whisky or gin?'

Life, we sensed, was definitely looking up.

Two hours later, the traumas of the day had been all but eclipsed by a warm glow of well-being, induced by generous quantities of gin and piping-hot baths. All three of us were installed in palatial splendour and comfort, George on a luxurious bed of thick pile shaving and Catherine and I amidst the chintzed elegance of two guest rooms overlooking a lovingly tended walled garden.

Our introduction to the Barclays had come through a cousin of Charlie Barclay, Selwyn Pryor.

'Charming chap, Charlie. Quite mad, of course.'

Captain Barclay had recently married for the second time, and Selwyn had intimated that for both husband and wife hunting was a keen interest. It soon became apparent that here was no interest, here was fanaticism. Entire bookcases and cabinets were devoted to the display of hunting directories and trophies, while all the pictures appeared to have been chosen not by any criterion of artistic merit, but for the number of hounds and huntsmen they featured.

It was a world that Catherine knew, and she felt at ease immediately. For my own part, I had always harboured the city-dweller's suspicion of country pursuits; the jolly bravura of those hunting types I had met previously had rather intimidated me. I had half expected similar alienation at the Barclays: an alienation that would in no way originate from our hosts themselves – they could not have been more welcoming – but from my own innate insecurity. To my surprise I experienced no such thing. I was beginning to realise that George and the journey for START had provided me with instant credentials to move in almost any circle, and this realisation boosted my confidence enormously. I didn't feel like an interloper, I felt like a guest.

'Got some pretty good billets,' muttered Captain Barclay at breakfast the next day as he glanced through our stabling list. 'Staying with Tony Warre, eh? Get hold of his port. He's not a Warre for nothing. The Duke of Grafton too. Hmm. You'll have to brush up your intellect there. Ah! Cousin Selwyn. You'll enjoy it there. Charming chap, Selwyn. Quite mad of course. I must say, I'm so glad you're staying another night!' he grinned as he tucked with schoolboy relish into eggs, bacon, sausages, mushrooms and tomatoes. 'I'm not allowed a decent breakfast normally.'

My morale was as high as my cholesterol level that morning, for not only was Mrs Barclay to ride with me, so too were the chairman and another member of the Uttlesford branch of the Essex British Horse Society, in what would be the first of a continuous series of mounted escorts throughout the county. For the time being at least I could forget my navigational fears.

When we reached Rickling church, Barbara and Nancy were already waiting for us, twin paragons of horsemanship with their regulation hard hats, matching Uttlesford BHS sweatshirts and polka-dotted neckerchiefs neatly tied at a forty-five degree angle. Both their horses had been immaculately groomed, and both sets of tack lovingly polished. Two neatly-packed picnic lunches in matching Tupperware containers completed their kit.

After a pleasant exchange about pargeting and other architectural matters, the conversation turned to the charity and the subject of fund-raising. Barbara and Nancy glanced at one another conspiratorially, their eyes gleaming strangely.

'You ought to hold people up!' declared Nancy.

'Yes!' cried Barbara. 'Like highwaymen!'

Her eyes alighted on a potential victim standing innocently outside Henham Post Office.

'See that man over there? You just watch!'

After that there was no stopping them. Once Barbara and Nancy had scented the kill no motorist or pedestrian was safe. By the end of the day their bloodcurdling cries of 'Stand and deliver!' had so terrified the population of Essex that my saddlebag was creaking under the weight of well over £60 worth of coins. As we parted company with our two highwaywomen *manquées* at Great Dunmow, I could not help agreeing with Nancy's pronouncement that it had been a 'Smashing day!'

Relieved of the burdens of mapreading, it had been my first real opportunity to enjoy the landscape and to reflect on the changes it had undergone since Celia's day. In 1698 it would have taken Celia only a couple of hours to ride out of London. At that time the population of the capital was between 600,000 and a million people. So small was the area it occupied that the open country between Westminster and the City of London was only just being developed, and as late as Queen Anne's reign it was still possible to shoot woodcock in the area now occupied by Regent Street. Suburbs now regarded as lying near the centre of London were then distant villages. Thus Celia referred to the journeys from 'London to Bednal Green' (Bethnal Green) and from 'London to Highgate'.

Three hundred years later it had taken George and me a good fifteen hours of intensive riding to clear London. Only now, two days into the journey, did I feel that I was in the countryside. Even so, the landscape had a distinctly suburban feel. As Celia wrote of Essex, 'you pass but half a mile ere one comes to two or 3 houses all along the road'. Here was an inviting, cosy, make-yourself-at-Home-County, with gently rolling countryside where prosperous villages of colour-washed cottages and timber-framed houses clustered round ancient churches, greens and duckponds. The villages had once depended on the wool trade for their wealth. Now one sensed that the money came from well-to-do retired couples or commuting executives. All the houses looked freshly painted;

smart estate cars were parked in the drives. I had my doubts as to whether many descendants of the original inhabitants still lived at places like Quendon, Ugley, Henham and Broxted.

The next morning Catherine and I felt rather sad to be taking our leave of Brent Pelham.

'We must take a photograph of Mighty and the girls in front of the house!' suggested Mrs Barclay, her enthusiasm to capture George's image for posterity matched only by her concern that he should not trample the lawn. Accordingly, George was led the long way round, across the yard, down the drive and over the rough grass to the most photogenic spot in front of the house.

'That's pretty,' remarked Catherine, pointing to an exotic-looking sapling with fan-shaped leaves.

'Yes, it's my pride and joy. It's a ginkgo. Do you know, they take simply ages to grow.'

Captain Barclay had finished focusing the camera, and now pointed it towards us with the words, 'Say cheese!'

'Cheese!' we all cried, grinning at the camera – all of us that is except George, whose attention seemed entirely devoted to the mastication of a large green shoot covered with fan-shaped leaves.

'Do you think it was a wedding present from Captain Barclay to Mrs Barclay?' asked Catherine, once we were all aboard the lorry and en route.

'Don't.'

Such a thought was too dreadful even to contemplate.

Thanks to Mrs Barclay's son-in-law Andrew, our team had now been increased to four by the addition of a tiny hunt terrier by the name of Bleeper. Barely six months old, he had been so bullied by the other dogs that Andrew, who looked after them, was only too delighted to entrust him to our care for the summer.

Thanks to an ancestral indiscretion with a dachshund, Bleeper had inherited inordinately short legs for the task of supporting his body, while his terrier parentage had left him so hirsute at the muzzle that he looked more like Yosemite Sam than a hunt terrier. That he was not house- or lorry-trained rapidly became apparent,

as did a distinctly unpleasant bodily odour, the power of which was quite out of proportion to the diminutive frame from which it emanated. But we had already fallen in love with him. Who could fail to adore the tiny little form that now lay with its head on Catherine's lap and its bottom supported by the gear-lever box? Who would not melt at those soft dark eyes?

Certainly not the Rayne Riding Centre, who had volunteered to accompany us on the next two-day stretch of the journey. Not only were they smitten with Bleeper, they quite fell for George, and took endless photographs of him with their Shetland pony, Tarzan. They even tried to talk us into swelling our menagerie still further with the addition of a ten-week-old piglet, Miss Piggy. Bleeper was beginning to develop quite enough porcine tendencies of his own for one lorry, and Miss Piggy looked as if she might well need a second lorry once she had reached full size. With great reluctance, therefore, we declined the offer.

Everyone from the Rayne Riding Centre went to enormous trouble on our behalf, from washing George and cleaning our tack to turning themselves out as smartly as Olympic dressage competitors for our ride to Braintree. Away from the scrutiny of the cameras, I had resorted to wearing breeches and a Barbour. Shamed, however, by the sartorial show of our new companions, I furtively discarded my waterproof in favour of a thin hacking jacket. No sooner had we set off than a great black cloud rolled across the sky to a point directly above our heads, and proceeded to deluge us with one of the heaviest rainstorms of the year. Valiantly we continued, but a further trial awaited us at Braintree, in the form of the local morris-dancing troupe. Over the past few days George had shown himself to be a horse of considerable courage and composure, but whether because of the jingling bells, the fluttering white hankies or the pagan fervour with which the dancers slapped their thighs at every opportunity, George's *sang-froid* entirely deserted him, and it was all I could do to restrain him. As I desperately tried to find a purchase on the slippery wet reins, I couldn't help thinking of the advice of Thomas Beecham: 'Try anything once, except incest and morris dancing.'

The rain continued for most of the remaining journey through Coggeshall, Great Tey and on to Colchester. The Essex BHS had managed the entire route, and now here we were, at the end of our first week, in one piece and riding into Colchester for three nights' rest. Even the rain couldn't dampen our elation.

Over the past two thousand years, the Trinovantes, Romans, Saxons, Danes and Normans have all left their mark on the town, and I had the impression that if the Colchester Borough Council were to have its way the Americans, Japanese, Scandinavians, French and Germans would be taking photographs of those marks for the next two thousand years. The local bookshops, gift shops and newsagents seemed to be overflowing with a plethora of guide books, leaflets and maps, all of which invited the visitor to discover for himself the town's Roman origins. But as I walked round Colchester I discovered little evidence of this earlier occupation. Here and there, sardined between an urban highway and a super-market, I came across the odd pile of stones. However, without having been alerted to their historical significance, it would have been as easy to attribute their presence to the neglect of some moonlighting builder as to the architectural prowess of the Roman Empire. More interesting and more tangible was the Dutch quarter, a part of the town predominantly occupied in the late sixteenth and seventeenth century by Flemish weavers. This was the Colchester that Celia described.

> 'the whole town is employ'd in spinning weaveing washing drying and dressing their Bayes [baize] in which they seeme very industrious; there I saw the Card they use to comb and dress the Bayes, which they call them testles which are a kind of rush tops or something like them which they put in frames or laths of wood; the town looks like a thriveing place by the substantiall houses, well pitched streetes which are broad enough for two Coaches to go a breast . . . the low grounds all about the town are used for the whitening their Bayes for which this town is remarkable, and also for exceeding good oysters, but its a dear place and to grattifye my curiosity to eate them on the place I paid dear'

Oysters are still grown around Colchester even now. But, riding through the town, the only evidence I found of them was the Oyster Fish Restaurant in St Botolph Street. I suspected however that its menu, limited for the most part to cod 'n' chips and plaice 'n' chips, would scarcely have gratified Celia's curiosity.

After a press call at the Garrison Saddle Club and the presentation of a cheque for £100 made out to START by the Essex BHS, George was finally relieved of his saddle and allowed to rest. The last five days had clearly taken their toll, for not only was he still sluggish, he had developed a small lump on his back. Applying a salt-water swab to the affected area, we could only hope that two days of saddleless inactivity would provide the cure. With George thus ensconced at the Garrison, we set off for our own stabling, with Selwyn Pryor and his family at Bures on the Suffolk border.

'Will you navigate?' asked Catherine, starting up the lorry.

All too soon she was to regret her act of delegation. Within

35

minutes we found ourselves up a narrow residential road, lined with parked cars.

'Let's keep going,' I suggested lamely. 'There's bound to be a way out.'

And so there was, but not for us. A ninety-degree corner, also lined with parked cars, ruled out any further progress, as did the considerable queue of oncoming cars building up ahead of us.

Slowly Catherine began to inch the lorry back down the street, past the stationary cars, bemused pedestrians and curious house-holders peering out from behind their net curtains, until she reached a junction where a large skip lorry was parked. Both Catherine and I misjudged the length of the tailboard, and our hearts sank as the purring note of our engine was counterpointed by the unmistakable sound of fibreglass crunching against brake-light. Luckily the driver, who had been having his lunch in his cab, seemed more interested in his sandwiches than his lorry, and we were soon on our way again, marvelling at how Celia could describe Colchester's streets as 'broad enough for two Coaches to go a breast'.

It was Catherine's birthday on the Sunday, so in celebration the lorry was tidied and decorated, and the Pryors were invited in for champagne and 'birthday cake' – a Mars Bar studded with twenty-seven miniature candles. As a memento of the ride, Catherine and I had brought with us a rather beautiful leather-bound visitors' book. In effect it turned out to be a visitees' book, since more often than not the signatories were our hosts. The Pryors not only signed their names, they also composed a limerick, and then offered us a St Kildare sheep and a bantam to accompany us on the rest of the journey. The logistics of keeping a sheep in so confined a space seemed insurmountable, but we leapt at the idea of the bantam. So did Bleeper. Scarcely had the Pryors made their generous offer than Bleeper appeared from the direction of the hen-house with a brown feather clinging to his muzzle and a limp object hanging from his mouth. The Pryors couldn't have been more charming and philosophical about the episode, but the idea of taking a pet bantam aboard was quietly dropped.

By Monday George's back hadn't improved. We were expected

at the 'Blue Peter' studio in White City that afternoon, so a vet was hastily called to look at the swelling and to decide whether it warranted cancelling our appearance. He thought not, but recommended that the sore be treated with Lasonil and that a piece of foam with a hole cut out of it be placed over the lump to minimise the pressure from the saddle.

Although we had set off in fairly good time, neither Catherine nor I had anticipated the tailbacks all along the A12, so it was not until three-thirty that we finally arrived. Since asbestos dust had been found in the usual 'Blue Peter' studio at White City, the programme had been relocated to a second-floor news studio a mile away at Shepherd's Bush. George would have to travel in the scenery lift.

'Don't worry, darling,' gushed Biddy Baxter, the editor of 'Blue Peter'. 'It's taken an elephant before now!'

Thanks to the foam rubber pad, both run-through and transmission went very smoothly, despite the laxative effect of the studio lights on George. Even Bleeper, whose chastisement after the bantam episode had left him more sheepish than the St Kildare, perked up and behaved on screen as if he had been a media personality all his life.

The sense of achievement was rather coloured afterwards by George's antipathy towards a second journey in the scenery lift, and by the discovery that two engineers from Banbury Boxes had spent the last four hours waiting for us in the Television Centre carpark at White City. Once both horse and men had been placated, and the overhauling of the lorry indefinitely postponed to a more convenient moment, we loaded up George and set off back to Colchester.

The next day saw a deterioration in George's back, so it was decided that I would ride not on a saddle but on a blanket tethered by an elasticated girth. This was the first time I had ever ridden bareback, and within a quarter of an hour I had slithered off twice. Suffering nothing worse than a severe case of grass staining on my breeches, I climbed back on and continued the ride to Dedham, a village of timber-framed and Georgian buildings. Constable attended the local grammar school in the late eighteenth century, and immortalised the pinnacled church of St Mary in the main street in many of his paintings. Tied up outside while Catherine went to admire the interior, Bleeper decided to immortalise the church in his own particular way, much to the chagrin of one parishioner armed with a bunch of chrysanthemums and a deadly-looking pair of secateurs.

'I hope you are going to clear this up,' she hissed, her glowering expression presaging the most terrible nemesis should Bleeper ever darken St Mary's doorstep again.

That Bleeper was growing up fast became abundantly clear while we were staying with our next hosts at Manningtree, who owned a particularly sleek and beautiful greyhound called Sadie. Bleeper's puppyish antics soon gave way to such forceful amorous advances that Catherine and I felt it best to separate the two dogs, for fear that Bleeper's ardour might overcome any logistical problems arising from the difference in height between him and Sadie. Our hostess, I believe and hope, was quite oblivious to the attempted rape going on in her front garden.

Unflagging hospitality every evening and George's immense appetite were taking their toll on Catherine. Five feeds slotted around eight hours of riding meant that George had to have breakfast not just at 8 am, but at 5 am as well. By the end of the first week she was exhausted. More and more it was she who was having to shoulder all the responsibility of the ride. Once the task of organising it was over, I had been only too happy to take on a more passive role. While I simply sat on George's back all day, occasionally steering, Catherine had the worry of looking after not only George and the lorry, but me as well. More than that, although our hosts would welcome us both warmly, as initiator of the project I was the one who was singled out for special treatment. It was I who would be put in the best guest room and to whom the majority of remarks would be addressed, and it was in my experiences that they would be most interested. Had our roles been reversed I'm sure I would have felt indignation and frustration. It is a great tribute to Catherine that she exhibited neither.

Once we reached Suffolk, things seemed to improve. Without escorts, I was left to my own navigational devices, and found that my mapreading was really quite passable. Catherine had brought her bicycle and would ride alongside me chatting while a rather terrified Bleeper lay in the pannier, ears flapping in the wind.

North of the finely etched silhouette of Manningtree and the grey wash of the Stour estuary, flatness gave way to undulating lushness. Clouds of shimmering white butterflies danced about the hedgerows while cornfields disappeared amidst a swaying red mass of poppies, as if Jackson Pollock had passed by, his paint-brush dripping with scarlet.

For the first time I felt really relaxed, at one with the landscape and united in fellowship with Catherine, George and Bleeper. Our five-minute appearance on 'Blue Peter' had also created another bond, for every child we passed would giggle in delighted recognition at the 'white horsey and the little doggy', while carloads of blue-rinsed ladies would wave at us with beatific smiles. Although I had worked in the world of television for years, only now did I realise what a rarefied existence it had been. I had grasped the basics of camera angles, light exposures and editing techniques, but I had lost touch with the basic reason for my craft: the viewer. I had forgotten that peculiar alchemy whereby a person addressing a small, purple, studio eye could be transported across the ether to the sitting room of a Scilly Isles tomato grower and the kitchen of a Hebridean sheep farmer in the same split-second. I had forgotten the almost religious fervour with which most people still regarded the box in the corner of their living room. The memory of the viewing public is reputedly short. Here, I thought, would be an opportunity to test that theory. Perhaps six million people would have seen us on 'Blue Peter', more than the entire population of

England in 1698. How many of them would remember us by the
end of our five-month journey?

At Belstead, just south of Ipswich, we stopped to say hello to a
gathering of old-age pensioners at the village hall.

' 'E's a right booty. Would 'e loike a bidof sugar?'

While they patted George and spoke nostalgically of the days of
the Suffolk punch, a cross-eyed man called Nigel, who had been
painting an impressionistic view in purple of a distant copse, asked
if he might paint George.

'I love horses!' he cried, and set to work in blue and yellow on an
equally impressionistic rendering of George.

It felt good to be in the country, to hear a different accent and to
have left London and the manufactured rusticity of Essex far
behind us. Towards the end of the day I felt in such a good mood
that I wanted to share it. Vodafone had sponsored the journey by
lending us portable telephones for both the lorry and my saddlebag. While Catherine and I had agreed not to abuse Vodafone's
generosity, and to use the telephone only for business relating to
the ride, I couldn't help showing off this marvellous new acqui-
sition. Much to my annoyance, everyone I rang was out, but I had
an interesting exchange with the switchboard at St Stephen's
Hospital, where my brother was working.

'No one answering on that extension,' came the bored reply,
then, 'Hey, can you hear a horse in the background?'

'Yes. I'm on it.'

'You're on it?'

'Yes.'

Click.

It was still only the beginning of June, but our reprieve from the
bad weather proved a short one. At Ipswich the following morning
our press call at Christchurch Park would have been very dispirit-
ing had it not been for the beauty of the mansion and its gardens
and the presence of a class of anoraked children from Ipswich High
School, who had braved the rain to see us on our way.

In the sixteenth century, Thomas Tusser, the agricultural writer
and poet, thought Ipswich a rival to paradise. A century later, Celia

Fiennes found it 'very clean' but 'a little disregarded and by enquiry found it to be thro' pride and sloth'. On that inhospitable June morning, I thought the town centre uninspiring and grey, the victim not of pride and sloth, but of ruthless town planners and a vicious one-way system.

My companion for the next stretch of the journey was Ken, a cinema projectionist from Ipswich who rode western-style, dressed in a stetson, cowboy boots and a red-and-blue anorak that had clearly never seen the inside of a washing machine. Equally filthy was his horse, Merlin, a name inspired by Rolls-Royce technology rather than Arthurian legend. Ken took a keen interest in the Great Journey, and after a few minutes withdrew from his pocket a somewhat crumpled and Marmite-smeared cutting entitled 'Charity Horsewoman in Essex', which he had cut out for me from the *Suffolk Star*.

As we neared Woodbridge, Ken decided to take the scenic route, only to lose his bearings up a tiny high-banked lane overgrown with briars and lush, dripping vegetation. As we puzzled over the map, I discovered that he and I had a lot in common when it came to navigation.

'You've got to look at it the way you're going, never mind whether it's upside down or not. That way what's left is left and what's right is right. You're lucky you're travelling north.'

Ken's theories on horology were even more unorthodox. When I asked him what the time was, he replied 9.32, even though it was 11.32, explaining that although he had owned the watch for some years he hadn't yet worked out how to programme it to read the correct time. Another watch of his, by contrast, kept perfect time on his wrist, but would lose twenty minutes every hour if he put it down his trousers. I was going to suggest he might try the trouser treatment on his other watch, but thought better of it.

Somehow we managed to reach Hasketon at lunchtime as arranged. George, who had refused both his breakfasts, now took no interest in his lunch. He looked very listless, and seemed to be wasting away even as we looked at him. There was clearly something seriously wrong which required the attention of a vet. Leaving Ken and Merlin at Hasketon, we loaded George into the lorry and drove him to Philip Ryder-Davies at Woodbridge, a big burly man with muttonchop sideboards and a braying laugh who, by coincidence, had spent some time a few years earlier looking after the Whitbread shires in London.

George stood patiently as the vet peered, poked and prodded. After a quarter of an hour Philip said he was afraid George might have the beginnings of azoturia, an equine complaint that caused a stiffening of the limbs and sometimes proved fatal. If it wasn't that, then George had suffered what could only be described as a minor nervous breakdown caused by the shock of so strange and irregular a lifestyle. In any event, George's diet would have to be radically changed, his feed supplemented with electrolytes to replace lost nutrients and the ride indefinitely postponed. It couldn't have been worse news.

'ordinary people'

Woodbridge to Wangford

Under the circumstances the best plan seemed to be to take George directly to his next stabling, so we loaded him up and set off in the driving rain along the A12. Our destination was Glemham Hall, owned since 1923 by the Cobbolds, an East Anglian brewing family. It had been arranged that George would be stabled on the estate's farm, and here we made him as comfortable as we could before presenting ourselves at the hall. A curving sweep of drive soon revealed an enormous house with Elizabethan and Palladian styles apparently thrown in at random. The eighteenth-century facelift, with its sentinel-like rows of sash windows, could well have been disastrous, had it not been for the softening influence of a luxuriant ivy and the warm and subtle colours of the Suffolk brick, which made the effect quite pleasing.

For many years the hall had been owned by Lady Blanche Cobbold, a daughter of the ninth Duke of Devonshire and a powerful matriarchal figure. Whilst dancing with one young man at a ball given at Glemham, she is reported to have said: 'Of course it is terribly difficult holding a ball like this at Glemham.'

'Oh, yes, I'm sure it must be,' replied the young man, 'so many rooms.'

'No, no, my dear, not enough rooms. It's terribly cramped here after Chatsworth.'

Tall and birdlike, with an air of whimsical elegance and a finely tuned wit, it was her son Patrick who now owned the Hall and who welcomed us on our arrival. Since continuing the journey for the

43

time being was out of the question, he immediately suggested that rather than move on to the next night's stabling as scheduled, we should stay at Glemham until George was better. It was a generous offer, and in the light of George's condition, one which we were hardly in a position to refuse. The next morning we telephoned Whitbread's to break the news about George. Both Catherine and I had been afraid that they might whisk him back to London, but they seemed satisfied to hear that he was under the supervision of Philip Ryder-Davies, and even joked that their drayhorse had been 'nobbled by Cobbolds'.

It is a strange truth that adversity unites, and Catherine and I became much closer during the days we spent at Glemham. I couldn't help but admire her pragmatism and capable approach to life, and when she suggested that if George were unable to continue we should complete the journey by bicycle, I could have hugged her.

On the Saturday Patrick Cobbold gave us a tour of the house and garden.

'I always think kitchen gardens are a bore,' he said, as we walked through an avenue of Irish yews towards the brick-walled rose garden. 'Much easier to go and buy a cabbage.'

During the war a group of nine-year-old evacuees from London had probably played in that very avenue, for they had been sent to Glemham to escape the Blitz. At a local shoot, however, some of them were unfortunately mistaken for rabbits. All the children were summoned back to London by their anxious mothers, who felt that their offspring would be safer dodging the German bombers than the guns of Glemham.

The house yielded up all sorts of treasures, from fine Oriental porcelain to exquisitely lacquered cabinets and Queen Anne chests inlaid with intricate marquetry and delicate geometrical designs.

'The birds get in during the summer, which is a bit of a nuisance,' explained our host as we ascended the great staircase lined with gilt-framed and guano-spattered pictures. Upstairs was more chinoiserie, a rather fine crayon portrait of Patrick Cobbold's grandfather – 'He died of hiccups' – and an enormous howdah-like four-poster bed, canopied in chintz and situated to our surprise in the ballroom.

In one of the maids' rooms on the third floor he pointed out a Davy escape, an antediluvian contraption by which a person could be lowered to the ground from an upstairs window in the event of fire. Apparently Patrick Cobbold's father had once tried to test the efficacy of this device, using his daughter as a guinea pig. Peering through the window at the forty-foot drop below, our host added thoughtfully: 'She's still got a gammy leg.'

The real jewel in Glemham's crown was tucked away in an unprepossessing corner of the house. Behind a small door in one of the upstairs corridors, in a space no bigger than an airing cupboard, was the most superb collection of potties – row upon row of them, in every conceivable shape, size, colour and material.

'Of course they're not used now,' added Patrick Cobbold, shutting the door with a serious expression.

George's appetite still hadn't returned, but under the tender supervision of Mrs Adlam, the farm manager's wife, he did manage to eat some baby calf mix. He was also responding well to the electrolytes and to being allowed to graze for up to two hours a day. On Saturday another vet from Philip Ryder-Davies' practice came to see him, and he brought the excellent news that the test for azoturia had proved negative. It was now a case of simply letting George recover in his own good time. The showmix, pony cubes and bran were all dropped from his diet. From now on he was to eat oats, barley, sugar-beet, chaff, and plenty of hay and grass whenever possible. Gone also were the two breakfasts. He would continue to be given five feeds, but the 5 am one would now be moved to the evening. Catherine and I were relieved beyond measure, and asked the vet to stay for tea in the box. A tiny ex-jockey with a bemused expression and a leprechaunish manner, he accepted our invitation with alacrity, and within minutes had consumed half a packet of biscuits. Fearing that he might not have eaten for some time, we offered him the other half, which disappeared with similar rapidity, as did two packets of crisps and a Mars Bar.

His capacity for food was clearly matched by his skill as a vet. By the next day George was looking better, and had even managed to eat a little. This called for a celebration, so we invited Patrick

Cobbold into the box for a lunch of bread, cheese and Cup-a-Soup. He had just been to a meeting at Ipswich Town Football Club, of which he was chairman, and as soon as he entered the box he took from his pocket a small floral-print paper bag.

'I've brought you both a present.'

Inside were two pairs of skimpy white nylon knickers bearing the legend 'I've scored at Portman Road.'

'It's one of those jokes one thinks is frightfully funny when one has had a good lunch,' he said in a rather embarrassed way. But no explanations were necessary. Within seconds the knickers had been pinned up in a place of honour on the wall.

On Sunday it was agreed that we should move to our next stabling just south of Beccles, with a certain Charles Stewart. Again, this had been arranged through someone else, and my only contact with Charles Stewart had been by telephone, when he had come across as a rather charmless and reclusive bachelor in his fifties, with about as much idea about horses as I had.

'Don't worry about the feed,' I had said, 'we'll bring it with us.'

'No, please don't. There'll be plenty in the house for you and Catherine to eat.'

That lunchtime we had been asked to take George along to the Butcher's Arms, a Whitbread pub in Beccles. After posing in costume with him for the local press I hitched up my train, slung it over one arm and strode into the bar with Catherine and two START collecting tins. A few minutes later we had raised £25 and a few eyebrows.

'Blimey! You look just like Margaret Lockwood in *The Wicked Lady* – pass the tin.' It takes a certain personality to enjoy collecting money. While Catherine and I met with moderate success in most cases, neither of us relished the task, never quite managing to conquer those feelings of rejection when people refused to give. Somehow being in costume made it worse, especially when I didn't have eighteen hands of horse to distance me from the people whose money I was requesting. The wisecracks were usually amusing, and I would always laugh back. Deep down, however, I found them rather embarrassing.

It was with some relief, then, that we set off from Beccles to

Charles Stewart's farm near Wangford. A long potholed drive led to a number of farm buildings, overgrown outhouses and a red-brick farmhouse outside which were parked an ancient pickup truck, a rusting Austin, a filthy Nissan Patrol, a large slug-shaped Rover and a Rolls-Royce with running-boards and lamps like frog's eyes.

Knocking on the door, we were surprised to find it ajar, and walked inside to discover a cluttered kitchen full of knick-knacks, antiques, prints and photographs. A number of the photographs featured a man with grey hair and a misanthropic expression, whom I took to be Charles Stewart. After calling up the staircase a few times it was clear that he wasn't at home. Catherine and I thought this behaviour rather off-hand, especially as we had explained to him on the telephone how ill George had been, and that he needed as much rest as possible. Looking around outside we could find no stable, so Catherine suggested that I ride George for half an hour or so while we waited for our host to return.

I had been riding along the road for about twenty minutes when a car drew up alongside.

'You must be Alison. I recognised you by the horse.' The door opened and out stepped not the irascible quinquagenarian of the photographs but a pleasant-looking young man in his early thirties.

'Hello! I'm Charles Stewart.'

Charles turned out to be quite the best fun of anyone we had stayed with, and also one of the most interesting. Apart from being a farmer, he was an historian and was studying with the Open University for a Ph.D in Astrophysics while writing a novel about an obscure mythological character called Erichthonius. He also claimed an interest in cooking, but as the only evidence of his culinary expertise we tasted was a horribly tough piece of venison, we decided that his aspirations exceeded his abilities, and that in this respect at least he was refreshingly normal. Two of Charles' other interests were shooting and champagne, and after supper one evening he suggested that we have an impromptu shooting contest. Lining all our empty champagne bottles along his garden wall, we each took it in turns to try and hit them with his 12-bore pump-action shotgun. Once all the bottles had been smashed, we graduated to moving targets, using a child's wellington boot and an old washing-up bowl as clay pigeons. Two hundred and fifty cartridges later and Catherine and I were passable shots.

During this time I managed to fit in seven hours' riding a day. Suffolk seemed isolated from the rest of England. It wasn't on the way to anywhere, and little seemed to happen apart from the extensive cultivation of sugar-beet, wheat and barley. Sometimes I would ride for hours and see no one, the only signs of life being the aerial antics of terns and waders or the wind rasping mysteriously through the dry heather and bracken.

Most mysterious of all was the tiny village of Dunwich. Once it was the capital city of the ancient kingdom of East Anglia. A major shipbuilding centre and supplier of royal galleys, it was cited in the *Domesday Book* as having a population of four thousand. But storms struck it again and again, causing continual flooding and erosion, and over the years one of the east coast's busiest towns was reduced to a handful of cottages, a beach café, an inn and a general store. The last of Dunwich's nine churches disappeared into the sea earlier this century, and fishermen say that on a neap tide, when the wind is in the east, they can still sometimes hear the tolling of the bells of the nine churches.

One day George and I followed a sandy coastal track north of Dunwich. The shambling, shimmering outline of the town was still visible behind us, while all that separated us from the grey haze of the sea was a herd of sleepy cows. Then the track turned sharply west and we found ourselves beneath a canopy of ancient trees in the shadowy cool of Dunwich Forest. The paths were all clear, but to either side great trunks lay slowly rotting amid the living vegetation, casualties of the hurricane of October 1987.

Passing a car parked deep in the forest, I suddenly realised how safe I felt. Had I been alone, seeing a car in such a desolate setting might have made me slightly uneasy. After all, in so dense a forest who would hear my screams if the driver turned out to be a psychotic rapist? On George, however, I felt as though nothing could harm me, and I hoped that in time I might inspire similar confidence in him.

Charles and Catherine were waiting to meet us at Blythburgh

church, where we spent lunch lying on the grass eating cheese and ham rolls and taking it in turn to hold George's rope while he grazed. As with so many of the places we had seen in Suffolk, the magnificence of Holy Trinity church seemed quite disproportionate to the size of the surrounding village, whose population in 1988 could not have numbered more than four hundred people. Rising from the marshy estuary of the River Blyth, the church seemed to float on the glistening mudflats like a great liner. Oliver Cromwell and his henchmen had shown little respect for the beauties of Blythburgh's cathedral of the marshes, and in 1644 they set about the systematic destruction of the church. Hundreds of bullets were fired into the heavy oak doors, and hundreds more into the carved wooden angels high above in the roof, pitting the serene faces with a pox of musket shot. Brasses were removed from tombstones and statues were destroyed. The remains of tethering rings in the pillars of the nave and trampled brickwork in the flooring below show where the riders tied up their mounts in the church.

I was curious to know the origin of some clawmarks on the south door and, finding no commentary in the guide book, asked Charles.

'Them be the marks of Black Shuck, the devil dog,' he replied, rolling his eyes in mock horror. 'They do say in these parts that he's thirteen foot high or more, with glowing luminous eyes and that he roams the marshes preying on human flesh, especially that of girls riding round England for charity . . .'

'At least he only *scratches* at church doors,' chipped in Catherine drily as she tickled Bleeper's tummy. Even if Bleeper had forgotten his indiscretion at Dedham, Catherine had not.

I mentioned to Charles how very insular Suffolk had struck me as being. He agreed, adding that he knew of one cowman who had always lived within a mile of his place of birth. The man had never been out of Suffolk, and his mother, who had died just two years earlier, had never seen a traffic light. 'But then, who's to say they're any more insular than you or me?' said Charles.

I was about to contradict him, but stopped. In the past I had always thought of myself as having a very broad outlook on life. Now I was not so sure. When I really considered it, my world was in fact rather small. I had gone directly from school to university and then to the BBC. All my friends dated back to those university days and were of the same age and background as me. Most worked in similar jobs. Even moving to my home – a one-room flat in Pimlico – had in no way extended my horizon. Beyond a next-door neighbour who looked after my spare key, the local grocer and the launderette attendant, I knew no one. The cowman may never have been to London, but was his world really any smaller than mine?

That afternoon we visited the county primary school at Ilketshall St Lawrence, where we were greeted by a score of seven-year-olds.

'Cor! He's big!'

'Can we pat him?'

'How many joints does a horse have?'

'How big is the biggest horse in the world?'

'Is Mighty the biggest horse in the world?'

The questions came from every direction, giving me no chance to answer, but eventually I was able to take advantage of a split-second pause following one little girl's question:

'What's it like up there?'

'It's lovely.'

'Why?'

'Because you can see everything.'

'What can you see?'

'Well, right now I can see your heads. I can see for example who's bald . . .'

This met with a wave of titters.

'. . . or if you've got dandruff . . .'

'I've got dandruff!' cried one little girl proudly.

'So have I!'

'Me too!'

'And me!'

Within seconds the air was filled with a chorus of piping voices, as every single child claimed to have dandruff.

There was more evidence of the Cromwellian occupation of East Anglia at Kirby Cane, a tiny village with a tenth-century round-towered flint church and a fine seventeenth-century hall with a Georgian façade. We had stopped on a farm track and, poring over my map to find our next turning, I hadn't noticed the approach of a dashing, military-looking figure wearing a regimental stable belt and an expression of proprietorial indignation.

'Can I help?' he asked pointedly.

On hearing about the Great Journey and all the people we had stabled with so far, he soon softened and introduced himself as Simon Crisp, an ex-squadron leader in the Household Cavalry, and proceeded to escort us across his land, shortening our journey and increasing our local knowledge considerably. En route he pointed out the longest barn in Norfolk, which had, like Blyth-burgh church, served as a stable for Cromwell's cavalry while Cromwell himself was supposed to have stayed at Kirby Cane Hall.

'I say. You're not going to write a book about all this are you?' he suddenly asked.

'Well, yes, actually, I am,' I replied.

'Oh, good! You will put us all in won't you? You know, me, the Cobbolds, Charles Stewart. No need to worry about libel or any-thing.'

As it was our last evening with Charles, Catherine and I decided to take him out to dinner, so the three of us drove to a restaurant in a nearby village. The place was empty and the meal was awful. The scallops were rubbery and cold as pickled eyeballs, the wine was tart and the vegetables as canned as the music, but it was surpri-singly enjoyable, especially when Charles suddenly stood up and exclaimed, 'Let's dance!'

It was well after one by the time we left. I drove back home across the marshes while Charles operated the foot brake. Catherine just sat in the back of the car laughing.

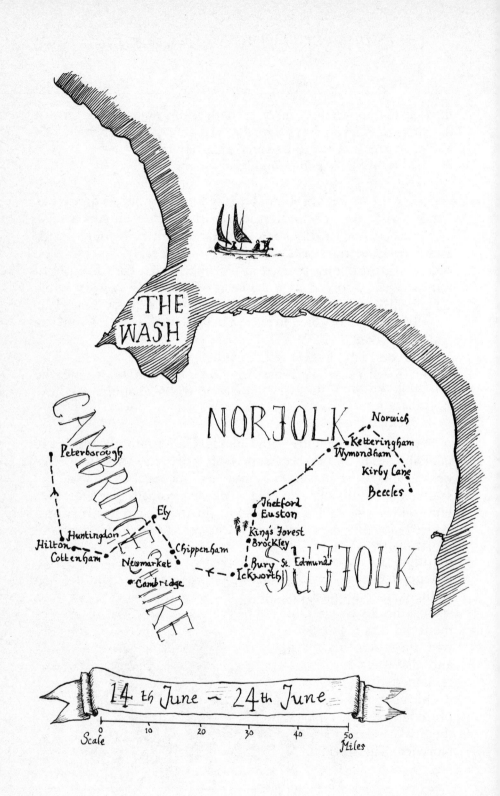

THE
WASH

CAMBRIDGESHIRE

NORFOLK

Norwich
Ketteringham
Wymondham
Kirby Cane
Beccles

Peterborough

Ely

Thetford
Euston

King's Forest
Brockley

Huntingdon
Hilton
Cottenham
Newmarket
Chippenham
Cambridge

Bury St. Edmunds
Ickworth

SUFFOLK

14th June ~ 24th June

0   10   20   30   40   50
Scale   Miles

52

6

Wangford to Newmarket

'and so to Norwich . . . which is walled round full of towers, except on the river side which serves for the wall; they seeme the best in repaire of any walled citty I know . . . there is a very large Market place and Hall and Cross for fruite and little things every day, and also a place under pillars for the Corn market. The building round here is esteemed the best and here is the Town Hall . . . the whole Citty lookes like what it is, a rich thriveing industrious place'

As we rode into the town, little seemed to have changed. The looms, combing shops and twisting mills of Celia's day had been replaced by other industries, but the essence of Norwich was still the same, retaining not only its prosperity but its beauty. 'Norfolk do different,' say the people in these parts, and it is perhaps this independence of spirit that saved the East Anglian capital. Thanks to the conservationist policies of Norwich during the fifties and sixties, the city escaped the fate of so many other towns. Development did occur, but not within the medieval nucleus of the city, with the result that the cathedral, the castle, the twisting streets and alleyways and the vast permanent market place at its heart remained intact.

Our visit to the city that June morning had another historical precedent, besides that set by Celia Fiennes. In 1599, Will Kemp, the Shakespearian actor, morris-danced his way from London to Norwich. The so-called 'nine daies wonder' in fact took twenty-three days, with Kemp averaging three miles an hour. The mileage was meticulously recorded by George Sprat, while the music was provided by Kemp's taberer, Tom Slye, and his servant William Bee. Kemp completed his epic dance with a great leap over the churchyard wall of St John Maddermarket, only to find that Sprat had lost sight of him in the crush and insisted on his repeating the dance across the city the following Tuesday.

While Catherine tacked up George behind the city hall, I changed into my costume, contorting almost to a kneeling position to avoid the prurient gaze of an ageing commissionaire. A group of small children from Bignold First School had gathered on the steps of the city hall to welcome us, flanked by various civic dignitaries and the mayor, who was confined to a wheelchair. Having ridden round the corner, I had just dismounted to greet them, when the 'Look East' cameraman suddenly said, 'Sorry, luv. Can you possibly do it again? Run out of tape.'

Catherine's arms were becoming as muscular as an Amazon's from all the leg-ups she had given me, but without complaint she hoisted me up again, smiling as I whispered to her that at least we would not have to wait until next Tuesday to complete this leg of the journey, unlike poor Will Kemp.

Once the press call was over, I changed out of my costume and left Catherine with George while I went off to buy toothpaste and shampoo. I hadn't been into a shop for over two weeks, and I found the experience a strange one. On the one hand it was something of a luxury to blend unnoticed into the crowd. Everywhere we had passed through, I had been invested with the status of a minor celebrity. It was amusing and flattering, but it carried with it far greater diplomatic responsibilities than I would ever have imagined. Even when one felt tired and fed up, one always had to be charming and polite. Here I was just another shopper in the centre of Norwich. If I had stuck out my tongue and sworn no one would have cared. On the other hand, I suddenly found myself missing George, missing him not just for his company, but for the immediate passport he provided into other people's worlds. After two weeks of being on his back it felt odd to be on foot. No one spoke to me and no one smiled, and I felt quite relieved when I eventually arrived back at the box.

*

My companion for the next stretch was Margaret, a long-distance rider of such accomplishment that she had won the coveted Golden Horseshoe Award. Our footling twenty miles a day paled into insignificance when compared with her usual sixty miles. It is all too easy to label people, and I am as guilty of it as anyone. Now, however, with so much more time to talk to them, I was discovering that most people defied categorisation, and Margaret more than most. Not only did she ride long distance, she was a teacher, wrote poetry for the bereaved and had a daughter who had posed nude in *Playboy*.

'She was Centrefold of the Year in the United States,' added Margaret proudly, exploding into a thousand pieces the mental pigeonhole I had made for her.

Beautiful as Margaret's daughter undoubtedly was, I wondered how readily our next host would succumb to her charms:

'I've seen so many sheep with mastectomies that I just don't get excited by page three girls anymore!' he declared within ten minutes of our meeting.

A champion sheep-shearer and a percheron horse authority, Roger Peacock, with his fuzzy sideboards, sanguine complexion and naughty twinkling eyes, looked just like a toby jug. Somehow it came as no surprise to learn that for thirteen years he had been Wymondham's pantomime dame. As soon as we arrived we had a border-cross ewe thrust into one hand and shears in the other and were given our first lesson in sheep-shearing while Roger regaled us with local wisdom:

'Have you heard the old Norfolk saying about the sky? "Red sky at night, shepherd's delight. Red sky in morning, shepherd's warning. Red sky at lunchtime, shepherd's pie." Watch that teat!'

Roger was fascinated by our route, and it soon emerged that he knew practically everyone we had met so far in East Anglia.

'Very nice, that chap . . . Bit snooty, that one . . . Aha! That's the one who's been having it away with the barmaid at the Swan.'

It seemed extraordinary that, after four years of living in London, I knew only one of my neighbours, and yet here was a man who knew the most intimate details about almost everyone living within a fifty-mile radius. Charles' words about my own insularity came back to me. I was also beginning to realise that one of the delights of riding so slowly through the country was that one had time to really savour each region, and to pick up all sorts of information about it, architectural, social, historical, agricultural, or just plain gossip.

Roger had quite a reputation in the area as an after-dinner speaker, and we soon realised why. With each glass of wine his face grew ruddier, his stories more risqué and his gesticulations wilder, until he was cavorting round the room employing nearly every chair, table and ornament as a prop for each new story. All we could do was clutch our sides in an agony of laughter.

He had bought a copy of *The Illustrated Journeys of Celia Fiennes*, and as I set off the next day he brought it outside and pointed to the section about Wymondham, in which Celia had described how 'the road on the Causey was in many places full of holes'.

'Nothing's changed!' declared Roger. 'The potholes are still there. The only difference is that they paint white circles round them. They're just council potholes now. You watch out, and take care.'

It wasn't the potholes, however, that delayed us that day. Going into Wymondham Station to ask the ticket collector for directions, Catherine had met with an expression of blank incomprehension.

'Ketteringham?' he had replied. 'Nope, never heard of it.'

She arrived for lunch half an hour late, incensed to discover, on consulting my map, that Ketteringham was only five miles from Wymondham. Celia had complained of the same phenomenon in 1698:

> 'generally the people here are able to give so bad a direction that passengers are at a loss what aime to take, they know scarce 3 mile from their home, and meete them where you will, enquire how farre to such a place, they mind not where they are then but tell you so farre which is the distance from their own houses to that place.'

I doubted whether this was a trait peculiar to East Anglians. For my own part I live in the centre of London, but would be hard-pressed to direct anyone from Trafalgar Square to Piccadilly Circus, let alone to a place three miles away from my flat.

George was in excellent form. I was glad for him that we were still in East Anglia. Norfolk, with its undemanding contours, seemed the ideal place for him to grow stronger and to develop his stamina for the hills ahead. Since his illness he had become far more affectionate, and I found myself growing increasingly fond of him – proud, too. Just outside Wymondham, we had negotiated our first level-crossing without assistance. It had taken twenty minutes of coaxing and cajoling, but we had managed. I was so delighted that I spent the next hour patting him, complimenting him on his cleverness and bravery. George couldn't understand what all the fuss was about.

The television coverage we had received on 'Blue Peter' and in Norwich now meant that half the people we passed knew who we were. 'Are you the lady riding round England?' they would ask, pressing money into our hands. Some motorists even stopped their cars to make a donation, and occasionally people working in their gardens would offer us coffee and carrots. The cathode ray seemed to be working its magic.

Our route now led us back to Suffolk and Euston Hall, a few miles south of Thetford. With gardens designed by John Evelyn, the hall was built between 1666 and 1670 for the Earl of Arlington, who in 1685 passed it to his son-in-law, Henry Fitzroy, first Duke of Grafton and son of Charles II by Barbara Villiers. When Celia Fiennes visited Euston Hall its owner was the second Duke of Grafton, described by Swift as 'almost a slobberer without one good quality'. An eye-witness once described how he saw the duke 'at fisticuffs' in the Strand with a coachman 'whom he lamb'd most horribly' over a disputed fare, having concealed his Garter ribbon in the coach to avoid recognition.

Such behaviour seemed very far indeed from the urbane charm of the present Duke of Grafton. We arrived at Euston at teatime, to be greeted in the courtyard by the duke and duchess and a few tourists.

'Have you got any collection buckets?' asked the duchess almost immediately, and, indicating a straggle of sightseers with a gracious sweep of the arm, added, 'These people won't want to sponsor you, but they'll give a straight donation.'

Once the collection had been made, the duke said, 'What about a cup of tea?' and ushered me into the old kitchen where jolly, roly-poly ladies in smocks were serving tea and home-made cakes.

'Find any good business today?' asked the duke, perching elegantly on a trestle table.

'No, not very good, Your Grace. It's the weather. They don't like it.'

The story was the same inside the house, for apart from another clutch of cuddly ladies, this time acting as attendants, the place was fairly empty. Fire and extensive remodelling had altered the house out of all recognition since Celia's day, but the Van Dycks and the Lelys were still there, and one could immediately see why they should have inspired Celia to such uncharacteristic enthusiasm. Had she been able to see the exquisite *Mares and Foals* by Stubbs painted in 1763, who knows of what rapture she might have been capable.

'Of course, I don't know why we've got Nell Gwyn's picture up here. She's the enemy. Cromwell too, I suppose,' continued the duke. 'Shouldn't give them house room, but they're really rather nice pictures.'

The following morning's ride was delayed by running repairs. While George received his first set of shoes since leaving London, the lorry batteries were being laboriously charged up by a tractor, having run flat for the third time since Glemham. Leaving Euston Hall by the Duke's Ride, cleared by a previous incumbent so that he might have his own private road to take him to Newmarket races, we soon bore left along the Icknield Way. It was amazing to think that this tiny sandy track with its grassy camber dated back to prehistoric times. If one were to continue along the Peddar's Way and the Ridgeway it was possible even now to travel from north Norfolk to the Dorset coast, with hardly a stretch of tarmac the whole way.

Stoats, hares, partridges, even a deer crossed our path, taking cover at our approach in the luxuriant undergrowth of nettles, ferns, grasses and young saplings. Not so timid were the flies, which troubled George greatly and clung irritatingly in a sticky swarm about my hat. I rolled my map into a stout cylindrical swat, and soon found this to be the most efficient use to which my maps had been put since we set off from London.

Bearing south-west we found ourselves in the stillness of the King's Forest, dense, coniferous and criss-crossed by rides that seemed to disappear into an infinity of green without even a pinprick of light at the end to suggest a glade or forest boundary. So evocative was the soft thud of George's hoof-fall, so intoxicating the bitter-sweet aroma of the ferns and pine needles, that one could easily imagine the place to be populated by the denizens of Narnia. Perhaps the susurrations in the undergrowth were the whisperings of two fauns, and the flash of russet in the trees a watching satyr? Perhaps at any moment the White Witch herself might appear to tempt me with sugary Turkish delight piled high on a silver bon bon dish . . .

By lunchtime I was rather wishing that she would. George and I had reached our appointed rendezvous at Brockley, but Catherine and the lorry were nowhere to be seen. Taking off the saddle, and replacing his bridle with a halter, I let George graze on a triangle of rough grass in the middle of the village, while I tried to ignore the rumblings of my stomach. This was an easier task than I had expected. The diuretic effects of the four cups of coffee I had drunk for breakfast at Euston were now beginning to manifest themselves, and the resulting pressure on my bladder proved a far keener sensation than any hunger pangs. What could I do? Our tiny island of grass could hardly have been more exposed, surrounded as it was by thoroughfares on all sides. Leaving George alone was unthinkable. Riding him to a suitably sheltered location was a possibility, but we were some distance from any fields. If Catherine were to pass by and find us gone there was little likelihood that she would wait. Since an hour had already elapsed since our proposed meeting time she would naturally assume that we had continued on our way. I couldn't take the risk of that happening. George's back was looking sore and desperately in need of Catherine's attention. By now my own discomfort was unbearable, and I was about to throw all caution to the wind and

59

lower my breeches when the door of a nearby cottage opened, and out stepped my salvation.

Seeing Mighty from her living-room window, Patricia's curiosity had got the better of her, and now she came over the road to discover more about us.

'How far have you ridden today?' she asked after I had explained our presence there in as intelligible a manner as I was able in my present predicament.

'Euston.'

'Euston? Oh. That's a long way . . . London, isn't it? Would you like a cup of tea?'

Despite this small lapse in her local geography, Patricia seemed sensible enough, so thrusting George's rope into her hand I blurted, 'Yes, please, but would you mind if I used your loo? He's awfully good and I'm bursting.'

The relief was indescribable. By the time Catherine appeared some thirty minutes later, I had consumed so much tea in celebration that I had to go through the whole performance again. How much easier life was now, I reflected, than in Celia's time. Had she been similarly stricken, she would have been forced to hitch up her skirts there and then and find relief behind the nearest bushes. Yet such a measure would probably have been preferable to the more standard forms of seventeenth-century lavatory: the overflowing earth closet or the chamberpot emptied out of the window into the street. Water closets were then still sufficiently novel a concept to merit the most detailed and reverent recording by observers. In 1678, John Aubrey, after a visit to Francis Carew's house in Bedington, Surrey, described

'a pretty machine to cleanse an House of Office, viz. by a small stream of water no bigger than one's finger, which ran into an engine made like a bit of a fire-shovel, which hung upon its centre of gravity, so that when it was full a considerable quantity of water fell down with some force'

and Celia herself, in 1712, felt moved enough at Windsor to mention

'a closet that leads to a little place with a seate of easement of
marble with sluces of water to wash all down'

It had apparently taken five men and a crane to shut the ramp on
the lorry at Euston, and then a visit to the Mercedes garage in Bury
to fit a new battery had delayed Catherine still further. Even now
she wasn't convinced that our problems were over, and kept under
her seat the brick given to her by Mr Adlam, the Glemham farm
manager, to keep the accelerator depressed while the battery was
being charged.

George's back had never properly recovered from Colchester, so
most of the time I rode him bareback.

'Poor you!' people would say feelingly, but I rather enjoyed the
sensation of being so close to George, and was pleasantly surprised
to find him so comfortable. Riding a shire horse bareback was,
however, not without its disadvantages, as I discovered to my cost
near Bury, when I foolishly let my map slip from my hands.
Looking round, I could see no motorist or pedestrian I might ask
for help. There was nothing for it but to dismount, pick up the map
and then worry about how best to clamber onto George's back.
With the most ungainly contortions I had coped with the problem
in the past, but only with the assistance of a gate or high bank. The
long tree-lined stretch of road on which I now found myself offered
no such impromptu mounting-block. So, with the map in one hand
and George's reins in the other, I set off on foot, prepared if
necessary to walk all the way to Bury. About a mile further on we
passed a rough-cast bungalow, separated from the road by a low
crazy-paved wall. For about ten minutes I tried to hoist myself up,
observed, to my acute embarrassment, by the two elderly occupants of the bungalow, who were watching the pantomime
through the net curtains. Smiling at them pathetically, I was about
to admit defeat when they disappeared, to re-appear at their front
door carrying a wheel-back chair, which they proceeded to place at
my disposal as a mounting-block.

One of the drawbacks of the journey was that there was never any
time to dismount and spend time looking at buildings, as I felt

keenly the following day when I rode through the grounds of Ickworth. Landscaped by Capability Brown, it was a park of great oaks in which was set one of the most magnificent examples of Georgian architecture. I would have loved to have been able to explore properly the elegant outer pavilions and elliptical domed rotunda, 104 feet high and modelled on the Pantheon in Rome, but had to content myself with simply riding past.

But there were advantages too. Each day saw my confidence in my navigational and equestrian abilities growing, and now, with George in such good form and the weather so glorious, I felt quite intrepid. To begin with I had avoided bridleways, hoping that by keeping to tarred surfaces I would be spared problems. Now I almost courted those problems. What could be more exhilarating than to battle through the jungly undergrowth under a hot June sky? What did it matter if the track turned out to be impassable and we had to retrace our steps? As long as George came to no harm, it was all part of the adventure.

The landscape began to flatten out considerably as we passed from Suffolk into Cambridgeshire. Ahead of us lay Newmarket, capital of the horse world since the first recorded race in 1619. Here were the National Stud, the National Horse Racing Museum and that august arbiter of racing destinies, the Jockey Club. I wondered if George could sense the presence of the great equine ghosts that must surely haunt this place. Passing one private stud, we caught sight of a few sinewy thoroughbreds, visions of speed and grace as they galloped across a white-fenced paddock. Looking down at George it seemed incredible that he should be of the same species.

Celia was more interested in Chippenham Park than the races, and this was where we were to stable for the next three nights. So relatively long a stay made it an ideal *poste restante*, and we arrived to find a deluge of letters. Among them was one from my father, who, realising that a proper job was impossible for the present, had hit upon another means of offsetting my overdraft:

'YOU HAVE three to four months IN WHICH to COIN MONEY for START. DO ADVERTISEMENTS on TELEVISION. You could do ONE A DAY,' and he proceeded to suggest various slogans that we might adopt, such as: 'I sing to my horse as I go along and we both enjoy a Hamlet cigar,' or 'I ride round England but I fly Air France to Paris,' or 'I still read the *Independent* as I ride along,' or 'I use Lanvin scent. Mighty loves Arpège.'

Looking at my putrid, torn, mud-spattered and grass-stained Barbour and breeches I suspected that Lanvin might perhaps have better ways of promoting their image.

The remainder of the letter contained a description of the Trooping of the Colour ('Please marry a chap in the Household Brigade'), a brief synopsis of the state of the stock market, a military-style briefing on the run-up to the French election and a few comments on television presenters: 'Fiona Armstrong has RUINED her hair and looks like Widow Twankey. Julia Somerville is barely recognisable. Lots of love Daddy xxxxx xxxxx.'

Reading my father's letter made me realise just how out of touch I had become. I never watched television and rarely had time to read a newspaper. The country could have been at war for the past three weeks for all I knew.

In Celia's day Chippenham Park had belonged to Edward Russell, who in 1697, just one year before Celia's visit, had been created Lord Orford in recognition of his victory at La Hogue. Obviously something of a *bon viveur*, for one of his parties Lord Orford allegedly had a large hole specially dug, into which punch was poured and a boat launched. So great was the quantity of punch prepared that two thousand lemons were required in the recipe. The revels continued until five in the morning, by which time the boat still hadn't touched bottom.

Lord Orford's hospitality was not extended to everyone, however. During his occupancy of Chippenham Park he had the surrounding village razed to the ground and relocated outside the park so that he wouldn't have to share it with the hoi polloi. Lord Orford and his family had long since gone, but it was exciting to think that the stable block, 'built over with a high lanthorn where hangs the clock and ball . . . built round a court very handsome', had not changed since Celia's visit, and that perhaps in some strange way she was there with us now, watching over us and guiding our steps.

On the Monday Charles Stewart turned up to see us. He had

telephoned three days earlier to say that I had left my pyjamas at his house. He was going to be in the Newmarket area on Monday, and would be very happy to deliver them in person. Catherine and I were delighted. Familiar faces had become a rarity.

He arrived at about midday, and it was decided that the reunion should be celebrated with a picnic. Once George had been fed and watered, we duly set off in Charles' car to a supermarket in Newmarket's High Street in order to buy the provisions.

'That's for you,' said Charles casually, pointing to a brown package in the well in front of the passenger seat. Picking it up I found it to be a bulky manila envelope bearing the words, 'For the eyes of Miss Payne only'. Inside were not merely my pyjamas, but another envelope, also addressed to me.

'Go on,' urged Charles, 'read it!'

And so I did.

'Dearest Miss Payne,

What an unparalleled joy it has been for me to have you and Catherine to stay for the last few days; and to have been bought such an excellent dinner by two such beautiful and charming girls was a treat that I had never expected to enjoy upon this tiny globe.

DID YOU KNOW that hamsters were first introduced to this country in 1930 from Syria, and that all the furry pets are descended from that first litter?

DID YOU KNOW that a pig was tried, convicted and executed for murder in Falaise in 1386?

DID YOU KNOW that Napoleon Bonaparte, later to be Napoleon III, said whilst in the company of others, and whilst trying to bring off his abortive coup in the town of Grenoble, *'Ma sacrée toux'*, which as you know, being a linguist, scholar and thoroughly delightful person, means 'My damned cough'? One of his minions misheard this statement and thought the great man had said *'Massacrez tous'*, which the putative general proceeded to do.

DID YOU KNOW that an eighteenth-century Sultan of Morocco used to decapitate his grooms whenever he mounted his horse? Don't try to emulate him! Catherine might not be pleased.'

The letter continued in a similar vein, with a further eight or so entertaining and intriguing facts, similarly prefaced with the words 'Did you know'. The final one was slightly different, however.

'DID YOU KNOW that I have not been able to eat or sleep properly since I met you? I have looked up this condition in my medical dictionary and it suggests that I am madly in love with you and I am now typing on my knees in order to ask for your hand in marriage. Perhaps a quiet ceremony in Macao, or jazz and clam chowder in New Orleans? What are your thoughts? I eagerly await an affirmative response. In the meantime, please find enclosed a pair of jimmy-jammies!
With all my love,
Charles Stewart
Je vive en espoir'

I was speechless.

7

Newmarket to Leicester

The following day we set off for Ely.

> '8 mile . . . which were as long as the 12 I came from St. Edmundsbery [Bury St Edmunds], the wayes being very deep its mostly lanes and low moorish ground . . . fendiks which are deep ditches with draines; the Fens are full of water and mudd; these also encompass their grounds, each mans part 10 or a dozen acres a piece or more, so these dicks are the fences, on each side they plant willows so there is 2 rows of trees runns round the ground which looks very finely to see a flatt of many miles so planted, but it must be ill to live there'

The miles seemed even longer to me than they had to Celia. Scored by a grid of drainage channels and dissected by solitary, straight causeways, here was an empty, strange quarter. As if designed by a geometrician with a setsquare, it was a landscape devoid of any curves or other visual relief. There were no obliging verticals to interrupt the flatness; no houses, no hillocks, not even a tree to soften the harsh horizontal of the skyline. And it was still – deathly still. Apart from the blind, tuberous growth of potatoes beneath the soil, one could almost believe that nothing lived here.

It was a hateful ride that day. I had cursed the rain before; now I longed for it. From a sheer expanse of cloudless sky, a blinding sun beat relentlessly down on us. There was no shade at all, and as the day wore on it grew unbearably hot. So did George. His thick coat was ill-suited to such heat, and he dripped sweat from every pore. I could have put up with it more easily had I not been riding bareback. But the sweatier he became, the wetter my breeches grew, resulting in the most disagreeable irritation. Thus we continued on our way, with only tedium and discomfort to keep us company. Not surprisingly, perhaps, my thoughts drifted, as they had many times during the preceding twenty-four hours, to Charles, our weekend near Beccles and his letter.

To say I was confused would be the grossest understatement. Even now I still hadn't taken it all in. Certainly the weekend Catherine and I had spent with him had been wonderful – relaxed, fun, and a total antidote to the worries and routines of the ride. We had both liked him immediately, and by the end of our stay we had grown to like him even more. Had we stayed a week, I admit, my feelings might have developed still further. But we hadn't. We had stayed only three days. I had hoped that we would meet again, but never for a moment did I imagine that our reunion would be quite so precipitate or quite so intense. I must have read his letter a hundred times that day on the way to Ely. I didn't know what else to do.

The monotony of the journey was relieved towards the middle of the afternoon by the hazy promise of Ely Cathedral's lantern and tower beckoning us in the distance. It was to be another three hours before we eventually rode into the city, but it was an enormous help to have something on which to focus my gaze.

Celia had been similarly inspired by the shimmering prospect of the cathedral, but on closer inspection Ely had proved the sorest of disappointments. It was, she wrote,

'the dirtyest place I ever saw, not a bitt of pitching in the streetes so its a perfect quagmire the whole Citty, only just about the Palace and Churches the streetes are well enough for breadth but for want of pitching it seemes only a harbour to breed and nest vermin in, of which there is plenty enough, so that tho' my chamber was near 20 stepps up I had froggs and slow-worms and snailes in my roome – but suppose it was brought up with the faggotts – but it

67

cannot but be infested with all such things being altogether moorish fenny ground which lyes low; its true were the least care taken to pitch their streetes it would make it looke more properly an habitation for human beings, and not a cage or nest of unclean creatures, it must needs be very unhealthy, tho' the natives say much to the contrary which proceeds from custom and use, otherwise to persons born in up and dry countryes it must destroy them like rotten sheep in consumptions and rhumes . . . they are a slothful people and for little but the takeing care of their grounds and cattle which is of vast advantage'

The cathedral she dismissed as 'a curious pile of building', and she could find nothing favourable to say about its diocesan governor either.

'The Bishop does not care to stay long in this place not being for his health; he is the Lord of all the Island, has the command and the jurisdiction: they have lost their Charter and so are no Corporation but all things are directed by the Bishop and its a shame he does not see it better ordered and the buildings and streetes put in a better condition'

Our experience of Ely was to be very different. No quagmires awaited us as George and I entered the city, but tidy streets of well-kept houses and an atmosphere of modest prosperity. Through the Garden History Society we had been invited to stay with the current Bishop of Ely, Peter Walker, and his wife Jean. Clearly of a healthier disposition than his seventeenth-century predecessor, he greeted us with warm animation before ushering us hastily into the garden of the Bishop's House, through the elaborately carved Prior's door and into the cathedral to hear Evensong.

Passing a curious stone obelisk, he pointed it out enthusiastically as Ovin's Stone. Although the cathedral was founded in 673 by St Ethelreda, the only physical link with this Saxon period was Ovin's Stone, originally the base of a cross. At one point it disappeared for centuries, only to be rediscovered in the eighteenth century out-side an inn in Haddenham, where it had been used as a mounting-block.

'Who knows!' declared the bishop with boyish glee, 'Celia herself may have used it!'

My bottom, I had discovered on rapid and discreet inspection, now looked like a dot-to-dot puzzle, and it felt like a furnace. All I really wanted to do was to soak in a bath and treat the affected area with whatever soothing ointment I could lay my hands on. Yet so heavenly was the singing, so uplifting the beautiful architecture of the cathedral, that such base thoughts were soon forgotten as I felt myself transported on a wave of joy and gratitude that we should have come this far on so strange a journey.

After Evensong the bishop took us into his study, where he showed us a delicate miniature jade horse and read us a few poems by T. S. Eliot, Geoffrey Hill, Philip Larkin and W. H. Auden. 'I knew him during his last six months. Rather a battered man, but I liked him.' He then photocopied for us the poems we had most enjoyed and gave us each a Maundy coin before entrusting us to his wife for a tour of the garden and house.

A note of infectious gaiety and youthfulness characterised Jean Walker's conversation. She described everything with the same vital enthusiasm, shocking us with occasional irreverences.

'Yes, the cathedral is beautiful, but of course it's hopelessly lopsided,' she declared between showing us the second-oldest wistaria in England and a prizeworthy row of Canterbury bells. So lovingly tended was her garden that I suspected that not even there would we find the slightest trace of Celia's 'froggs and slow-worms and snailes'.

The Bishop's House, where they lived, was built in 1280 as a refectory for the monastery. Originally a single huge room, it had since been converted into a house, although the roof timbers and corbels had been left intact and exposed. Having moved into the house on her husband's appointment as bishop, Mrs Walker recounted how she had been just about to take her first bath there when she suddenly had the uneasy feeling that she was being watched. Glancing round she discovered that a pair of eyes were indeed trained on her, but they belonged not to a peeping tom but to one of the corbels, a tonsured monk with the most disapproving expression imaginable. 'It was absolutely priceless!' laughed Mrs Walker.

Also suffering the scrutiny of the disapproving corbel, I had a hot bath that evening and went to bed thinking of Charles. It would have been difficult not to. I had arrived at the Bishop's House that evening to find an enormous bouquet awaiting me.

'I think they must be from an admirer!' Mrs Walker had said as I opened the small envelope attached to them. Inside was a small Interflora card, sprigged with a floral motif and carrying the message, 'SAY YES.'

The following day went dreadfully. In my state of now constant abstraction, I had forgotten to give Catherine precise instructions about our lunchtime rendezvous. As a result we eventually found each other an hour later than intended, which in turn made us late for a press call just outside Cambridge. I further compounded my crime by then directing Catherine along quite the wrong road. She was understandably infuriated, and my apologies only irritated her further. Reading in a guide book that there were nearly thirty Cambridges around the world, I thought of citing this as a defence for my poor mapreading. Stealing a sidelong glance at Catherine's stony face, I thought better of it. Bleeper, lying between us with his bottom on the gearstick, seemed quite oblivious to the cold war being waged above his head.

From Ely, George and I had headed south towards Cambridge and then west through Cottenham and Longstanton towards Huntingdon. The geometrical regularity of the fens now gave way to a gently haphazard configuration of ridges, valleys, rivers and copses. In 1698 Celia branded the inhabitants of this region 'a lazy sort of people, and are afraid to do too much'. Three hundred years later the reverse seemed the case. Every available acre of land was given over to the intensive growing of barley, carrots and sugar-beet and, on a smaller scale, the cultivation of flowers, salad vegetables and fruit. Riding past one smallholding I struck up a conversation with a strawberry grower who insisted on my accepting half a pound of luscious strawberries the size of small apples.

'They'll last you all day, they will. What about the old fella? He's got a long way to go.'

He had indeed – 1200 miles still separated us from our eventual return to London. It seemed rather rash to speculate on George's chances of completing the Great Journey – too many things could go wrong – but with the passing of each day my faith in his abilities grew, as, I suspect, did his in mine. Broken as a dray-horse, George had been taught to respond only to vocal commands delivered in the gruff monosyllables of the Whitbread grooms. My soft tones meant nothing to him, and every time I addressed him I would have to lower my voice by at least an octave and affect a Cockney inflection. Thus 'Go on!' became 'GWARN!' and 'Calm down' became 'STAIR-dee ol'boy! STAIR-dee!' Two months of practice had, I felt, made almost perfect. George and I had developed a depth of understanding that I would never before have imagined possible.

There are few states of mind more dangerous than complacency, as I was to discover to my cost just west of Hilton. It was just after lunch. We were heading in the direction of Huntingdon, and our route took us along a narrow road with deceptively deep ditches, all but camouflaged by tall grasses, on either side. At first I had always drawn up the reins, held George tight with my legs and talked to him whenever a large vehicle passed us. As time went by I had gradually relaxed the physical control, relying simply on my voice to hold him. I was soon to realise what a grave mistake this was. Seeing a lorry of modest proportions approaching us, I thought that a gravelly 'STAIR-dee!' would be sufficient to calm him. Compared with the pantechnicons, cement mixers and milk containers we had already encountered that day, so small a lorry seemed to constitute no threat at all, and indeed George himself did not seem in the least perturbed by it. But neither George nor I had reckoned on the lorry's slipstream, and it caught us unawares. Terrified by this invisible assailant cutting a swathe across his path, George panicked and blundered towards the only familiar thing he could see – grass.

It is difficult to remember the precise sequence of the next few moments, but five seconds later I found myself lying at the bottom of a six-foot ditch covered in mud, with George's enormous white bottom crashing through the undergrowth ahead of me. Pulling myself out, I ran along the verge and headed him off some fifty yards further along, all the while desperately trying to counteract the tremulous quaver in my voice with a reassuring bass. Then, quite suddenly, he stopped. I lay down on the grass and, leaning into the ditch, stroked him and talked to him. With nostrils dilated and his breath coming in rasping gasps, he rested his head on the crook of my arm. I felt terrified. Then he shut his eyes, which made me even more frightened, only to open them again two seconds later. In a rush, the full realisation of what had happened came over me. Here was my horse at the bottom of a six-foot ditch, probably injured and possibly lame, with no visible means of extricating himself or being pulled out, and all because of my foolhardiness. For a cowardly moment I thought with dread of Whitbread's and Catherine's reactions to my ineptitude, and of the bearing the incident might have on the completion of the journey: but somehow none of it seemed important anymore. The priority was George's well-being. If anything were to happen to him I would never forgive myself.

Not knowing what to do, but sensing that I should at least attempt to get George out of the ditch somehow, I grabbed hold of his reins and, partly coaxing, partly tugging, tried to pull him out. For a moment the air was filled with a confusion of flailing legs and then he was out, dripping with sweat and kneeling with his front legs on the road.

Perhaps in the light of such a mishap it is ridiculous to talk of fate, but it did seem rather odd that the first car to draw up was that of a vet. Examining George's legs, he declared him in perfect health, but predicted a little stiffness the following day.

'I'd call it a day now, if I were you. Good luck.'

My Vodafone had been either lost or stolen, so there was no way of telephoning Catherine to alert her. I had no option but to hobble back into Hilton in the hope that she might still be there and had not driven off to our next rendezvous, eight miles away.

When we did eventually reach the picnic spot, the lorry was nowhere to be seen. We couldn't ride anywhere, so the best thing seemed to be to stay where we were and hope that fate might once more come to our aid. And so it did, in the shape of Doreen, Betty and Pat.

'Ooh!' cooed the apronned and curlered Doreen, a cigarette dangling from her bottom lip, 'Luvvely horse!'

'Ooh!' gasped Betty, ''E's the one on the telly! Does'e bite?'

'Ooh!' exclaimed Pat, registering my mud-stained clothes and expression of despair, 'Are you all right?'

Replying as lucidly as I was able, I drew my map out of my pocket to explain what had happened.

'Ooh!' shrieked Doreen, pointing at me, 'BLOOD!'

'Ooh!' swooned Betty.

'Ooh!' cried Pat.

I quickly looked down at myself to find the cause of their horror. The whole of my map from Biggleswade to Bourn was saturated in what could only be blood, which dripped with eerie and unnerving regularity onto my faun cords. Terrified that I had been so badly injured as to have lost all sensation, I put my hand into my pocket and discovered the source of the flow – half a dozen Cambridgeshire strawberries crushed to a liquid pulp.

Noticeably relieved, Doreen, Betty and Pat did all they could to help. While Betty tried to telephone Catherine and Doreen fetched a washing-up bowl of water for George and a floral deckchair for me, Pat ushered us both into the tiniest garden I had ever seen.

'It'll save me mowing it,' she said as George attacked the grass with nervous relish. My right foot was beginning to balloon most painfully, so I was glad to take advantage of Doreen's deckchair and sit down for a few minutes.

The batteries of Catherine's Vodafone had clearly run down, as Betty came back saying: 'The woman said the contact I was trying to subscribe to was not available and can I phone later.'

The prospect of an imminent reunion with Catherine was looking very unlikely. Then Keith appeared. A neighbour of Pat's, he had heard all the commotion and was now offering to go and find Catherine in his car. 'I feel like a run in the car,' he smiled, as he got into his Cortina and disappeared up the road.

Half an hour later George was safely loaded into the back of the lorry. As we waved goodbye to Doreen, Betty, Pat and the cluster

of neighbours, friends and relatives who had by now gathered in
the little garden, it was hard to believe quite how lucky we had
been. Despite a searing pain in my foot whenever I tried to move it,
George and I were unscathed. The only casualty had been my
dictaphone, into which I would describe the landscape, adding at
the same time any anecdotes I might have forgotten to enter into
my notebook the previous evening. In the confusion it fell out of
my saddlebag and now lay somewhere at the bottom of the ditch.
Defying all the laws of gravity, my notebook had miraculously
escaped a similar fate, and I found it precariously balanced on top
of a few blades of grass, inches from the muddy water.

My good fortune continued that evening, for one of the dinner
guests turned out to be an orthopaedic surgeon. Nothing was
broken, he assured me on examining my foot, but I should take
things easy and put no undue strain on it. Riding, however, should
pose no problems.

'Forgive my mentioning it,' he added a few moments later, 'I've
only read a little of the Celia Fiennes book, but didn't she have a
narrow escape in Cambridgeshire too?'

In all the commotion it had quite slipped my mind, but after
dinner I reread the Cambridgeshire section of the diary.

> 'the raines now had fallen so as in some places near the
> Citty the Caussey was covered and a remarkable deliver-
> ance I had, for my horse earnest to drinke ran to get more
> depth of water than the Caussey had, was on the brinke of
> one of these diks but by a speciall providence which I desire
> never to forget and allwayes to be thankfull for, escaped;
> that bridge was over the River Linn which comes from
> Norfolke and does almost encompass the Island of Ely.'

Barely a handful of miles separated Celia's near-disaster from
mine. Could it be that the same 'special providence' that had
intervened on her behalf had come to my aid?

A moratorium was declared on the next day's ride, and while
George rested we turned our attention to the lorry. Catherine
launched an assault on the back and I attacked the inside, carrying

out a commando raid on the floor, windows, sink and fridge, which after a month of electrical inactivity resembled the site of a messy biological experiment. Once the lorry looked and smelled passable, we loaded up and set off for Peterborough and the East of England Showground. But when we arrived we discovered to our horror that the ramp was stuck, with George inside the box. There was no means of lowering the ramp, so all we could do was check that the fans in George's compartment were working, make sure that he had enough hay and then telephone Banbury Boxes. After about half an hour Catherine managed to get through to one of the engineers, who promised to come straight to Peterborough and who, in the meantime, gave step-by-step instructions on how to release the oil valve.

Two of the East of England Show workers had taken pity on us, and while they had no experience of hydraulics they offered to crawl under the lorry and release the oil valve for us. After an hour of Catherine relaying instructions to the two pairs of overalled legs projecting from under the lorry, the ramp slowly began to descend and the two show workers pulled themselves out, covered in shiny black oil and looking as if they had just walked off the set of an avant-garde production of *Porgy and Bess*.

It was enormously relaxing to stay in a hotel that night. Increasingly, the most exhausting aspect of the journey was proving to be not the riding but the socialising. Catherine and I would find ourselves recounting the same tired old anecdotes each evening or resorting to the same uninspired litany of compliments: 'What a lovely house you have. What lovely children. What a lovely dog. What a lovely dinner . . .'

If we found ourselves boring, how much more tedious we must have seemed to our hosts.

Celia does not say in her journal where she stayed in Peterborough, but she admired the city and found it 'looked very well and handsomely built . . . a very industrious thriveing town'. From what I could see as we drove through it still looked very much like a city whose prosperity was based on industry. But there was an air of moneyed brashness to the place, and the pedestrianised precincts and shopping centre seemed to make a grotesque mockery of the cathedral with its three soaring arches and pinnacled towers. Perhaps I was being uncharitable, as my foot was hurting badly and I was judging the city on no more than a few minutes' acquaintance through the lorry windscreen, but it seemed to me that Peterborough had lost its soul. I was glad to reach our hotel, hobble to my room and turn on the television. I had no wish to sightsee that evening.

The next day's ride took us over the Cambridgeshire border into Northamptonshire and then to Leicestershire. Charles had joined us for the day, and while I rode he would overtake me in his Nissan Patrol and then walk alongside me chatting, opening gates and holding my hand. I felt every bit as confused as before, but I was surprised at quite how much I was enjoying his company.

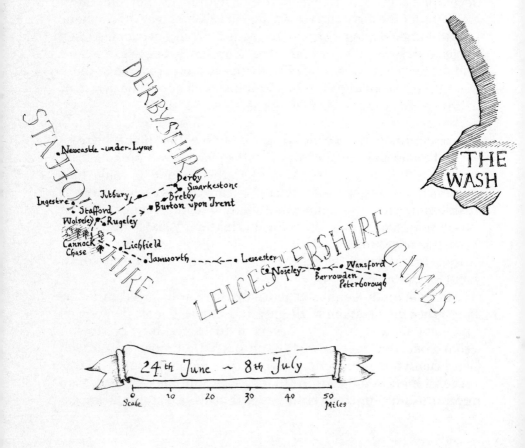

Something else that was beginning to surprise me was the sheer diversity of the English countryside. It seemed extraordinary to think that in a country only half the size of Italy, and a quarter that of France, it was possible to encounter such extremes. In the space of only a few miles we had travelled from what seemed the flattest, bleakest landscape imaginable to the cosy counterpane world of Leicestershire with its rolling sweeps of chequered wheatfields and soft pastureland. Home of the Belvoir and the Quorn Hunts, it was an area well served by bridleways, and our route that day took us through lush fields and gladey rides dripping with foliage. The honeystone villages were attractive and unspoiled, but I sensed that this lack of development was the result not of rustic apathy but of fierce local lobbying. If the local gentry were to disapprove of any local development, then one had the feeling that there would be no development.

Perhaps little had changed since Celia's time. Even in 1698, Leicestershire was well established as one of the most powerful of the central shires.

> 'all the houses and walls are built of stone as in Glocester-shire; this river and bridge enter'd me into Leicestershire which is a very rich country, red land, good corne of all sorts and grass both fields and inclosures; you see a great way upon their hills the bottoms full of enclosures woods and different sort of manureing and herbage, amongst which are placed many little towns, which gives great pleasure of the travellers to view; pretty hard good way to Coppingham [Uppingham], which is a neate market town; Satturday is their market which is very good affording great quantetys of corn leather yarne and cattle, such a concourse of people that my Landlord told me used to have 100 horse set up at his inn, and there were many publick houses here; you see very large fine sheep and very good land'

Celia broke this part of the journey at the Swan in Wansford. George and I continued on to Barrowden, where we were to stay with Major and Mrs Warre. Just outside the village a car drew up in front of us and out stepped a middle-aged man with a rubicund

77

complexion and a jocular smile, whose first words to me were: 'If you see my wife for God's sake don't laugh! I'm Tony Warre, by the way. We'll see you later.'

With that he got back into his car and drove off. I was wondering what he meant by so enigmatic an introduction, when I caught sight of a tiny cavalcade coming over the brow of the hill, led by a very striking woman seated sideways in her stockinged feet on a small grey horse and dressed in a huge black straw hat, gypsy earrings and a bolero jacket and skirt.

'Oh! We thought you were going to be in all your finery!' she cried, her face dropping visibly at my shabby attire. Within a second, however, she had quite regained her composure and introduced herself as Jeanetta Warre and her band of followers as the Barrowden Reception Committee. 'We thought it would be nice to give you a proper welcome!'

'Yes, yes,' said Major Warre, reinforcing his wife's words some thirty minutes later. 'Don't worry about being on parade. Come down in your knickers if you like. I don't mind!'

'Warre', I began to realise, was not an altogether inappropriate name for the major. A severe case of shooting deafness meant that he could only hear half of what was said, so his response to most utterances would be the drawling interrogative, 'Warre?' Once or twice I tried raising my voice only to be countered by the response, 'You don't have to shout, I'm not DEAF, you know!' At times I suspected that Major Warre deliberately exaggerated his disability. Discussing his grandchildren the next day, I asked him: 'How many have you got and what are they?' to which he replied: 'Four. They're all white if that's what you mean, and I think it's damned uncivil of you to ask what colour they are.'

Sometimes Mrs Warre would protest at his affected obtuseness, but her remonstrances would be silenced with a 'Hmm! To hell with the lot of you! Silly sods! I'm going to put my bedroom slippers on,' or some similar rejoinder.

The night before we left, Major Warre made a bet with me that George would be unable to complete the journey and that we would need another two horses before we arrived back in London. I staunchly defended George's stamina, but secretly I wondered whether he really would complete the journey. The odds seemed increasingly stacked against him. He looked tired already, and as each day passed the terrain was becoming noticeably more hilly.

Our next host was also an inhabitant of Leicestershire. Tall, bespectacled and silver haired, Lord Hazlerigg's benevolent appearance belied a wickedly playful sense of humour. He lived at Noseley Hall, just east of Leicester, where he shared a wing of the house with two long-haired terriers called Kiri and Woo who were as brutal as they were tiny. Kiri's name had been inspired by Lord Hazlerigg's admiration for the New Zealand singer Kiri te Kanawa, but apart from an extraordinary vocal range she had little in common with the operatic soprano. Verdi, Mozart and Puccini meant nothing to Kiri and Woo. What they loved more than anything else was to sink their incisors into a juicy bit of leg, much to the amusement of Lord Hazlerigg who seemed actively to encourage the savaging of postmen and visiting tradesmen. It came as no surprise to learn that Noseley Hall had been blacklisted by the workforces of various companies and institutions throughout the county, and that in the canine public enemy shortlists compiled by the Leicestershire Constabulary, Kiri and Woo ranked equal first. Miraculously both Catherine and I escaped the jaws of Lord Hazlerigg's dogs, but I suspect that this was largely due to our wearing wellington boots and giving them a berth of at least fifty yards.

Although Celia Fiennes never visited Noseley, her father Nathaniel would certainly have known Sir Arthur Hazlerigg, who was one of Cromwell's generals. Cromwell on the other hand did stay at Noseley, and legend has it that on the eve of the Battle of Naseby he slept in the room in which I was put. Lord Hazlerigg pointed out a small, pitted, grey shaving mirror that had belonged to Cromwell himself, adding darkly that its owner was reputed to haunt that wing of the house along with a petulant poltergeist called Isobel. Something did indeed wake me in the middle of the night, but I have to confess that in the shadowy gloom I was far more terrified of the teeth of Kiri and Woo than the nocturnal perambulations of Isobel and Cromwell.

When we continued on our way once more, heavy rains had left

79

the earth sticky and waterlogged, slowing down our progress by at least a couple of hours. Celia had met with similar vexations, and complained of

> 'very deep bad roads; from hence [Uppingham] to Leister full of sloughs, clay deep way, that I was neer 11 hours going but 25 mile – as they reckon it – between Wansford and Leicester town, a footman could have gone much faster than I could ride'

But the day was not without its compensations. Someone had asked us to call in at a tiny village near Leicester that had been purposely built for the mentally handicapped. As soon as the inhabitants heard the clip clop of George's hoofs they all rushed out to meet him, beaming with delight at the size of his feet. They pressed coins into my hands, and one boy gave me ten pence and then asked for change.

'How much do you want?' I asked him.

'Two pounds!' he replied gleefully, at which the assembled company responded with whoops of laughter, thrilled that I should so easily be their dupe.

Within a few hours we had reached the southern outskirts of Leicester. John Evelyn described the city in 1654 as an 'old and ragged Citty . . . despicably built', and a little later Daniel Defoe was to condemn it as 'an old stinking town'. Individualist as ever, Celia declared that:

> 'Leicester town stands on the side of a little riseing ground tho' at a distance from the adjacent hills it looks low, but its a good prospect; it has 4 gates, the streetes are pretty large and well pitch'd, the Market place is a large space very handsome with a good Market Cross and Town Hall'

It was not merely the architecture that interested her. She was fascinated by the idiosyncrasies and oddities of each place she visited, and these she sought out in Leicester with all the avidity of a modern-day tourist:

'There are two Hospitalls [Holy Trinity and Wigston's] one for old men and the other women 24 in number, they are allow'd 2s.8d. per weeke, candle, fewell, oatmeale, butter and salt; I saw the Library there was one book all written hand by a scribe before printing was found out, it was a fine vellum; and there was another Book of the New Testament in Chineaze Language and Caractour . . . St. Martins Church which is one of the biggest (there is none very big and none fine) but here I saw Hyricks tomb who was Major of the town and was married to one wife 52 years, in all which tyme he buried neither man woman nor child tho' most tymes he had 20 in his family, his age was 79 and his widdow 97 at her death, she saw 142 of her posterity together'

It is no accident that Celia should have been so interested in the subject of longevity, for in 1698 it was a rarity. Celia herself lived to the age of seventy-nine, but she was very much an exception. Not only was she a woman with a hardy constitution, she came from a social class which could afford to live well but was not given to excess. Most of her contemporaries were not so lucky. Because of the high rate of infant mortality at the end of the seventeenth century, the average life expectancy would have been some thirty years lower than it is today. The Great Plague of 1665 had also taken immeasurable toll of the country's population. The Battle of Naseby resulted in 900 deaths, 700 royalists and 200 parliamentary soldiers. Each day the Great Plague of 1665 caused the same number of deaths. Indeed, the monthly plague casualties in London alone were equal to Cromwell's New Model Army of 21,000 men. To have been alive at all in 1698 must have seemed something of a miracle.

Leicester to Eaton

It was 29 June. We had already ridden through nine counties and covered a distance of some four hundred miles and were now on the point of recreating Celia Fiennes' loop into Derbyshire. Entering Staffordshire had marked a turning point in my relationship with Catherine. Whether it was because we had grown used to each other's faults, or whether our roles had become more clearly delineated I wasn't sure, but the tension had disappeared, and I found that I not only admired and respected her, but that adversity had created a bond which went beyond friendship.

A press call had been arranged in the three-spired shadow of Lichfield's magnificent red sandstone cathedral. A small knot of photographers had gathered by the time we arrived, along with two representatives from Ordnance Survey and Canon John Turner from the cathedral. Looking round the Close, I had the impression that little had changed in the course of three hundred years.

> 'the town has good houses, the Close has the Bishops and Deanes and Prebends houses which are good, the streetes are very neate and handsome, the breadth and length very well and the building handsome; the Minster is a stately structure but old, the outside has been finely carv'd and full of Images as appears by the nitches and pedistalls which remaine very close all over the walls'

Celia had been every bit as interested in the local festival as in the detail on the cathedral's west front.

> 'they have in this town a custome at Whitsontide the Monday and Tuesday call'd the Green Bower feast by which they hold their Charter; the Bailiff and Sheriff assist at the Cerimony of dressing up Baby's with garlands of flowers and greens and carry it in procession through all the streetes and then assemble themselves at the Market place and so go on in a solemn procession through the great streete to a hill beyond the town where is a large Bower made with greens in which they have their feast; many lesser Bowers they make about for the conveniency of the whole company and for selling Fruite Sweetemeetes and Gingerbread which is a chief entertainment'

I asked John Turner whether the Green Bower Feast was still celebrated today.

'Oh yes, it's still celebrated. We even open the cathedral gates specially for it.'

'But it's a pagan feast, isn't it?'

'Well, yes, I suppose it is. All to do with fertility rites. That kind of thing. But the Christian Church is awfully good at embracing paganism.'

Meanwhile the photographers were snapping away, but despite the imposing setting they seemed dissatisfied with the composition; not even George inadvertently standing on my train and pulling my skirt off seemed to excite their interest.

'It's not right. It needs something else,' lamented one of their number. At that moment a group of yellow-capped choristers emerged from a door in the west front.

'Is he real? Is he real?' asked one immaculate little boy with fair hair and glasses.

'Course he is, stupid,' retorted another, his grey socks concertina'd into a slough about his ankles. The photographer was elated.

'Over here, boys! How would you like your pictures taken? Just say cheese!' After the choristers had said cheese at least thirty times, the photo session came to an end. There was just time for the

canon to show us quickly round the cathedral, which he did, pointing out among other things the 'Sleeping Children' tomb, a Victorian marble affair in the south aisle.

'It's nice enough if you like that kind of thing. Personally I find it a bit too twee and holy.'

Our journey now took us through Cannock Chase. Once a royal hunting forest and refuge for outlaws, its 20,000 acres now offered refuge to walkers, picnickers and birdwatchers. Although half the Chase has been colonised by Forestry Commission softwoods, the rest is still indigenous birch, oak and heather. Ferns also grow in the forest, which was of special interest to Celia in 1698.

> 'In Kank wood . . . there is also great quantetys of ferne, which tho' it overruns their ground and so spoiles the grass where its much, yet the usefullness of it renders it necessary to be preserv'd; when its at its maturity which happens just before harvest or hay tyme the whole Country are employ'd in cutting it up and burning it in heapes for the sake of the ashes, which they make fine and rowle them up in balls and so sell them or use them all the year for washing and scouring, and send much up to London'

It used to be said that there were so many trees in Cannock Chase that a stranger might lose himself in half an hour. With no landmarks to guide us, and so many unmarked and mysterious tracks, it was a miracle that we didn't lose ourselves within two seconds. I hoped to see some deer, but all we encountered was a tenacious swarm of flies and a herd of spotted ramblers. To my chagrin I later learned that Catherine, during a five-minute ride through the forest on her bicycle, had seen three deer.

Celia spent six weeks of her Great Journey in the area, staying with her uncle, Sir Charles Wolseley, at his estate near Rugely. She described the seat as 'wonderfull pleasant', but her highest praise was reserved for the gardens. In 1697, during another visit, she had written:

> 'the Gardens are good both gravell and green walks, there is a good River runns by it which has dwarfe trees and honeysuckles and bines on the bancks, there is a great deale of good fruite and there are severall walks, one shady with high trees which my Aunt told me my Mother liked to walke in and so was call'd her walke'

The hall in which Celia stayed no longer exists, and for many years the gardens were forgotten. In 1988 Sir Charles Wolseley, the eleventh baronet, decided to recreate them as a leisure and tourist attraction. A small press launch had been arranged at Wolseley to unveil the site chosen for the gardens, and by one of the bizarre coincidences that were beginning to characterise our journey, the date set for it was 1 July, the very day on which I was to ride past Wolseley.

Looking round the waste of bulldozed mud and rubble, it was difficult to imagine that within a year this would be the site of twenty-five theme gardens, a gourmet restaurant, a theatre, a series of craft workshops, a café and a garden centre.

'My motives for creating this theme park include jumping on the leisure bandwagon to make money,' declared Sir Charles to a group of journalists, with disarming honesty. 'This land has been my family's for over a thousand years. I want to create something of horticultural and botanical excellence and with a strong sense of history.'

I felt sure that the second Sir Charles Wolseley would have approved of such pragmatic sentiments. A member of Cromwell's House of Lords, he was also one of his greatest confidants and would often invite him to stay at Wolseley, where they would play crambo and write verse together. After the Restoration, however, Sir Charles prudently retired from political life and remained at Wolseley with his wife and seventeen children, devoting his energies to improving the hall and gardens.

Not so fortunate was the third baronet, Sir William Wolseley. An extensive traveller, some years before his death in 1728 he acquired four Arabian mares in Persia. Whilst there, he was told by a fortune teller that he would meet his death by drowning, with the same four horses. Anxious not to tempt providence, Sir William took the precaution of sending the mares home by ship, while he himself returned overland. All arrived safely, but on the night of 17 July 1728, when he was crossing the brook at Longden on his way home from Lichfield, the mill dam burst and Sir William and the four mares were drowned.

The nasal intonations that had been so apparent at Tamworth and Lichfield were gradually being replaced by the warm bluffness of the Staffordshire accent as we bore south-east of Rugeley towards Burton-on-Trent. The countryside was changing too. Lush, green and wooded, these were the first real hills we had met, and each one afforded a still more breathtaking view of a landscape that embraced both the promise of rural England and the realities of industrialisation. In the glancing rays of a golden sun, with the cloud shadows moving slowly across their concave torsos, even the giant chimneys of distant Rugeley possessed a certain magnificence.

We could smell Burton-on-Trent almost before we could see it. Even on the town's outskirts the air seemed heavy with the sickly aroma of hops and malt. It curled invisibly around every corner; it insinuated itself into every window and doorway; it clung with leaden pungency to the great red triangle of the Bass Charrington tower. The very inhabitants of Burton-on-Trent seemed to smell of it.

It was with the building of the Trent and Mersey Canal in the eighteenth century that the town really established itself as one of England's most important centres of brewing; for the canal provided a key ingredient for the industry's success: a swift and cheap means of transport. Burton's history as a brewing town dates back to the thirteenth century, when a local abbot used water from the local wells to make beer.

No doubt Celia would have drunk beer here in 1698, but she would have seen little reason to chronicle the fact. Beer was then the universal English beverage not only for men and women, but for children as well. At Westminster School at the end of the seventeenth century, for example, each boy was given a daily allowance of four pints of beer. This would have been small beer, brewed according to the same principles as ordinary beer but lower in alcohol. That beer was so commonly drunk is not surprising, when one considers how polluted most waterways were with sewage and waste. In York the water was so cloudy that house-holders were forced to keep it for several days in large pots or tanks until the sediment had sunk to the bottom. There were few viable alternatives to beer. Wine was expensive and difficult to obtain because of the tariff wars with France, while coffee and tea were still limited to the fashionable and rich circles of society.

Drinking habits have changed since then, but even in 1988 Burton still seemed firmly rooted in the brewing tradition. There were few parts of town that did not in some way reflect the influence of the Bass dynasty. St Paul's Church, St Margaret's Church, the Victorian-Gothic Town Hall and various other public buildings were all given to the town by Michael Bass, who was to become Lord Burton, while the history of the brewing industry is celebrated at the Bass Museum.

With its dour architecture, Burton is by no means beautiful but there is a cheeky charm about its inhabitants that was refreshing to one more used to southern guile. Children waved and people smiled as I rode past, and at one set of traffic lights two denim-jacketed wisecrackers called out: 'Better not try and skip those red lights, Tonto!' I was to make another discovery in Burton. I couldn't understand why I should be so surprised to see so many gaunt Indian women in anoraks and saris pushing prams. Then I suddenly realised. For a whole month Catherine and I had not seen a single black face. Living in London, I had grown so used to seeing a mixture of nationalities that it now came as quite a shock to realise that the population of England really was predominantly white.

Without a doubt, the highlight of Celia's sortie into Derbyshire was Bretby, built during the reign of Elizabeth I and then rebuilt in 1656 by Philip Stanhope, second Earl of Chesterfield. It was not the house, however, that most aroused Celia's enthusiasm:

> 'that which is most admired – and justly so to be – by all persons and excite their curiosity to come and see is the Gardens and Waterworks; out of the billiard roome the first was with gravell walks and a large fountaine in the middle with flower potts and greens set round the brimm of the fountaines that are paved with stone; the pipes in the fountaines play very finely, some of a great height, some flushes the water about, then you come to a descent of several steps which discovers another fine garden with fountaines playing through pipes, besett on the bancks with all sort of greens and flower trees dwarfes honey-suckles in a round tuft growing uppright and all sorts of flower trees and greens finely cutt and exactly kept; in one garden there are 3 fountaines wherein stands great statues, each side on their pedistalls is a Dial, one for the sun, the other a Clock which by the water worke is moved and strikes the hours and chimes the quarters, and when they please play Lilibolaro on the Chymes – all this I heard when I was there'

Perhaps it isn't surprising that with all the excitement Celia needed a glass of wine before continuing on her way.

A very different prospect awaited us from the avenues, green-houses, aviaries and gravel walks described by Celia. Only the dower house remained of the buildings, while the gardens had reverted to rolling parkland. Our hosts were tax exiles living on the Channel Islands, which meant that while George was installed next to a string of elegant racehorses, Catherine and I were based in the horsebox.

The next few days were gloriously slothful. Charles came up and we spent the time eating, drinking, exploring and doing cross-words. Since we had parted at Newmarket, Charles had rung me every night on the Vodafone, and we would talk until the batteries ran flat. I had grown to love these conversations. The anticipation of them would spur me on during the day, while the prospect of yet another visit from him would lend a sweet excitement to the passionless routine of our itinerary. Charles continued to stand by his proposal. He would playfully call me his fiancée and try and lure me into jewellers' shops to choose an engagement ring. It was lovely, and both Catherine and I adored his eccentric attentions, but I had no idea what the outcome would be. Apart from the flimsy framework of our journey, life was so unsettled and dis-orientating that for the next four months at least it seemed best to take each day as it came.

Bleeper clearly adhered to the same philosophy: some days he was good, some days he was bad and some days he was very bad, but it was completely arbitrary which day would be which. Quite apart from a fairly cavalier attitude to hygiene he was still in his chewing stage, and anything he could get his teeth round or into, whether it was a map, a chocolate bar, a jumper or a table top, he would attack with gusto. Experience taught us to remove from reach everything but the most permanent fixtures. Unfortunately our circumspection did not extend to my tricorn hat. When I wasn't wearing it, the hat normally hung from one of the hooks near the door. At first this had been an ideal spot, for it was easily accessible to me but safely out of Bleeper's reach. Gradually however, as the weeks went by, the hook also became home to an accumulated jumble of jackets, map-cases, binoculars and halters. Losing more and more of its purchase every day, the hat must have eventually relinquished its post, for we returned one afternoon from Burton to find Bleeper licking his lips, surrounded by a trail of chewed braid and mangled ostrich feathers.

The fine weather continued into the beginning of the following week, causing swarms of pollen beetles to cling to my fluorescent tabard, presumably mistaking it for rape flower. My companion for this Derbyshire leg of the journey was a very jolly and sensible woman called Jackie, who took me through some of the loveliest country we had yet seen. I rather agreed with her that if she ever went to heaven it would look something like south Derbyshire, with its undulating fields of rustling corn and distant hills of hazy blue woodland.

Celia had also been moved by the 'fine prospect of the Country, enclosed good lands admirable corne of all sorts, good grass', but Derby town itself was clearly not her idea of heaven.

> 'this is a dear place for strangers notwithstanding the plentyfullness of all provision my dinner cost me 5s. and 8d., only 2 servant men with me and I had but a shoulder of mutton and bread and beer; here they make great quantetys of gloves, I did not observe or learn any other trade or manufacture, they had only shops of all sorts of things; they carry much of their carriages on sledges to secure their pitchings in the streetes.'

According to Jackie it wasn't unscrupulous restaurateurs who were the scourge of modern-day Derby, but a totally different breed of citizen.

'Watch out for flashers! It happened to me the other day. A chap in a gold Ford Ghia.'

Had it been a very distressing experience, I wondered.

'Not at all. I wrote down his number and he got a fifty quid fine. It was great fun. I keep looking out for him, but I haven't seen him since.'

South-east of Derby Jackie drew my attention to a bridge over the Trent, identifying it as Swarkestone. According to legend there lived on the north side of the river two very beautiful women, who were betrothed to two knights away on the Crusades. When the Crusades were over the knights returned to claim their brides, only to be swept to their deaths when they tried to cross the river. So heartbroken were the two women that they never married and on their deaths left their money to the nearby monastery, so that a bridge might be built across the Trent. Looking at the graceful seventeen-arched causeway in the distance, I must have murmured 'How romantic,' for Jackie immediately retorted: 'Nonsense! It's the most terrible bottleneck.'

The halcyon weather was not to last. As George and I made our way back over the border into Staffordshire it began to pour. By the time we had reached Tutbury we were cold, sodden and dispirited. In such a deluge it scarcely seemed worth the detour to go and visit Tutbury Castle, described by Celia as a 'great fortification but all decay'd', but I pulled George to the right and followed the signs to the castle. I was hardly prepared for the imposing spectacle of this ruin, perched high above the River Dove on an isolated projection of rock. As we entered the gateway, I saw that someone had scratched into the stone the words 'Ace Woz 'ere'. So too had been Mary Queen of Scots, James I and Henrys II, III, IV and VI, but now Tutbury was in the hands of the Manpower Services Commission who were in the process of giving the castle a facelift under the direction of Barry the custodian.

'Ooh! 'es got a 'tache, a 'tache – just like me!' cried Barry, forgetting the rain in his delight at seeing George.

Plying me with coffee, Barry explained how appropriate it was for me to have brought my horse to the castle, for it was near this very spot that the Bolingbrokes had first started to breed the English shire. Barry's clothes were soon clinging to his body with the wet, but he continued to tell me more of the castle's history and would accept no money for the guide book and postcards he gave me. Instead he thrust a twenty pound note into my saddlebag for START, and taking both my hands in his, thanked me for visiting his castle.

The rain persisted over the next two days as we made our way to Newcastle under Lyme. Like Celia, we called in at Ingestre Hall near Stafford, a rose-brick Jacobean house built in 1601. Until 1960 it was the home of the Earls of Shrewsbury, but now it was the home of the Metropolitan Borough of Sandwell's Department of Education. The façade had changed very little since Celia's visit:

> 'the front lookes nobly; noe flatt roofed houses in this country but much in windows; two large bow windows on each side runns up the whole building, the middle the same, besides much flatt window between so that the whole is little besides window'

In the past two decades the interior must have changed out of all recognition. The Yellow Drawing Room was the setting no longer for *tête-à-têtes* over cucumber sandwiches, but for drama work- shops and improvisational music classes, while the Mortlake tapestries, gilt candelabra, Queen Anne escritoires and Sèvres dinner service had long since been replaced by institutional furniture and canteen crockery. Only a few family portraits remained, a rather pathetic reminder of the time when Ingestre was not a residential arts centre but a home.

The following two nights found Catherine and me sleeping in the box, while George was stabled at the Westlands Riding Centre in Newcastle under Lyme. Apart from the fact that the shower didn't work, it was never irksome to stay in the box. Indeed by this stage in the journey Catherine and I had come to value these evenings on our own, when we could relax, listen to some opera or Motown, clean the tack over a glass or two of wine and then giggle and gossip our way through more wine and an impromptu meal of pasta and Mars Bars. Disorientating as it was to wake up surrounded by piles of books, dirty washing, files and maps, the bed above the cab was surprisingly comfortable even if one needed the skills of a trapeze artist to actually climb into it. For easy access to George and Bleeper, and perhaps because she didn't relish scaling the cab overhang with a hangover, Catherine had opted for the bed-seat near the door.

That the box was home went without saying. It was also the office, the changing room, the lunchtime canteen, the tack room and the kennel: in short, the nerve centre for the entire journey. Next to the Ipswich Town Football Club knickers, on the only available space of wall above the seat, we had pinned a large-scale map of England on which we would plot our progress with red pins. Very quickly this map became the focal point of the lorry interior.

Although the lorry was cosy, and we were very grateful to Banbury Boxes for having granted us the use of it, we decided after five weeks that it might be improved if certain design features were modified or dispensed with altogether. The brass catches on the cupboards, for example, looked most decorative and drew gasps of admiration from the owners of lesser boxes, but were in fact totally impractical once the lorry was in motion. Should Catherine turn left the catches on the starboard side of the lorry would leap open and the cupboards would disgorge an avalanche of socks, breeches and bras onto the floor below. Should she turn right the 'high-tec' cupboard on the port side would fly open, catapulting Vodafone batteries, dictaphones, Sony Walkmen and all manner of other lethal projectiles across the gangway. The only solution we discovered was to tie a shoelace round the offending fitments, although that was not without its disadvantages, especially when one of us needed a jumper or a roll of film in a hurry.

Next to the sink was a smart pine cupboard in which were housed the fridge and microwave. Like the fridge, the microwave had never fulfilled its proper function, but performed sterling service as a storage cupboard for pasta, chocolate and packet soup. The only design fault was that the microwave was not quite flush with the shelving units, so that any food which happened to slip down the side was utterly irretrievable. The shower/lavatory and the kitchen sink similarly didn't work, but also served as excellent storage spaces – the shower for our clothes, START leaflets and brochures, vet box and dog food, and the sink as an anti-spillage device for opened cartons of orange juice and half-finished bottles of wine. Amazingly, both gas rings worked, as did the grill, although lighting it one needed the bravery of a Scaevola, for on contact with a burning match it would ignite with the violence of a blowtorch, shooting out tongues of hair-singeing flame. When it wasn't in use as an incendiary device, the grill pan served as a convenient hiding place for the cash float, but if Catherine turned a corner too sharply a flurry of five pound notes would be sent spiralling to the floor, a race between Bleeper and myself ensuing as to who would reach them first.

To our enormous relief the tapedeck and radio usually did work, since they had been connected to the lorry battery and not to the same circuit as the fridge, microwave and television. Even if the television circuit had functioned there was little likelihood of the set itself working, since the aerial, a saucer-like affair attached to the highest point of the roof, had been knocked off at the lorry's first brush with a low-lying branch. All that remained of it now were two bare wires.

Celia's visit to Newcastle under Lyme had been inspired by her interest in pottery.

'I went to this Newcastle in Staffordshire to see the makeing the fine tea-potts cups and saucers of the fine red earth, in imitation and as curious as that which comes from China, but was defeated in my design, they comeing to an end of their clay they made use off for that sort of ware and therefore was remov'd to some other place where they were not settled at their work, so could not see it'

Pottery has been made in the region since the Bronze Age, although it was only with the Industrial Revolution that the area collectively known as the Potteries achieved world fame. All the great names of today – Wedgwood, Spode, Coalport, Minton – are associated with that period. During our stay in Newcastle under Lyme I discovered that all the present factories could be visited. Time was, however, very short. Rather guiltily, I decided to omit the factory tour, and set off for Nantwich the next day feeling at least a little vindicated by the fact that Celia's desire to see pottery-making at first hand had also been thwarted.

From Nantwich Celia continued north-west towards Chester

'14 long miles the wayes being deep; its much on enclosures and I passed by severall large pooles of waters but what I wonder'd at was that tho' this shire is remarkable for a greate deale of greate Cheeses and Dairys I did not see more than 20 or 30 cowes in a troope feeding, but on enquiry find the custome of the country to joyn their milking together of a whole village and so make their great Cheeses and so it goes round.'

From the Potteries we had now travelled to the rich, rolling pastureland of Cheshire. Green seemed an inadequate epithet with which to describe the intensity of colour that now surrounded us. I had been riding along daydreaming when the noise of a cow lowing interrupted my reveries. Looking over a hedge I realised to my horror that the cow, rolling and heaving on her side a few feet away from me, was about to give birth. Casting round helplessly for assistance my eyes alighted on the bobble-hatted form of a

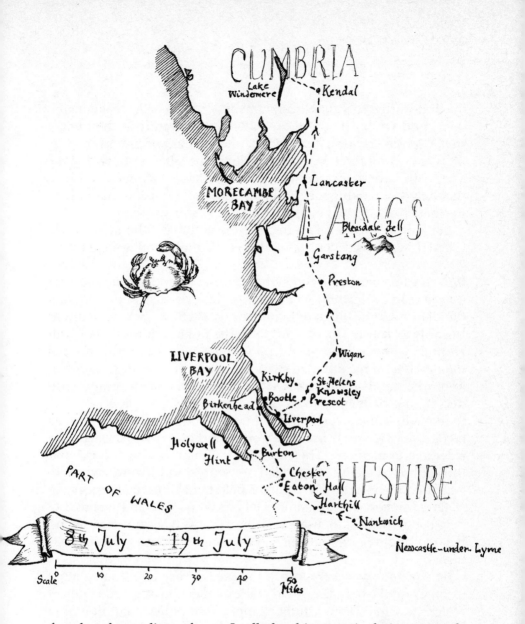

CUMBRIA

Lake Windemere

Kendal

MORECAMBE BAY

LANCS

Lancaster

Bleasdale Fell

Garstang

Preston

Wigan

LIVERPOOL BAY

Kirkby

St. Helens

Knowsley

Birkenhead

Bootle

Prescot

Liverpool

Holywell

Hint

Burton

Chester

Eaton Hall

CHESHIRE

Harthill

Nantwich

PART OF WALES

Newcastle-under-Lyme

8th July — 19th July

Scale   0   10   20   30   40   50 Miles

farmhand mending a fence. I called to him, gesticulating urgently
in the direction of the cow. Very slowly he put down his tools,
ambled across the road, and ponderously climbed over the gate,
pausing to check whether its bailer-twine knot was secure before
continuing on his way towards the cow. By now I was frantic, for
the cow seemed to be bellowing with pain. Once he had reached
the animal, the man methodically began to roll up his sleeves, and
then, with both hands, grabbed hold of the tiny legs now protrud-

ing and started to pull. Never in my life had I seen anything being born, and while George picked away indifferently at the hedge-row, I looked on transfixed. Once the calf had been born and its mother was contentedly licking it clean, the labourer turned to me and, with a barely perceptible nod of the head, grunted. Realising that he was thanking me, I called back. 'No, I'd like to thank you. I've never seen a calf being born before. It was wonderful.'

Looking at me as if I were a certifiable lunatic the man slowly rolled down his sleeves, did up his cuff buttons and walked off.

We were to meet with a somewhat warmer reception a little further up the road at Harthill. As I rode through the village, I could hear the distorted mufflings of a loudspeaker which, as we advanced towards its source, turned out to be the public address system for Harthill School's Summer Fair. It was like one of those events one remembers from childhood, with children in fancy dress, goldfish in bowls, mums in sundresses, ice creams in cornets, grannies in deckchairs, dads in cahoots, babies in prams, sweets in jars and toddlers in tears. Nearly all the children, mums and grandparents recognised George from 'Blue Peter', and our arrival caused considerable excitement. The three-legged race was postponed and the country dancing suspended as George and I were invited to walk into the middle of the games field to be officially introduced: 'This is Mighty, the shire horse who is walking round England to help people with skin diseases. When Class 2B has finished saying hello to Mighty, will they all sit down and let Class 3A have their turn.'

By the time we were ready to leave, every child had patted George and the organisers had made a collection of £26, the bulk of which they had thoughtfully changed into notes to cut down on the weight.

'Where are you off to next?'

'Eaton Hall.'

'Good luck!'

While I was organising the trip, several people had suggested that I write to the Duke of Westminster because of start's connection with Westminster Hospital. I had typed a fairly standard letter, personalising it with the heading 'From Belgravia via Chester and back again for Westminster.' Two days later there had been a telephone call from the duke's personal assistant, Mr Carter at Eaton Hall, asking me to suggest a convenient time to come and see the duke at his London office in Davies Street.

A handsome man with a tendency to dissolve into fits of boyish giggles at the slighest provocation, the Duke of Westminster struck me not so much as the richest man in England as the model for a character out of *Just William*. Enthusiastic and charming, he was full of suggestions about the ride.

'Liverpool's going to be pretty tricky. How are you going to manage that? Of course you must stop off at Eaton Hall. I wonder if you pass any of my other houses?'

By the end of our meeting I had acquired an extra ten nights' stabling, as well as introductions to the Merseyside mounted police and to all the editors of the Chester and North Wales Newspaper Company.

'Please don't go to an awful lot of trouble,' I said as he saw me to the door.

'Don't worry!' he giggled down the stairs, 'I'll get someone else to do it!'

All that afternoon I had been curious to know just what our reception at Eaton Hall would be like. I was soon to find out. We had barely left Harthill behind us when a car suddenly drew up and out stepped Mr Carter himself. Introducing himself in anxious Cheshire tones he declared with no small urgency, 'You won't know this but the outer defences close at five. We'd better hurry.'

Quite what the outer defences were was never explained, but from the very mystery that surrounded them, one sensed that the security measures for Eaton Hall would resemble those of Fort Knox. Speed was clearly of the essence, but Mr Carter seemed most concerned about whether the bridge leading to the hall would take the weight of the horsebox. After long deliberations it was decided that another route would have to be taken, so off we set with Mr Carter in front and Catherine following in the lorry. What with circumnavigating the hall and park, driving into the outskirts of Chester and returning once more to the open country, the journey to Eaton, which would otherwise have been less than a mile, actually exceeded the total mileage George and I had covered that day.

I had chosen to sit in Mr Carter's car and was regaled during the journey with all manner of statistics about Eaton Hall, its environs and the Grosvenor empire in general.

'His Grace's park alone covers 900 acres,' declared the personal assistant proudly.

Passing through a gate, I was expecting to have to show my papers at any moment, or at least to see a few gun emplacements, but there wasn't even a padlock in evidence. Once inside I was surprised to find not the desolation of no-man's land, but an area of green and beautiful parkland in which cricket and golf were being played around what looked like a small village. Having thus penetrated the outer defences we disembarked outside a magnificent stable-block. This, announced Mr Carter, indicating the very box that had been occupied by Arkle, the legendary steeplechaser, was to be Mighty's stable. If during his stay Mighty should want for anything, a girl groom was always at hand. As for us, if we decided to stay in the lorry, the facilities consisted of a tack room where we could boil a kettle, a hosepipe and a gents which was locked between seven at night and seven in the morning. Should we decide to stay elsewhere he recommended the Grosvenor Arms at Pulford. Either way we would have to decide before seven, as after that the outer defences would be shut and passage in and out of the park would be impossible.

The patrons of START had offered to pay all our legitimate expenses, including bed and breakfast should the need arise. Until this moment it had not. If we now chose to stay at the Grosvenor Arms, START would be contributing, however indirectly, to the funds of the Grosvenor Estates. It seemed ridiculous to run up bills for the very charity for which we were supposed to be raising money. Besides, we needed to be around to give George his three evening feeds. Catherine and I decided to stay in the box.

Once George had been settled we were just about to sit down for a cup of tea when a tiny, piping voice exclaimed, 'Oh look, Mum! Whose dog's done a doings on the doorstep?'

Without bothering to check whether Bleeper was in the lorry

Catherine strode off purposefully in the direction of the voice, returning within seconds with a shivering bundle under her arm and a chirpy seven-year-old at her side, who introduced himself as Peter, the son of one of the under gardeners. Much to our delight Peter soon made himself at home in the lorry, chattering away like a little bird, taking an interest in everything. Before long his mother Debbie also came and introduced herself, welcoming us to Eaton and offering to do any washing for us. Catherine and I felt at home immediately.

The following day a press call at the Old Trooper Inn took us into Chester. Celia's feelings about the place had been mixed:

> 'the town is walled all aboute with battlements and a walke all round pav'd with stone; I allmost encompass'd the walls; the streetes are of a greate breadth from the houses, but there is one thing takes much from their appeareing so and from their beauty, for on each side in most places they have made penthouses so broad set on pillars which persons walks under covert, and is made up and down steps under which are ware houses; tho' a penthouse or pallasadoe be convenient and a security from the sun or weather and were it no broader than for two to passe one by the other it would be well and no dissight to the grace of the streetes, but this does darken the streetes and hinder the light of the houses in many places to the streete ward below'

For once she was in accord with Daniel Defoe, who declared that the Rows made the city 'old and ugly'. Few others can have agreed, for the centre of Chester has scarcely changed since 1698. The city walls, the maze of narrow streets, the half-timbered buildings: all were still intact, along with the Rows, those medieval two-tiered shopping arcades that had been so disliked by Celia, now barely visible beneath the swarms of admiring tourists buzzing about with automatic cameras and guide books.

More striking than the Rows was the nominal presence of our host – in less than an hour we had seen the Grosvenor Precinct, the Grosvenor Court, the Grosvenor Gardening Centre, the Grosvenor Museum, as well as numerous other similarly entitled interests. Our host's name seemed to dominate the city – as did his face. On the shelves of W. H. Smith we found it staring up at us from the cover of *Cheshire Vista* magazine.

Notwithstanding the honour of occupying Arkle's stable, George was not happy. The lump on his back had grown and, calling in the vet, we were advised to let him have an extra day's rest. To my great disappointment this meant that the north Wales leg of the journey would have to be left out. Having spent my own childhood and adolescence in south Wales, I had been fascinated to see whether there was any truth in Celia's vitriolic pronouncements on some of my compatriots in the north.

'its [Holywell] a very ragged place many villages in England are better, the houses all thatched and stone walls but so decay'd that in many places ready to tumble down . . . they speake Welsh, the inhabitants go barefoote and bare leg'd a nasty sort of people'

As it happened we did to go to Wales – not on an official visit but on a raiding party across the border to the nearest Chinese takeaway. As far as the charge of barefootedness was concerned, there seemed to be no substance to Celia's accusation, since all ten of the people we saw appeared to be wearing shoes. She was however partly vindicated over the question of bare legs, for we did see two girls walking about in miniskirts with no tights. The question of language was rather more difficult. Certainly there seemed to be an inordinate number of unpronounceable consonants on all the signposts, but of the two people with whom we conversed, one spoke in broad Liverpudlian while the other used an unintelligible distillation of pidgin English and downtown Hong Kong: 'For'y thlee, Eigh'een an' plawn clackers. O.K.?'

We managed to penetrate not only the outer defences at Eaton Hall, but the inner ones as well. Quite by chance our stay coincided with a charity open day at which, in exchange for a nominal fee, the gardens were opened to the public for a few hours. It was well worth the money, for they were lovely, with sweeping vistas and lakeside plantations providing a lyrical backdrop to the temples, pavilions and formal designs of the Dragon, neo-Italian and Tea-House Gardens. It was difficult to say as much about the house. The fourth to be built on the site itself, it looked more like a third-world airport terminal than a ducal seat, but perhaps it was no worse than its predecessors. The second Eaton Hall, built in 1802, was the most extravagant house of the Regency period, an ecclesiastical Gothic confection costing the then vast sum of £75,000, while its replacement in 1882 led the first duke to say to his daughter-in-law: 'Now that I have built a palace, I wish that I lived in a cottage . . . we had better let this daily.'

Our departure was fixed for Wednesday morning. Mr Carter had already said goodbye, and we were just about to leave when Peter and Debbie rushed out of their cottage to wish us luck and to give us some flapjacks, which they had made especially for us.

'I hope the duke didn't scratch your horsebox,' said Debbie. 'These past few days he's been driving round here at a hell of a pace.'

He must have missed us, we replied, adding that we on the other hand were most sorry to have missed him, for it would have been nice to have thanked him for letting George stay in so illustrious a stable.

'Oh, we never see much of him,' replied Debbie. 'Occasionally the duchess waves.'

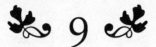

Eaton to Lancaster

It was Wednesday 13 July. George's back had still not recovered and the vet had cautioned against more than two hours' riding that day. Rather than miss Liverpool we therefore decided to box George all the way there, so that I would at least be able to ride him through the city. Celia's journey from Flintshire to Liverpool was an altogether different affair.

> 'I forded over the Dee when the tide was out all upon the sands at least a mile which was as smooth as a die being a few hours left of the flood; the sands are here soe loose that the tydes does move them from one place to another at every flood, that the same place one used to foard a month or two before is not to be pass'd now, for as it brings the sands in heaps to one place so it leaves others in deep holes, which are cover'd with water, and loose sand that would swallow up a horse or carriages, so I had two Guides to conduct me over; the carriages which are used to it and pass continually at the ebbs of water observes the drift of sands and so escape the danger; it was at least a mile I went on the sands before I came to the middle of the channell which was pretty deep, and with such a current or tyde which was falling out to sea together with the wind the horses feete could scarce stand against it, but it was but narrow just the deep part of the channell and so soone over; when the tyde is fully out they frequently ford in many places which they

marke as the sands fall, and can go near 9 or 10 mile over the sands from Chester to Burton or to Flint town almost; but many persons that have known the foards well, that have come a year or half a year after, if they venture on their former knowledge have been overwhelm'd in the ditches made by the sands, which is deep enough to swallow up a coach or waggon.'

Nor was she by any means safe once she had reached Burton.

'From Burton which was on the side of England the shore I went to the ferry 9 miles to the river Meresy, another great river indeed much broader and a perfect sea for 20 miles or more; it comes out of Lancashire from Warrington and both this and the Dee empts themselves into the sea almost together a few leagues from Leverpoole which poole is form'd by a poynt of land that runs almost round the entrance from the sea, being narrow and hazardous to strangers to saile in in the winter, the mouth of the river by reason of the sands and rocks is a gate to the river; this I fery'd over and was an hour and halfe in the passage, its of great bredth and at low water is so deep and salt as the sea almost, tho' it does not cast so green a hew on the water as the sea, but else the waves toss and the rocks great all round it and is as dangerous as the sea; its in a sort of Hoy that I ferried over and my horses, the boate would have held 100 people.'

The modern-day equivalent of Celia's ferry appeared to be the M53 which, cutting a great swathe through the Wirral Peninsula, swept along through a limbo of cranes, derricks, gasometers, chimneys and high-rise flats. Once at Birkenhead, we were quickly swallowed up by the tunnel only to be ignominiously disgorged a few minutes later on the other side of the Mersey. Compared with Celia's heroic struggles, our journey to Liverpool seemed embarrassingly easy. Our first impressions of the city were also to be different. In 1698 Celia wrote:

'Leverpool is built on the river Mersy, mostly new built houses of brick and stone after the London fashion; the first original was a few fishermens houses and now is grown to a large fine town and but a parish and one Church, tho' there be 24 streetes in it; there is indeed a little Chappell and there are a great many Dessenters in the town; its a very rich trading town the houses of brick and stone built high and even, that a streete quite through lookes very handsome, the streetes well pitched; there are abundance of persons you see very well dress'd and of good fashion; the streetes are faire and long, its London in miniature as much as ever I saw any thing'

In 1988, Liverpool seemed to have little in common with London, unless one were to compare it with, say, Brixton. The city seemed to be in the process of a dockside facelift, but beyond a nip here and a tuck there, the majority of the features were decaying and ravaged. It all seemed very far removed from the 'fine town' described by Celia. We stopped in Bootle in a street desolate of people apart from a handful of overall-clad workmen hosing down huge container lorries in a compound. As Catherine and I tacked George up a shambling figure disappeared into the working men's pub on the corner where the promise of a weekly ninety minutes of tasselled titillation was pasted to one of the windows: 'Exotic Dancing every Wednesday 12.30–2.'

One almost longed to indulge oneself and wallow in the bleak-ness of it all, but it was impossible. No sooner had the workmen in the compound heard George's hoofs ringing on the tarmac than they flocked to the mesh fencing of the compound, bandying wisecracks and volunteering all their loose change for START. Similarly everyone flocked out of the pub to admire the great drayhorse, from the most hardened bar-propper to a singularly unexotic dancer with a long black wig and false eyelashes, to whom we explained that we were collecting to help people with skin cancer, burns and psoriasis. 'Scirrhosis? Yeah. That's a good cause, that is. Yeah. I'll give to that.'

Our expectations were similarly frustrated in Toxteth. Asking directions from a cyclist we had been told: 'Straight up there, luv.

Turn right and you're in the heart of Toxteth. That's where you lock your doors and windows – especially when you're IN the car.'

His words seemed to be reinforced by the wasteland in which we soon found ourselves, with its craters of rubble, boarded-up slums and peeling hoardings bearing fluorescent evangelical messages: 'Repent! The end is nigh!' Yet somehow the end seemed far from nigh. For every house with corrugated iron over the windows there would be another three that looked bright and cheerful, with occupants to match. Pulling into a narrow street of tiny red-bricked terraced houses we were amazed to see every door open as the residents came out to see George and to wish us well. Such was the warmth of the reception, such the fun of the occasion, that the event turned into something of a street party. Nearly every inhabitant of the street was there, and those who weren't were quickly sent for: 'Tracy! Go and get your gran! She'll kill us if she misses this.'

Our collecting tin had already doubled its weight when one elderly widower called Sam invited us into his house to show us holiday snaps of his wife and pictures of his son winning the first prize in a Warner's Holiday Fancy Dress Contest.

At the end of the day we boxed George up and set off for our next night's stabling at Knowsley,

> 'the Earle of Darbys house which looked very nobly with many towers and balls on them; it stands amongst tall trees and lookes like a pleasant grove all about it; its an old house runs a large compass of ground'

The surrounding areas of St Helen's, Prescot and Kirkby have since 1698 merged almost into one sprawling extension of Liverpool. What effect would this have had on Knowsley, we wondered? At the very least we had expected to find some sizeable diminution of the 'large compass of ground' seen by Celia. Instead we discovered one of the largest estates I have ever seen: two thousand acres of parkland girded by twelve miles of wall. For six centuries the site had been in the hands of the Stanley family, the Earls of Derby, with the oldest part of the hall dating back to the fifteenth century. Somehow it came as no surprise to learn that the family motto was 'Sans Changer'.

In answer to my initial enquiry in February, Lord Derby had immediately sent a very warm letter wishing me luck with the ride and suggesting that I contact his farm manager about stabling arrangements. Mr and Mrs Dive were as welcoming as their employer. Once they had conveyed Lord Derby's best wishes they helped us to settle George into his stable and regaled us with a tea fit for a lord, after which Mr Dive showed us the estate.

In just an hour we saw nearly everything. From the 600 sheep and 200 cows to the sawmill, granary and ornamental lake, Mr Dive pointed out everything with the same enthusiastic pride. Over to our left, for instance, was the greenhouse, from which figs were always sent up to Scotland while the family was there for the shooting season: 'It's a tradition.'

Over to the right was the garden where Edward Lear had written many of his *Nonsense Songs and Stories* for the children of the house: 'I can't take you in, I'm afraid. The countess might be walking there.'

Mr Dive showed us the 'New Hall', built sixteen years earlier by the earl: 'The queen's apartments are in the front.' And the stretch of open ground where the twelfth earl used to hold horseraces: 'The name Derby means something to everyone all over the world.'

When we finally returned to his own house, Mr Dive showed us a book which had been inscribed quite simply by Lord Derby with the words 'To Dive'.

'People of his lordship's standing always call me Dive. It would be demeaning to call me anything else.'

Taking our leave of the farm manager, we felt that even though we hadn't met the Earl of Derby, his distant, gracious presence had nevertheless pervaded the whole of Knowsley.

The next day was ghastly. Celia had encountered her own problems on this particular stretch of the journey, as she made her way:

> 'mostly in lanes and some hollow wayes, and some pretty
> deep stony way so forced us upon the high Causey many;

but some of the way was good which I went pretty fast, and yet by reason of the tediousness of the miles for length I was 5 hours going that 14 mile, I could have gone 30 mile about London in the time; there was pretty much woods and lanes through which I pass'd, and pass'd by a mer or lake of water; there are many of these here about; but not going through Ormskerk I avoided going by the famous Mer call'd Martin Mer that as the proverb sayes has parted many a man and his mare indeed; it being neare evening and not getting a Guide I was a little afraid to go that way it being very hazardous for Strangers to pass by it'

My preoccupations were of a somewhat different nature. The ride, although it was going to plan, was raising far less money than had been expected. The main problem was collecting manpower. Notwithstanding the generosity of those we had met along the route, there was a limit to what two people could raise on their own. Catherine and I collected as much and as often as we could, but even on the most optimistic forecast it was clear that we would return to London far short of our target of £100,000.

Added to that, I was confused about Charles, who continued to propose to me relentlessly. Our telephone conversations still sustained me, yet while I looked forward to them all day and felt awful once the batteries had run flat and cut us off, I was worried at how dependent I was becoming on them. With such a volatile and peripatetic lifestyle, I knew that I was far more vulnerable emotionally than I had ever been before. Half of me wanted to say something encouraging to him; the other half shrank from any commitment.

I was to feel even more upset that morning. As we rounded a sharp corner my typewriter had suddenly hurled itself from the bed above the cab and struck me on the arm, landing on the floor with keys and springs flying in all directions. It wasn't as if the typewriter constituted a very important part of the luggage – I hadn't once used it since we left London. But in my current frame of mind this was irrelevant. I wanted to be angry, and with no difficulty whatsoever found all sorts of arguments to fan my rage.

'Lucky it wasn't your head,' said Catherine quietly.

'I wish it had been,' I replied, trying to invest each syllable with as much bitterness as I could muster.

Catherine must have been glad to see the back of me that morning, for I set off in the blackest of moods, made still worse by my dropping my cassette of *Tosca* into the path of an oncoming juggernaut. The prospect of another three and a half months of this plodding journey seemed unbearable. I longed desperately for privacy and anonymity, to shut myself away and forget about the ride, Celia Fiennes, fund-raising, the typewriter and Charles. It was all too complicated and tiring. I rode to Preston that day, but remembered nothing of the journey. Feeling emotionally battered, I dismounted from George that evening sure only of one thing: that I would have to call things off with Charles and never see him again.

After a good night's sleep, my spirits were greatly lifted. Catherine cycled alongside me for half the morning and then rode George for the remainder, while I took a spin on her bicycle. After George's lolloping gait, this new-found mobility was exhilarating and I behaved like a child with a new Christmas present all morning. It was a sunny day, but in the distance a shadowy ridge of hills sat hunched and brooding beneath a dark mantle of cloud. Looking at it, I felt not only apprehension at the climb ahead, but also an overwhelming sense of excitement. The south was now unequivocally behind us. In two days we would be in the Lake District.

We had heard that Grize Dale to the north-east of Garstang was especially beautiful, so it was arranged that Catherine would intercept me en route for a picnic lunch. The day was fine and hot and judging by our progress that morning, George and I would have plenty of time to reach the proposed rendezvous. Unfortunately we had not reckoned on the River Wyre. On the map fording the Wyre east of Garstang had looked an easy enough operation. However, once George reached the water's edge he needed no more than a glance at the eddying black water to convince him that this was as far as he intended to go. All my entreaties were in vain, and I was about to turn back when I saw an elderly lady crossing the footbridge above us. Would it be possible, I wondered, to take George the same way?

'I don't see why not,' she replied. 'It's very strong and there aren't any steps. I've crossed it hundreds of times myself.' Since the only other conceivable way across the river would add at least another hour to our journey, the decision was simple. Dismounting, I began to lead George slowly along the bridge. Although narrow, it seemed solid enough and in good repair. It had even received a recent coat of green paint. There were barely three inches to spare on either side of his flanks, but George remained very calm as I talked him over. I was beginning to congratulate myself on my resourcefulness when I suddenly saw that just ahead the bridge terminated not in a well-trodden path, but in four steps.

Once again, through sheer thoughtlessness I had jeopardised George's safety. All too late I realised that I should not have relied on the information of the old lady. After one and a half months in the saddle, even I knew that the things one notices as a rider are quite different from the things one sees as a pedestrian. Of course the old lady would never have noticed the steps, for they presented no obstacle to her. The last thing I wanted was to risk George becoming lame, so, calming myself as far as I was able, I stroked his head, told him he was a good boy and then, very slowly, started to push him back along the bridge. To my amazement George needed no encouragement, and began to walk back of his own accord, every now and then looking anxiously over his shoulder as his flank rubbed against the balustrade or one of his hoofs glanced metallically against the railing. For the most part he kept his gaze steadily on me, his large brown eyes faintly quizzical but filled with trust. I felt totally unworthy of his confidence. By the time we reached the other side, I was the one who was sweating. George was quite calm, the only physical evidence of his ordeal being a few tiny flecks of green paint along his side. Feeling very embarrassed and foolish, I resolved to tell no one of the incident.

Celia's experience of Garstang had been altogether better:

> 'here it was I was first presented with the Clap bread which is much talked off made all of oates; I was surpris'd when the cloth was laid they brought a great basket such as one uses to undress children with, and set on the table full of thinn waffers as big as pancackes and drye that they easily

breake into shivers, but coming to dinner found it to be the only thing I must eate for bread; the taste of oate bread is pleasant enough and where its well made is very acceptable, but for the most part its scarce baked and full of drye flower on the outside . . . Gascoyn [Garstang] is a little market town, one Church in it which is a mile off from the town, and the parish is 8 miles long which discourag'd me in staying there being Satturday night and so pressed on to Lancaster; I perceive most of the parishes are a great tract of land and very large and also as beneficial, for all over Lancastershire the revenues of the parsonages are considerable, 2 and 300£, 500 and 800£ apiece'

All hopes of meeting Catherine for lunch faded entirely when we met with a further delay near Grize Dale. A bridleway that was to take us over both an electrified railway and the M6 turned out to have been closed for fifteen years, even though it was still marked on the map. Luckily, after an abortive attempt at a detour, the wife of the farmer who owned the land took pity on me and, unlocking the gates, led us across the grassy bridge. The noise from below was deafening.

'Is it always like this?' I shouted once we were a hundred yards clear.

'Yes!' she yelled back, 'Except on Christmas Day. We all look forward to Christmas round here.'

By the end of the afternoon we were about three hours behind schedule. We had eaten nothing all day – not even an underdone wafer of clap-bread. Turning to Celia's journal that evening I was gratified to read

'I was about 4 houres going this twelve mile and could have gone 20 in the tyme in most countrys, nay by the people of those parts this twelve mile is as long and as much tyme taken up in going it as to go from thence to Lancaster which is 20 mile; and I can confirm this by my own experience'

So, I thought, could I.

Our stablers that night lived high on the fells at Bleasdale. We arrived rather late, and after diving in and out of the same bath water, hopping into our tights and pulling on the most presentable clothes we could find, we descended the stairs to be met by Father Dominic Milroy, a friend of our hosts and headmaster of Ampleforth.

'Would you like gin or whisky?' were his first words.

Thereafter all our memories falter somewhat, but I seem to recall that by the end of the evening it had been decided that our next adventure should be a journey across the Andes with Catherine riding, me tagging behind and Father Dominic handling the P.R. and catching the fish for supper. It would be hard to think of a more congenial companion, and we were very tempted to hold poor Father Dominic to his word.

Our host was an entertaining man with an irrepressible smile, who enjoyed nothing more than a good joke. However, when the conversation turned to foreign news and politics, all levity disappeared from his voice as he realised with horror that neither Catherine nor I had the slightest idea what was going on in the world.

Since we saw no television and rarely listened to the radio, our only information came from what we read. Of the two of us Catherine was probably the more interested in current affairs, but once she had scanned the headlines and scoured the Engagements column, she would be more than happy to relax with a Mills & Boon. I had brought along the entire contents of my travel library, such as it was, but the Patrick Leigh Fermors, Jan Morrises and Jonathan Rabans remained unopened and I found myself coasting along on a newspaper diet of crosswords, horoscopes and gossip. We rarely talked about the news with our various stablers. They were usually far too interested in George's appetite, his shoes and the appalling weather we had encountered along the way. The only other channel through which the events of 1988 were filtered through to us was my father's letters. Only that week, for example, I had received a letter from him referring not only to the Piper Alpha oil-rig disaster in the North Sea, but also to various other events in which he thought I might be interested.

'There is an exhibition in Cardiff Museum about the jour-

neys made through Wales 800 years ago by GERALD CAM-
BRIENSIS. His ARSE must have been as sore as yours.

Bank rate is 10½ per cent. PUT IN (AND KEEP IN) as much
money as you *possibly* can.

Daddy xxxxx xxxxx

P.S. What news of the gas meter???'

Apart from his rather idiosyncratic view of world events, I had
no idea whatsoever what was going on.

'You mean you don't even know who was standing in the
Kensington by-election?' persisted our host. 'I thought Cynthia
Payne was a relation of yours!'

After dinner he escorted us to the garage where nailed to the wall
was a wooden shield bearing the most magnificent rhinoceros
head. 'It's one of our family's most treasured possessions,' he
declared solemnly, adding that as students of the region we might
be interested to read the inscription beneath it.

'Believed to be the only Rhinoceros shot in the "wild" in the
British Isles. Destined for Blackpool Zoo, Bigi Nicki, as he
was affectionately known by the Masai Children of the
Ngora Ngora, was parked in a railway siding at Garstang
station of the 28th March 1923. He is thought to have been
panicked by the passage of the Coronation Scot en route
from London to Glasgow at 1.05 am. Breaking out from his
reinforced container he made for the hills and was sighted 2
days later on the Bleasdale Fells. Cornered and eventually
shot at the Arbour by a police marksman from the Lancashire Constabulary using double ball and wad. 1.4.1923.'

It seemed too extraordinary an incident not to be recorded, so,
having fetched my notebook, I began to copy it down verbatim. It
was only when our host said 'Now you must come and see the
elephant's tooth,' that I realised I had been duped. I laughed so
much I got hiccups, which persisted until I went to bed, despite the
solicitous attentions of Father Dominic, who exhorted me to take
sixteen sips from a glass of water backwards while holding my
breath.

The following day I felt terrible. With uncharacteristic foresight, a few days earlier I had put a packet of Panadol into my saddlebag, and it was to this I now turned to relieve the throbbing above my right eye. Spirits always give me a migraine, so I comforted myself with the thought that if the degree of pain had been commensurate with the amount of alcohol I had consumed, three hatchets would now be embedded in my forehead instead of just one. The Panadol seemed to work at once, although this was perhaps due more to its unpleasant taste than its analgesic properties. The mere thought of having to take another one without water was painkiller enough.

Although looking at the changing countryside each day was an absorbing occupation, the contents of my saddlebag also helped pass the hours. Apart from the Panadol, I had with me a second dictaphone to replace the one I'd lost in Cambridgeshire. For the most part the dictaphone commentary was inaudible when played back, since what was not drowned by the clatter of George's hoofs was usually distorted by the crackling of the prevailing wind. In addition to the recorder I would sometimes carry a book with me in case Catherine was late for a rendezvous; but my main entertainment was a Walkman and a set of opera cassettes, to which I would listen in mono, partly so that I could still hear the traffic and partly because it was just too uncomfortable to wear both earphones under my hat. The remainder of the bag's contents consisted of a camera, a spare roll of film and a tube of high protection factor sunblock. Of all my luggage this must surely have been the most superfluous. Since Leicestershire the weather had progressively deteriorated. Indeed, only that morning I had read in the newspaper that the rainfall for the first thirteen days of July was three times the average, and that the bookmakers William Hill were offering odds of 5 to 1 against punters predicting the next forty-eight hour dry spell.

We were now south-east of Lancaster. Gone were the loitering river valleys and languid hills of the lowlands. All that surrounded us now was damp, spongy moorland and fells, their flanks jagged with outcroppings of rock. There were no people and no houses. We were passed by only one car all morning. The only other signs of life were the hundreds of black-faced sheep which would bounce away into the sedge grass at our approach, tails wagging and bottoms wiggling. Since seven o'clock that morning it had been raining, and still it continued. Cold and spiteful, the stinging drops insinuated themselves into every chink and crevice of clothing. The very air seemed heavy with moisture. Feeling the water squelching in my right boot, I thought to myself that if William Hill were to visit Appletree Fell that day, he would probably raise his odds against a dry spell to 100 to 1. It kept raining all the way to Lancaster.

Celia had apparently been dogged by similar weather, for:

'when I came into the town the stones were so slippery crossing some channells that my horse was quite down on his nose but did at length recover himself and so I was not thrown off or injured, which I desire to bless God for as for the many preservations I mett with'

It was all I could do to hold George as we picked our way through the rivulets of water plaiting and weaving their way down towards the market square, and I found myself sorely looking forward to my rendezvous with Catherine at the castle. Celia's opinion of Lancaster was that it was 'old and much decay'd', but she approved of one recent innovation:

'they have one good thing in most parts off this principality (or County Palatine its rather called) that at all cross wayes there are Posts with Hands pointing to each road with the names of the great town or market towns that it leads to, which does make up for the length of the miles that strangers may not loose their road and have it to goe back againe'

That Celia should have seen fit to mention something so common-place in today's roadscape as a signpost is not as strange as it seems. In the seventeenth century the romance of the road was as yet unappreciated, and the word 'travel' still had strong semantic

114

links with the French noun *travail*, implying hardship, discomfort and often danger.

There was the ever-present risk of highwaymen. Women travellers would go to the lengths of carrying a spare purse with them, ready to hand over at the first sign of trouble. Sometimes the purse would act as a deterrent against physical attack. Sometimes it would not. One sixteen-year-old heiress is reputed to have been attacked eleven times by footpads and highwaymen.

The roads themselves often presented insurmountable difficulties. The majority were so bad that for most wheeled vehicles they were impassable, and frequently they were so rough and potholed that even single riders had difficulty getting through.

Most problematic of all however was the lack of any comprehensive English road atlas. Celia would certainly have referred to John Ogilby's *Britannia* of 1675, which consisted of strip maps of the country's major roads and featured villages hills, bridges, streams, forests and the direction of each by-road. But while Ogilby's atlas was the best of its kind, it was still very limited, certain parts of the country being omitted from it altogether. Even the most detailed of his strip maps was not without its disadvantages. If a traveller should for a moment stray beyond the roads illustrated, he ran the danger of becoming completely lost, unless he had the fortune to stumble on the services of a local guide. And that was unlikely. At the end of the seventeenth century, as Celia affirmed, most people knew 'scarce 3 mile from their home'. It was not until the statute of 1697 that signposts were introduced to England. Their advent understandably met with widespread rejoicing, for they were to change not only the face of the landscape, but the whole nature of road travel.

A one-way system now led us through the town towards the forbidding grey battlements of the castle. Following what seemed to be the appropriate signs, we found ourselves at the entrance not of a Norman fortification, but a multi-storey carpark. Too late I realised how misleading the signpost had been. We should have turned off earlier. Now we would be forced to complete a whole circuit of the city's one-way system before once again reaching the correct turning. We were already an hour behind schedule, and it was to take another hour before we eventually met up with

Catherine. As I emptied the water from my boots I reflected on Celia's words. The 'Post with Hands' had indeed carried the appropriate information. But whether it had helped this particular stranger not to lose her road 'and have it to goe back againe' was another matter.

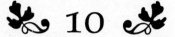

10

Lancaster to Ullswater

It was 16 July. We had now been on the road for seven weeks and had covered well over 600 miles. Two rest days lay ahead of us before we crossed into Cumbria to begin the most arduous part of the whole journey, and it seemed like a good time to take stock. So far we had suffered no severe casualties, although the lorry had received further minor damage near Lancaster when the plastic skylight above George's area of the box had been knocked off after an altercation with a tree. Torrents of water had poured in until Catherine had had the initiative to drape the hole with the jacket Musto Waterproofs had given me as sponsorship for the journey. Musto would have been proud of their product, for even though it sagged ominously under the weight of the accumulated water, it never let a drop into the box.

As far as George was concerned, all his softness had been replaced by lean muscle and we felt confident that he could at the very least make a creditable attempt at the next leg of the journey. As for Catherine and me, whether by design or accident we had settled into our different roles, respecting one another's strengths and putting up with one another's weaknesses. 'Do you still get on?' people would ask us, to which I would instinctively blurt out an affirmative and Catherine would reply 'Yes,' with a measured tone and a half smile. It did not seem too bad a basis on which to continue for the next thirteen weeks.

It also seemed a good time to reflect on the journey itself. Before the ride I had rather arrogantly assumed that I knew my own

117

country better than most. A third of the way into the journey, I now
realised how wrong I had been. My first mistake had been to think
of England as an indivisible unit. My experiences over the past
seven weeks had shown me what a fallacy this was. In fact England
was a composite of entirely differing identities.

Physically, the diversity of the country was overwhelming. Each
county seemed to possess a recognisable and distinct 'look', and in
some counties that 'look' could be subdivided still further. The
spirit of Suffolk, for example, was distilled not simply from the
lonely tracts of coastal heath to the east but from the agricultural
prosperity and solidity of the west. One of the exciting discoveries
of the ride for me was that such variations were so quickly
apparent. George and I travelled no faster than four miles per hour,
yet in the space of a few days we had experienced the flatlands of
Cambridgeshire and the fells of Lancashire. And we had still to
encounter even greater extremes with the Lakes, the Pennines, the
Cornish coastline and the plains of Wiltshire.

I had been equally mistaken in my perception of England's
inhabitants. Since 31 May we had met almost as many people as I
had previously met in my entire life. I had expected these people to
be fairly homogeneous as a population, but now I was reeling at
their variety. The only topic on which everyone seemed agreed
was the appallingness of the weather; otherwise a multitude of
social, economic, occupational, moral, religious and linguistic
factors differentiated the people we had met along the route. From
bishops to belly-dancers, from publicans to policemen, from col-
onels to cowboys – in seven weeks we seemed to have encountered
an entire cross-section of society. Moreover, we had crossed bar-
riers on this journey that at any other time in our lives would be
closed to us. In one day in Liverpool, for example, we had received
hospitality from a Toxteth pensioner and a peer of the realm. How
many people, I wondered, could make a similar claim?

As usual, the START office had arranged for us to spend Sunday
lunchtime raising funds at a Whitbread pub, and this particular
weekend we were expected at the Royal Lion Hotel at Burton-in-
Kendal. However, by a tragic twist of fate the visit was suddenly
cancelled. Only three days earlier the Royal Lion had been gutted

31 May 1988. George and I setting out from Hyde Park, at the head of the Household Cavalry.

The lorry – for five months our mobile office, horsebox, tackroom, kennel and home.

George in action: forging through a forest with uncharacteristic speed . . .

. . . and searching for an overgrown bridleway in a field of corn.

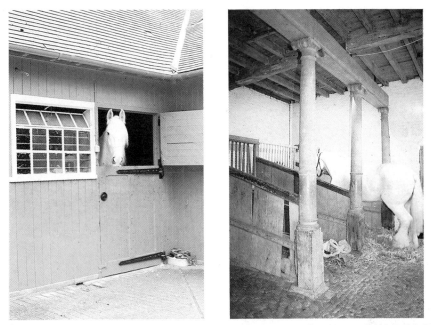

Often George's accommodation was more luxurious than ours; (*left*) Arkle's box at Eaton Hall; (*right*) the Doric pillars of Dunham Massey.

George greets an admirer in Toxteth.

150 feet above Ullswater. Seconds after this picture was taken, we almost plunged to our deaths.

Kirkstone Pass. The threatening clouds lifted as we reached the summit.

Ullswater

Coming into Corbridge at the end of the longest, wettest, weariest day of the journey.

George, once more in the lap of luxury, surveying the view from his sash-windowed stable at Ombersley.

Despatch riders in Leeds, apparently unimpressed by my alternative form of transport.

The Cremyll Pedestrian Ferry. Catherine soothes a nervous George while I attempt to interest him in the feed bucket.

Mount Edgcumbe. In 1698 Celia Fiennes wrote: 'its scituation makes it esteemed by me the finest seat I have seen'.

George, Bleeper and Puppy.

Mabel Mudge, the oldest pub landlady in England, supported by two of her regular customers.

My abiding memory of the journey – the English countryside framed by George's ears.

London at last, after five months on the road.

The end of the journey. George greets his old friends Musketeer and Pikeman on Putney Bridge.

by fire, leaving the landlord's son seriously burned. Learning that he was in intensive care in Preston Infirmary, we sent a note to his father expressing our deep sympathy. It seemed all too ironic that the very charity for which we would have been raising funds at the hotel was dedicated to helping those with terrible burn injuries.

Since the next two days were now free, I decided to travel down to London on the Sunday evening so that I could meet Charles on the Monday and tell him of my decision. It seemed strange to be on a train. I had grown so used to being outdoors all day that the airless confinement of the Intercity 125 made me feel almost claustrophobic. Stranger still was the prospect of going back to London, which I hadn't seen since our visit to 'Blue Peter'. Although Catherine had been home during the past seven weeks, I had not. Nor had I intended to do so for the remainder of the journey. To really see the country and to recreate Celia's journey as authentically as possible it had struck me as imperative not to cheat. In fact I hadn't even been tempted to. Each day was proving to be so intense an experience that I had scarcely a thought about home. Strangest of all, however, was the prospect of seeing Charles again. Although I was dreading the confrontation, in a perverse way I was still looking forward to seeing him. It was all too perplexing, and I tried to take my mind off it during the train journey by writing letters.

By the end of each week there would not only be an enormous backlog of thank-you letters to write, but also all the other correspondence that would have built up at our various *postes restantes* to attend to. Usually this would include a short letter from my mother and at least four ten-page epics from my father. My friend Claudia had moved into my flat during the summer, and this clearly pre-occupied my father greatly. Opening one of the five letters on the table before me I read:

'Darling Alison
YOU PAIN IN THE ARSE OF A FINANCIAL IDIOT. On 23rd April 1988 you had an ESTIMATED BILL. 24081 on the meter. Last reading 23101. Electricity was then 5.45 pence a unit (IT HAS GONE UP TO 5.850 pence a unit NOW). YOU ARE

A BLOODY FOOL NOT TO HAVE HAD A LEAVER'S READING. You sort this out with Claudia at once. I WILL BRAIN BOTH YOU AND CLAUDIA IF MY ELECTRIC KETTLE AND TOASTER HAVE EVEN FINGER MARKS ON THEM and I will disinherit you if the chairs are damaged or my table scratched.

E.R.P.

P.S. Please come and see me en route so I can spoil you and Catherine. Leave out the Gloucester and Bristol section. It is BUM BORING – and you would MISS NOTHING.'

I wrote back explaining that it might be rather difficult to cancel three days of the trip. Had Celia experienced similar parental pressure during her journeys, I wondered? Somehow I thought not.

It was lovely to see Claudia, lovely too to see my flat again, now a thousand times cleaner than I had ever kept it and as free from fingermarks as a bank vault after a professional raid. London, however, was a rude shock. Even though the prospect of a break from them had not seemed altogether unpleasurable, I found myself missing George, Catherine and Bleeper. Most of all I missed the countryside. London now seemed so big, so noisy, so disorientating. Even my own flat seemed strange to me. What struck me most of all though was the smell. I had never really noticed it before, but it was unmistakable: the noxious odour of exhaust fumes, petrol, takeaways and refuse and, most pungent of all on that hot July day, the warm, fetid smell of the Thames at low tide. For the first time I felt like a stranger in my own city.

I had arranged to meet Charles for lunch and so spent the Monday morning looking at the shops in Oxford Street. I felt very alone without George. My sense of isolation grew in John Lewis's, when my signature was challenged by a sullen assistant who insisted on my signing my name again in front of another assistant. By the time I reached Charles' flat I felt awful. He knew full well why I was there, and as I inarticulately explained my reasons for not wanting to see him, he seemed as depressed as I was.

'Oh well,' he sighed, 'I never expected it to be too easy. I'll just have to switch to plan B.'

Neither of us could eat lunch. My train went at four o'clock and Charles came with me in the taxi to the station. As I was getting out he kissed me and said, 'I know this is a strange time to ask, but will you marry me?'

Grabbing my luggage, I fled into the station.

Catherine was waiting to meet my train at Oxenholme.

'Well, what happened? You didn't really call it off, did you?'

Yes, I replied, I really had. For ten minutes she thought I was joking, convinced that my true feelings for Charles would eventually have conquered all my doubts and insecurities. When she realised that I was in earnest, she relapsed into appalled silence. I felt wretched.

The momentous decision, which I had supposed would be the solution to all my worries, had only served to make me yet more depressed and confused. What was more, I missed Charles desperately. By eleven o'clock that evening I could bear it no longer and telephoned him.

'You've made me the happiest man in the world!' he cried, 'But somehow I knew this would happen,' and he went on to explain how just a few minutes after saying goodbye to me he had seen seven geese flying in a 'V' from left to right. What better omen could there be? We chatted until the battery began to run down. The line became indistinct, and as we were saying goodbye I could just make out above the crackles the faltering question 'Will you marry me?' With that the telephone went dead.

Despite rain and low lying fog on the Tuesday, morale was high as we began the Lake District leg of the Great Journey. I was joined that day by a local called Ray, a good-natured pessimist with an endless supply of cautionary tales about equine demises.

'Flippin' 'eck. You'll see nothing in this weather!' he exclaimed as we set off. Visibility was such that we could barely see more than the blanket of fog around us, but Ray was undeterred.

'Of course, if you'd come on a better day you'd have seen Kendal over there to the left and a cracker of a view of the fells up to the right.'

When in the afternoon the fog did lift to reveal a tumbling green landscape of meadows, copses and mossy dry stone walls, Ray suddenly said, in the casual way countrymen have when pointing out a natural wonder to a town-dweller: 'Oh, look, there's a stag.'

I spun round excitedly, scanning the hillside for a tell-tale glimpse of antler.

'No, no,' said Ray. 'Over there! The Triumph Stag. You can see its tail-lights just ahead of us.'

That evening we stabled with a delightful lady in her seventies called Mrs Cropper. Set in a Milly Molly Mandy garden, heady with the scents of jasmine and honeysuckle, Mrs Cropper's was a cottage of floral-sprigged nooks, beamed crannies and patchwork-quilted beds with plump downy pillows. This was Beatrix Potter country, and looking out of the deep-silled window one expected at any moment to see an apronned Mrs Tiggywinkle hanging up her washing on the line or Jemima Puddleduck disappearing through the garden gate to do her shopping in Kendal. Celia herself might also have done some shopping in the town.

> 'Kendall is a town built all of stone, one very broad streete in which is the Market Crosse, its a goode tradeing town mostly famed for the cottons; Kendall Cotton is used for blanckets and the Scotts use them for their plodds [plaids] and there is much made here and also linsiwoolseys and a great deale of leather tann'd here and all sorts of commod-ityes twice a weeke is the market furnished with all sorts of things.'

The 'cottons' mentioned by Celia were in fact woollens. For six centuries the woollen industry flourished in Kendal, giving rise to the town's motto – *Pannus mihi panis* – 'Wool is my bread'. Now the industry has been superseded by footwear, hosiery, carpets, insurance, engineering industries and tourism. A visitor shopping in Kendal today would probably buy, as we did, a bar or two of Kendal Mint Cake, a rather sickly concoction that purports to be essential for scaling Everest, so packed is it with energy-giving calories.

In 1698 things would have been very different. Beyond a sample of 'Kendall Cotton', souvenirs would have been virtually impossible to come by, for there was simply no call for them. Apart from intrepid travellers like Celia Fiennes whose natural curiosity drew them to the area, few people visited the Lakes. Indeed, the majority of travellers went to great lengths to avoid what was commonly regarded as a bleak and inhospitable region, 'eminent', according to Defoe, 'only for being the wildest most barren and frightful of any that I have passed'. Such a view persisted long into the eighteenth century, when formalised notions of landscape beauty were suddenly turned on their heads with the introduction of a new aesthetic category: the picturesque. Coined by William Gilpin, the term 'picturesque' signified anything in the landscape that was rough or irregular. Thus mountains, lakes and waterfalls, previously dismissed as troublesome obstacles, now became objects of artistic and literary veneration. So compelling was the cult that by the end of the eighteenth century visiting the Lake District had become as popular as the Grand Tour.

It did not take long for the inhabitants of the region to tap this vast source of potential income. Inns doubled and even trebled their prices, fishermen would charge to take parties out onto the lakes to listen to the echoes, and in every village and hamlet self-appointed local guides hired out their services. At Keswick, transformed almost overnight from a mean village into a prosperous town, Peter Crossthwaite, 'formerly Naval Commander in India', cut steps into the rocks for the convenience of tourists visiting Scale Force, sold maps, prints and guide books and even opened a museum of antiquities and curiosities which included a lamb with claws and the hat of a sailor from Captain Bligh's ship, the *Bounty*.

Riding through Windermere the following day to a press call in Bowness, I had the impression that little had changed since those early days of crude commercialisation. Here was a resort more reminiscent of the seaside than a lakeshore retreat, with all the kitsch-me-quickness of a Blackpool or a Clacton. Every gift shop thronged with anoraked tourists, all the grey-stoned guest-houses displayed their 'No Vacancies' signs and all the fish and chip shops looked well set to be frying that night.

Perhaps Celia would have approved, as it was her love of fish as much as her curiosity to 'see the great water' that took her to the lake.

> 'At the Kings Arms one Mrs. Rowlandson she does pott up the charr fish the best of any in the country, I was curious to have some and so bespoke some of her'

Sadly Mrs Rowlandson was unable to satisfy Celia's craving, since it was not the season for charr. But her cooking must still have found favour, for Celia commented on her 'very good dinner'. Unlike Celia, we were indeed lucky enough to dine on charr, prepared for us not by Mrs Rowlandson but by Mrs Cropper, who had managed to procure two charr from a local fisherman by bartering a pheasant. As we savoured the rich red trouty flesh I could almost see Celia watching us, her nostrils twitching with envy.

Away from the postcard emporiums of Bowness and Windermere, the landscape became progressively more bleak, as we headed north to Kirkstone, at 1476 feet the highest of all the Lakeland passes. As we climbed into the cloud, Lake Windermere was suddenly swallowed up behind us in a shroud of primeval grey mist, so that soon there was nothing but grey all around. Were it not for the steep gradients and the occasional muffled whines of an overtaxed car engine, we might almost have been anywhere. George too was beginning to wheeze with the strain, and on several occasions we had to pull into a layby, where he would nibble abstractedly at the tight-cropped grass as he tried to regain his breath. Towards the top, visibility gradually improved to reveal the pass as Celia must have seen it in 1698.

> 'I rode in sight of this Winander Water [Windermere] up and down above 7 mile; afterwards as I was ascending another of those barren fells – which tho' I at last was not halfe way up, yet was an hour going it up and down, on the other side going only on the side of it about the middle of it, but it was of such a height as to shew one a great deale of the

PART OF SCOTLAND

NORTHUMBERLAND

DURHAM

CUMBRIA

NORTH YORKS

Aitchison Bank
Gretna
Longtown
Naworth
Gilsland
Thirlwell
Carlisle
Halbwhistle
Corby
Hexham
Newbrough
Corbridge
Newcastle
Chester-le-Street
Durham
Penrith
Ullswater
Askham
Lowther
Brothers Water
KIRKSTONE PASS
Lake Windermere
Bowness-on-Windermere
Darlington
Richmond
Catterick
Boroughbridge

19th July ~ 9th August

Scale   0   10   20   30   40   50   Miles

Country when it happens to be between those hills, else those interposeing hinders any sight but of the clouds – I see a good way behind me another of those waters or mers but not very bigge; these great hills are so full of loose stones and shelves of rocks that its very unsafe to ride them down. There is good marble amongst those rocks; as I walked down at this place I was walled on both sides by those inaccessible high rocky barren hills which hangs over ones head in some places and appear very terrible'

Few sheep had ventured into this boulder-strewn wilderness, and the place seemed empty and forsaken. The only natural

125

movement was that of the cloud shadows, contorted by the corrugated mountainside into dark demonic shapes.

By the time we had reached the summit all the clouds had disappeared. Peter Smales, the P.R. man from Whitbread's, had come north with his son Jack to see how we were getting along, and now they met us on the highest point of the pass with their bicycles. As we surveyed the Helvellyn and High Street massifs stretching into the distance and the road before us snaking its way down to vibrant green pasture land and the shimmering blue of Brother's Water, he said: 'You know, we had a chap ring up the other day, asking if we could lend him a horse to ride from Scotland to Land's End.'

'What did you say?'

'Sorry, old boy, but it's been done already.'

I felt so moved I couldn't say a word.

For the next two nights we were to be the guests of the Earl of Lonsdale. I had mislaid his telephone number during the ride and rang the operator, asking whether she could supply a number.

'The Earl of Lonsdale . . . That's a pub, isn't it?'

In 1698 Celia herself had stayed at

> 'Lord Landsdown's [Lonsdale's] house call'd Louder-hall [Lowther Castle] which is four mile from Peroth [Penrith]; I went to it through fine woods, the front is just faceing the great road from Kendall and lookes very nobly, with severall rows of trees which leads to large iron gates, into the stable yard which is a fine building on the one side of the house very uniform, and just against it as such another row of buildings the other side of the house like two wings which is the offices; its built each like a fine house jutting out at each end and the middle is with pillars white and carvings like the entrance of a building, these are just equal and alike and encompass the two sides of the first court which enters with large iron gates and iron palasadoes in the breadth; there is 4 large squares of grass in which there is a large statue of stone in the midst of each and 4 little Cupids or little boys in each corner of the 4 squares; this is

just the front of the house where you enter a porch with pillars of lime stone but the house is the red sort of stone of the country.'

So magnificent was Lowther Castle that it was described by one observer of the time as 'such a palace-like fabric as bears the bell away from all'. Even the stables, recorded another, were 'finer than the royall palace in Scotland'.

If the façade of the castle was magnificent, then the interior was opulence itself.

'The staircase very well wanscoated and carv'd at the top, you are landed into a noble hall very lofty, the top and sides are exquisitely painted by the best hand in England which did the painting at Windsor [Antonio Verrio]; the top is the Gods and Goddesses that are sitting at some great feast and a great tribunal before them, each corner is the Seasons of the yeare with the variety of weather, raines and rainbows stormy winds sun shine snow and frost with multitudes of other fancyes and varietyes in painting, and looks very natural – it cost 500£ that roome alone'

The castle was burnt down in 1720, but in 1807 another castle was built on the site by Sir Robert Smirke, designer of the British Museum. Battlemented, towered and turreted, for over 130 years it was home to the Earls of Lonsdale, including the fifth earl, who was not only the first president of the AA, but gave his name to the Lonsdale belt, one of boxing's most coveted trophies. Eventually the family moved to nearby Askham Hall, and in 1957 Smirke's castle was finally demolished. All that remains of it now is the spectacular façade, a fairy-tale castle perched high above the wooded slopes of the River Lowther.

Askham Hall proved surprisingly cosy for a fourteenth-century fortified tower, despite the wyverns snarling in stony silence at the door. Dinner the first evening was rather grand and very delicious with avocado in strawberry mayonnaise, salmon and summer pudding; but every bit as enjoyable was the kitchen supper the following evening, with the Lonsdales and their two youngest children, Marie-Louisa, aged twelve, and Charles, aged ten. Armed with the *Ha Ha Bonk Jokebook* Charles bombarded us throughout the meal with conundrums and riddles and then spent the next half hour mercilessly catapulting his father with a rubber band, as the earl read *Sporting Life* over a cup of coffee.

Celia relates in her journal how 'the lady Lansdown sent and treated me with a breakfast, cold things and sweetmeats all serv'd in plaite, but it was so early in the morning that she being indisposed was not up'. Our hostess clearly didn't share the indolent leanings of her forbear, for she was up very early, supervising the preparations for Marie-Louisa to go riding. Marie-Louisa had asked if she might accompany me for a day, and since her parents seemed to approve of the idea I was delighted to agree. The next leg of the journey was to take us from Patterdale along the shore of Ullswater. In her journal, Celia described the 'formidable heights' to which the fells soared on all sides, but her journey seems to have passed pleasurably enough.

> 'I rode the whole length of the water by its side sometyme a little higher upon the side of the hill and sometyme just by the shore and for 3 or 4 miles I rode through a fine forest or parke where was deer skipping about and haires which by meanes of a good Greyhound I had a little Course'

In all probability she had ridden along the western edge of the lake, following what is now the route of the A592. I elected instead to ride along the eastern side, along a tortuous bridleway that promised to be the most spectacular ride of the whole journey. I had been warned that it was stony and steep in parts, but having scaled the Kirkstone Pass I was blithely confident of George's abilities. Besides, it was a beautifully clear day with Ullswater shimmering benignly in the heat. What could possibly go wrong?

And so we set off, full of good spirits and bad jokes, with Marie-Louisa bringing up the rear on a pony called Humming Bird. We had been on the track for no more than a few minutes when it started to climb sharply. The path became narrower and stonier, with the result that soon only a precipitous cliff separated us from the water below. Striking a small boulder with his hoof, George sent a frightening avalanche of scree and flint tumbling down the mountainside. We had stopped telling jokes by this stage. It was all I could do to even acknowledge Marie-Louisa's cheerful observations, for my attention was now totally focused on George and on helping him to pick the safest route through the boulders and angled flints that now scattered our path. Far worse than the climbs were the downhill sections. Worn smooth by centuries of weathering, the rocks had become slippery. While Humming Bird's hoofs were small enough for him to pick his way daintily between them, George would slither clumsily, snorting in alarm as his weight added terrifying momentum to his lurchings.

Reaching a small plateau at Silver Point, I felt so nervous that I asked Marie-Louisa to hold George for me while I walked on ahead and reconnoitred the route. In my heart I knew full well that it made little difference what I saw. We would have to go on. Far below, a tiny, gaily-painted pleasure steamer was describing a gentle arc across the lake's sparkling surface. Such was the leisurely pace of its engines, such the distance that separated us, that the little boat seemed to be suspended in motionless silence. As a child, the subtle movements of clock hands had always fascinated me, and now, in the same way, I found myself transfixed for a few moments by the barely perceptible progress of the tiny steamer. How curious to think that its captain and passengers should be so oblivious to the drama being played out above their heads. How I longed to be with them. It had already taken us over two hours to cover a mile, and another three and a half miles still separated us from our lunch rendezvous. Telling myself that my 'recce' was no more than a cowardly luxury, I turned back and rejoined Marie-Louisa. She seemed happily unaware of my apprehensiveness as we set off once more, and her chatter helped to calm me slightly, even though her presence increased the burden of responsibility that was now weighing so heavily on my shoulders.

We had dismounted because of the steepness of the track and I was looking for a space wide enough in which to remount, when George suddenly turned round. Quite how he managed it in so confined a space was impossible to say. My problem now was how to turn him back again. Leading him on a little further we came to a slightly wider section of track. 'You won't find anything better than this,' I told myself. 'Go on, do it here.'

At that moment a party of German hikers filed past, glowing with health and Teutonic heartiness. 'Tag! Gut morning! Hev you a problem?'

'No, thank you,' I replied smiling, thinking how strange it was to keep so stiff an upper lip when my lower one was so close to trembling. Patting George on the neck, I slowly started to pull him round, my small, feeble frame tugging against his. At first he wouldn't move, but perhaps like me he began to reason that while to go on seemed an impossibility, to turn back would be worse. All at once the rein slackened and he began to move. His about-face took me quite by surprise, for in a second I had lost my balance and was slithering down on my back. Suddenly George was floundering above me, his front hoofs on the path while his back legs struggled desperately to find a purchase on the crumbling earth of the cliff edge.

'God!' I cried, pulling the now taut reins with all my might. For a moment it looked as though I would lose him, but with a great bound he heaved himself up and in an instant was standing beside me, facing the right direction. Only then did it occur to me how close I too had been to disaster. An inch further over and George would have trampled me to death with his hoofs. Hugging and patting him, I realised that while I had jeopardised his life George had saved mine.

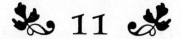

Ullswater to Chester-le-Street

The following day we took our leave of the Lonsdales and headed off towards Penrith.

> 'Tuesday is the market day which was the day I came thither . . . The stones and slatt about Peroth [Penrith] look'd so red that at my entrance into the town thought its buildings were all of brick, but after found it to be the coullour of the stone which I saw in the Quarrys look very red, their slatt is the same which cover their houses; its a pretty large town a good market for cloth that they spinn in the country, hempe and also woollen; its a great market for all sorts of cattle meate corne etc.'

It was on a Saturday that George and I arrived at Penrith, the day not of the market but of the Penrith Show. The START office had advised us to spend the whole morning collecting, and since the local fire brigade had offered to help, the conditions could hardly have been more favourable. The main events at the showground had not yet started, so the crowds were still milling about the town, rattling the change in their pockets in anticipation of the day's entertainments.

'You should think of every punter as a pound,' called the fire chief as he clambered aboard the engine. It soon became apparent that his brigade was as adept at bringing in the money as it was at putting out fires, for the entire exercise was carried out with military efficiency. Once we reached the main shopping area the chief ordered his men to arm themselves with a yellow bucket each and to spread out in a pincer movement along the pavements. The fire engine crawled alongside, lights flashing, while George and I brought up the rear. The 'punters' were only too delighted to have something to spend their money on, and within an hour the buckets were full. The total came to over £300, and we celebrated back at the station with big white cups of steaming hot tea. We were even allowed to slide down the pole. 'Actually, we always use the stairs,' confided one young fireman once I'd reached the bottom. 'They're so much quicker.'

It was now 23 July, and Catherine had gone home for three days, appointing Charles as under-groom in her absence. Although he was wonderfully good with both George and the lorry, I found myself missing Catherine, not just for her company and wit but for her level-headedness and organisation. Only now that she was gone did I realise just how much she did. Quite apart from following and keeping an eye on George and me during the day, her responsibilities included keeping the lorry in good order; attending to George's ailments and organising his fortnightly shoeing; feeding him five times a day; stocking up on feed when our supplies ran low; mucking out George's stable every day; keeping the back of the lorry clean and finally grooming George every day to keep him looking reasonably white. Had we been sponsored for the sheer acreage Catherine had already groomed, we would already have added thousands to our fund-raising total. All this she did efficiently and with good humour, volunteering in addition to help me graze George each day and clean the tack. By the time she returned we were exhausted, even though we had just had two rest days.

Our host during this period lived at Corby Castle, a striking red sandstone Georgian house set high above the River Eden. The gardens, he had told us, were well worth seeing, so very early one morning I sneaked out and descended the deep stone steps that led down the wooded escarpment to the water's edge. It was a beautiful walk. The air was cool and woody, and through the trees I could see the river glinting like a gold ribbon in the sun. Seeing a delicate pink flower, I decided to pick it and press it between the pages of my notebook. To my right a cascade of water tumbled down through an ornamental archway, where it was channelled through the fangs of a gibbous-eyed Cerberus before falling down into the River Eden below. So fascinated was I by the gruesome stone likeness that it was some moments before I became aware of a figure standing behind me. Embarrassed by my furtive behaviour and thinking that it might be a protective gardener or, worse still, my host, I decided to brazen it out and had already spun round with a cheerful 'Good morning!' before I realised that I was in fact addressing a statue. He was missing an arm, and his face was badly chipped beneath its five o'clock shadow of moss and lichen, but it was unmistakably a Cyclops that was now fixing me sternly from beneath a disapproving eyebrow.

The feeling of guilt was more than I could bear, and at breakfast I decided to come clean.

'A pretty pink flower?' repeated my host quizzically. Then realisation dawned across his face. 'You must be joking! It's that damned balsam weed. It's everywhere. I only wish you'd picked more – you'd be doing us a great favour!'

We took our leave of Corby's jungle of balsam weed the following morning. Polyphemus had clearly not forgiven me, even if our host had, for without any warning the lorry stubbornly refused to start. At any other time this would have presented a minor problem. On this particular day it was a disaster, for George and I were expected in Carlisle at 8.45 am for a live interview with Radio Cumbria. As my interview was supposed to begin in half an hour we decided that Charles should drive me to the studio while Catherine set about finding an accommodating vehicle to which she could attach our jump leads. Without George clopping and jangling in the background, the interview was a disaster. Desperate to fill the eight-minute chasm of silence that threatened to separate the last record from the pre-news weather report, the presenter switched tactics and started to question me not about my horse but about Celia Fiennes. Here for a minute at least I was on safe territory, as Celia had been only too vociferous in her comments about Carlisle.

> 'The wayes from thence [Penrith] to Carlisle over much heath where they have many stone quarrys and cut much peate and turff, which is their chief fuel; its reckon'd but 16 mile from Peroth to Carlisle but they are pretty long, and I was a great while rideing it; you pass by the little hutts and hovels the poor live in like barnes some have them daub'd with mud-wall others drye walls . . . there remaines only some of the walls and ruines of the Castle which does shew it to have been a very strong town formerly; the walls are of a prodigious thickness and vast great stones; its moated round and with draw bridges; there is a large Market place with a good Cross and Hall and is well supply'd as I am inform'd with provision at easye rates, but my Landlady notwithstanding ran me up the largest reckoning for allmost nothing; it was the dearest lodging I met with and she pretended she could get me nothing else, so for 2 joynts of mutton and a pinte of wine and bread and beer I had a 12 shilling reckoning; but since, I find tho' I was in the biggest house in town I was in the worst accomodation, and so found it, and a young giddy Landlady that could only dress fine and entertain the soldiers.'

'Oh, so she didn't think much of Carlisle then,' said the presenter, clearly horrified that she would again have to change tack. 'Where will you be stabling tonight?' she continued, with forced jollity. It was at that very instant, as the girl held the microphone expectantly before my lips, that I realised the terrible truth. We had nowhere to stay. I must have muttered something inarticulate in reply, for the microphone was whisked away, the interview swiftly terminated and 'Little Donkey' by Nina and Frederick put on the turntable.

By the time Catherine and Charles arrived I had grasped the cause of our predicament. According to the itinerary we had been scheduled to stay an extra night at Corby. Through some aberration I had decided that our departure day was not Wednesday but Tuesday, so we had packed up and left a day too early. There had been no reason for the others to question my decision, since throughout the journey the stabling arrangements had always been my responsibility. It did however explain why our hosts had looked so puzzled as we had waved goodbye that morning.

Kind as they had been, we felt we couldn't possibly inconvenience them further by telling them of my mistake. They had probably made alternative plans for the evening by now, and besides, it would mean having to prepare the stable all over again. Catherine and I needed no accommodation, since we could sleep in the lorry, and Charles had arranged to stay the night with his father at Lockerbie. The only problem was George. After much discussion we decided to throw ourselves on the mercy of our next hosts, the Earl and Countess of Carlisle.

The ride that day was very dull. Spoiled by the dramatic scenery of the Lake District, I found the countryside north of Carlisle windswept, flat and uninteresting. Celia had been even less impressed:

'all here about which are called Borderers seem to be very poor people which I impute to their sloth; Scotland this part of it is a low marshy ground where they cutt turff and peate for the fewell, tho' I should apprehend the sea might convey coales to them; I see little that they are employ'd besides fishing which makes provision plentiful, or else their cutting and carving turff and peate which the women and great girles bare legg'd does lead a horse which draws a sort of carriage the wheeles like a dung-pott and hold about 4 wheele barrows; these people tho' with naked leggs are yet wrapp'd up in plodds a piece of woollen like a blanket or else rideing hoods, and this when they are in their houses; I tooke them for people which were sick seeing 2 or 3 great wenches as tall and bigg as any women sat hovering between their bed and chimney corner all idle doing nothing, or at least was not settled to any work, tho' it was nine of the clock when I came thither, haveing gone 7 long miles that morning'

She broke her journey at Aitchison Bank, but even there could find little to her satisfaction, except for some imported French claret.

'the houses lookes just like the booths at a fair – I am sure I have been in some of them that were tollerable dwellings to these – they have no chimneys their smoke comes out all over the house and there are great holes in the sides of their houses which letts out the smoake when they have been well smoaked in it; there is no roome in their houses but is up to the thatch and in which are 2 or 3 beds even to their parlours and buttery; and notwithstanding the cleaning of their parlour for me I was not able to beare the roome; the smell of the hay was a perfume and what I rather chose to stay and see my horses eate their provender in the stable then to stand in that roome, for I could not bring my self to sit down; my Landlady offered me a good dish of fish and brought me butter in a Lairdly Dish with the Clap bread, but I could have no stomach to eate any of the food they should order, and finding they had noe wheaten bread I told her I could not eate their clapt oat bread, soe I bought the fish she got for me which was full cheape enough, nine pence for two pieces of Salmon halfe a one neer a yard long and a very large Trout of an amber coullour; soe drinking without eateing some of their wine, which was exceeding good Clarret which they stand conveniently for to have from France, and indeed it was the best and truest French wine I have dranck this seven year and very clear, I had the first tapping of the little vessell and it was very fine.'

Nor was she in the slightest bit tempted to venture further north.

'This is threescore miles from Edenborough [Edinburgh] and the neerest town to this place is 18 miles, and there would not have been much better entertainement or acco-modation and their miles are soe long in these countrys made me afraid to venture, least after a tedious journey I should not be able to get a bed I could lye in; it seemes there are very few towns except Edenburough Abberdeen and Kerk which can give better treatment to strangers, therefore for the most part persons that travell there go from one Noblemans house to another; those houses are all kind of Castles and they live great, tho' in so nasty a way, as all things are even in those houses, one has little stomach to eate or use any thing as I have been told by some that has travell'd there; and I am sure I mett with a sample of it enough to discourage my progress farther in Scotland; I attribute it wholly to their sloth for I see they sitt and do little'

It would have been hard to pass judgement on the twentieth-century descendants of the Borderers, for the entire region seemed deserted. Only at Gretna Green did we see any quantity of people. For the most part they seemed to be coachloads of Scandinavians, French and Americans who had come across the border in raiding parties to carry off tartan travelling rugs, horse brasses and repro-duction sepia marriage certificates. The only Scot I could see was the kilted piper posing for photographs outside the Aulde Smithy Restaurant as he played 'Scotland the Brave' for the twentieth time that morning.

By the time Catherine met us at Aitchison Bank it was already six o'clock. The engineers at the Mercedes garage in Carlisle had spent the whole day examining the lorry. Although they had fitted a new battery, they forecast further disasters unless some radical action were taken over the electrical circuits.

Catherine was clearly depressed at returning to all the problems of the lorry after so restful a weekend with her family. Leaving her to graze George by a roadside telephone kiosk, I rang Peter Smales at Whitbread to ask for his advice about our next move. His news was not encouraging. Banbury Boxes, it seemed, could not supply another horse box, and it would be at least four days before they could send an engineer. Peter himself was off on holiday with his family the next day, but he promised me that he would do his best to resolve the problem that very evening. Arranging to speak to him at about nine o'clock that night, I rang off in a very despondent mood. There was little we could do except load George into the lorry and set off for Brampton and Naworth Castle.

Celia did not stay at Naworth, but she

'pass'd by my Lord Carletons [Earl of Carlisle] which stands in the midst of woods [Naworth Castle]; you goe through lanes and little sort of woods or hedge rows and many little purling rivers or brooks out of the rocks.'

We arrived at about seven o'clock, to be met by Philip Howard, son of the earl and countess and estate manager for Naworth. Not only would the extra night's stabling be no problem, he said, but his parents were already expecting me up at the castle for dinner. Since the invitation had been extended only to me, I left Catherine with Philip and, with my stow bag in hand, walked towards the castle.

Built in 1335 by Ranulph Dacre, Naworth Castle was one of the great border strongholds, providing the setting for Sir Walter Scott's *Lay of the Last Minstrel*. In the seventeenth century it was converted by one of the earl's ancestors into a mansion, which is how Celia would have seen it in 1698. Looking up at the crenellated sandstone towers looming high above the central courtyard, I could see little evidence of its twentieth-century occupation apart from a television aerial perched high on the battlements. 'Harold Macmillan, when he came here, said it was a real castle,' declared the earl once I had been ushered up the stone spiral staircase to the drawing room. Both the Carlisles responded enthusiastically to all my enquiries about the castle. Only one question seemed to baffle them. Did they have an adaptor? Knowing I would have to telephone Peter Smales that night, I had brought the Vodafone with me, hoping to charge up the batteries from the castle's main supply. I had not however reckoned on its antediluvian system of wiring, and to my dismay could find only tiny round-pin sockets. 'I don't think we have anything like an adaptor,' said the countess doubtfully, and leaning towards me conspiratorially she confided, 'I don't understand anything about electrics.'

By chance I happened to notice a suitable socket in the hall and, retrieving the charger and batteries from my room, plugged them in downstairs. Once I had returned to the drawing room, the earl politely asked whether I had solved my problem.

'Yes, thank you,' I replied, 'the charger's in the hall.'

'In the hall?' The earl raised his eyebrows. 'What the hell's he doing in the hall? There is a stable, you know.'

Because of the castle's thick walls and its situation in a deep valley, the Vodafone still didn't work. Determined not to abuse the Carlisles' hospitality by asking to use their telephone for what promised to be lengthy long-distance discussions, I reconciled myself to the fact that the problem of the lorry would have to wait until the following morning.

That night I slept fitfully. What if the lorry were beyond repair? How long would it take to find a replacement? What if no replacement were available? Even a day's delay would throw our schedule out entirely. Peter Smales couldn't have been more supportive, but what if he were to go off on holiday before I managed to contact him? Since he hadn't heard from me that evening, he had probably assumed either that the problem had been solved or that we didn't need his help. I knew how irrational I was being, but all sorts of other worries and insecurities now crowded to the fore. We weren't raising enough money; George might not complete the journey; we desperately needed a blacksmith; and team morale was low. More than anything, I was tired. Tired of the journey, tired of the endless routine and tired of having no time to myself. I desperately wanted to call a halt, and for a few days at least step off the carousel and live like a normal person.

I needn't have fretted about the lorry, because when I managed to speak to Peter Smales the next morning I found that our worries were over. The Mercedes mechanics at Carlisle had told Peter that if the electrical system in the interior of the lorry was disconnected altogether, the battery would no longer run flat. It would mean that the fridge, television, microwave, electrical points and most of the lights wouldn't work, but since most of these had never worked in the first place, it seemed a small enough price to pay. The best news of all was that the engineers could carry out the disconnections that very day. So when I set off from Thirlwell later that morning en route for Corbridge, Catherine headed in the opposite direction along the A69 to Carlisle.

It was to be a long day for both of us, almost as long as it had proved for Celia.

> 'this I am sure of the more I travell'd northward the longer I found the miles, I am sure these 6 miles and the other 6 miles to Hartwhistle [Haltwhistle] might with modesty be esteemed double the number in most of the countys in England; I did not go 2 of those miles in an hour; just at my entrance into Northumberland I ascended a very steep hill of which there are many, but one about 2 mile forward was exceeding steep full of great rocks and stone, some of it along on a row the remainder of the Picts walls or Fortification'

Although she didn't know it at the time, it was along Hadrian's Wall that Celia was now travelling. She would have seen many reminders of the Roman occupation throughout her journey, but none as impressive as Hadrian's Wall.

It was in 122 AD that the Emperor Hadrian began to build his wall. His intention was not only to mark the northernmost limit of the Roman Empire, but to create a permanent defence against the Pictish invaders. Completed within eight years, the wall extended seventy-three miles, from Wallsend to Solway Firth – but it was more than just a wall. Fifteen feet wide and nine feet high, it was flanked by a military way, measuring twenty feet wide by ten feet deep. Forts at intervals held between 500 and 1000 men each, and lookout turrets were sited all along its length. It even had its own heated baths. For over 250 years the Romans held the wall, but after 383 AD it lost its importance for them, and over the centuries it crumbled into disrepair. Great chunks of it still remain. At Gilsland I saw part of it which had been landscaped into a domestic garden, and a little further up the road another section had been incorporated into a railway embankment. Beyond Gilsland, however, the wall seemed to shake off its benign character, and for the rest of the day it was to prove an austere travelling companion.

If my journey to Lancaster had been bad, then the ride to Corbridge along the wall was a thousand times worse.

> 'its a sort of black moorish ground and so wet I observ'd as my man rode up that sort of precipice or steep his horses heeles cast up water every step and their feete cut deepe in, even quite up to the top; such up and down hills and sort of boggy ground it was, and the night drawing fast on, the miles so long, that I tooke a Guide to direct me to avoid those ill places.'

All day the rain fell, and with such sheeting force that it was impossible to read my map. Even when the rain abated it was still difficult to read, as the various features were thrown into distorted magnification by the quivering raindrops.

At a small farm I was given a cup of coffee in the pouring rain by a woman called Iona, whose daughters ran their own bakery business supplying the tourist cafés at the forts along the wall with biscuits, quiches and pies. They held George for me while I used their loo. Despite their holding a teatowel over it, the saddle was soaking by the time I climbed back on, and so it remained for the rest of the day. By the time I reached Newbrough, Catherine and lunch, I could scarcely speak for cold. The landlord of the Red Lion, taking pity on me, dried my Barbour in front of the open fire, and while we waited for his wife Nancy to bring us our order of cottage pie and chips he made me accept a glass of his best brandy: 'It's champion that, when you're cold.'

That afternoon Nancy rode some of the way to Corbridge with me, keeping us warm with stories of visiting American tourists, who would ask whether the sheep were brought in at night, but soon she turned back and we were alone again. And so we remained until the early evening, when we arrived drenched and exhausted at Corbridge.

It would be difficult to imagine a more relaxing haven than the Ramsays' house at Corbridge, where for the next two days my boots and hat slowly steamed themselves dry on the Aga. It was all very different from Celia's experience of border hospitality:

> 'there was one Inn but they had noe hay nor would get none, and when my servants had got some else where they were angry and would not entertaine me, so I was forced to take up in a poor cottage which was open to the thatch and no partitions but hurdles plaister'd; indeed the loft as they called it which was over the other roome was shelter'd but with a hurdle: here I was forced to take up my abode and the Landlady brought me out her best sheetes which serv'd to secure my own sheetes from her dirty blanckets, and indeed I had her fine sheete with hook seams to spread over the top of the clothes, but noe sleepe could I get, they burning turff and their chimneys are sort of flews or open tunnills that the smoake does annoy the roomes.'

Two nights sleeping between Mrs Ramsay's flannelette sheets proved the best restorative imaginable, and by the end of our stay I was feeling fitter than I had for a long time. My arms and legs were certainly in the best shape they had ever been, but my waist had gradually begun to disappear, partly because of the riding and partly because of all the excellent food we had been eating. My increasing inches had put an inordinate strain on the scarlet riding habit, which in any case had been made for someone with a considerably slighter frame than mine. It now took no small effort to do up the gilt braid buttons, while an alarming tension was discernible in the back panels. George, too, was looking fitter and fatter thanks to the Ramsays. Teasing at the stable bolt with his prehensile lips, he managed to free himself on the second night, and set about demolishing half the Ramsays' kitchen garden, including a bed of prize marrows. It was only when the fourth one had disappeared that his breakout was discovered.

*

It was now 29 July. We had been on the road for sixty days, covered almost 800 miles and were about to start heading south again. Our next destination was Newcastle-upon-Tyne. As early as 1698 Celia had been struck by its industrialised appearance:

'As I drew nearer and nearer to Newcastle I met with and saw abundance of little carriages with a yoke of oxen and a pair of horses together, which is to convey the Coales from the pitts to the barges on the river; there is little sort of dung-potts I suppose they hold not above 2 or three chaud-ron; this is the Sea-coale which is pretty much small coale though some is round coales, ye none like the cleft coales; this is what the smiths use and it cakes in the fire and makes a great heate, but it burns not up light unless you put most round coales, which will burn light, but then its soone gone and that part of the coale never cakes; therefore the small sort is as good as any, if its black and shineing that shews its goodness; this country all about is full of this Coale the sulpher of it taints the aire and it smells strongly to stran-gers; upon a high hill 2 mile from Newcastle I could see all about the country which was full of coale pitts.'

George and I were to be confronted by a twentieth-century version of the same view. Beneath a cat's cradle of pylon wires the city's sprawling entrails stretched far into the distance. Huge industrial hangars, volcanic-looking slagheaps and tall and squat chimneys had colonised the north-western approach to the city, while on the other side of the Tyne endless streets of grimy red-brick terraced houses lined the hillside like articulated pink snakes.

In 1698, the centre of Newcastle had struck Celia as

'a noble town tho' in a bottom, it most resembles London of any place in England, its buildings lofty and large of brick mostly or stone; the streetes are very broad and handsome and very well pitch'd and many of them with very fine Cunduits of water in each, allwayes running into a large

143

stone Cistern for every bodyes use . . . There is a very
pleasant bowling-green a little walke out of the town with a
large gravel walke round it with two rows of trees on each
side makeing it very shady; there is a fine entertaineing
house before which is a paved walke under pyasoes [piaz-
zas] of bricke; there is a pretty garden by the side shady
walk, its a sort of Spring Garden where the Gentlemen and
Ladyes walke in the evening; there is a green house in the
garden; its a pleasant walke to the town by the walls; there
is one broad walke by the side of the town runns a good
length made with coale ashes and so well trodden and the
raines makes it firm; there is a walke all round the walls of
the town, there is a good free Schoole, 5 churches.'

Even the market met with Celia's approval, being

'like a faire for all sorts of provision and goods and very
cheape: I saw one buy a quarter of lamb for 8 pence and 2
pence a piece good large poultry; here is leather, woollen
and linnen and all sorts of stands for baubles'

How little she would recognise today, I thought, in this concrete
wasteland slashed by motorways and vandalised by overzealous
town planners. Even the market had been superseded by an ugly
shopping centre. I felt appalled at the way in which Newcastle had
been treated. And yet, just as in Liverpool, it was impossible to be
totally depressed by it, such was the warmth and humour of its
inhabitants. But it was not until the following day that we were to
have our first proper introduction to the Geordie mentality.

A press call had been arranged at the Black Horse in Chester-le-
Street, where Irene, the landlady, had gone to enormous trouble to
whip up support for us. By the time George and I arrived she had
ushered a sizeable number of hardened regulars out onto the
pavement to greet us. 'Come on lads. Empty your pockets. The
poor lass is drenched!'

In no time two tins were full. Putting George in the lorry to eat
his lunch, we went inside the pub, where Irene offered us sandwiches on the house. As I took my seat at a barstool, I was suddenly

tapped on the shoulder, and turning round found myself looking up at a strapping Geordie lad in a denim jacket.

'My, you're a bonny lass! Wheor yer from, hinny?' he asked, introducing himself as Wonka, and his mates as Neash, Plum, Berry, Dug and Mick the Madman. Within seconds there seemed to be hundreds of them crowding round, all with equally strange names, and all firing questions at us. It was soon clear that conversation was going to be a problem, for they couldn't understand our accents, and we couldn't understand theirs.

'Hoy-yer-hamma-ower-heor!' cried Wonka suddenly, raising aloft his pint of Newcastle Brown Ale.

'Hoy-yer-hamma-ower-heor!' echoed his entourage in deafening unison.

'Weel larn yer Geordie, pet!' exclaimed Wonka, as Irene sniggered from behind the bar.

And so our lesson began. After Catherine and I had mastered the basic vowel sounds Wonka judged us ready to graduate to more demanding stuff.

'Haway then! Hoy-yer-hamma-ower-heor! Now you.'

Our efforts drew murmurs of approval from our tutors, so we were taught two more phrases: 'Tappy-lappy-doon-thi-ali' and 'Divven-drop-yer-dottle-on-thi-proggymat'.

Emboldened by our success, I asked Wonka exactly what the phrases meant, reasoning that if they were profanities it might be just as well to find out before we tried them on the unsuspecting senior citizens of Chester-le-Street.

'Weel it's simple man!' cried Wonka. 'They mean "Hoy-yer-hamma-ower-heor", "Tappy-lappy-doon-thi-ali" and "Divven-drop-yer-dottle-on-thi-proggymat"!'

By the time we were ready to leave, Wonka had taught us another three phrases, Berry had collected a further £30 for START and Mick the Madman had proposed marriage both to Catherine and to me.

'Wouldn't you like us to teach you how to speak like us?' we suggested as we said goodbye to Wonka.

'Haddaway to hell! That's for lasses, man!'

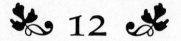

12

Chester-le-Street to Boroughbridge

There is something uplifting about travelling south. You feel your journey will be that much less arduous – after all, you're travelling downhill; and in the northern hemisphere, at least, there is the added promise of warmer climes and more hospitable terrain. I knew such thoughts were irrational. There was no reason why the next stretch of our journey should be any easier than the preceding ones. Psychologically, however, once we had started to head south from Newcastle it was as if an obstacle in our way had been toppled.

Before we had begun the journey, the northernmost stretches of England had been an unknown quantity. To a city-dweller from the south they had held all manner of bleak and inhospitable associations. Now, with George's help, I had met the challenge. Not only had I ridden across them, I had come to appreciate their dour beauty. And that wasn't all. There had been a subtle change in the dynamics of our small team. Coming so close to death at Ullswater had made me grow up considerably. Even if I wasn't yet equal to the responsibilities the ride had thrust upon my shoulders, I had become far more aware of my own strengths and weaknesses. More importantly, I had come to appreciate George's limitations. Having jeopardised his life through my own foolishness and inexperience had changed my relationship with him. Before, I had thought of myself as his friend. Now I felt like his parent as well.

Catherine, I think, sensed all this. At the beginning of the journey George and I had been totally dependent on her. The very fact that she now felt able to go home for a long weekend suggested that she felt we could fend for ourselves, for a few days at least. As well as being more relaxed, she was happier too. Although we were far from complacent, it seemed as if the lorry really had been repaired. Nothing untoward had happened since the electrical circuits had been disconnected at Carlisle, and it looked as if it would stand up well to journey south. The auspices for the next twelve weeks looked good.

Perhaps Celia had also felt this sense of achievement and anticipation. Her impression of the borders had been most unfavourable. Newcastle and Durham were to herald a complete change of tone.

'Thence I proceeded a most pleasant gravell road on the ridge of the hill and had the whole country in view, which seemes . . . like a fruitfull woody place and seemes to equal most countys in England . . . I pass'd over the river Weire [Wear] which runns to Durham, over a pleasant road and country that resembles Black heath, you see the towns and country's round full of woods; one sees the Citty of Durham four mile off from a high hill . . . Durham has about 7 Churches with the Cathedrall, its a noble place and the aire so cleer and healthy that persons enjoy much health and pleasure.'

We saw more evidence of pleasure than health at the top of the cathedral's central tower, where our fellow-sightseers obviously found that the exertions of scaling 218 feet of spiral staircase took the breath away every bit as much as the view at the top did. But it was worth it. High above a steep-banked wooded curve in the River Wear, the cathedral seemed to rise out of the very rock. It was magnificent.

The town's importance dates back to the monks who, forced by Viking raids to flee Lindisfarne, founded a shrine for the body of St Cuthbert at Durham in 995. Pilgrims' offerings brought prosperity, and Durham became one of the most important and powerful Christian settlements in Britain. That power had not in any way diminished when Celia visited the city in 1698.

'The Castle which is the Bishops Pallace stands on a round
hill . . . there are very stately good roomes parlours drawing roomes and a noble Hall but the furniture was not very
fine, the best being taken down in the absence of my Lord
Crew who is not only a Barron of England but is a great
Prince as being Bishop of the whole Principallity off
Durham and has a great royalty and authority, is as an
absolute Prince and has a great command as well as rev-
enue; his spirituall is 5 or 6000£ and his temporalls since his
brothers death makes it much more; he comes sometymes
hither but for the most part lives at another Castle [Bishop
Auckland] which is a noble seate about 12 mile off which is
very well furnish'd and finish'd; he is the Governour as it
were of the whole province.'

For centuries, Durham's prince bishops had unique powers, for
they were lay as well as religious leaders and were entitled to have
their own parliament, army, nobility, coinage and legal system.
These privileges were ended in 1836, but buildings about the
Palace Green which once housed hospitals, almshouses, resi-
dences or courts still bear witness to the former power of the
palatinate.

When Celia visited Durham, the city was in the throes of an
election.

'There was great striveing in the choice of the parliament
men, which I had the trouble of in most of my journey, the
randan they made in the publick houses, indeed I happen'd
to get into a quiet good inn, and good accomodation, two
maiden sisters and brother kept it, at the Naggs Head.'

Since we had time to spare, Catherine and I tried to discover
whether the Nag's Head still existed, but our enquiries met with no
response. Only in the cathedral did we find a lead, when the
chaplain, pointing to a frail lady steward at the postcard stand,
declared, 'She might know. Oh dear! She'll probably give me a slap
now!'

Surprisingly, the lady turned out to be something of an oracle in matters relating to public houses, but to her great frustration even she was unable to locate the Nag's Head.

'Got friends who recommended it, have you?'

'Sort of,' we replied.

'Well, let me see. It might give us a clue to know when they went there. Recently, was it?'

'1698.'

'Oh, I'm afraid I don't understand the continental clock. When would that be?'

'Three hundred years ago.'

'Oh dear. Well, I don't think I can help then.'

Celia's stay at Durham had put her in such good spirits that a minor accident the following day scarcely seemed to inconvenience her.

> 'From thence to Darlington which is good way, but by the way I lost some of my nightcloths and little things in a bundle that the Guide I hired carry'd'

By this stage Catherine and I would willingly have thrown away half our clothes. After the vicissitudes of the journey and a succession of unfamiliar washing machines, they had all acquired the same grey, lacklustre appearance. Far more pressing a problem for me was the state of my backside. I had never really recovered from the injuries I had sustained at Ely. I now found that, whatever I wore, by the end of the day I would be in considerable discomfort. My saddlesores had become a source of great mirth to Catherine, but, taking pity, she had made an expedition to Boot's in Darlington, and had come back triumphantly waving a large grey tub of nappy-rash cream.

'Rather a cheeky little number,' she quipped, 'but fundamentally very effective.'

That evening we stabled at Low Fold Farm, where the Braes Pony Club was holding its annual camp. Even though we were later assured that there were no more than thirty children in residence, there seemed to be thousands of them swarming about the yard when we arrived, from overconfident, overweight little girls of eight to gangly boys of sixteen with prominent Adam's apples and retiring manners. They were not to remain in the yard for long. No sooner had someone announced 'The tuck shop's open!' than the entire complement of pony-campers stampeded across the yard and disappeared into a nearby barn.

Food was evidently a major preoccupation for everyone, for only a few minutes later they had all been summoned to the makeshift refectory, and were sitting down at trestle tables on bales of straw in preparation for supper. Bleeper was ecstatic. Sneaking in half-way through the meal he found a slops bowl full of half-eaten catering pies, jelly, peas and ice cream, and set about demolishing the contents with indiscriminate gluttony. The children, delighted to discover anything with a greater appetite than their own, quite lost interest in their own meals and spent the next five minutes trying to tempt Bleeper with the rest of the leftovers.

Invited to eat supper with the grown-ups, Catherine and I had hoped to be spared the catering pies, but sat down to exactly the same meal as the children. The only difference was that it was washed down by Liebfraumilch. 'A box of wine and a bottle of whisky every two days gets us through,' said one woman, with a tired smile.

Bleeper's dyspepsia had got the better of him by ten that eve-ning, and he mooched about listlessly as we played a game of Scrabble in the lorry. The children were supposed to be asleep in various trailers, caravans and dormobiles scattered about the yard, but deep into the night we could hear the sounds of giggling and scampering as they decamped from one vehicle to the next on a never-ending movable midnight feast.

There was more food the following morning when the children consumed Brobdingnagian quantities of bacon, egg and fried bread.

'Do you like it here?' I asked, catching one small girl between mouthfuls.

'Mmm. Yeah.'

'What do you like about it?'

'The baths.'

'But there aren't any, are there?'

''xactly. Some of us haven't washed since we came here.'

'Is there anything you don't like?'

'Mmm. Yeah,' she replied as she wiped up the last smear of egg from her plate with her fried bread. 'The food – 's awful.'

The ride around Darlington had been very dull and flat. Heavy industrial traffic made the roadwork tiring and unpleasant, and what few bridleways there were seemed either to be blocked or to go in quite the wrong direction. Towards Richmond the landscape changed dramatically. This was Zetland Hunt country, intensely green, with plunging valleys and villages of warm, cream-coloured stone.

'I passed over Crafton [Croft] Bridge which crosses the river Teess, and soe entred the North Rideing of Yorkshire in which is that they call Richmondshire a shire of 30 miles; the way was good but long. I went through lanes and woods an enclosed country . . . Richmond town one cannot see till just upon it, being encompass'd with great high hills, I descended a very steep hill to it from whence saw the whole town which it self stands on a hill tho' not so high as these by it; its buildings are all stone the streetes are like rocks themselves, there is a very large space for the Markets which are divided for the fish market flesh market and corn; there is a large Market Crosse, its flatt on the top and of a good height; there is by it a large Church and the ruines of a Castle the pieces of the walls on a hill.

I walked round by the walls the river [Swale] running beneath, a great descent to it, its full of stones and rocks and soe very easye to make or keep up their wires [weirs] or falls of water, which in some places is naturall, that the water falls over rocks with great force which is convenient for catching Salmon by speare when they leap over those bayes'

We had arranged to stable that night with the Queen's Royal Irish Hussars at Catterick Garrison. Paragons of politeness, the officers disguised their dismay when Catherine and I walked through the door of the mess, bringing with us the unmistakably sickly aroma of horse, manure and dog.

151

'How about baths first?' suggested Captain Toby Maddison. 'There aren't any bolts on the doors, I'm afraid. You'll just have to whistle if you hear anyone coming.'

The warning system proved an effective deterrent, sparing both our modesty and the officers' olfactory nerves, and an hour later we emerged considerably more presentable than when we had gone in.

Of all our dinner companions, Toby was by far the oldest at twenty-seven. Noticeably younger, the rest were introduced to us as Simon, Aiden, David, Jeremy, Jamie and Boomer. Boomer was in fact an eighteen-month-old labrador at whom tennis balls would periodically be hurled with frightening velocity. His particular skill was to catch them in his jaws before they ricocheted off the regimental silver and sent a battery of cut-glass tumblers flying across the room. Dinner was served by two women in maids' uniforms, whom the officers treated with the same respect and consideration they might have shown a retired nanny: 'We were a bit worried about breaking with tradition and having women in the mess, but they look after us brilliantly,' explained David.

Despite the formality of the setting, the evening was decidedly relaxed, with mercifully few questions about the ride. The meal was excellent, and as the alcohol intake rose so did the spirits of our hosts. Simon was soon relating a cautionary tale about another mess dinner, at which an officer had surreptitiously relieved himself in one of the empty wine bottles, subsequently offering its contents to the girl sitting next to him. Peals of laughter rang round the table as Simon revealed that the girl had not only taken a large draught of the liquid but had also declared it delicious.

'I should think his kidneys were pumping out a hundred per cent grape by then!' sniggered Simon. Then, turning to me with a straight face he asked, 'More wine?'

There was more Boomer-baiting after dinner, when the conversation turned to the regiment and the youthfulness of its junior officers.

'Some people in the City are much more juvenile than us,' claimed Jamie with a solemn expression as the tennis ball flashed past his left ear, closely followed by Boomer. Did they all envisage themselves staying in the regiment for good, I wondered.

'Oh no,' replied one. 'I'll probably go into the City after a year or two.'

The atmosphere the following morning was in complete contrast to that of dinner. All evidence of the preceding evening's revels had been removed. Catherine and I walked into the dining room to find it as silent as a monastery, with all the officers variously bowed in concentration over *The Times*, the *Telegraph*, the *Daily Mail* and the cornflakes. Even Boomer was distinctly subdued and lay in a corner quietly gnawing his tennis ball. Breakfast was clearly sacrosanct. Catherine and I didn't say a word.

For the ride to Boroughbridge that day I was joined by Tracey, a very capable young woman from Bedale who, like her mother Jennifer, was a member of the Side Saddle Association. Jennifer believed most fervently in the merits of hard work. 'We don't have any of what's called social spongers in Bedale. If you haven't got a job round here, you find summat else to do.'

Tracey had obviously inherited all her mother's determination, for she not only had a job at a nursery school, but had already secured a loan from the bank to buy the school out. After the engaging boyishness of the officers at Catterick, her sober single-mindedness and initiative seemed all the more remarkable. Did she mind my asking how old she was?

'Not at all. Eighteen.'

It struck me afterwards that in the space of twenty-four hours I had met two not dissimilar products of Mrs Thatcher's Britain. For all their regimental loyalty, the officers at Catterick, while subscribing to the age-old tradition of serving Queen and Country, expected to be rewarded for that service. They would stay with the regiment for a few years and then move to the City and become rich. It was a natural progression: it was their due. Tracey, for all her northern bluntness, was not so very different. She would probably have to struggle a little more than the officers, but I sensed in her the same cult of the individual. Success was her right.

The following four nights were spent with a friend of Catherine's at Myton-on-Swale, a small village just outside Boroughbridge. The weather had improved immeasurably, and apart from tidying out the lorry and catching up on thank-you letters, we had a very slothful time. George was probably glad of the rest too, for he had just been given his vaccination against equine influenza and the vet had ordered complete rest from riding until at least the following Tuesday. Charles arrived to see us on the Monday, and to celebrate we decided to have a boozy pub lunch at Boroughbridge. Finding a suitably appealing pub, we soon found ourselves in the midst of a local celebration. Nearly every single man in the bar appeared to wear a badge bearing the legend 'The Battle of Boroughbridge'. Charles explained to us that it was here that, in 1322, Edward II defeated Thomas, the Earl of Lancaster. It seemed strange that these men should be celebrating an event which, beyond its name, could have held no significance whatsoever for them. Strangest of all was the fact that it wasn't even a proper anniversary. The Battle of Boroughbridge had been fought on 16 March. Today's date was 8 August. It seemed to be another example of the regional oddities we were encountering all over England. The Battle of Borough-bridge may not have had any bearing on the lives of the town's twentieth-century inhabitants, but at least the celebration of it was unique to them.

So absorbing was the general conversation about catamites and red-hot pokers that it was some time before we realised that Bleeper had disappeared. We were not immediately alarmed. He had often wandered off before, but since he invariably homed in on the nearest food source he was usually easy enough to find. Panic began to set in when, after a thorough search of the kitchens and dustbin area, he was still missing. Deciding that the best plan would be to systematically comb the town, we split up and set off in different directions.

'Have you see a little terrier with short legs?' I asked everyone I saw, but apart from one man who replied, 'I've just seen a bulldog if that's any help,' I had no luck.

After half an hour we had found no trace of Bleeper. Charles and I stood in the middle of the road outside the pub wondering how best to break the news to Catherine. The prospect of losing the little dog was very sad, and we knew that Catherine, for all her tough exterior, would be heartbroken. She was the one who had always fed him and given him water. She was the one who had taken him for walks, dewormed him and made up a little bed for him out of an old chaff sack. She was the one whose knee he liked most to sleep on, and against whom he would snuggle when he was lying in the lorry with his bottom on the gear-lever stick. We were both on the verge of tears when the pub door opened and Catherine emerged with a huge grin on her face and a bundle of fur in her arms. Apparently Bleeper had inadvertently wandered into the Ladies and been unable to get out again. It had taken thirty minutes for him to be discovered, much to the disapproval of the elderly customer who found him cowering with fright in the corner of her cubicle.

'He might at least have gone into the gents!'

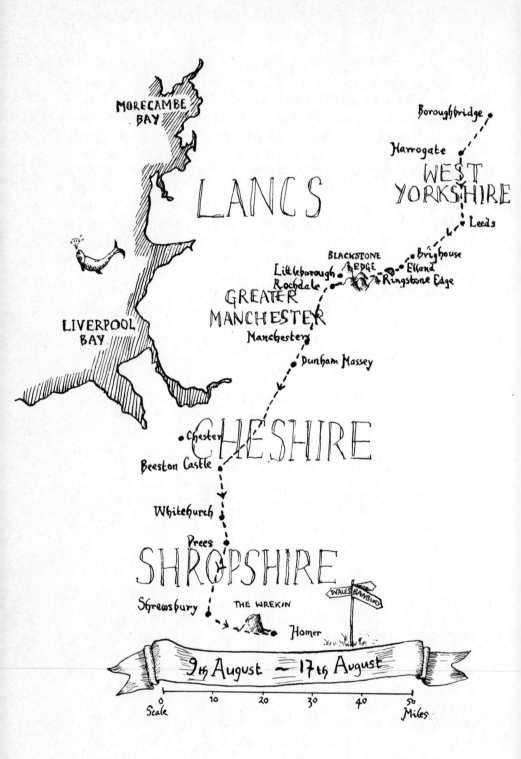

MORECAMBE BAY

LANCS

WEST YORKSHIRE

Boroughbridge

Harrogate

Leeds

BLACKSTONE EDGE

Brighouse

Elland

Littleborough

Ringstone Edge

Rochdale

GREATER MANCHESTER

Manchester

LIVERPOOL BAY

Dunham Massey

CHESHIRE

Chester

Beeston Castle

Whitchurch

Prees

SHROPSHIRE

WALES BANBURY

Shrewsbury

THE WREKIN

Homer

9th August ~ 17th August

0   10   20   30   40   50
Scale   Miles

156

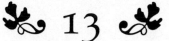

13

Boroughbridge to Ringstone Edge

George had suffered no adverse effects from the equine jab, so on Tuesday 9 August we set off for Harrogate, where the mounted police, local fire brigade and North Yorkshire Ladies Side Saddle Costume Display Team had volunteered to help collect money for START.

No sooner had we arrived and unboxed George for the preliminary press call than the firemen were called away to tackle a blaze at a joinery works in Knaresborough. All was not lost, however, for the spectacle of the North Yorkshire Ladies Side Saddle Costume Display Team far exceeded our wildest expectations. Harrogate stopped in its tracks at the sight of our extraordinary procession. Every colour of the spectrum, and every marvel of the tailor's art seemed to be represented in the dazzling costumes. Chocolate-box confections of braid and ostrich feather, the hats were outrageous, but more extravagant still were the dresses whose flounced furbelows and panoplies of petticoats all but eclipsed the horses beneath. The authoress of these remarkable creations was the delightfully flamboyant Dolores Craven who, with her husband, had helped to mastermind our fund-raising ride through Harrogate.

'I hope we're not going to gallop, Alison,' she called out to me as the cavalcade set off, 'I've only got my lacy bra on.'

Eight collectors accompanied us on foot, and they darted amongst the crowds distributing START leaflets and asking for donations. In no time the buckets were practically overflowing with coins, largely thanks to the energetic efforts of Sarah, who not only charged for leaflets, but also sold kisses for a pound a peck.

Celia's experience of Harrogate had been altogether less pleasant.

> 'From thence [York] we went over to Haragate which is just by the Spaw . . . its all marshy and wett and here in the compass of 2 miles is 4 very different springs of water: there is the Sulpher or Stincking spaw, not improperly term'd for the Smell being so very strong and offensive that I could not force my horse near the Well, there are two Wells together with basons in them that the Spring rises up in, which is furr'd with a White Scumm which rises out of the water, if you keep it in a cup but a few hours it will have such a White Scum over it, notwithstanding it rises out of the Spring very cleare, and so being a quick Spring itt soone purges it self cleare againe, it comes from Brimstone mines for the taste and smell is much of Sulpher, tho' it has an additionall offenciveness like carrion or a jakes; the Ground is Bitumus or the like that it runns over, it has a quality of changing Silver into the coullour of Copper, and that in a few minutes, much quicker than the Baths in the West Country in Somersetshire; its a quick purger and very good for all Scurbutick humours; some persons drink a quart or two – I dranke a quart in a morning for two days and hold them to be a good sort of Purge if you can hold your breath so as to drinke them down'

Celia was by no means the only person to complain about the nauseousness of Harrogate's sulphur spa. According to Joseph Taylor, an observer of the time:

> 'a mixture of Gunpowder, Ink, Gall and Verjuice would have given a more pleasant relish . . . I had a repetition of it 20 times in my stomach'

Such opinions had little effect on Harrogate's success as a spa. By 1698 'taking the waters' was firmly established as an integral part of

English life. The first British spa came into existence almost a century earlier with the discovery of the Tunbridge water by Baron North, who declared it a powerful restorative after all the good living at Court. In no time England's spas were being lauded as one of the country's many 'Wonders'. Everybody wanted to take the waters. When one considers the incompetence of seventeenth-century doctors and the repellent nature of their prescriptions, it is hardly surprising that the spas met with such favour. But they were more than a sop to the hypochondriac. They provided the moneyed and leisured classes with a good excuse to have a holiday. By the eighteenth century, taking the waters had become a fashionable cult.

Celia was interested in spas for their medicinal powers, and had various theories as to which waters were 'spiritous' or 'diaretick', which were 'good for all scurbutick humours' and which were 'stincking spaws'. Nor was her interest confined to tasting the various waters. She would bathe in them as well. At St Mungo's Well near Harrogate, she explained how

> 'I used my Bath garments and so pulled them off and put on flannell when I came out to go into the bed, which is best; but some came at a distance, so did I, and did not go into bed but some will keep on their wet Garments and let them drye to them and say its more beneficial, but I did not venture it; I dipp'd my head quite over every tyme I went in and found it eased a great pain I used to have in my head, and I was not so apt to catch Cold so much as before, which I imputed to the exceeding coldness of the Spring that shutts up the pores of the body'

To my secret relief, there was no time either to taste or bathe in the sulphur spa at Harrogate. I did however take the waters later that evening in Dolores' gilt-topped Jacuzzi. Somehow I felt that Celia would approve of the novelty, if not the luxury, of this twentieth-century spa.

If we had looked strange in Harrogate, we must have cut even more curious figures the following day, when Dolores led our motley cavalcade through the streets of Leeds. In 1698 Celia described Leeds as:

'a large town severall large streetes cleane and well pitch'd and good houses all built of stone, some have good gardens and steps up to their houses and walls before them; this is esteemed the wealthyest town of its bigness in the Country, its manufacture is the woollen cloth the Yorkshire Cloth in which they are all employ'd and are esteemed very rich and very proud'

Three hundred years later Leeds had acquired a few urban motorways and angular office blocks, but the atmosphere had not changed. The air of civic confidence Celia had observed was still very much in evidence in the Victorian pomp of the Town Hall and Corn Exchange. It was apparent also in the grandiose proportions of the nineteenth-century warehouses and mills still scattered about the town, monuments to Leeds' dominance in the textile industry. When they were built they represented far more to their industrialist owners than mere factories or repositories. They were a celebration of power and prosperity, and this was often reflected in the ostentatiousness of their designs. Giotto's campanile in Florence for example was the model for one brick chimney, while an Egyptian temple provided the inspiration for one of the mills.

Other manufacturing industries have now taken over from textiles, but Leeds still seemed to exude an air of wealth and pride as we rode through it that August day. The shops looked busy and well-stocked, and the people seemed as prosperous as any I had seen so far, bearing out Celia's observations three hundred years ago:

'they have provision soe plentifull that they may live with very little expense and get much variety; here if one calls for a tankard of ale which is allwayes a groate – its the only dear thing all over Yorkshire, their ale is very strong – but for paying this groat for your ale you may have a slice of meate either hott or cold according to the tyme of day you call, or else butter and cheese gratis into the bargaine, this was a general custom in most parts of Yorkshire but now they have almost changed it, and tho' they still retaine the great price for the ale yet make Strangers pay for their meate, and at some places at great rates, notwithstanding how cheape they have all their provision; there is still this custome on a Market day at Leeds the sign of the Bush just by the bridge, any body that will goe and call for one tanckard of ale and a pinte of wine and pay for these only, shall be set to a table to eate with 2 or 3 dishes of good meate and a dish of sweetmeates after; had I known this and the day which was their Market, I would have come then but I happened to come a day after the Market, however I did only pay for 3 tankards of ale and what I eate and my servants was gratis'

On the way to Elland that afternoon, I became aware of the flipside of Yorkshire's textile revolution. Here were many more mills and warehouses, but they were all disused and abandoned, their windows boarded up or gaping black like hollow eye-sockets. Halifax, Sowerby, Brighouse and Elland appeared almost to merge into one, separated only by steep-sided Pennine hills, on which scrubby grass provided a meagre subsistence for sheep and the odd pony tethered to a peg in the ground. Apart from heather, nothing seemed to grow on these exposed and barren heights. Most striking of all was the grime. It was impossible to tell the original colour of most of the older buildings, so encrusted were they with soot; even the dry-stone walls were jet black beneath their coating of pollution. I found it rather shocking at first, but then I reasoned that my reaction was understandable. I was, after all, a product of the age of smokeless fuels. Until a few years ago, such pollution would have been considered as unfortunate, but inevitable. In Celia's day all cities would have appeared blackened. Chimneys were inefficient and smoked, and the universal use of tallow candles added to the filth in the atmosphere. Not even fine new buildings remained clean for long. Even before St Paul's had been completed, Sir Christopher Wren complained that it was 'already so black with coal smoke that it has lost half its elegance'. When Celia travelled through industrial Yorkshire it would probably have been just as dirty as I found it in 1988. The difference is that Celia wouldn't have thought it worth mentioning.

It was 10 August. We had covered over 800 miles, ridden through nineteen counties and now, after seventy-two days, had reached the halfway point of our journey. It seemed like a good time for a party. We finished at Jagger Green early that evening and set off for Ringstone Edge, where George was to stable in the cow byre of a tiny windswept hill farm situated at the bottom of a steep, flinty track. Since it was inaccessible to the lorry we decided to make our base half a mile further up the road in a layby overlooking Ringstone Reservoir, and we parked there for the night, having made a quick sortie into Elland for party supplies.

It was beginning to rain as a souwestered Catherine cycled off into the gathering gloom to feed George, while I turned the Motown tape up to full volume and started the party preparations. By the time I had cleared the seat of saddles and maps, lit a saucerful of household candles and laid the two-foot by one-foot table with knives, forks and a small vase of heather, Catherine had returned. Aiming the bottle out of the door into the darkness we cracked open the champagne and began our banquet of fish and chips and Toblerone. The tape must have been played at least five times as we giggled and danced our way through two bottles of Lanson and a litre of wine, intoxicated as much by a sense of disbelief at our achievement as by the alcohol.

I volunteered to take George his feed later that evening. The exposed hillside offered little protection from the wind and rain but the inside of the cowshed was dry and George's breath felt warm and moist as I patted him in the darkness. I stayed for a few moments to listen to the soothing, rhythmic sound of him eating and then, picking my way up the track, remounted the bicycle and set off towards the lorry. I still felt quite drunk and elated, and before rejoining Catherine I stood for a few minutes in the heathered darkness, looking at the rain-puckered expanse of reservoir and the distant hills cloaked in the night.

I thought back over the past two and a half months. Quite apart from the physical distance we had covered, so much seemed to have happened. In Catherine I had made one of the best friends I would ever have. It was a relationship that transcended the normal ties of friendship for it had been forged in adversity. Even if we were never again to see one another after the ride, I knew we would always be friends. I had made another friend in George too, and in Charles I had found, if not a husband, then someone for whom I would always hold the tenderest feelings. Even Bleeper now occupied a place in my heart.

But the ride had given me more than all that. It had given me not only an insight into Celia Fiennes and the reasons that impelled her to make her journey in the first place, but an insight into her England and, by extension, my own. At first hand I had experienced the sheer diversity of the country, both through its geography and its people. Compared to the rest of the globe England was tiny, but I had learned in the past ten weeks that its variety was infinite.

The most curious discovery of all, and something that I would never have foreseen, was the effect the journey had on me. Whether it was being responsible for others and for animals, meeting so many different people; risking death in the Lake District or simply the chance to prove others' opinions of me wrong, I didn't know. Perhaps it was a combination of all these things. All I knew was that I was less insular and more self-assured now than I had ever been in my life. As much as anything the Great Journey had been a journey into myself. I felt that I had grown up at last.

That night my father telephoned to find out how I was and to check whether the gas bill for my London flat had been paid. It had not, and he was far from pleased.

'No wonder you're riding round England,' he concluded, 'you still haven't passed your driving test. For God's sake, Alison, when are you going to start acting responsibly and behaving like an adult?'

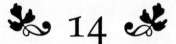

14

Ringstone Edge to Homer

From Elland Celia turned her collar to the elements and rode to Rochdale via the moor of Blackstone Edge. The moor had a formidable reputation, its treacherous bogs and volatile weather having laid claim to many an unwary traveller. Crossing the Edge in August, Daniel Defoe and his companions had suddenly found themselves in the midst of a snowstorm, from which they considered themselves lucky to escape with their lives. It was to be one of the most daunting rides of the whole journey, and I was glad not to be riding alone. My companion was Sarah. She was a local girl, but she knew as little as I did about Blackstone Edge.

Sarah worked as a medical research assistant at Halifax General Hospital, and for the first hour or two we chatted about her job. One of the major diseases into which she researched was AIDS, and she told me that, out of a total population of 150,000, Halifax had five recorded cases. I suppose I had become used to hearing and reading about the high incidence of the disease in London, for I commented on the lowness of the figure. Sarah seemed shocked. Even one case, she argued, was one case too many.

Celia would have understood such fears, for in many respects AIDS is to the twentieth century what the Great Plague was to the seventeenth. Celia was only three when it broke out in 1665, but the memory of it would still have been fresh in 1698. Indeed, such had been its impact on England that it was to lurk at the back of the national consciousness until well into the eighteenth century.

Death is one of the great twentieth-century taboos; but this was not always so. In the seventeenth century, death was regarded as just another aspect of the natural cycle. The infant mortality rate was so high, and life expectancy so low, that people couldn't afford to be sentimental. This attitude is reflected in Celia's dispassionate descriptions of an anatomical hall in Newcastle, where she described the cadavers as matter-of-factly as she did the view out of the window:

> 'I went to see the Barber Surgeons Hall which was within a pretty garden walled in, full of flowers and greenes in potts and in the borders; its a good neat building of brick, there I saw the roome with a round table in it, railed round with seates or benches for the conveniency in their disecting and anatomiseing a body and reading lectures on all parts; there was two bodyes that had been anatomised, one the bones were fastned with wires the other had had the flesh boyled off and some of the ligeaments remained and dryed with it, and so the parts were held together by its own muscles and sinews that were dryed with it; over this was another roome in which was the skin of a man that was taken off after he was dead and dressed and so was stuff'd the body and limbs, it look'd and felt like a sort of parchment; in this roome I could take a view of the whole town, it standing on high ground and a pretty lofty building.'

When it came to the plague, things were very different. Its cause was unknown and as the disease spread, panic set in. All dreaded becoming contaminated, and anyone even remotely suspected of having the disease would immediately be locked up in his own house, and a red cross would be painted on his door beneath the words 'Lord, have mercy upon us'. Such incarceration meant certain death. As the plague strengthened its grip on the population, so fear and ignorance gave rise to all sorts of superstitions. People likened it to a Biblical scourge, a punishment for society's wickedness, and accused anyone who contracted it of moral turpitude. The parish register at Great Coggeshall in Essex, for instance, records that on

'August 10 Lore Smith wife of John Smith was buried, the first to die of the Plague.

This Lore Smith was the instrument of the Lord used to bring the infection of the Plague into this town. She was the first that died of that infectious sickness and the most of those that followed dyed of the same, until the Winter time came, when the Lord in mercie stayed the same. The woeman was comanlie noted to be a notable harlot.'

Such callousness may seem barbarous to us, but as I talked to Sarah I wondered if things had really changed. We put our AIDS sufferers in hospital, but beneath our veneer of humanity are we not as terrified of this new plague as our forebears were?

As if to reflect such dark thoughts, the landscape had changed dramatically. Striking off west across the Pennines, we had left the sheltered cosiness of the Colne River valley far behind us. A frighteningly sheer ascent had brought us to a desolate moor, shrouded in a low-lying, clammy mist. We had reached Blackstone Edge,

'noted all over England for a dismal high precipice and steep in the ascent and descent on either end; its a very moorish ground all about and even just at the top, tho' so high that you travel on a Causey, which is very troublesome as its a moist ground, soe as is usual on these high hills they stagnate the aire and hold mist and raines almost perpetually; as I ascended the morning was pretty faire but a sort of mist met me and small raine just as I attained the top which made me feare a wet day and that the aire would have been so thick to have quite lost me the sight of the Country'

Occasionally we would find ourselves on an ancient packhorse route or a half-forgotten Roman causeway, its stones barely visible beneath the two-thousand-year-old colonies of moss and bog grasses. More often than not we would be following a track no wider than a sheep trail, which would thread in and out of the boulders, bracken and marsh grass, sometimes disappearing for several yards at a time. Most oppressive of all was the silence. The spongey ground muffled the thud of the hoofs, and when the wind dropped there would be no sound at all. Once our horses spooked at an eerie rasping. A few yards further on we suddenly came upon two walkers, their forms barely human beneath the layers of waterproofs. The regular swish on swish of nylon followed us long after the kaghoulish glow of their garments had been swallowed up in the mist once more. Another time the mist lifted long enough for us to catch sight of a distant reservoir, its surface sinister and lifeless beneath the slate-coloured sky. The weather worsened as the day wore on, until all at once we found ourselves on a high and windy promontory:

'but when I attained the top where is a great heap raised up which parts Yorkshire, and there I entred Lancashire, the mist began to lessen, and as I descended on this side the fog more and more went off and a little raine fell, tho' at a little distance in our view the sun shone on the vale which indeed is of a large extent here, and the advantage of soe high a high which is at least 2 mile up, discovers the grounds beneath as a fruitfull valley full of inclosures and cut hedges and trees; that which adds to the formidableness of Blackstone Edge is that on the one hand you have a vast precipice almost the whole way both as one ascends and descends and in some places the precipice is on either hand; this hill took me up much tyme to gaine the top and alsoe to descend it and put me in mind of the description of the Alps in Italy, where the clouds drive all about and as it were below them, which descends lower into mists then into raines, and soe tho' on the top it hold snow and haile falling on the passengers which at length the lower they go comes into raine and so into sun-shine at the foote of those valleys fruitful the sunshine and singing of birds; this was the account my Father gave of those Alps when he passed them and I could not but think this carried some resemblance tho' in little, yet a proportion of that.'

We had crossed Blackstone Edge. Littleborough, Rochdale and Manchester lay before us.

Our next destination was Dunham Massey. I had been advised against riding George through Manchester, so we loaded him into the lorry and set off along the M63. Halfway to Altrincham, the telephone rang. Catherine picked it up.

'Who? . . . I'm sorry, I can't hear you. Who? . . . No, of course I can't give you a map reference. I don't know how to do them . . . We're on the M63 going to Dunham Massey . . . All right . . . See you there.'

'Who was that?' I asked.

'Dunno,' she replied, laughing, 'but we'll find out soon enough!'

Approached from the north, our first glimpse of Dunham Massey was of a low and very plain red-brick house apparently dating back to the first half of the eighteenth century. Celia would have recognised little of the 'old fashion building' she saw in 1698, for early in the next century the Tudor mansion was completely encased. The radical change in Dunham Massey's appearance was authorised by George Booth, the second Earl of Warrington, who, remotely related to Celia through his grandfather, the first Baron Delamere, had married the daughter of Celia's Aunt Bridget. Despite the connection, Celia either wasn't invited to stay at Dunham Massey, or chose not to. In all probability no invitation was extended by the second earl, who even at the age of twenty-three was renowned for his misanthropic and cantankerous disposition. When he succeeded to the title in 1694, there were lengthy legal wrangles over his father's will which culminated in a petition to Parliament by his sister and brother on the grounds that they had been left destitute. In 1702, the earl married Mary Oldbury, the daughter of a London merchant, in the hope of restoring the family fortune. But, apart from £40,000, she brought him little contentment, for they 'quarell'd and lived in the same house as absolute strangers to each other at bed and board', and in 1739 the earl published a pamphlet advocating divorce on the grounds of incompatibility of temper. Far more attractive a character was the sixth earl, George Harry Grey, who at the age of eighteen inherited two earldoms and a rent roll of £90,000 a year. Whilst still at Cambridge he became attached to Bessie Billage, the daughter of the Trinity College bootman, and in 1848 he swept her off to Brighton and married her. Much to the family's relief, Bessie died of a seizure in 1854. The deliverance was shortlived. In 1856 the earl was married again, this time to Kitty Cocks, the celebrated equestrienne and circus performer. Despite the difference in background, their tempers were most compatible, and they remained devoted to one another until the death of the earl in 1883, after which the countess became a great benefactress to the tenants on the estate.

The identity of our mystery caller was revealed when we drew into the carpark of Dunham Massey.

'Hello!' cried a jolly voice.

We looked round, but could see nothing apart from a white car.

'Hello!' came the salutation once more, 'I'm over here!'

Peering in the direction of what we took to be 'over here', we discovered the source of the disembodied voice. His upper torso projecting like a tank commander's out of the sunroof of his white Opel Kadett, a young man with a military haircut and naughty, boyish grin now addressed us with the words, 'Hi! I'm Patrick!'

Just a few miles south-west of Dunham Massey, Celia had one of the narrowest escapes of the Great Journey:

'here I think I may say was the only tyme I had reason to suspect I was engaged with some Highway men; 2 fellows all on a suddain from the wood fell into the road, they look'd truss'd up with great coates and as it were bundles about them which I believe was pistolls, but they dogg'd me one before the other behind and would often look back to each other and frequently justle my horse out of the way to get between one of my servants horses and mine, and when they first came up to us did disown their knowledge of the way and would often stay a little behind and talke together then come up againe, but the Providence of God so order'd it as there was men at work in the fields hay makeing, and it being market day at Whitchurch as I drew neer to that in 3 or 4 mile was continually met with some of the market people, so they at last called each other off and soe left us and turned back; but as they rode with us 3 or 4 miles at last they described the places we should come by, and a high

pillar finely painted in the road about 3 mile off of Whitchurch which accordingly we saw as we pass'd on, which
shew'd them noe strangers to the road as they at first
pretended.'

Could history be repeating itself, I wondered? Looking at the
lanky figure now bounding towards us with a black labrador
puppy at his heels, it seemed unlikely. It emerged that I had
corresponded with Patrick about the possibility of our stabling
with his family in north Wales. In the event we had stabled at the
Duke of Westminster's, but Patrick had decided to track us down
nevertheless while he was on leave from his post in Germany as a
second lieutenant with the Royal Engineers. There was time only
for the briefest of introductions before George and I had to present
ourselves at the house for a press call and to meet Clive Alford, the
custodian of Dunham Massey.

The house seemed to contain more historical objects than most
National Trust properties, and Clive enthused about them all in the
same engaging and knowledgeable manner. Responsible for 1000
pieces of furniture, 1000 textile items, 1500 drawings and 250 sets of
china, he was surprisingly self-effacing about his role as custodian.
Its keynote, he explained, was simply variation. 'One day I might
be showing the Lelys to the Duke of Grafton and the next cleaning
out the gents.'

Our tour must have lasted an hour, during which we saw such
treasures as the second earl's silver-plated chamberpot, a cruci-
fixion carved by Grinling Gibbons and five remarkable bird's eye
views of Dunham Massey painted between 1695 and 1751. So
convincing was the perspective in the paintings, by Adriaen van
Dienst and John Harris the Younger, that on more than one
occasion visitors to the house had asked Clive whether the little
white building on the horizon was Burton Aerodrome.

'This place is endless. My job is to show the house to visitors and
make it interesting. But I can't deny that I love it in winter when
there's no one here and we have it to ourselves.'

So authentic was the refurbishment in all thirty of the rooms on
display that it was easy to see why Dunham Massey had acquired a
reputation for being haunted. Some years earlier a National Trust

catering manager had apparently stayed the night in the Oak Room. Descending ashen-faced to breakfast the following morning, he recounted how in the middle of the night he had felt himself hemmed into his bed, and looking up had been terrified to see three female faces gazing down at him.

I asked Clive whether he thought Dunham Massey really was haunted. I had expected a cynically dismissive response, but to my surprise he gave no answer at all, and related another story. One night while his wife and children were away, he decided to disprove the haunting theory and had camped in the Oak Room in his sleeping bag. Drifting off to sleep at about eleven, he had suddenly awoken in the dead of the night with an overwhelming feeling of nausea. The sensation would not subside, so he made his way slowly back to his own room, where to his astonishment he immediately felt quite well again. Surely that was proof enough, we insisted.

'Well, who knows,' replied Clive. 'It might just have been indigestion.'

The countryside flattened out considerably as we headed towards Whitchurch the next day. The Cheshire border seemed to mark not only a topographical divide but a social one as well. The standard of living was improving with each mile; the population was growing in density and the inhabitants seemed increasingly reserved. All of a sudden we had found ourselves back in the south. It was curious to cross the tracks of our journey north at Beeston Castle, and I wondered whether Celia's sense of achievement at having come so far was tempered, like mine, by a sense of nostalgia for the north she was leaving behind.

We stabled that night at Prees Heath, just outside Whitchurch. I was quite taken aback when, within five minutes of our arrival, the son of the house invited me up to his bedroom and suggested that we have a bath together. I could only attribute his forwardness to a four-year-old's excitement at meeting strangers. The next three days were most restful despite being woken every morning by two children jumping on me yelling: 'Get out of bed, lazybones!' Although these assaults took place at dawn, it was far more agreeable to be jolted into consciousness by high-decibel nursery rhymes than by the usual intergalactic bleeping of my digital quartz alarm clock.

Patrick was proving to be a most agreeable temporary addition to the team. It clearly amused him to help two damsels in distress, or 'DIDS', as he called us, and he set about repairing all the minor structural damage the lorry had suffered since 31 May. His skills as an engineer were to prove invaluable as he patched up the gaping skylight with polythene and Agritape, made fast any fixtures that had worked themselves loose during the journey, and mended the roller-blind catches that had been gnawed by Bleeper. He even remedied the problem of George's back by buying some sticky-backed orthopaedic felt. It was an ingenious idea, and for a while it displaced the pressure of the saddle and allowed the air to circulate freely round the sore area, its gluey surface preventing it from sliding about and chafing George further.

Once all the chores had been carried out we all felt in need of a rest. It was the hottest day so far of the journey, and a neighbour of our hostess had suggested that we call round for a swim. We accepted the offer with alacrity. The invitation had been extended by a very attractive woman in her late thirties, and we arrived to find her draped in semi-clad elegance across a poolside *chaise longue*. Rising languorously to meet us, she asked our names.

'This is Catherine. She's the groom and drives the lorry. I'm Alison. I do the riding. And this is Patrick.'

'And what does Patrick do?' she breathed.

There was a momentary silence.

'Oh, I see,' she continued with a seductively curling half-smile, 'Patrick's the Toyboy.'

Not even total submersion could entirely dispel the blushes that now engulfed Patrick's frame.

On 18 August it had been arranged that we would box George down to Banbury for a fund-raising ride from Banbury Cross to Broughton Castle, seat of the Fiennes family. Celia didn't visit Banbury during her Great Journey, but since she was so closely connected with the town and its nursery rhyme, it seemed too good an opportunity to miss. START and Whitbread's hoped that a high-profile visit would act as a fillip to our coverage in the national press, but I had a different reason for wanting to go. While Celia had never lived at Broughton, it was home to her manuscript. Since my only contact with her had been through her writing I could not help feeling that if her spirit was to be found anywhere, it would most probably be in the leather-bound pages of the octavo volume. In a sense, then, the trip to Broughton was a pilgrimage, a way of paying my respects to a woman who had died 300 years before my birth, but who had inspired me more than any person living.

Morale was high as we drove to Banbury. George had clearly benefited from his rest, and it was exciting to pass so many signposts to places we had already visited en route. While George was stabled at a nearby farm we were guests that night of the Saye and Seles at Broughton Castle. For more than 600 years the castle had been in the hands of the Saye and Sele family. When Celia visited it, she described it as:

> 'an ancient Seate of the Lord Viscount Say and Seale; its an
> old house moted round and a parke and gardens, but are
> much left to decay and ruine, when my brother came to it'

When we came to it some 300 years later nothing could have been further from the truth. Canvas-draped scaffolding extended the whole length of the castle, testimony to a fifteen-year restoration programme initiated by the twenty-first Baron Saye and Sele.

'It's going to cost three and a half million,' he explained as he led us through the porch to the kitchen, 'but nothing substantial will need to be done for another 400 years.'

I found it remarkable that anyone could entertain such long-term plans. Beyond a vague idea that I might one day have children, and possibly grandchildren, my own outlook was very much rooted in the present. To think more than a few years ahead seemed almost a luxury that humanity could no longer afford. Yet here was a man whose vision of the future was firmly founded in stone and extended nearly half a millennium. It was curiously reassuring.

The most striking thing about Broughton's interior was that it felt lived in. While it looked like a castle, the stone vaulting and echoing flagstones were offset by an overwhelming atmosphere of homeliness. Ironically, the fact that it was still able to continue as a private house was entirely due to its being open to the public. Seventeen thousand people visited the castle each year, revealed Lord Saye and Sele, and it was through their entrance fees that the annual running costs of the building were met. The Saye and Seles would themselves often take money at the gate or act as guides around their own house. Occasionally they would even be asked to point out the lord. 'The fact that I look so insignificant helps,' declared Lord Saye and Sele, with disarming modesty.

The remainder of the £35,000 running costs were covered by private functions and by location fees from television, film or advertising companies. In the past the castle had been used for such productions as *The Slipper and the Rose*, *The Scarlet Pimpernel* and even the Morecambe and Wise Christmas show. Pointing to the new carpet in the drawing room, Lady Saye and Sele said, '*Joseph Andrews* paid for that.'

Celia might not have approved of the film, but I felt sure she would approve of the practicality of her descendants.

We ate dinner that night in the sixteenth-century double linen-fold panelled dining room. I had met the Saye and Seles before, and it was relaxing to relate to them our various adventures in the hoof-tracks of their ancestress. Saye and Sele knew a good many of the people we had stayed with along the route, and he would interrupt our account with such comments as: 'They've got rather a gin and tonic problem, I hear,' or, 'He's quite a lad, they say. The staider members of the aristocracy don't quite approve.'

Over the past weeks I had settled into the habit of reading Celia's journal each night before I went to sleep. That evening was no exception, apart from one difference. Mine was a twentieth-century edition; at Broughton I read the original. It was a thrilling experience. So exciting was it simply to hold the manuscript, to inhale its intoxicating mustiness and to hear the delicate crackle of its pages under my fingers, that I felt almost giddy. Two hours after I had put Celia's journal down, my hands were still shaking. I had never felt so close to her.

'Banbury is a pretty little town the streets broad and well pitched, the whole Country is very pleasant and the land rich, a red earth'

Banbury was still quite pretty 300 years later, but as I rode to our press call at the town's cross the following morning, I reflected on some of the more regrettable changes it had undergone. A nursery rhyme and a cake had helped to make Banbury's name, so it seemed rather sad that the original cake shop should have been pulled down as recently as 1967, and the original Banbury Cross destroyed in the seventeenth century by Puritans. The present cross proved to be a very unattractive and cumbersome Victorian replacement, but it served our purposes well enough that day. Both the START office and Whitbread's had made a concerted effort to attract the press to the event, and we were met by a sizeable contingent from the media. The next half hour must have resulted in tailbacks of at least five miles as the through-traffic was halted to allow George and me to walk round the cross.

'Just one more time. Sorry, luv . . . For the *Banbury Guardian*.'

The mayor presented us with the Sword of Banbury, while a brace of diminutive civic dignitaries, posing for a photograph, were almost crushed beneath George's hind hoofs. Travelling back to Banbury later that evening, we decided that the day could have been far worse. Not only had we paid our respects to Celia, but the Sword of Banbury, a six-inch silver-plated paper knife bearing the town's coat of arms, now hung beside the Ipswich Town Football Club knickers in a place of honour on the wall.

From Whitchurch we travelled the next day to Shrewsbury, about which Celia conceded:

> 'its true there are noe fine houses but there are many large old houses that are convenient and stately, and its a pleasant town to live in and great plenty which makes it cheap living; here is a very good Schoole for young Gentlewomen for learning work and behaviour and musick.'

Shrewsbury's centre seemed scarcely to have changed at all, but I doubt whether Celia would have been so complimentary about the town had she been caught, as we were, in a fast-moving one-way system that added at least fifty minutes to our journey.

She was less impressed by the Wrekin, the hump of rock that rises abruptly out of the flat Severn plain like a beached whale:

'and soe I rode by the great hill called the Reeke noted for the highest piece of ground in England – but it must be by those that only live in the heart of the kingdom and about London, for there are much higher hills in the north and west, and alsoe not 40 mile distant from it Manborn [Malvern] hills seems vastly higher; this hill stands just by it self a round hill and does raise its head much above the hills neare it, and on the one side does looke a great steep down; but still my thoughts of the fells in Cumberland and Westmoreland are soe farr beyond it in height that this would not be mentioned there; it is seen 20 mile off and soe may many other hills, but when I rode just under it I was full convinc'd its height was not in competition with those in other parts that I have seen'

Disparaging though she may have been, Celia was quite correct. At 1334 feet, the Wrekin is not even the highest hill in Shropshire, let alone England. What makes it remarkable is not its height, but its situation. So remote is it from the nearest range of hills that people used to believe giants had deposited it there. The truth is almost as strange as the fiction, for the Wrekin was in fact formed from the lava ash and debris disgorged from a volcano 900 million years ago. Even more remarkable are the entrances to Heaven and Hell on its summit – the inner and outer entrances of an Iron Age fort, tribal capital of the Cornovii and one of the last strongholds to resist the Roman invasion.

All day the weather had been very volatile, alternating between bright sunshine and heavy showers. Towards the end of the afternoon a great shaft of light suddenly rent the tattered clouds and, glancing gold off the telegraph wires, threw every hillock and tuft of grass into dazzling relief. For some reason I chanced to look up into the sky, where I saw two perfect rainbows extending from the darkening form of the Wrekin to the village of Homer just ahead of us. It seemed as if Providence were smiling on our little odyssey.

SHROPSHIRE

• Uyke Equestrian Centre
Homer • Wrottesley
Ironbridge • Wolverhampton

HEREFORD

Kidderminster

Ombersley • Droitwich
Leominster
• Worcester

Stretton
Grandison   Stony
Stoke   Cross   • Great Malvern
Edith
Ledbury

& WORCESTER

Newent

GLOUCESTERSHIRE

Gloucester

17th August ~ 8th September

Scale   0   10   20   30   40   50 Miles

• Badminton

SEVERN ESTUARY

AVON

• Bristol
        • Bath
    • Netherbridge

Wookey Hole
• Wells

• Glastonbury

SOMERSET

• Taunton

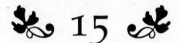

15

Homer to Leominster

A pot of gold really did lie at the end of our double rainbow, for we arrived at our stabling that night to find the following notice pinned to the entrance gate:

> 'Meet TV's Alison Payne. Garden Party. Here Friday
> 19th August 7.30 pm.
> Wyke Equestrian Centre.
> Everyone welcome
>
> Skin for Life Research Appeal.
>
> Help us to support them by supporting us.'

I have to confess that both Catherine and I shrank at the prospect. The last thing either of us felt like after so long a day was to be sociable to what promised to be a large number of strangers. I felt embarrassed too at the description 'TV's Alison Payne', which suggested that I was a star of at least the magnitude of a Sue Lawley. Besides, our rainbows had long since disappeared and the angry black clouds overhead didn't seem the best augury for a garden party. But there was no turning back. George was tired and we had no other stabling. We decided to brazen it out.

In fact our reservations proved unfounded. The garden party had been prudently relocated into a large covered school, every square foot of which was taken up by stalls and attractions. All along one length of the wall were trestle tables creaking under a display of home-made cakes, assorted groceries, indoor plants, second-hand books and jumble clothes, while along the other wall huge notices written in felt pen tempted one to try one's skill at tug-o-war, skittles, tossing the horseshoe, apple dunking, hula hoop, darts and soaking-the-student. There was even a belly-dancing fortune teller called Gypsy Rose Lee. Dressed in a black wig and diaphanous yashmak she looked at my hand and said in a tremulous voice: 'Aaah! the mists are clearing. You've been a long way, a very long way, and you're going to go a long way.'

Then, taking Catherine's hand, she put her arm to her forehead and with eyes rolling emitted a yet more plaintive moan: 'Woooaaah! You've been a long way, a very long way, and you're going to go a long way, a very long way. AAAh!'

Then she caught sight of Bleeper. 'AAAAH! The canine crystal clears. This dog has travelled a great distance . . . a very great distance. And he has many miles before him still.'

Suddenly her face dropped, and standing up she suddenly gasped.

'What is it?' we asked anxiously, afraid lest the whorls in Bleeper's paw presaged some dreadful disaster.

'Ooh, I am silly!' replied Gypsy Rose Lee, 'I forgot to ask you to cross my palm with silver. That'll be £3 consultation fee, please.'

One of the best things about the evening was that nobody really wanted to talk to us. George was the celebrity, and they crowded round his stable until well into the night discussing tungsten-tip horseshoe nails, electrolytes and equine therapy. They would have asked him to present the prizes if they could, but had to make do with me instead. By 9.30 all the awards had been handed out except the one for the horseshoe tossing.

'Well done!' I congratulated the winner, a skinny boy with freckles. 'How did you do it?'

'I cheated.'

If it had been up to me I would have given him ten prizes.

A grand auction was held at the end of the evening to clear every stall of its remaining produce and to sell off any sausages or hamburgers into which Bleeper hadn't sunk his teeth. So persuasive was the auctioneer that everyone was soon bidding outrageous sums of money for objects they might more sensibly consign to a dustbin. Catherine and I bought less than most, but even our purchases ran to five packets of dwarf peas; an outsize purple wool dress; two geraniums; a tin of carrots; a cracked soapdish; a library's worth of Mills & Boons; three tins of Spam; the 1978 *Kojak Annual*; a bottle of elderflower wine and a chipped porcelain bell in the form of two blue tits. It came as no surprise to learn the following morning that the auction had raised £300.

For the next three nights we were stabled near Wolverhampton. Celia spent some time in the area, drawn especially by the gardens of Patshull Park, 'talk'd off as the finest and best kept'. Patshull Park has since been converted into a convalescent home, so we stayed at Wrottesley, another house to which Celia referred in her journal. Wrottesley is now divided up into flats, and the park converted to a golf course, but a pall of mystery surrounded it while it was in the hands of the Wrottesley family. The troubles date from the sixteenth century, when Guy Wrottesley was thrown from his horse while out hunting. Unconscious and badly injured, he would have died had it not been for Vivienne, the forester's daughter, who had him taken back to her father's cottage and nursed him back to health. Guy fell in love with his beautiful saviour, and when he eventually returned to Wrottesley he announced that he was going to take her as his wife. His parents were outraged at the prospect of acquiring so lowly a daughter-in-law, and to thwart the marriage declared Vivienne a sorceress. A trial was held and Vivienne was sentenced to death by burning. As the flames began to lick around her, Vivienne pointed towards Wrottesley and cried:

'First by the King,
And then by the State,
And then by something thrice as great
Shall Wrottesley Hall be made fuel for fire.'

The curse was soon forgotten, but some years later the Wrottesley land was suddenly confiscated by Henry VIII. It was eventually returned to the family, only to be re-confiscated in the seventeenth century by Oliver Cromwell. Uncanniest of all was the third blow that was to strike the house and family, for soon afterwards it was destroyed by lightning. All that remained were the Tudor cellars, and it was over these that a new house was built in 1696, standing one storey high and constructed from the original bricks. This was the house Celia saw in 1698 and declared so 'stately'. Wrottesley, it would seem, had found peace at last. Not so Vivienne. The Wrottesleys no longer live at the hall, but on the eve of every marriage connected with the house, she appears before the bride. Had it happened to our hostess, I wondered?

'Well, as a matter of fact it did,' she replied, 'but it wasn't scarey. In fact it felt rather super to be part of the hall's history.'

Since she was on the verge of marrying for the second time I could only assume that what she said was true.

Bored with our own cooking, Catherine and I ate one night at the Dil Shad, a Tandoori restaurant in the centre of Wolverhampton. It was an excellent meal and we were soon speculating as to what the puritan palate of Celia would make of the spicy concoctions. Regional variations of all types fascinated her, especially those of a dietary and culinary nature, and she would go to great lengths to sample them.

So keen an interest in regional specialities is all the more under-standable when one considers how restricted the choice of food was in the seventeenth century. To a certain extent the cold climate was responsible, as only a few crops were indigenous to the country. The main factor, however, was poverty. The majority of the population came from poor, peasant stock. Apart from the occasional offal-based dish, most people simply couldn't afford to eat meat and so lived on cereals – a diet not dissimilar to that of many third-world countries today. Bread was a staple food and one in which Celia was especially interested. At Garstang and Lake Windermere she described the making of Clap bread, 'which is much talked off, made all of oates . . . the taste is pleasant enough and where its well made is very acceptable'. Not so acceptable was rye bread, which she came across

in Lancashire Yorkshire and Stafford and Shropshire and so Herriford and Worcestershire which I found very troublesome in my journeys, for they would not own they had any such thing in their bread but it so disagrees with me as allwayes to make me sick, which I found by its effects when ever I met with any tho' I did not discern it by the taste; in Suffolke and Norfolke I also met with it'

Fish was another food source, but was for the most part available only to those who lived near the coast. The relish with which Celia described Windermere Charr, Scottish salmon and Colchester oysters suggests how seldom she ate them.

Having speculated on Celia's reaction to Indian food, I wondered what she would make of English food today. A higher standard of living has led to greater choice. Paradoxically, it has all but eradicated what regional variations once existed. A handful of local dishes like Yorkshire pudding and Lancashire hotpot remain, but how many people make bread at home when they can go and buy a loaf of Hovis? How many go to the trouble of preparing fresh fish when they can buy a packet of fish fingers? That England has little cuisine of its own is all too clearly demonstrated by the inability of the English language to come up with a word for an eating place. Instead we are forced to use such imports as 'restaurant', 'bistro', 'buffet' and 'café'. I could only conclude that, were Celia to come back today, she would find the English lazy and their food unimaginative.

It was during our stay at Wrottesley that we first met Puppy. A six-week-old bundle of lurcher with a sleek body and an ingenuous manner, his charms were difficult to resist.

'We can't keep him,' said his owners, scenting a potential sale. 'Why don't you buy him? Would £20 be reasonable?'

The very idea was preposterous. He already towered over Bleeper, and the chunkiness of his leg joints suggested that his present appearance was but a hint of the stature he would achieve once fully-grown. Space was already at such a premium in the lorry that to take a growing lurcher on board was quite simply out of the question. Besides, looking after Bleeper was in itself a Herculean task. However would we manage with a second dog? Tempting though the idea was, we agreed that to take Puppy on would be

folly of the sheerest kind. Our decision was unanimous – we paid the £20 there and then.

The first question was what to call this latest recruit to the Great Journey. As soon as he had set eyes on the interior of the lorry he had headed straight for the only seat, which he now occupied with an attitude of wanton indolence, his head lolling lazily against a cushion.

'What about "hog"?' suggested Catherine; but somehow 'Puppy' suited him as well as anything, and so, for the time being at least, the name stuck.

'After all,' said Catherine, 'we've got until he's fully-grown to think of a name.'

There could be few sights more formidable than that which greeted me as I stepped out of the lorry the following morning. Dressed in a long navy coat, black leather boots, and wearing an arsenal of weaponry about his person, was the incarnation of Oliver Cromwell himself. Glowering at me from under his visored helmet, he cleared his throat with a terrifying growl and said, 'Lovely morning, isn't it? I'm Mike. You must be Alison.' As he himself said later that day, 'It's amazing what a Parliamentary glare from under a lobsterpot can do!'

Quite apart from his job as the local BHS bridleways officer, Mike was a cavalryman with the Sealed Knot, the society dedicated to re-enacting the Civil War. It was clear on which side his allegiance lay.

'We're much better behaved than the Royalists. They normally come from the stockbroker belt near Guildford.'

Whatever the persuasions of its five thousand-odd members, I quickly realised that the Sealed Knot went far beyond the realms of play-acting. 'For most of us the twentieth century is just a hobby,' admitted Mike. 'We really live in the seventeenth century.'

So fanatical was one member that he had his name changed by deed poll to that of the Cromwellian general he most admired, while Mike himself admitted that he would much rather spend a holiday metal-detecting for cannonballs at Edgehill than sunning himself in Spain.

Living in the seventeenth century at twentieth-century prices was not without its drawbacks. Simply kitting himself out had cost Mike over £700, even though much of his equipment was home-made. It was heavy, too. With his powder flask, musket and assorted weaponry, Mike's load alone weighed 94 lbs, while his mare had a further 120 lbs to carry in addition to her rider.

We were just nearing the outskirts of Kidderminster when a man called out to Mike from the pavement, 'You like to ride in bondage, do you?'

Mike obviously didn't hear this defamation, for he smiled blankly and rode on. A few moments later he asked me what the man had said.

'Bondage!' spluttered Mike, his face purple with rage beneath its lobsterpot helmet. 'I'd have bunged my sword up his backside if I'd heard!'

Puppy had settled into lorry life very quickly, despite what seemed to be pathological cowardice. If anyone so much as brushed against his tail, the decibels would start ricocheting from one wall to the other as he let out the most piercing shrieks and yelps. Even when, after ten minutes, he realised that he had in fact sustained no injury, he would affect a pronounced limp and, taking up his customary pose on the seat, would regard us with reproachful eyes. Not unfairly, perhaps, we toyed with the idea of calling him 'Weedy' or 'Windy', but he was still a puppy, and it seemed rather cruel to brand him before we had discovered of what metal he was really made.

Bleeper was developing in quite the opposite direction. That Puppy had brought out his bullying streak was all too apparent, and for the first three days it was rare for Puppy's head not to be gripped sadistically between Bleeper's incisors. Day four brought about a turning point. Puppy had gradually realised that retaliation was possible and now focused his counter-attack on the fleshiest part of Bleeper's ears. By day five, Bleeper realised he had met his match. He also realised that a truce might better suit his long-term plans: having so tall an accomplice was an advantage he was going to exploit to the full. With Bleeper's brains and Puppy's height nothing in the lorry was safe from their grasp, as we were to discover when we returned to the lorry after an absence of five minutes to find Puppy's and Bleeper's jaws firmly clenched about my tricorn hat. It was clear that a constant vigil was going to be necessary if we were to return to London with the lorry and its contents intact.

George was an altogether different problem. While the orthopaedic felt pad supplied by Patrick, or 'Toyboy' as we now called him, had prevented any further deterioration in the state of George's back, constant riding meant that it never had a chance to heal. More worrying still was George's general attitude. Since Dunham Massey he had grown reserved and moody. For no apparent reason he would stop in mid-track, and even a sharply delivered 'Gittorn, you lazy bugger!' would often fail to move him. Although she didn't show it, I could tell that Catherine was also alarmed at his recalcitrant behaviour. It was 24 August. Nearly sixty days and 600 miles still separated us from London. Up until two weeks ago, I had been certain that we would succeed. Now I was not so sure.

From Kidderminster Celia had headed towards Ombersley. I wondered what Mike would have made of this staunchly Royalist stronghold with its magpie-timbered houses arranged in a neat cluster about the Crown and Sandys Inn. That night we were the guests not of the publican but of its landlord, Lord Sandys, owner of the grandest of all the stables we had yet seen. Built in 1810, they were constructed in the shape of a square, with sash windows overlooking a central cobbled courtyard. Although they were over 170 years old there was a spotless elegance and symmetrical purity about the buildings that seemed untouched by time. Every mechanism worked as if it had been installed that very day, from the gleaming door latches to the semicircular revolving mangers, which at the merest touch would glide silently into the wall. Mercifully no such act was necessary for George, for despite his contrary disposition, his appetite remained unaffected.

He continued to be sluggish over the following days, and it was only after the most tedious of journeys that we eventually came to Worcester. Celia had had vexations of her own along this route. Apart from describing it as 'a very sad heavy way, all sand', she complained that:

> 'All the way from the Seven Starrs where we baited to Ambusly the road was full of the Electers of the Parliament men coming from the choice of the Knights of the Shire, which spake as they were affected, some for one some for another, and some were larger in their judgments than others, telling their reason much according to the good liquors operation and of these people all the publick houses were filled that it was a hard matter to get Lodging or Entertainment'

Things improved somewhat when she reached Worcester:

> 'a large Citty, 12 Churches, the streetes most of them broad, the buildings some of them are very good and lofty; its encompass'd with a wall which has 4 gates that are very strong; the Market place is large; there is a Guildhall besides the Market house which stands on pillars of stone'

Like Ombersley, Worcester was also a Royalist stronghold during the Civil War, being the first city to declare for the king and the last to surrender in 1646. An inscription over one door, 'Love God, honour ye King', commemorates Charles II's flight here after his defeat at the Battle of Worcester. The city's unswerving loyalty to the House of Stuart is also celebrated in the Guildhall. This is not the Guildhall that Celia saw, but a Queen Anne replacement of stone-dressed brick. Three niches contain statues of Charles I, Charles II and Queen Anne, but most significant of all is the gruesome effigy of Oliver Cromwell, nailed by its ears above a doorway.

Worcester's Royalist tendencies still seemed prevalent. Walking into one newsagent's, I found myself visually assaulted by pictures of the Duchess of York grinning from at least ten magazine covers while the Princess of Wales coyly batted her eyelids from another six. I wondered what Celia would make of these twentieth-century icons. When she visited Worcester in 1698, England had already experienced a decade of constitutional monarchy. An ardent Whig, Celia was very much in favour of this new régime, for as well as bringing peace and stability to the country it had resulted in a radical reduction in the powers of the monarchy and a total devaluation of its hitherto divine status. As I looked round the magazine racks it struck me that Celia would find the England of today a very retrogressive place. Not only did its inhabitants revere their royal family, they had elevated them once again to the status of godheads.

Finding no contacts in the area, we had arranged to stay that night at a dairy farm that offered stabling to itinerant horses. It was a long way from the regal setting of Ombersley Court. Pulling into the driveway, we soon found our wheels sinking into the muck of a large farmyard. The place seemed deserted. Near the farmhouse was a jumbled assortment of barns and outhouses, while ranged at the far end of the yard a fleet of cream and blue 'Mr Yorky' ice cream vans was parked. Seeing a movement inside one of them, I knocked on the door to be confronted by a choleric-looking man with a high colour and a low-slung belly wearing bedroom slippers.

'You'll find him that way, I expect,' he replied curtly in answer to

my enquiry about the farmer's whereabouts, and then climbed
back into the van. Our host was more sympathetic. His daughter
had recognised George from 'Blue Peter', and it clearly amused
him to have a TV personality in his stable.

'You don't mind if I get one or two of my mates round to look at
Desert Orchid here, do you?'

We didn't mind in the least. George adored the attention, while
Catherine and I were only too glad to have the evening to
ourselves.

Since we were free agents, we decided to spend the evening at
Droitwich Spa. Although Celia had only passed by it, she had
commented on

> 'the 3 salt springs divided by a fresh spring that runs by it; of
> this salt water they boyle much salt that turns to good
> account.'

Salt was being produced at Droitwich long before Celia's visit, for
the radioactive brine springs had been discovered in prehistoric
times. Salt production was continued under the Romans, who
called the town Salinae, but it was not until the nineteenth century
that Droitwich became a spa. In 1828 a far-seeing businessman
called John Corbett recognised both the therapeutic benefit and the
financial potential of the springs, and built the St Andrew's Brine
Baths, remodelling the sixteenth-century Raven Hotel and various
other establishments about the town as luxury spa hotels. By 1876
Corbett had become known as 'the salt king' and Droitwich established as one of Britain's most fashionable resorts, a mecca for
those seeking a cure for gout, sciatica, lumbago and arthritis.
Corbett's baths no longer exist, but in 1985 a new Brine Bath was
opened on the same site, and it was there that we presented
ourselves at seven o'clock that night. A party of rather generously
proportioned ladies had apparently made a block booking, for
when we peered through the glass doors we could see some of
them floating about in the pool, while others lay in various states of
undress on the poolside sunloungers, chatting over biscuits and
coffee like models for a Beryl Cook painting.

'Nothing beats the first time,' said one lady with envy as

Catherine and I gingerly tested the water. The salt gave the surface of the water a waxy, almost viscous consistency which was not immediately appealing. It was also quite hot. I thought of St Catherine of Vigone scalding herself in the hot springs as a preparation for Purgatory, and withdrew my foot from the water.

'It's lovely once you're in,' continued the lady encouragingly. 'It's got 2½ lbs of salt per gallon. That's saltier than the Dead Sea.'

Eventually we submerged ourselves, and to our surprise found the experience quite exhilarating. I could well believe our companion's comment about the salt content, for all efforts to swim or walk were futile and Catherine and I found ourselves floating around the pool like bobbing corks. I had been a little afraid that the salt might irritate my saddlesores, but the overriding sensation was one of extreme well-being and relaxation, and I slept better that night than I had done for a long time.

Bearing south-west the next day George and I headed towards the Malvern Hills and Stretton Grandison. This was Elgar country, and at nearly every turn in the road we came upon signs bearing the symbol of a violin and the words 'Elgar Route'.

I was reflecting on how sad it was that even music should be turned into a tourist attraction when a battered red Cortina drew up in front of us. Its driver was a swarthy man with a heavy growth of beard and sharp, yellow teeth.

'Is that for sale?' he muttered, nodding at George.

'No!' I replied indignantly, and fixed him with a disapproving glare until his Cortina had finally rattled off round the corner with a belch of exhaust fumes. A few minutes later another car drew up, this time a white Metro.

'What a lovely horse!' declared its driver. 'You know that tail's worth a lot of money.'

I was about to make some disdainful reply when he revealed that he was a violinist. Up to 150 horsehairs might go into a single bow, he explained, and since a good bow could cost up to £1000 I should forgive him for taking so lively an interest in George's tail. His musical interests were nothing if not eclectic. Not only had he been the co-leader of Covent Garden and leader of a string quartet, he had played with Stephane Grappelli and toured with a number of punk rock bands. What did he think of Elgar, I asked.

'Can't bear him.'

The day took on a hot, white stillness as dusty tracks led us past endless fruit plantations and through orchards lined with avenues of poplars. The Malvern Hills were now just a shimmer of blue gauze in the distance. George and I moved like somnambulists that morning, too tired even to pick the ripening fruit that hung across our path, and it seemed hours before we reached our destination. Catherine was waiting for us at the Crown Inn at Stony Cross, and while she attended to George I went to ask the landlord for water. His only other customers were three punks with henna'd hair and earrings, a study in dispirited torpor as they sat in a dark corner drinking beer.

'What's with the bucket?' one asked dully.

When they realised it was for a horse, they all trooped out into the carpark and spent the next half hour gazing at George in awe.

'He's great!' was the general consensus, although all three were careful to keep their distance.

'My brother got bitten by a donkey once. You can still see the teeth marks. I'm staying well back.'

'Me too,' said another. 'They can take a man's arms off, they can.'

He was right. A stallion at Newmarket did bite its trainer's arm off once. Looking at George as he leaned against the side of the lorry, his eyelids heavy with tiredness, I knew that with this horse at least the three punks would be in no danger at all. No one else came to this pub that lunchtime and I had the impression that few people ever did. When I asked the landlord where the ladies was, he replied: 'Oh dear, I'll have to unlock it. You see, there's not really the call for it that often.'

Throughout the day we had passed field upon field of what I thought were giant yellow raspberries or ripening loganberries. They seemed at least ten feet high, with canes suspended from an overhead wire.

'Raspberries?' spluttered our mild-mannered host that evening.

'They're hops, not raspberries! It's easy to see you're no country girl.'

To compound my crime, it turned out that our host owned a hundred acres of the crop himself. So mortified was he that they should be mistaken for raspberries that he insisted on taking us on a tour of his farm. One and a half hours later we could not only string a bine, but we were passing experts on Alpha acid analysis, verticillian wilt and the latest in hopper technology.

The farmhouse itself was of even greater interest to me, for it had belonged to one of Celia's relations:

> 'my Cos'n Fiennes has made a very convenient habitation at this place, which contrary to its name was an old built house timber worke; but by his alterations and additions of good brick walls round the Court and 4 pretty gardens with good walks, grass platts, much good fruite of which the country does easily produce, and if persons are curious in planting may have the best, which my Cosen has here'

The half-timbered house had changed scarcely at all since her visit, and one could imagine her picking her way along the dark-beamed, stone-flagged passage before ascending the creaking, rickety staircase to her room. What few concessions there were to the twentieth century within the house seemed confined to the kitchen and bathroom, although even there they seemed to co-exist with the seventeenth century in a higgledy-piggledy fashion. Rotting timbers had caused subsidence in one wing, with the result that the upstairs bathroom was on such a slope that the bathwater seemed to be at a 45 degree angle to the bath.

The stable too had changed very little. When I led George into it at the end of the day's ride I had the strangest sensation, for I knew that Celia had been there before me, that she too had led her horse in and stood on the very spot on which I now stood, breathing in, as I did, the wholesome mustiness of the place. I had often imagined her in various places, fancifully projecting an image of her in my mind's eye. Nowhere had I felt her presence so keenly as now. I shuddered involuntarily, and turning round half expected to see her watching me from the cobwebby recess of the manger.

But there was no one to be seen apart from George, tugging away at his hay net while he waited for Catherine to bring him his supper.

After the spectacular scenery around Malvern, the following day's ride was as tedious as Celia's had been.

> 'this is the worst way I ever went in Worcester or Herriford-shire – its allwayes a deep sand and soe in the winter and with muck is bad way, but this being in August it was strange and being so stony made it more difficult to travell.'

Despite the nappy rash cream my saddlesores were intensely painful, and my mood wasn't improved by the rain, which persisted throughout the afternoon. We met nobody along the route apart from a gouty old brigadier with an empurpled face and startlingly white moustache, who warned me darkly to 'Avoid Ledbury!'

Catherine and I had elected to stay in the lorry during our stay at Stretton Grandison, and that night I had the most horrible nightmares in my cab perch. In one dream the queen was stabling us at Windsor. Before I could check myself the fearful litany of automatic compliments came tumbling out of my mouth. 'What a lovely house you have, ma'am, what a beautiful garden. What lovely children – you must be so proud of them. What charming corgis . . .' I woke in a cold sweat and couldn't get back to sleep again for hours. Counting sheep proved useless. Far more successful was counting shire horses, although for verisimilitude I had them crash through rather than jump over the five-bar gate.

Hayes Farmhouse, mentioned in the *Domesday Book*, was at least 900 years old, claimed our next host, Mr Maddox. We had every reason to believe him, for within the first few minutes of our arrival he had revealed a startling propensity for the assimilation and subsequent recall of information of all kinds. Did we realise, for example, that if the entire population of China were to stick its collective bottom in the sea, it would cause a tidal wave of such massive proportions that whole countries would be submerged?

Had we ever considered the fact that cannibals had no need of greens since theirs was a perfectly balanced diet? And surely we had already calculated for ourselves that in the course of the thousand miles we had covered so far, George had taken approximately 1,760,000 steps. By the time we went to bed our heads were reeling.

George and I had been invited to lead the Leominster Procession the following day, so at the appointed hour we presented ourselves as requested at the Leominster Gas Works where the procession was to muster before setting off for the showground. The combination of the milling crowds and the canned recording of 'Knees up Mother Brown' blaring from the loudspeakers was clearly making George very tense, but once the Leominster Youth Band let rip with the first oompah of 'E Viva Espagna' all semblance of self-control departed him and we reached the showground in record time, leaving the trombones, tubas, police and floats far behind us.

Once George had performed his lap of the ring, we put him in the box, gave him some lunch and set off on foot to explore the show. Conversation was impossible above the cacophony of gossiping chatter, buzzing biplanes, sobbing children, bleating livestock, clanking steam engines and jingling carousels. Above it all the loudspeaker whistled and crackled its way through the day's events, calling into the ring the competitors for the small mountain and moorland in hand, announcing the results of the working hunter classes and commenting on the entrants for the heaviest commercial beast and the British Toggenburg Female Goat Section. 'There is no reason why if everyone else goes through both rings the goats can't – even if they have got shorter legs.'

Inside the tents everything seemed more peaceful. After gasping at the Gargantuan dimensions of the marrows, we made our way to the trestle tables bearing the entries for the Floral and Handicraft Sections. Division Three of the Floral Section seemed to be one of the most highly subscribed classes, for there were endless examples of corsages ranged the whole length of the table. Neatly placed next to each entry was a small square of exercise-book paper on which the judge had written her comments in a schoolmarmish hand. To adjudicate between such an embarrassment of floral offerings, and to find something positive to say about each one, seemed an unenviable task. Yet the diplomatic skills of the Foreign Office could not have rivalled the discretion of the corsage judge. Compliments abounded, while all criticisms were rendered inoffensive by the disarming use of the exclamation mark: 'A very well made corsage, but the small yellow petals have let you down!' Even the most advanced cases of petal fatigue were tactfully summed up as 'interesting!' and 'eye catching!' Not so kind was the judge of Class 77 of the Handicraft Section, whose distaste was thinly concealed: 'Garment has been worn. Marks show at underarms.'

We stayed at the show for some hours, but like most people we were eventually driven away by the rain. Our final glimpse of the Leominster Carnival was of the Labour Party's float, 'The Old Bazaar in Cairo'. As its fezzed and yashmaked cast looked on in bedraggled helplessness, a tractor was trying in vain to pull it out of the mud.

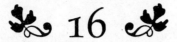

16

Leominster to Glastonbury

It was on the morning of 30 August that George and I reached Gloucester. Celia's feelings about the city had been more than a little mixed.

> 'Glocester town lyes all along on the bancks of the Severn and soe look'd like a very huge place being stretch'd out in length, its a low moist place therefore one must travel on Causseys which are here in goode repaire; I pass'd over a bridge where two armes of the river meetes where the tyde is very high and rowles in the sand in many places and causes those Whirles or Hurricanes that will come on storms with great impetuosity; thence I proceeded over another bridge into the town whose streetes are very well pitch'd large and cleane; there is a faire Market place and Hall for the assizes which happened just as we came there, soe had the worst Entertainment and noe accomodation but in a private house – things ought not to be deare here but Strangers are allwayes imposed on and at such a publick tyme also they make their advantages'

We had hoped to redress the balance and impose on a few strangers ourselves by making a street collection for START. The local fire brigade was all primed to help us, and we were on the point of setting off when it was discovered that we had no collecting permit. I left Gloucester feeling depressed and frustrated with just £10 in my collecting tin. My destination was Badminton.

Even after three months of travelling and hospitality, Catherine and I still had no idea what to expect at each new stabling. Our philosophy was that so long as George had a stable, we would be perfectly happy to stay in the box. Should our hosts extend the offer of stabling to us as well and offer us a bed and a bath, then that was an added bonus, and one for which we were most grateful. In reply to my initial enquiry, some people had written back saying they would be delighted to put the three of us up; others, perhaps unintentionally, had replied in rather more ambiguous tones. Thus we arrived at Badminton not quite knowing whether we would be staying in the house itself or in the stable yard with George.

The day's ride had been wonderful. Under a Wedgwood blue sky with porcelain clouds, we had found ourselves in a landscape of trim little villages of pale gold stone, where portmanteau names like Wotton-under-Edge and Ozleworth Bottom bore witness to twisting green river valleys and steep-sided wooded hills. The journey culminated in a three-mile ride along a magnificent grass avenue of beech trees, extending from Worcester Lodge to the Palladian splendour of Badminton House itself, set, as Celia had described it:

> 'in a Parke on an advanc'd ground with rows of trees on all sides which runns a good length and you may stand on the leads and look 12 wayes down to the parishes and grounds beyond all thro' glides or visto of trees; the Gardens are very fine and Water works.'

Once George and I had reached the deer park and lake, we bore away from the avenue along a narrow road and, after negotiating our way through a succession of magnificent courtyards, found ourselves outside a grandly appointed stable block at the back of the house, where Catherine was waiting for us in the lorry.

The head stableman had indicated to Catherine which box had been made up for George, and his wife had insisted that we knock on her door if we should need anything. It all seemed to suggest that a night in the box was in store, but the head stableman had added that we were expected at the house and should present ourselves at the front door when we were ready.

After twelve weeks of travelling in a horsebox, it is impossible not to look untidy. On this particular night I, for one, looked even worse than usual. My cotton jersey was not only discoloured with grime, it had developed an alarming number of holes and ladders in the most compromising of places. My leather boots were also battered out of all recognition. Once I had been able to see my face in them; now I could hardly tell what colour they were meant to be, so caked were they with mud and scuffed with wear. Worst of all was the sickly sweat smell of horse-box, an aroma so penetrating that it clung not only to our clothes and hair, but to all our books, maps and papers – even to the Vodafone.

Only when one circumnavigates a house of Badminton's size on foot does one fully realise its sheer size. After what seemed half an hour we eventually came to what we supposed to be the front door, a weighty affair that looked as though it hadn't been opened since William Kent put it there in 1740. Beside it was suspended a correspondingly impressive bell-pull, which we proceeded to ring. A plangent chime resounded from the very bowels of the house, followed by a still more awesome silence. Finally, after some five minutes, we heard the jangle of chains, the heavy clank of keys and the grating echo of bolts being drawn across. Then came a wheezing creak worthy of any Hammer Horror film as the mighty door was slowly pulled back to reveal two ancient retainers who now blinked at us suspiciously from the gloom.

'Yes?' asked one, eyeing our nylon stow bags with distaste.

'We've come to see the duchess.'

'Well, this is the wrong door. You want the other side of the house. But she won't be there. She'll be at the servants' quarters for the Olympic dinner.' And with that he swung the great door shut. It was not an auspicious beginning. Picking up our bags, we scrunched our way once more across the vast expanse of gravel until we discovered a more promising entrance to the citadel.

'Hello! You're here! Let me take your bags! We're going out for dinner! Can you be ready in half an hour? I'll show you to your rooms! You're in the Crimson Room, and Catherine's in the Pigeon Hole! Oh, and you've got to telephone some pub – the message is downstairs!'

In a second the duchess had greeted us, shaken us enthusiastically by the hand, seized our bags and was now purposefully striding up a great sweep of staircase. It was all we could do to keep up with her.

There was no time to take in the four-poster bed with its embroidered hangings or the rich dark flock wallpaper as I plunged in and out of the bath and then set about trying to flatten out by hand my creased change of clothes. Twenty minutes had passed when there was a knock at the door. Flinging a towel about me, I opened it to find a small-framed woman who introduced herself as Mrs Nettles.

'Can I do anything for you? I'm so sorry, I didn't know you had arrived or else I would have unpacked your luggage. Let me at least do some ironing.'

I joyfully bundled my clothes into the hands of my deliverer, silently thanking whichever power had interceded on my behalf to delay Mrs Nettles' discovery of our arrival. Not even Pandora would have been tempted to open the sordid blue stow bag that had variously served as overnight luggage container, dirty-washing receptacle and dog bed.

'I'll see to these straight away. If you need anything else you'll find my number by the telephone.'

And so it was, along with a framed list of some eighteen other telephone numbers, including those of the Billiard Room, the Kitchen, the Chinese Room and the Library – Desk End.

The dinner turned out to be the British three-day event team's farewell party before they set off for Seoul and the 1988 Olympics. Apart from Captain Mark Phillips and Catherine's aunt, Jane Holderness-Roddam, I recognised nobody, although from the way Catherine's eyes shone that night, I had the impression that the majority were probably rather famous. At dinner I found myself sitting next to an urbane man of about sixty with classic looks and dark-lashed blue eyes, with which he regarded me with no small amusement when I confided to him the reason for our presence at dinner.

'And you're really doing it all on a shire?' he asked incredulously. 'How extraordinary!'

Despite its being in the servants' quarters, the high-ceilinged hall in which we dined was rather a grand setting. Displays of weaponry glinted on the wall while a herd of stags' heads regarded us with glassy stares from wooden shields. We had even passed a suit of armour on the way in to dinner, and I found myself irresistibly reminded of an Agatha Christie murder story. Emboldened by his twinkling blue eyes, I said as much to my companion. With so many reputations at stake at Seoul, jealousy would provide the perfect motive. Which of the team did he think the most likely candidate to be bumped off? And more important still, by whom? My companion hazarded no guesses but agreed that it was not so outrageous a scenario. And so the conversation continued, with the result that by the time the coffee had arrived we had systematically poisoned the entire Olympic team.

'Who were you sitting next to?' asked Catherine as we discussed the dinner later that evening.
   'Someone called Patrick Beresford.'
   'Patrick Beresford? You idiot! Don't you realise who he is?'
   'No. Who?'
   'Only the *chef d'équipe*. He's responsible for the welfare of the entire Olympic three-day event team!'

The following morning Catherine and I descended the stairs for breakfast to find armies of overalled cleaning ladies but no sign of the duchess anywhere. There was not even the faintest whiff of toast to set us on the right track, and we wandered aimlessly from one room to the next vainly searching for a cup of tea. Eventually we found ourselves in a rather grand little salon lined with Regency stripe wallpaper and encrusted with gilt-framed portraits and mirrors. In the middle of the room stood a table on which lay a silver cigarette case; a silver-edged bowl of matches; a pair of spectacles; freshly-ironed copies of the *Telegraph* and the *Daily Mail*; a plate neatly flanked by a gleaming silver knife and fork; a cup and saucer; a bowl of marmalade and a small flat dish on whose centre a pristine square of butter had been placed with mathematical precision: in short, the table had been laid for breakfast, but for one person's breakfast only.

'I bet it's for the duke!' whispered Catherine, giggling.

Neither of us had yet met him, but somehow the breakfast table seemed too intimate a setting at which to rectify that.

'Let's go!'

We were just about to make a run for it when, without warning, one of the bookcases suddenly swung open to reveal a dark-suited man in his thirties.

'Can I help?'

I explained that we were looking for breakfast, to which he replied: 'Are you staying on this side of the house or the other?'

'We're actually staying on this side of the house,' replied Catherine, 'but we can easily go over there.'

Insisting that we stay, the man disappeared for a few moments behind a door disguised as a bookcase containing Gibbon's *Decline and Fall of the Roman Empire*, and returned with the wherewithal for two more place settings.

'Will you be requiring a full breakfast?'

'Oh no!' we cried in nervous unison, 'Just toast, please.'

From the care with which the table had been laid, it was clear that, to the duke, breakfast was sacrosanct. What heinous crime were we about to commit by defiling his butter and soiling his marmalade spoon? At any moment we expected him to emerge from behind a curtain, a sideboard – even the door. Never had I felt such sympathy for Goldilocks.

'You chicken!' laughed Catherine as she piled marmalade onto her thickly buttered corner of toast, 'you're too scared even to have butter!'

It did seem cowardly, but I noticed that even Catherine, whose capacity for breakfast was legendary, limited herself to one piece of toast and seemed every bit as happy as I was to high-tail it out of the room once we had drained our teacups.

In fact we met the duke later that morning, and in the very same room.

'You must meet my husband before you go,' the duchess had insisted, and leading us through a labyrinth of antechambers brought us to the Regency-striped inner sanctum itself, where a bespectacled figure was poring over the paper, toast in hand.

'David. This is Alison Payne and this is Catherine Bullen. They're the ones doing the wonderful ride round England.'

Putting down his toast, the duke rose from his chair with a smile. As he reiterated his wife's welcome and chatted about the ride, I chided myself for having misjudged him. The Duke of Beaufort bore not the slightest resemblance to any of the three bears.

From Badminton Celia had travelled to Bath, but since it seemed more logical to visit Bristol first, we headed for Ashton Court, where a press call with the Lord Mayor of Bristol had been organised. For nine centuries there had been some kind of building on the site, but I had my doubts about whether Celia would recognise the 'olde large house' she saw in 1698. Given a Gothic facelift by the Victorians, it looked more like a railway station than a manor house.

Ashton Court now belonged to Bristol City Council, its grounds annually playing host to the Bristol Horse Show, the North Somerset Agricultural Show, the Bristol International Balloon Fiesta and various traction and veteran car rallies. Even the house itself had been refurbished to cater for conferences, training seminars, trade fairs, product launches, Georgian banquets and wedding receptions.

It was also the home of Bristol City Council's State Coach and carriage and it was in this that it had tentatively been arranged that the Lord Mayor should greet us. Catherine and I arrived in good time to find the Lord Mayor's groom preparing the carriage with two pressmen in close attendance. At ten o'clock sharp a black limousine glided up, out of which stepped a pleasant looking couple with heavy gold chains about their necks, who introduced themselves as Derek and Pamela Tedder, the Lord Mayor and Lady Mayoress of Bristol.

'Who's in charge?' asked the Lord Mayor once all the introductions had been made. Civic guidance was provided by the newspaper photographers, who proceeded to orchestrate the entire photocall, right down to having the Lady Mayoress feed George. 'Just one more sugar lump, Lady Mayoress, please. That's right – lovely!'

Once the pressmen had gone, the lord mayor, an ex-TUC official, confessed that he had only just been appointed to his new office.

'It's terrible. You've got to be nice to everyone,' he lamented. 'And as for this,' he pointed to his mayoral chain, 'I'm still not used to it. That's nine and a half pounds' worth. Here, feel the weight.'

Even in Celia's time the responsibilities of governing Bristol must have weighed heavily on its mayor's shoulders.

> 'This town is a very great tradeing citty as most in England, and is esteemed the largest next London; the river Aven, that is flowed up by the sea into the Severn and soe up the Aven to the town, beares shipps and barges up to the key, where I saw the harbour was full of shipps carrying coales and all sorts of commodityes to other parts; the Bridge is built over with houses just as London Bridge is, but its not so bigg or long, there are 4 large arches here; they have little boates which are called Wherryes such as we use on the Thames, soe they use them here to convey persons from place to place; and in many places there are signes to many houses that are not Publick houses just as it is in London; the streetes are well pitch'd and preserved by their useing sleds to carry all things about.'

The sleds were used in preference to wheeled traffic so as not to disturb the underground sewers, a much admired rarity in the late seventeenth century. Even in the capital the provisions for sewage disposal were primitive, to say the least. Names such as Dung Wharf still commemorate the laystalls or refuse heaps that lined the River Thames. Streetsweepings, ash, rubble, offal, vegetable scraps and the contents of thousands of chamberpots would all be dumped onto these sites, and often years would elapse before they were cleared. One such laystall spread to eight and a half acres, the entire area now bounded by Argyle Street, Euston Road and Gray's Inn Road. Only in the nineteenth century was it finally carted away, when the landowners sold the heap to Russia as building material following the destruction of Moscow in 1812.

As even the basic principles of sewage disposal had not been mastered, it's hardly surprising that seventeenth-century hygiene in general was so poor. Even at Bath, where she took the waters, Celia complained that:

> 'the pump is in one of these galleryes at the Kings bath which the Company drinks of; its very hot and tastes like the water that boyles eggs, has such a smell, but the nearer the pumpe you drinke it the hotter and less offencive and more spiriteous; the baths are all emptyed as soone as the company goes out, which is about 10 or 11 of the clock in the morning, then by sluces they empty at once the bath, so it fills againe, I have seen all the springs bubble up as thicke out of the ground when the baths have been empty, the bottom is gravell; so they will be full for the evening if Company would go in againe; if so they empty them againe at night, and they are filled against the morning; and there will be such a white scum on the bath which the guides goes and scimms off cleane before any Company goes in, if they go in while this scum is on it gives them the bath mantle, as they call it, makes them breake out into heate and pimples; the like will be on them if they go into the bath before they have purged, especially in the hotter bath.'

The bath authorities saw no reason to provide a separate source of water for those who wanted to drink rather than bathe in it. Thus, like Celia, people would find themselves drinking the very water which had been bathed in by those seeking cures from debility, obesity, gout, digestive disorders, orthopaedic conditions and rheumatism. As Samuel Pepys commented in 1668, 'methinks it cannot be clean to go so many bodies together in the same water'.

I had decided to avoid the dangerously steep hills of Bath and so on Tuesday 6 September skirted the town and set off for Wells. Gradually we left the precipitous green valleys and warm-toned villages of Avon behind, and crossing the county border found ourselves in the undulating countryside of Somerset. There is an appropriately sleepy burr to the word, for it means 'land of the summer people' and dates back to the times when the Saxons would bring their flocks down from the uplands to graze on the lush marsh-grass of the river valleys. Every bit as sleepy was the behaviour of its present-day inhabitants, as I was to find out when I met Catherine for lunch at Netherbridge.

Going into a roadside pub to buy drinks and to fill George's water bucket, I found myself in a dimly lit snug, where two rubicund and gouty old men were ensconced in hearthside chairs, drinking whisky. The only other person in sight was the publican, whose complexion was similarly bibulous. Leaning amicably over the bar, he asked for my order. 'Orange 'n' zoda?' he repeated slowly. 'Hmm. We don' 'ave zoda. Don' get azked for it. Bit like that perrier stuff. Ended up drinkin' it all myzelf.'

Curious to know why his custom had been swelled by a third, he asked what had brought me to Netherbridge.

'A charity ride, is it? Well, we'll raise zome money for you. We'll have a dizco.'

Thanking him, I left the bar as quickly as decency allowed. The thought of the two customers prising themselves from their chairs and twisting to Chubby Checker was too much so early in the day.

The same languid atmosphere was discernible at Wells:

> 'which . . . is what must be reckoned halfe a Citty, this and the Bath makeing up but one Bishops See; the Cathedral has the greatest curiosity for carv'd work in stone, the West Front is full of all sorts of figures, the 12 apostles, the King and Queen with angells and figures of all forms as thick one to another as can be, and soe almost all round the Church'

England's tiniest city, Wells derives its name from St Andrew's Well in the Bishop's Palace ground, which is fed by underground streams from the Mendips. It was this freshwater supply that led to a church being built on the site more than a thousand years ago, and the ecclesiastical precinct gradually developed around it.

When Celia visited it,

> 'the assizes was in the town which filled it like a faire, and little stands for selling things was in all the streetes; there I saw the Town Hall – the streetes are well pitch'd – and a large market place and shambles'

Three hundred years later, not even the tourists photographing the west front could disturb the tranquillity of the place. The city's sundials bear the motto *'Horas non numero nisi serenas'* ('I count only the peaceful hours'). Even in 1988 it seemed appropriate.

Three hundred and eighty-six angels, apostles, kings and queens populate the elaborately carved west front of Wells Cathedral, their chipped beards, bluff noses and missing arms testimony to almost seven centuries of Somerset weathering. Every bit as extraordinary were the fanciful shapes and figures that inhabited the dank and dripping limestone caverns of Wookey Hole.

> 'Oacky Hole is a large cavity under ground . . . its full of great rocks and stones lying in it just as if they were hewen out of a quarry and laid down all in the ground; the wall and roofe is all a rocky stone, there is a lofty space they call the Hall and another the Parlour and another the Kitchen; the entrance of each one out of another is with great stooping under rocks that hang down almost to touch the ground; beyond this is a Cistern allwayes full of water, it looks cleer to the bottom which is all full of stones as is the sides, just like candy or like the branches they put in the boyling of copperace for the copperice to crust about it, this in the same manner so that the water congeales here into stone and does as it were bud or grow out one stone out of another . . .
>
> They fancy many Resemblances in the rocks, as in one place an organ, and in another 2 little babys, and in another part a head which they call the Porters head, and another a shape like a dog; they phancy one of the rocks resembles a woman with a great belly which the country people call the Witch which made this cavity under ground for her enchantments'

Evidently the patter had changed very little since Celia's visit to Wookey Hole. Our guide was a theatrical young man with dyed hair and an earring, who would periodically train the beam of his torchlight on some crystalline deposit or dripping stalactite and with a thespian flourish invite us to compare it with a dog, Joan of Arc, or a track-suited priest. 'That's the ghost of Father Bernard, who was supposed to have exorcised the witch from the caves, that's the reason he's wearing a track suit – he was taking some exorcise.'

As each wave of polite titters passed round the huddled company, the young man would suddenly pick on the person with the loudest laugh and declare in strangulated and staccato tones: 'You were smiling, sir! I wouldn't smile . . . Just where you are standing they found the old woman's bones . . .'

Despite the self-indulgent monologues of our young guide, it was difficult not to be impressed by the echoing mystery of the caves. More extraordinary than the arbitrary likenesses to witches and cowering dogs were the colours of the pale limestone rock, shot through with black manganese, grey lead and vermilion iron oxide. Bright green ribbons of hart's tongue, mosses and algae provided more colour in the lightest of the chambers, but greenest of all were the slow limpid waters of the River Axe, secretly flowing through the labyrinthine network of fissures, shafts, tunnels and caverns.

From Wookey Hole, Celia had ridden to Glastonbury, 'a pretty levell way till just you come to the town'. I was amazed that Celia could dismiss in four words a journey that to me had seemed unending. Throughout the afternoon I could see the ghostly grey outline of Glastonbury ahead, but the day dragged on, hot and interminable. Again and again I was reminded of Cambridgeshire as a laboriously angular route took us across inky black peat flats. Silent and stifling, it was an oppressive place, and I was only too glad when we left its drainage scars and pollarded willows and found ourselves approaching Glastonbury.

Many pilgrims still believe that Joseph of Arimathea buried the chalice used at the Last Supper on the slopes of Glastonbury Tor; that when he thrust his thorn staff into the ground of a nearby hill it miraculously took root; that he built a church of daub and wattle at Glastonbury and that he made there the first conversions to Christianity in Britain. These, briefly, are the tenets of the legend of Glastonbury. So potent was the legend in the seventh century that a monastery was built on the site. One of the richest and most beautiful in the land, it was larger even than Wells Cathedral, and was to dominate the surrounding landscape and the spiritual consciousness of the country for the next nine centuries. With the dissolution of the monasteries its fortunes were to change radically.

> 'Glassenbury tho' in ancient tymes was a renowned place where was founded the first monastery, its now a ragged poor place and the Abbey has only the Kitchen remaining in it, which is a distinct building round like a pigeon house all stone; the walls of the Abby here and there appeares, and some little places and the cellar or vault which if they cast a stone into the place it gives a great echo, and the country people sayes its the Devil set there on a tun of money, which makes that noise least they should take it away from him'

The original holy thorn which blossomed on Christmas Day and fell on 6 January was destroyed by a Roundhead, said to have hacked off his own leg in the process. An offshoot had previously been planted in a tavern garden, and it would have been this that Celia saw in 1698. By that time it had become fashionable to carve one's name in the bark and to take surreptitious cuttings from it as souvenirs, a practice sorely lamented by Celia.

> 'this the superstitious covet much and have gott some of it for their gardens and soe have almost quite spoiled it'

It seems latter-day pilgrims were less subject to such kleptomaniacal tendencies, for in 1988 grafts of the thorn still flourished in Glastonbury. Many of the people who now visit Glastonbury are drawn by another legend: the Glastonbury Pop Festival. To judge by the ubiquitous 'No Hippies' notices about the town, that particular event has traumatised the town far more than the damage to its holy thorn ever did.

We had now been on the road for 100 days and celebrated in the evening with a bottle of champagne. Catherine had gone home for her brother's wedding, and for the next few days Charles had agreed to stay and help me look after George. I had grown so used to the ambling pace of the West Country that it came as some surprise to discover in a letter from my father what had been going on in the world. Most prominently featured was something with which Celia would have identified: the troubles in Ireland.

'I am dismayed and saddened by the terrible murders of our young soldiers. Thank goodness you have already had your escort from the Household Cavalry. The IRA has threatened to Kill "*anyone* with the soldiers" and they mean it.'

After the usual exhortations to 'TRY HARD to be a FINANCIAL WIZARD NOT A FINANCIAL IDIOT (TRY TO SAVE)' the letter concluded:

'I hope you are well, not sick of it, that you have bathed your arse in methylated spirits and that you are STILL ALIVE. Are you? As we expect a postal strike and "go slow" I must get this letter off at once.
Daddy xxxxx xxxxx
P.S. I enjoyed your letter but it seems devoid of men. Don't you meet any nice ones?'

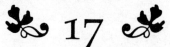

17

Glastonbury to Plymouth

Catherine and the dogs returned on the Tuesday morning to find us in remarkably good spirits.

'Have you won the pools or something?'

'No, but we've got to buy some champagne!' announced Charles.

'What? She hasn't said yes, has she?'

'No, but almost as good. She's said MAYBE!'

There was no time to elaborate, for we were due at Exeter Cathedral for our first press call in Devon.

It was as if we had been transported back to the Middle Ages. Standing before the magnificently ornate Gothic lantern of Exeter Cathedral, dwarfed by its arcaded and traceried façade, was a crimson-robed delegation of civic and ecclesiastical dignitaries.

'Oyez, Oyez!' rang out the stentorian tones of the town crier. 'Oyez to Alison Payne and Mighty. God speed and may your ride raise much money!'

Various television crews, radio and newspaper reporters had turned up to witness the spectacle, and as George and I circled the Close four times for the cameras the town crier repeated his salutation. The only person who remained unimpressed by the proceedings was the cathedral gardener, who with his elbow resting on his mower looked on in outraged silence as his beloved turf was wantonly desecrated.

It seemed too early in the day to celebrate with champagne, so

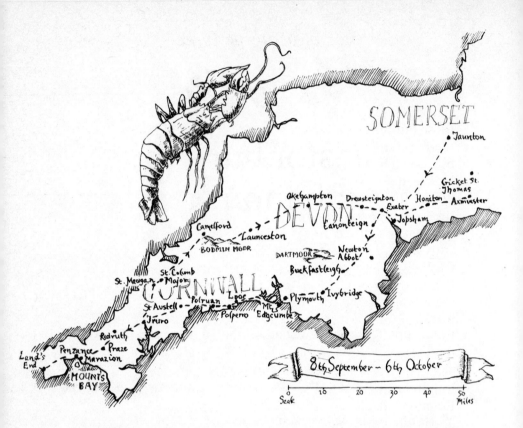

SOMERSET
• Taunton

Cricket St. Thomas

DEVON
Okehampton Drewsteignton Honiton Axminster
Exeter
Canonteign • Topsham
Camelford
Launceston
BODMIN MOOR
DARTMOOR Newton Abbot
Buckfastleigh
St. Columb Major
St. Mawgan CORNWALL Plymouth Ivybridge
St Austell Polruan Looe Mt.
Polperro Edgcumbe
Truro
Redruth Praze
Penzance
Land's End Marazion
MOUNTS BAY

8th September – 6th October

0 10 20 30 40 50
Scale Miles

we decided to go instead to Tinley's Tea Room across the Close to toast ourselves with a pot of tea. The counters seemed to sag under ramparts of rock cakes and crenellated stacks of flapjacks, and a rich aroma of coffee filled the air. Originally a hostelry for travelling priests, Tinley's had since been patronised by such secular celebrities as Mick Jagger and the Beatles, and even claimed among its clientèle a poltergeist by the name of Fred. There were no pop stars there that morning; only three old ladies intently comparing ailments over a pot of Earl Grey and a selection of Danish pastries. Not even Fred hurling the willow-pattern from its magnolia alcove could have disturbed the trio, so engrossed were they in each other's rheumatic joints.

We were between press calls, and filled in the remaining half hour before setting off for Newton Abbot by buying champagne and restocking our supply of glasses, now seriously depleted after the buffetings of nearly fourteen weeks of travelling. The post-war city centre we saw in Exeter that day was a legacy of the 'Baedeker Raids' of 1942. Apart from its Cathedral Close, Exeter in 1698 would have been a very different place:

'This Citty does exceedingly resemble London for, besides these buildings I mention'd for the severall Markets, there is an Exchange full of shops like our Exchanges are, only its but one walke along as was the Exchange at Salisbury House in the Strand; there is also a very large space railed in just by the Cathedrall, with walks round it, which is called the Exchange for Merchants, that constantly meete twice a day just as they do in London; there are 17 Churches in the Citty and 4 in the subburbs; there is some remaines of the Castle walls; there is just at the market place a Guild Hall the entrance of which is a large place set on stone pillars; behind this building there is a vast Cistern which holds upwards of 600 hodsheads of water which supplyes by pipes the whole Citty, this Cistern is replenish'd from the river which is on purpose turned into a little channell by it self to turn the mill and fills the Engine that casts the water into the truncks which convey it to this Cistern; the Water Engine is like those at Islington and Darby as I have seen, and is what now they make use of in diverse places either to supply them with water or to draine a marsh or overplus of water.'

A reliable water source would have been crucial in seventeenth-century Exeter, for it was one of the key resources needed for the city's major industry:

'the whole town and country is employ'd for at least 20 mile round in spinning, weaveing, dressing, and scouring, full-ing and drying of the serges, it turns the most money in a weeke of anything in England, one weeke with another there is 10000 pound paid in ready money, sometymes 15000 pound'

Celia even risked her safety to visit one of the mills:

'the mill does draw out and gather in the serges, its a pretty divertion to see it, a sort of huge notch'd timbers like great teeth, one would thinke it should injure the serges but it

211

does not, the mills draws in with such a great violence that
if one stands neere it, and it catch a bitt of your garments it
would be ready to draw in the person even in a trice'

Such was the high quality of Exeter's serges that the majority were
sold in London. Successful as the industry was, it was not without
its more unsavoury side, particularly when the serges were fresh
off the loom:

'first they will clean and scour their roomes with them –
which by the way gives noe pleasing perfume to a roome,
the oyle and grease, and I should think it would rather foull
a roome than cleanse it because of the oyle . . . then they lay
them in soack in vrine [urine] then they soape them and soe
put them into the fulling-mills'

At Newton Abbot that day we lunched as guests of the Teignbridge
District Council. Its headquarters were at Forde House, a sumptuous manor built in 1610 for the Reynell family. Itinerant Italian
plasterers were responsible for the ornate ceilings, at their most
magnificent in the room that Charles I occupied during his stay
there in 1625, the year of his accession to the throne. His hosts
clearly felt deeply honoured by their monarch's visit, for the
preparations were as lavish as the ceiling. A list of the food
supplied for the King during his visit reads as follows:

'A buck, a doe, a hunted tagge [a doe of a year old], a
mutton, killed and dressed. The fish consisted of 160 mul-
lets, 42 whiting, 4 salmons, 7 peels, 7 dories, 21 plaice, 26
soles, 48 lobsters, 550 pilchards, etc.
    Among the fowls and game, 69 partridges, 5 pheasants,
12 pullets, 14 capons, 112 chickens, 4 ducks, 6 geese, 37
turkeys, 69 pigeons, 92 rabbits, 1 barnacle, 1 hernshaw, 12
sea larks, 11 curlews, 258 larks, 1 heath pult, 2 nynnets, 6
seapyes, 1 stone curlew, 4 teals, 3 peahens, and 2 gulls.
    6 oxen, 5 muttons, 2 and a half veals, besides several
entries of ribs of beef, quarters of mutton, chines, tongues,
sides of lamb, and a Westphalia gammon.

The liquor – 2 hogsheads of beer, one barrel canary wine, and 35 quarts of white wine.
The entertainment cost £55.5.0'

William, Prince of Orange, was also a guest at Forde House following his historic landing at Brixham in November 1688. The owner of the house was Sir William Courtenay, who, while he supported the Prince's mission, was keenly aware of the compromising position in which he himself would be placed should it fail. Thus it was, when William arrived at Forde House on the second day of his progress towards London, Sir William Courtenay was 'not at home'. The cautious host had discreetly absented himself, having first given instructions to his staff to feed the Dutch Prince and then to accommodate him, not in the best bedroom, which Charles I had occupied, but in a slightly inferior room on the first floor, known ever since as the Orange Room.

The Teignbridge District Council were evidently more circumspect about squandering their catering allowance than the Reynell family, for it was on a cold collation of meats, salad and chips that we lunched that day, while discussing the relative merits of Devonshire and Cornish clotted cream. The chairman of the council was a woman of warmth, energy and refreshing frankness. Like the Lord Mayor of Bristol, her appointment was a recent one and she shared his reservations about wearing the chain of office.

'The first time I bent forward, it bashed me on the back of the head.'

After lunch we were taken round the house by the deputy chairman, who seemed very proud of the recently refurbished reception rooms.

'It's a good way to entertain people,' he explained, indicating an enormous cabinet filled with bottles. 'You usually get the information you want after they've had a few drinks.'

While Forde House was reserved for entertaining, the District Council's administrative offices were located next door in an oatmeal stone building, overlaid with green tubular steel piping. It was one of the most pleasing examples of modern architecture we had seen during our travels, and an admirable complement to its seventeenth-century neighbour.

'From thence [Exeter] I pass'd the bridge across the River Ex to Chedly [Chudleigh], mostly lanes and a continual going up hill and down, and all these lesser hills rises higher and higher till it advances you upon the high ridge, which discovers to view the great valleys below full of those lesser hills and inclosures, with quicksett hedges and trees, and rich land; but the roads are not to be seen, being all along in lanes cover'd over with the shelter of the hedges and trees'

We stayed that night at Canonteign, an elegant white Georgian house built in 1837 by the first Viscountess Exmouth and overlooking the luxuriant woodland of the Teign River valley. Down a gorge a few hundred yards from the house, silver water cascaded in a series of spectacular races and falls to produce England's highest waterfall. The grounds were already open to the public as a nature trail, but the present viscount explained that he was hoping to develop the estate further.

'I wouldn't wish this lot on any son. I want to turn it into a giant fantasy park, with the house as an enormous Hamley's-type toyshop. That way it'll pay for itself.'

It had become a familiar story. Canonteign would not have existed when Celia made her Great Journey, but of those large houses that did, very few now remained in the hands of the original families. It seemed a sad but inevitable result of the twentieth century and its lack of continuity that the only exceptions I had come across in the course of my journey were Euston Hall, Knowsley, Naworth, Broughton and Badminton. Lowther was perhaps another, but while it still belonged to the Earl of Lonsdale, it was nevertheless a ruin. The giant fantasy park of which Lord Exmouth now spoke with such enthusiasm had at first filled me with apprehension, but when I considered the purposes to which some of the other big houses had been put, it did not seem so ignoble a fate. Canonteign would at least remain in the hands of those who had built it, while the grounds would bring pleasure to thousands more.

We discovered that the viscount's stepson, Charles, had just finished editing a book entitled *The Mystery of William Shakespeare*, in which the authorship of the plays was attributed not to William

Shakespeare, but to Charles Vere's own ancestor, Edward de Vere, the seventeenth Earl of Oxford. With passion and energy Charles proceeded to put foward the various arguments against William Shakespeare. How was it possible, he asked, for a man who could barely write his own name, and whose parents and children were illiterate, to have possessed twice the vocabulary of Milton? Was it even remotely feasible that a man whose preoccupations were wholly financial and who spent most of his life in a provincial backwater, could have been Ben Jonson's 'soul of the age'? Surely such a tangled web of paradoxes all pointed to one of the greatest cover-ups in history? Charles grew still more impassioned as he put forward the arguments in favour of Edward de Vere. Courtier, patron of the arts, classical scholar, poet, dramatist, sportsman, Italophile and favourite of Elizabeth I, what man could conceivably have possessed better qualifications for the authorship of the histories, comedies and tragedies than he?

The landscape changed markedly the following day as we climbed a thousand feet and found ourselves on an uncultivated and treeless plateau broken only by rocky tors. We had reached Dart-moor.

> 'on these hills one can discern little besides inclosures hedges and trees, rarely can see houses unless you are just descending to them, they allways are placed in holes as it were, and you have a precipice to go down to come at them'

Until a thousand years ago, when much of the surrounding lowlands were disease-infested swamps, the moor was quite densely populated. With the discovery of tin in the twelfth century it enjoyed a new age of prosperity. Freelance miners converged in a great tin-rush, and became so powerful that they instigated their own courts, laws, prison – even their own parliament, which would meet on the craggy heights of Crockern Tor. The Black Death in 1349, combined with the exhaustion of the surface tin, led to the end of the tin boom in the mid-fourteenth century. Poverty-stricken and denuded of people, this is the Dartmoor that Celia would have seen in 1698. It was a region for which she had little time.

> 'the lanes are full of stones and dirt for the most part, because they are so close the sun and wind cannot come at them, soe that in many places you travell on Causeys which are uneven also for want of continued repaire.
> From Chedly [Chudleigh] to Ashburton a poor little town, bad was the best Inn: . . . here the roades contracts and the lanes are exceeding narrow and so cover'd up you can see little about, an army might be marching undiscover'd by any body, for when you are on those heights that shews a vast country about, you cannot see one road; the wayes now became so difficult that one could scarcely pass by each other, even the single horses, and so dirty in many places and just a track for one horses feete, and the banks on either side so neer . . . I cannot see how two such horses can pass each other or indeed in some places how any horse can pass by each other, and yet these are the roads that are all here abouts; some little corners may jutt out that one may a little get out of the way of each other, but this is but seldom.'

Although some mining existed into the twentieth century, the moorland settlements never recovered. Now the majority of Dartmoor's population live in the surrounding lowlands, and their numbers increase by the day. George and I had our own taste of this rapid growth rate when we rode through Ivybridge, reputed to be the fastest-growing village in Europe. So many new houses and roads had been built in the preceding six months that even my 1988 Ordnance Survey map was hopelessly out-of-date, and we spent half an hour trying to navigate our way through a confusion of new estates and bulldozered wastelands.

After so peaceful a passage through Devon, Plymouth was to be a rude awakening. Thundering motorways and trunk roads dissected the city outskirts, and it was along these that we encountered the worst traffic of the journey – noisier, dirtier, faster and

more furious even than in London. It was a far cry from the
pleasant prospect described by Celia.

> 'Plymouth is 2 Parishes called the old town and the new,
> the houses all built of this marble and the slatt at the top
> lookes like lead and glisters in the sun . . . the streetes are
> good and clean, there is a great many tho' some are but
> narrow; they are mostly inhabitted with seamen and those
> which have affaires on the sea'

Somehow we managed to navigate our way through the traffic,
to find ourselves at Plymouth's quayside by the end of the afternoon. We had now covered nearly 1200 miles, and ahead of us lay
Cornwall, the south-westernmost tip of England and the penulti-
mate leg of our ride. To an outsider, it must have seemed as if
nothing could stop us. In reality we were about to encounter the
most difficult and dangerous part of the entire journey.

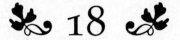

18

Plymouth to Land's End

When Celia had crossed the Tamar in 1698, she took her chances on the Cremyll ferry,

> 'which is a very hazardous passage, by reason of 3 tydes meeting; had I known the Danger before I should not have been very willing to have gone it, not but this is the constant way all people goe, and saved severall miles rideing; I was at least an hour going over, it was about a mile but indeed in some places, notwithstanding there was 5 men row'd and I set my own men to row alsoe I do believe we made not a step of way for almost a quarter of an hour, but blessed be God I came safely over; but those ferry boates are soe wet and then the sea and wind is allwayes cold to be upon, that I never faile to catch cold in a ferry-boate as I did this day, haveing 2 more ferrys to cross tho' none soe bad or half soe long as this'

The Royal Marines had agreed to take us over on a landing-craft, but events were to conspire against us. We arrived at the Cremyll ferry jetty in Plymouth's Barbican only to find that our proposed passage across the Tamar coincided with a training exercise. All the craft were in use and we would have to find some other means of reaching Cornwall. With no landing-craft to help us, we would never be able to cross the Tamar. After 1200 miles it now looked as if we would be thwarted by a mere quarter-mile stretch of water. I could have wept.

'You could try the pedestrian ferry,' suggested Catherine tentatively. She had reached the quayside a good hour before us, and had decided to reconnoitre the present Cremyll ferry to see if there was any chance that it might be able to accommodate one ton of shire horse.

'It's quite small,' she continued. 'Well, very small, but it's steady and the captain's said yes.'

And so it was decided. George would be transported across the Tamar in the *Queen Boadicea II*, a veteran of Dunkirk and one of Britain's tiniest ferries.

As we waited on the jetty for the ferry to return from the Cornish bank, Catherine and I were silently having second thoughts. Even the shallowest fords had fazed George in the past, and now we were attempting to take him across one of the widest rivers in England. It seemed like madness. This was the closest George had ever been to seawater and, as the breeze gently tousled his mane, he sniffed about him curiously, taking in the unfamiliar salty smell of the water, the pungent aroma of muddied seaweed and the noise of the gulls wheeling and diving above his head. Long before we did, he picked up the phut-phut of the returning ferry and, pricking his ears and focusing his gaze, followed its progress all the way back to the Devon quayside. As yet he suspected nothing.

'All right, girls! Whenever you're ready,' cried the captain.

Catherine had filled George's plastic manger with oats and, handing it to me, took his leading rein and began to pull gently. At first George looked at her uncomprehendingly and began to follow. Then, as he realised quite where Catherine was leading him, he suddenly braced himself and, with front legs apart, stood his ground on the jetty.

'Give him some oats!' called Catherine, relaxing her grip.

George quite forgot the ferry in his slobbering haste to eat the grain, enabling Catherine to pull him on a few more inches. So we continued for the next five minutes until, almost without realising it, George had been lured aboard the *Queen Boadicea II*. In a second the mooring rope had been untied, the engine coughed into action and we were away, leaving the narrow, sloping streets of Ply-

-mouth harbour behind us as we chugged towards Cornwall and the final leg of our journey. Perplexed by the sudden rush of wind, the noise of the engines and the unnerving sensation of floating, George buried his head in the plastic manger. Occasionally he would look up, the glistening grains caught in quivering suspension on his beard as he tried to understand quite what was happening. As he buried his head for the twentieth time in his manger, we felt a gentle thud and realised with joy and relief that we had reached the Cornish coastline.

We stayed that night at Mount Edgcumbe. Celia's first view of the house had been from the Plymouth shore, and she had been inspired to describe it as 'the finest seat I have seen, and might be more rightly named Mount Pleasant'. For almost five centuries the seat of the Edgcumbe family, the house was gutted in 1941 at the height of the aerial bombardment of Plymouth by a stray incendiary bomb. Three generations of family portraits by Reynolds were destroyed in the ensuing fire, the only picture to survive being that of Richard, the second Lord Edgcumbe, who as the black sheep of the family had had his likeness banished to the basement.

Under the joint aegis of the Cornwall County Council and Plymouth City Council, the house had been fully restored, and we learned that it was to be opened to the public for the first time that very night for a concert in aid of START. Mere thanks seemed a pitifully inadequate way to acknowledge the work of the members of staff and the string quartet, all of whom had forfeited their overtime and their expenses in order to swell the collection.

'You must think of yourselves as catalysts,' said Maggie Culver, the administrator. 'People like to help and do things, and you're giving them the opportunity to do exactly that.'

While George slept off the day's excitement in a stable especially constructed by Mount Edgcumbe's joiner, Catherine and I spent the night in an octagonal room overlooking the Tamar. Fugitive phrases and fragmentary notes from the concert kept drifting back as I undressed in the darkness. Just as Evensong in Ely Cathedral had done three months before, so the hovering melodies and passionate crescendos of the Mozart and Schubert pieces played that evening had transported me on a wave of euphoria and gratitude that we should have come so far. As my eyes grew accustomed to the darkness, my gaze was drawn through the large bay window, down the soft black pelt of rolling lawn, across the inky expanse of the Tamar and over to Plymouth, a friendly constellation of a thousand winking lights. Only 400 miles separated us from London. In less than five weeks we would be home.

Nor was my elation dampened the following day, when George and I set off along the coast to Looe.

> 'Here I . . . passed over many very steep stony hills tho' here I had some 2 or 3 miles of exceeding good way on the downs, and then I came to the steep precipices great rocky hills; ever and anon I came down to the sea and rode by its side on the sand, then mounted up againe on the hills which carryed me along mostly in sight of the South sea'

Like Celia we travelled close to the sea, where winding clifftop roads offered stunning perspectives onto languorous beaches strewn with great shards of rock. Every now and then we would see a soft, white 'v' of foam out to sea, as a tiny speedboat described a bumpy arc across the bay. Once we even glimpsed George's alter ego, a mane-tossed white horse cavorting in the spume and spray far below. At every step seemingly random configurations of trees, boats, cottages and hills would arrange themselves into compositions of such charm and loveliness that I was quite at a loss which to photograph. In the end I tried to take pictures of them all, exhausting the only two rolls of film in my saddlebag within fifteen minutes.

Towards Looe, a little of Cornwall's charm evaporated, as we found ourselves increasingly caught up in the last throes of the holiday season. Purpose-built holiday villages and regimented caravan parks clung like barnacles to every cove and promontory; amusement arcades and snack bars cluttered the beaches and ice cream vans seemed indigenous to every lay-by.

Looe, despite brazen commercialisation, still retained much of its haphazard quaintness, but it was a relief to leave its welter of trippers and traffic and head further west. Polperro we avoided altogether. Various roadside exhortations to visit the 'historic fishing village', call in at the 'Jolly Roger' or park our caravan were enough to convince me that it would be unwise to deviate from our route.

The day's ride was laborious enough. There seemed to be no bridleways, and we were forced to throw in our lot with the caravans, dormobiles and cars laden with flapping roofracks. The narrow winding B roads hugged every contour of the land, and it felt as if we were adding miles to our journey.

Celia had encountered difficulties of her own along the Cornish roads.

> 'Here indeed I met with more inclosed ground and soe had more lanes and a deeper clay road, which by the raine the night before had made it very dirty and full of water, in many places in the road there are many holes and sloughs where ever there is clay ground, and when by raines they are filled with water its difficult to shun danger; here my horse was quite down in one of these holes full of water but by the good hand of God's Providence which has allwayes been with me ever a present help in tyme of need, for giving him a good strap he flounc'd up againe, tho' he had gotten quite down his head and all, yet did retrieve his feete and gott cleer off the place with me on his back.'

Just east of Polruan we did in fact find a bridleway – not much of a short-cut but a welcome respite from the road. I had a long and fairly unintelligible argument with a farmer who insisted that no such track existed.

'Ain't no track marked on map,' he declared.

'Oh, but there is,' I retorted, showing him the map.

In his eyes, however, not even the Ordnance Survey map was admissible proof of the track's existence.

'Even THEY make mistakes, don'em?' was his only comment.

Realising that we were united at least in our intransigence, he swung open the rickety gate that led to the phantom track and wished us luck as we disappeared into a thicket of overgrown brambles and saplings. Scratched and sporting more foliage than a soldier in camouflage, we emerged half an hour later at a chicken coop, much to the delight of its owner.

'You're doing a charity ride round England and this was a short-cut!' she repeated incredulously. Her cackles followed us all the way to the Bodinnick ferry.

'You done this sort of thing before?' asked the ferry attendant suspiciously as Catherine and I held out our money for three tickets.

'Only on the Cremyll ferry.'

This was apparently sufficient qualification, and we were immediately allowed on at no charge. Almost six times as big as its Cremyll counterpart, the Bodinnick ferry posed few problems for George, who spent most of the voyage trying to empty the red plastic manger of its oats. The real problem was our lorry. As at Cremyll, Catherine was forced to reboard the ferry, retrieve the lorry on the eastern shore and set off westwards the long way round. The majority of Cornish roads were impassable to seven tons of Mercedes, so Catherine would travel along the A roads, cycling to meet us at lunchtime, with George's feed and an empty waterbucket in her bicycle basket and the dogs at her heels. When the distances were so great that that was impossible, I would take George's feed myself, wrapped in a plastic bag and strapped to the D ring of the saddle, and contrive to find water for us both along the way.

Thus we continued until we reached St Austell, where Celia was to encounter one of the most pleasant experiences of her entire journey:

'here was a pretty good dineing-roome and chamber within it, and very neate country women; my Landlady brought me one of the West Country tarts, this was the first I met with, though I had asked for them in many places in Somerset and Devonshire; its an apple pye with a custard all on the top, its the most acceptable entertainment that could be made me; they scald their creame and milk in most parts of those countrys and so its a sort of clouted creame as we call it, with a little sugar, and soe put on the top of the apple pye; I was much pleased with my supper'

Catherine and I also feasted on clotted cream at a local teashop, where we were served by a neat and bustling woman in a blue check overall.

'I'm afraid you won't get very far round here with a name like START,' she declared, once she had learned of our journey. 'In these parts START means The St Austell Round Table. That'll be twenty p extra for the jam please.'

Celia may have been pleased with her supper in St Austell, but she was not amused by

> 'the custome of the country, which is a universall smoaking, both men and women and children have all their pipes of tobacco in their mouths and soe sit round the fire smoaking, which was not delightfull to me when I went down to talke with my Landlady for information of any matter and customs amongst them'

While Celia referred to it as a Cornish custom, smoking was by no means limited to the West Country. Nor was it unusual for children to indulge in the habit, for in the seventeenth century tobacco was strongly believed to be a prophylactic against the plague. So widely held was this view that in 1665 one boy at Eton was flogged because he wouldn't smoke.

She was to see more children in the course of her stay at Austell, not playing but working in the nearby tin mines.

> 'I went a mile farther and soe came where they were digging in the Tinn mines, there was at least 20 mines all in sight which employs a great many people at work, almost night and day, but constantly all and every day includeing the Lords day which they are forced to, to prevent their mines being overflowed with water; more than 1000 men are taken up about them, few mines but had then almost 20 men and boys attending it either down in the mines digging and carrying the oare to the little bucket which conveys it up, or else others are draineing the water and looking to the engines that are draineing it, and those above are attending the drawing up the oare in a sort of windless as is to a well

. . . its a fine mettle thus in its first melting looks like silver, I
had a piece poured out and made cold for to take with me'

Celia was right to take a souvenir, for the feverish activity she
witnessed gave way to massive unemployment as the tin deposits
were gradually exhausted. George and I were to pass many tin
mines on our way to Truro; but they were not the working engine
houses Celia would have seen, but roofless and overgrown ruins,
silhouetted against the skyline. Somehow they seemed fitting
monuments to Cornwall's Age of Tin.

After taking the *King Harry* ferry across the Fal – an easy enough
achievement for George after his Cremyll and Bodinnick experiences – we bore north-west towards Truro,

'which is a pretty little town and seaport, formerly was
esteemed the best town in Cornwall now is the second next
Lanstone [Launceston]; its just by the Copper and Tinn
mines and lies down in a bottom, pretty steep ascent, as
most of the towns in these countrys, that you would be
afraid of tumbling with nose and head foremost; the town is
built of stone, a good pretty Church built all stone and
carv'd on the outside, and just by there is the Market House
on stone pillars and hall on the top, there is alsoe a pretty
good key; this was formerly a great tradeing town and
flourish'd in all things but now as there is in all places their
rise and period, soe this which is become a ruinated disregarded place.'

It was to be a very different Truro that we saw 300 years later. The
declining town observed by Celia was on the point of a transforma-
tion. High metal prices in the 1700s were to bring such prosperity to
the area that, by the end of the century, Truro would be established
not only as one of the major English mining towns, but as a focal
point for Cornish society as well. We were to see for ourselves in
the elegant Georgian and Regency terraces the legacy of that
renaissance, a renaissance that was to be continued through to the
twentieth century with the construction both of the railway and, in

1890, the cathedral – the first to be built in England since St Paul's. As I rode through the city that day, Truro exuded an air of confident self-sufficiency. Even its administrative offices seemed twice as big as the White House and I concluded that here, in all but name, was the capital of Cornwall.

Truro was also home to Radio Cornwall, who had asked us to call in at their station once we had finished raising funds for START in the city centre. Despite the help of a team of dustmen who rushed into all the shops collecting not just refuse but money for our buckets as well, eleven-thirty found us twenty minutes behind schedule.

'Come on, they're waiting for you!' motorists would cry, winding down their windows and pointing at their radios, 'You're supposed to be on air!'

We arrived at the gravel forecourt of Radio Cornwall with seconds to spare, much to the relief of the presenter, who panted into the microphone: 'And they've finally made it! Mighty and Alison on the last leg of their historic 1600 mile journey around England. Alison, how've you both coped with the weather?'

Compared with the rest of the country, our passage through Cornwall had been a surprisingly clement one. As I rode that day to Praze, our fortunes were to change dramatically. Just west of Truro a sulphurous gloom descended on the landscape and within seconds George and I were drenched. This was a face of Cornwall which I had not yet seen, but one with which Celia had been all too familiar:

> 'from thence [Tregothnan] I returned back, intending not to go to the Lands End for feare of the raines that fell in the night which made me doubt what travelling I should have . . . The next day finding it faire weather on the change of the moone I alter'd my resolution, and soe went for the Lands End by Redruth mostly over heath and downs which was very bleake and full of mines . . . so I went up pretty high hills and over some heath or common, on which a great storme of haile and raine met me, and drove fiercely on me but the wind soon dry'd my dust coate'

We were not to be so lucky. By the time we reached our night's stabling, my saddle was oozing with rainwater and George's forelock lay plastered and straggling across his eyes. It took us an hour to dry off.

Our host was a Cornish farmer, whose accent we found as unintelligible as he found ours. Most conversation was conducted through his wife, a tiny maternal woman who treated us like royalty. While her family ate in the kitchen, she waited on Catherine and me in the parlour, where a freshly-laundered lace tablecloth had been laid with home made pasties, sausage rolls, scones, clotted cream and jam, fruit cake, iced cakes and cheese and biscuits.

'And I don't want any of it left now!' came the friendly admonishment as she disappeared into the kitchen, shutting the intersecting door behind her. We dared not tell her that we had eaten a large lunch that day, and to spare her feelings, sneaked a third of the table's contents into my bucket bag. We thought we had been discovered when, in a mumbling burr, her husband later compared it to a nosebag. Fortunately the crime remained undetected, and over the next two days the bag's contents proved a far more agreeable lunch-source than our normal diet of crisps and Mars Bars.

From Praze we continued west to Marazion, a small, roughcast town, whose houses were so tiny that on George's back I found myself level with the upstairs windows. To our left we could now see the fairy castle battlements of St Michael's Mount:

> 'its on a rock in the sea which at the flowing tyde is an island
> but at low water one can goe over the sands almost just to it;
> its but a little way from Market Due [Marazion] a little
> market town; you may walke or ride to it all on the sands
> when the tyde's out; its a fine rock, and very high, severall
> little houses for fisher men in the sides of it just by the
> water; at the top is a pretty good house where the Govenour
> lives sometymes, Sir Hook his name is; there is a tower on
> the top on which is a flag; there is a chaire or throne on the
> top from whence they can discover a great way at sea and
> here they put up Lights to direct shipps.'

The landscape was becoming progressively bleaker as we neared Land's End, as Celia had observed in her description of Penzance:

> 'it lookes soe snugg and warme and truely it needs shelter haveing the sea on the other side and little or no fewell: turff and furse and ferne; they have little or noe wood and noe coale which differences it from Darbyshire, otherwise this and to the Lands End is stone and barren as Darbyshire'

There was nothing snug and warm about this approach to Land's End. Like an American freeway the final stretch of road was punctuated by signs announcing the location of 'The Last Inn in England' or 'The Last Fish 'n' Chips 400 yds ahead'. I could well understand why even in September the Sunny Bank Licenced Hotel was advertising 'full central heating' on its hoarding. The temperature had plummeted, and what little vegetation I could see was being buffeted by a sharp, chill wind. But I was soon to forget the cold. Reaching the crown of a hill, I suddenly saw the Land's End promontory laid out before me. In an instant I felt all the excitement Celia must have when she

> 'came in sight of the maine ocean on both sides, the south and north sea, and soe rode in its view till I saw them joyn'd at the poynt, and saw the Island of Sily [Scilly]; they tell me that in a cleer day those in the Island can discern the people on the maine as they goe up the hill to Church, they can describe their clothes'

I rode past the Land's End sign with all the pride and euphoria of a 'John O'Groater', and clenching my right fist, raised it to the sky in an impulsive gesture of triumph.

No one had told us that a press call had been arranged earlier that afternoon, and we arrived at the south-westernmost tip of England to find a photographer from *The Times* petulantly kicking his heels.

'You were supposed to be here at three-thirty,' he announced with bureaucratic gall, and proceeded to march us off to the observation post for a photograph. After taking a handful of shots against a suitably frenzied backdrop of churning spume, he bid us

a curt farewell and left us to the devices of a tartan-capped photographer from Whitbread's. Affable as he was, the Whitbread photographer met with little enthusiasm for his suggestion to pose me and George with a can of Heineken. Cold, tired and worried that George was missing his feed, I was as co-operative as the photographer from *The Times*. It was only later that I realised the full significance of our small tableau: Heineken refreshes the geographical parts other beers cannot reach.

It was 6.30 pm. Our antics had been observed in desultory fashion by a knot of anoraked and shivering trippers, who now dispersed, leaving England's south-westernmost tip to the sea-gulls. It was hardly surprising. At the height of every season an average of three people a week complete the 874-mile journey from John O'Groats – some on bicycles, some on foot, some in wheel-chairs. I even saw a noticeboard outside the gates devoted to the *John O'Groats to Land's End Association News*. During the twentieth century the journey to Land's End has been popularised to the point of debasement. In the seventeenth century things were very different. Rare were those who made it as far as Truro, let alone to the end of England, and even though Celia did not, as Defoe did, put her foot into the sea, her sense of achievement at reaching Land's End is apparent in her description of the promontory.

'The Lands End terminates in a poynt or peak of great rocks which runs a good way into the sea, I clamber'd over them as farre as safety permitted me; there are abundance of rocks and sholes of stones stands up in the sea, a mile off some, and soe here and there some quite to the shore, which they name by severall names of Knights and Ladies roled up in mantles from some old tradition or fiction the poets advance, description of the amours of some great person'

Even now the tradition still flourishes about the rocks, although I suspected that latterly such fictions had been advanced by enterprising locals and tour operators. To our left was supposed to be Dr Johnson's Head, to our right Dr Syntax's Head, and out to sea the craggy profile of the Armed Knight. That evening the granite outcrop bore more resemblance to bundles of tired asparagus, crumbling a little at the heads, but recognisably greeny-grey in their bath of bubbling water.

Today Celia would recognise little apart from the rock formations. With the advent of the steam train and the opening of the London to Penzance railway, Land's End became accessible to everyone. Parties would make their way from Penzance by staging coach to visit Grace Thomas's First and Last House for refreshments. By the turn of the century, the Land's End Hotel was a thriving concern, and was to become still more popular with the invention of the motor car and the introduction of the first John O'Groats to Land's End marathon. To discourage speeding, road records are no longer kept, but the journey has been made by a Ferrari in less than eleven hours. From London it had taken George and me nearly four months.

For many years England ended not with a bang but with a whimpering straggle of souvenir shops, ice cream kiosks and a threadbare network of clifftop paths. Early in 1988 Land's End underwent a facelift when it became part of Peter de Savary's Landleisure Group. Just as the Emperor Hadrian had marked the most extreme boundary of his empire with a wall, so Peter de Savary marked his with a purpose-built tourist resort. There was a whitewashed uniformity to the Land's End we saw that September, with its thirty-four bedroomed luxury hotel, Dollar Suspension Bridge, Shipwreck Play Area and Last Labyrinth audiovisual experience. Even the Land's End Custom House turned out to be just another part of the complex, an information centre with toilets and facilities for nursing mothers. I have to confess that despite the faintly sterilised, homogenised feel of the place, I rather liked the new-look Land's End. But I was gratified to discover that Land's

End still possessed a modicum of seaside tackiness; that it was still possible to have my photograph taken beneath the Land's End signpost, and that if I looked hard enough amongst the chi-chi household accessories and exclusive-range fudges, I could still find the odd shell-encrusted galleon or miniature vinegar cruet filled with mead.

'The people here are very ill guides,' Celia had complained in 1698. We were to discover the same thing. After a week in Cornwall, Catherine had developed a phobia about narrow roads. Such was her fear that when we discovered that George's stabling was to be down a winding lane, she grilled a local boy for five minutes to find out whether it would be accessible to the lorry. Adamant, the boy replied that it would. When some hundred yards later we heard the unmistakable grate of fibreglass against granite, followed by a still more unnerving metallic clatter, we realised the full import of Celia's words. Rather than risk another encounter with the Cornish lanes, we decided that night that I would take George his final feed by taxi. In the circumstances it seemed an admissible expense, and one which I was fully prepared to meet myself.

The hotel receptionist was most efficient, and was on the telephone at once. 'Is your mummy there?' she enquired in mellifluous tones. Then, a few moments later, 'Any chance of Tom taking a young lady down Newlyn Way?'

Evidently there was, and at eleven o'clock a slight man with Celtic colouring arrived at reception, introducing himself as Thomas Thomas, co-manager of the Sennen Cove Fish Bar and eponymous proprietor of Tommy's Cabs. Slightly taken aback at first to find his passenger dressed for dinner yet carrying a yellow bucket brimming with chaff, he soon engaged me in friendly conversation about my business in Newlyn. Once he had wrested the entire story from me, Tommy's demeanour changed instantly. 'I've never had a star in my cab before,' he said. I assured him that we were about to meet the real star, but Tommy was not to be deflected. Once we arrived at George's stabling I was allowed to do nothing, while he emptied the feed into the manger, filled up the two water buckets and then carried them into the stable. Nor would he accept a penny in recompense, merely replying, 'And if you're staying here tomorrow night, I'll do the same again.'

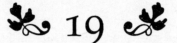

19

Land's End to Newton Toney

A watercolour wash of seeping grey had descended on the land-scape. Land and sky now fused into one and the air had grown cold and damp. Autumn had arrived.

It was 26 September. We had been on the road for 119 days, covered over 1300 miles, and now, like Celia, we were glad to be heading east:

> 'but the season of the year enclined to raine, and the dayes declineing I was affraid to delay my return, and these parts not abounding with much accomodation for horses, their being a hard sort of cattle, and live much on grass or furses of which they have the most and it will make them very fatt being little hardy horses, and as they jest on themselves, do not love the taste of oates and hay because they never permit them to know the taste of it; but my horses could not live so especially on journeys, of which I had given them a pretty exercise, and their new oates and hay suited not their stomach; I could get noe beanes for them till I came back to St Columbe [St Columb Major] againe'

I wondered if Celia's relief at nearing home was tempered, as mine was, by a feeling of melancholy. No sooner had we turned to the east than the whole mood of the ride changed. We were leaving behind us not only Land's End, but some of that sense of adventure that had so shaped the rest of the journey. Now only a month separated us from London and the end of the ride, and it seemed as if nothing exciting would ever happen again. Beginning with that very evening, the next four weeks were to prove me utterly wrong.

We were stabled at St Mawgan. Catherine and I had returned from a walk in the rain to discover Puppy scrabbling around in a shadowy corner of George's stable.

'Whatcha got there?' asked Catherine, good-humouredly. All of a sudden she lunged forward, and yanking Puppy away from the corner removed from under his nose a saucer of grey powder.

'Damn! Rat poison!' she cried.

'What can we do?' I asked, horrified.

'We can't do anything,' replied Catherine brusquely. 'If he dies, he dies.'

Catherine's apparent lack of concern belied a genuine worry, and a number of times I saw her desperately try to make Puppy throw up, but it was no use. Puppy wouldn't touch his supper. He simply lay on the seat, his head lolling listlessly as he fixed us with a beseeching gaze.

'He's always like that,' declared Catherine practically, but she still kept feeling his nose to check whether it was dry.

That evening we scarcely spoke. A pall hung over the lorry, and supper was eaten in silence. Even Bleeper was subdued and lay on the front passenger seat, eyeing us quizzically from under his gingery eyebrows. That night both dogs were allowed to sleep in our compartment.

At about three I was suddenly awoken. Down below I could hear Catherine padding about in the darkness.

'What is it,' I asked, fearing the worst.

'Puppy,' she hissed back in the stage-whisper people employ in the dark, even though there is no one left to wake.

'Is he dead?'

'No – he's eating his supper.'

George was also proving to be in good health. Like Celia's horses he had had 'a pretty exercise' over the past four months, but it had apparently done him no harm. He had grown lean and muscular, and his earlier recalcitrance had quite disappeared. There was also a spring in his step that I didn't recognise. It was almost as if he sensed that he was going home.

From St Mawgan we travelled through Wadebridge to Camelford.

> 'Combleford was a little market town but it was very indifferent accomodations, but the raines that night and next morning made me take up there, till about 10 oclock in the morning it then made a shew of cleering up, made me willing to seek a better lodging'

George and I met with a far more favourable reception. Despite the rain, the landlord of the Darlington Hotel came out to give me a stirrup cup of port and lemon, while Mr Prescott, the greengrocer, presented me with a corsage. Not even the Leominster Carnival Floral Section judge could have found fault with its delicate arrangement. Nor, it seemed, could George. Plucking it from my Barbour he devoured it with relish, spitting out the pin only after he had licked the last driblets of green saliva from his mouth. So diametrically opposed had my impression of Camelford been to Celia's that I wondered whether we had in fact visited the same place.

'Oh no!' insisted one resident, 'It's Camelford all right, although it's not the least bit surprising that she thought the place was called Combleford. When you think how thick the accent is round here and how most people have usually got half a pastie in their mouths, the amazing thing is how close her approximation actually was!'

There were to be further communication problems later that evening with the Vodafone. For much of our journey through Cornwall, reception had been poor. Now it was terrible.

'He . . . It's Rob . . . . bury Ten . . son,' came the voice at the other end. It was almost unintelligible, but it was enough. In an instant I knew that Robin Tenison was at the other end of the line. I had never met him, but since reading *White Horses over France*, the account of how he and his wife Louella rode two Camargue horses all the way from the South of France to Cornwall, he had become something of an idol for me. I had even written him a fan letter. In fact the letter was never sent and I tore it up, embarrassed that what was intended as genuine admiration might be mistaken for a schoolgirl infatuation. Perhaps I was a little infatuated, for when he suggested that he and Louella should meet me on Bodmin Moor, I could speak of nothing else.

'Have you got a crush on him or something?' joked Charles during one of our nocturnal chats.

It was on 28 September that George and I set off from Hamatethy towards the frowning crags of Rough Tor and Brown Willy. We very quickly left behind the last whitewashed cottage, and soon even its homely curl of chimney smoke was indistinguishable against the shred-torn cloud. All about us now was moor: brown, bleak, infertile. There were no trees, no bushes, not even heather, only coarse hussocky grass that squelched ominously underfoot. More ominous still were the patches of greener turf, for at the merest pressure they would suddenly ooze water and transform themselves into treacherous bog. Now and then we would pass the bleaching bones of sheep or cattle, their flesh long since picked clean by the foxes and buzzards. Standing stones also littered the moor, an eerie legacy of its prehistoric occupation. Yet even within living memory the moor was inhabited. As recently as eighty years ago a village lay at the foot of Brown Willy and wheat was grown on its foothills. Now, as we rode past them, even the foundations of the cottages had all but disappeared.

Three cottages however did remain, all empty, but within sight of each other. When they were inhabited, the occupants would always place a lighted candle in the upstairs window so that the other two families across the moor would know that all was well. The three cottages were abandoned long ago, but travellers lost since then on Bodmin Moor have often claimed they would have lost their bearings and perished, had it not been for three guiding pinpricks of light at the foot of Brown Willy.

It was at about eleven o'clock that I saw Robin and Louella. Astride their grey Camargue horses they were visible in the far distance as they cantered across the spongy sweep of moorland to meet us. Robin immediately slipped into the easy conversational style of one who is not only at home with strangers, but in love with the landscape as well, and the next hour passed quickly as he told me about the moor, its geology, its history and its legends. Louella's was a more taciturn charm as she exchanged anecdotes about travelling with a horse. 'The most tiring bit isn't the riding, it's having to tell people all about it each evening,' she declared with feeling. It was a sentiment I shared. To my relief, they didn't appear in the slightest bit horsey. Confessing I still didn't know for sure what a fetlock was, I was relieved beyond measure to hear Robin's jocular rejoinder.

'Oh Goodness! Neither do we! I think it's the hairy bit at the ankle, but I wouldn't swear to it.'

I had to conclude that Celia had followed a different and possibly easier route than ours, for she dismissed Brown Willy in no more than a few disparaging lines:

> 'as I travelled I came in sight of a great mountaine esteemed the second highest hill in England, supposeing the account Black Comb in Cumberland the first – but really I have seen soe many great and high hills I cannot attribute prehemi-nence to either of these, tho' this did look very great and tall – but I thinke its better said the highest hill in each county.'

Far more impressive in her eyes was Dozmary Pool:

> 'a large standing water called Dosen Mere Poole in a black moorish ground and is fed by no rivers except the little rivolets from some high hills, yet seemes allwayes full without diminution and flows with the wind'

Lying between Twelve Men's Moor and Temple, there was something very strange about the inland lake. For centuries it was believed to be bottomless. Its curious situation added to its mystery, and the legend grew up that it was into these peaty waters that Bevidere threw Excalibur. The legend was somewhat dis-credited in 1869 when the pool dried up and its depth was found to be no more than six feet. Yet even when I saw it, Dozmary Pool seemed to have lost none of its mystery. When the wind blew, rattling through the reed grass and puckering the sheet-like surface to a troubled grey, I almost expected to see a sword rise from the water, brandished by a thrice-waving hand.

From Dozmary Pool we rode to Jamaica Inn. Coaches and caravans cluttered the carpark and the bar was thick with tourists. We ate our lunch quickly and departed. With its atmosphere of contrived jollity, Jamaica Inn seemed too depressing a place to stay for long. There was just time to say goodbye and ask the Hanbury-Tenisons to sign our Visitees' Book, now almost completely filled. Robin and Louella not only signed it, but composed a clerihew for it:

> 'Alison Payne
> Didn't do it for gain,
> She wasn't a tart
> She did it for START.'

'You know,' said Robin after I had confessed my abortive correspondence with him, 'you should've sent that letter. I answer them all. They're rather good for cheering you up when you're depressed. I've got one girl who's been writing to me for years. She sends me sugarlumps.'

From Bodmin Celia headed east via Launceston to Okehampton, where she met with torrential downpours.

> 'A mile beyond I crossed on a stone bridge over a river, and pass'd through mostly lanes which were stony and dirty by reason of the raines that fell the night before and this day, which was the wettest day I had in all my summers travells hitherto, having had noe more than a shower in a day, and that not above 3 tymes in all except when I came to Exeter; as I came down from Taunton there was a small raine most of the afternoon, but this day was much worse, so that by that time I came through lanes and some commons to Oakingham I was very wet; this was a little market town and I met with a very good Inn and accomodation, very good chamber and bed, and came in by 5 of the clock so had a good tyme to take off my wet cloathes and be well dryed and warme to eate my supper, and rested very well without sustaining the least damage by the wet; these raines fully

convinced me of the need of so many great stone bridges whose arches were soe high, that I have wonder'd at it because the waters seemed shallow streames but they were so swelled by one night and dayes raine that they came up pretty near the arches, and ran in most places with such rapidity, and look'd so thick and troubled, as if they would clear all before them; this causes great floods and the lower grounds are overwhelm'd for a season after such raines, so that had I not put on and gotten beyond Lanston that day there would have been noe moveing for me till the flouds, which hourly encreased, were run off.'

Fortunately George and I were dogged by nothing worse than intermittent showers and a fractious bull, which threatened to give chase just outside Launceston. We were to enjoy a total reprieve from the rains as we rode through Drewsteignton and met Mabel Mudge, the oldest landlady in England.

While a local farmer held George, I went into the Drewe Arms to talk to her as she sat on a settle in the shiny magnolia passageway leading from the lounge bar to the snug. Her ninety-third birthday was less than a week away, but Mabel Mudge was as sharp as she had been on the day she took possession of the pub in 1919.

'So long as that's working,' she said, pointing at her wrinkled temple, 'I want to go on as long as I can.'

Lucidity notwithstanding, conversation was strained, for Aunty Mabel, as she was universally known, was as deaf as the stone flags on the pub's floor. I simply listened while she recounted how it had taken 'four and sixty horses' to transport the granite needed to build Castle Drogo, seat of Julius Drewe, the Home and Colonial Stores grocery King. 'Of course that was only yesterday,' added Aunty Mabel, shaking with laughter, '1910 at least.'

In the same way as it had done for Aunty Mabel, time now became telescoped for Catherine and me. Two rest days in Exeter passed rapidly, and soon we were on the road again, heading towards Honiton. In 1698 Celia had written of the town:

'here it is they make the fine Bonelace in imitation of the

Antwerp and Flanders lace, and indeed I think its as fine, it only will not wash so fine which must be the fault in the thread'

The weather that day would have been a good test for Honiton's lace, for the rain sheeted down, bouncing off the pavements like white pellets. In the distorting gloom of the downpour I could make out only one lace shop. Otherwise there seemed to be nothing but antique shops and bow-windowed tea rooms. We stabled that night at a nearby farm, where the drip of my clothes strung high above the Raeburn beat metronomic time to our kitchen supper.

Crossing our tracks at Exeter had marked a turning point in the journey. It was as if we had left behind us one of the final divides separating us from London. My thoughts were now with home, my friends, my family and most of all with Charles. Previously I had felt only the gentlest pull towards London. Now there was an urgency in our progress, and as each day passed it gathered momentum. The journey was no longer a journey for its own sake, it was a journey with an end.

That Celia had felt the same was apparent from the very economy with which she recorded these final miles.

'Thence [from Honiton] I went to Axminster, but not soe good way being much in lanes, stony and dirty, and pretty much up and down hills; beyond Axminster where I passed over the river Ax on a pretty large bridge I came to Somersetshire againe and the London Road by Chard, but I struck out of that road 2 mile off the town to Liegh, to a Relations house Mr. Hendleys which stands on a hill'

It was 5 October when George and I reached Axminster. Our stabling that night was also to take us to a house on a hill, not Leigh, but Cricket St Thomas. The name reflected its geographical situation, the word 'cricket' deriving from the Anglo-Saxon word 'cruc', meaning a hill or a ridge.

The manor or estate of Cricket St Thomas was described in the *Domesday Book* as:

'LAND OF THE COUNT OF MARTAIN
The Count of Martain holds CRICKET ST. THOMAS from
the king. Sheerwold held it before 1066; it paid tax for 6
hides (i.e. 720 acres), Land for 5 ploughs, of which 4 hides
are in lordship; 3 ploughs there; 2 slaves; 6 villagers and 5
smallholders with 3 ploughs and 2 hides. A mill which pays
12s; meadow 1½ acres; woodland 7 furlongs long and 2
furlongs wide; 14 cattle; 14 pigs; 124 sheep; 24 goats. The
value was £4; now 100s.'

When we came to Cricket St Thomas, both the value and the
occupants of the estate had changed somewhat. Since 1966 the
1000 acres of landscaped park, lakes and waterfalls had been home
not merely to cattle, pigs, sheep and goats, but to a menagerie of
elephants, zebras, flamingos, llamas, bison, camels, wapiti, walla-
bies, rheas and cranes. In addition to this wildlife park, the estate
also boasted a Countylife Museum, the National Heavy Horse
Centre and a Children's Adventure Playground. We stayed that
night at Cricket House itself, designed in 1804 by Sir John Soane for
the famous naval Hood family and more recently the location for
the television series 'To the Manor Born'. As I lay in bed and
listened to the distant barking of the sea lions, I wondered what Sir
John Soane would make of it all.

From Cricket St Thomas we continued through Beaminster and
Maiden Newton to Dorchester.

'and then from Liegh I went through narrow stony lanes up
hills and down, which steeps causes the water on raines to

trill down on the low ground, that for a few hours or a day
there will be noe passing in the bottom; which happen'd
while I was at Liegh, one nights raine put the cattle in the
meddows swimming and hindred us from going to
Church, the water would have came over the windows of
the Coach'

This was Hardy country, with its wooded pastures and vast tracts
of exposed heathland. To one familiar only with coastal Dorset, it
came as quite a surprise. Until now Dorset had meant for me a belt
of Georgian seaside resorts and thatched villages populated by
spaniels, retired majors and genteel old ladies. Now I was confronted by its huge interior. It seemed as devoid of people as
Northumberland, and I rode for hours without seeing a car. For the
most part the only sign of movement was the falling leaves which,
fluttering down as we brushed past the dripping vegetation,
would lodge themselves in George's mane. And so we continued,
alone and reflective, through the autumn landscapes of Dorset and
Wiltshire until we came at last to Newton Toney, the birthplace of
Celia Fiennes.
    Celia was born on 7 June 1662, almost certainly at the manor
house at Newton Toney, and it was from here that the majority of
her early tours began and ended. She eventually died in Hackney,
probably in the home of one of her nieces, but her will, written at
the age of seventy-six, contained precise instructions about her
burial, 'without ostentation only put into a leaden coffin', at
Newton Toney. It was to be 'as privat as can be a hearse and one
coach and to goe out early in the morning and goe the backside of
the Town to the Western road'. As for the stone, 'I forbid all
escutcheons or bearers'. The only memorial Celia desired was an
inscription on her father's monument. It seemed an inadequate
tribute to a woman whose achievements had been so remarkable,
but I was determined to see it and fixed on 13 October for my visit to
Newton Toney.
    Up until the end of September I had often ridden until about six
thirty in the evening. Two weeks into October the days had grown
so short that I rarely continued beyond five in the afternoon. It
meant setting off earlier, but neither Catherine nor I minded, for

she was as loath to drive along unfamiliar roads in the dark as I was to ride George in the half-light. I had intended to reach Newton Toney by five. In fact I was to arrive very much later.

A lunchtime press call and fund-raising session in Salisbury had taken far longer than I envisaged, and it was not until 3.45 pm that George and I finally set off for Newton Toney. Hold-ups along the main road and a blocked bridleway delayed us still further, so that by the time George and I were within half a mile of Newton Toney it was seven o'clock, and dusk had fallen. The grassy track of the bridleway had petered out and we found ourselves in a narrow lane lined on either side by black trees, with only a single light ahead to guide us into the village.

What little colour was visible in the dusky gloom soon disappeared as night settled all around. Even the violet glow of George's coat had given way to the most shadowy suggestion of his form, which vanished into the darkness altogether if I looked at it directly. Once we heard an owl hoot and sensed the leathery fluttering of a bat flying overhead. Otherwise there was no noise beyond the creak of the saddle and the metallic ring of George's hooves on the road as he picked his way down the slippery, worn surface.

Suddenly, two shafts of light seared the blackness ahead. It was only a car but it took us both by surprise. Not thinking, I relaxed my grip and in a second had slithered to the ground as George sank to his knees.

'George!' I cried instinctively, putting out my hand. I could barely see him for the darkness and the tears of frustration welling up in my eyes. Only ten days now separated us from the completion of our journey, and I had let him slip. What if he were hurt? What if he were lame? The journey itself was of no importance. What mattered was that I had not looked after him properly. Once again I had failed him.

Breathing heavily, George pulled himself up and stood beside me. I took his reins and led him, trying to tell in the darkness whether or not he was limping. But I could sense no imbalance in his step. The lane had flattened out, and his hoof-fall was clear and regular. We walked on a little further. As far as I could tell, he was unhurt and so, letting the left stirrup down to its last notch, I hauled myself up onto the saddle and rode him the last few yards into the village.

'They're here,' came a voice as we approached the first house. 'They've arrived.'

There seemed to be people everywhere, silhouetted in the black against open doorways or standing at garden gates. Some held torches. A few had their hands cupped round candles and every now and again I could make out the flickering suggestion of a face as the candlelight glanced off the bottom of a chin, the tip of a nose, and threw the hollows of the eyes into perfect crescents of gold light.

We must have reached the centre of the village, for we suddenly came upon a knot of people in the middle of the road.

'Welcome to Newton Toney, Celia. We're so glad you came.'

The next ten minutes passed in an instant as I was introduced by torchlight to each member of the welcoming committee, and George was patted by a group of children from Newton Toney Primary School. Then I was taken to the church to see the memorial plaque to Celia Fiennes.

'Feel free to stand on the pew to look at it,' said the church-warden, once he had found the right switch, 'we all do.'

It had been an extraordinary evening, and in its way magical; but it was only later that night, as I re-read Celia's journal, that I realised quite how extraordinary and magical it had really been. Describing the Newton Toney section of her journey she had written:

> 'the little raines I had in the morning before I left Newton-tony made the wayes very slippery, and it being mostly on chaulk way, a little before I came to Alsford forceing my horse out of the hollow way his feete failed, and he could noe wayes recover himself and so I was shott off his neck upon the bank, but noe harm I bless God, and as soone as he could role himself up stood stock still by me, which I looked on as a great mercy – indeed mercy and truth allwayes have attended me'

Somehow it seemed more than mere coincidence.

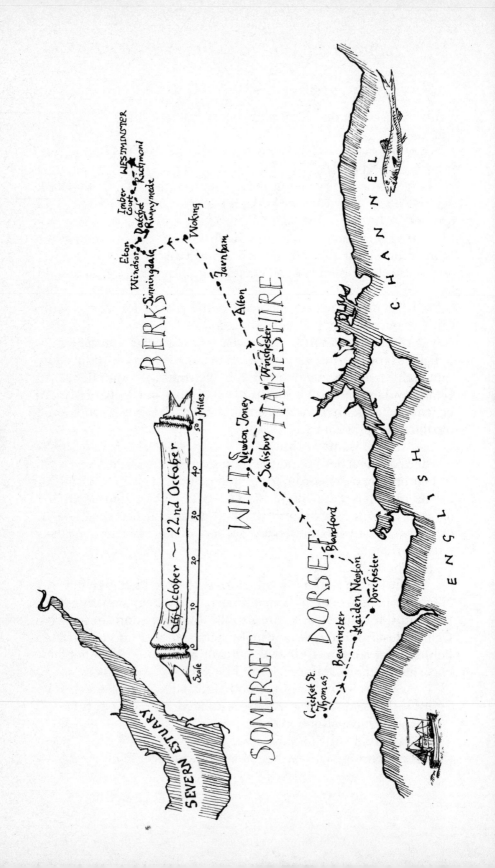

SEVERN ESTUARY

SOMERSET

BERKS

WILTS

HAMPSHIRE

DORSET

WESTMINSTER
Imber Court
Eton • Richmond
Windsor • Datchet • Runnymede
• Sunningdale
• Woking
• Farnham
• Alton
• Winchester
• Newton Toney
• Salisbury
• Blandford
• Maiden Newton
• Dorchester
Cricket St.
• Thomas
• Beaminster

Scale

6th October — 22nd October

0 10 20 30 40 50 Miles

ENGLISH CHANNEL

20

Newton Toney to Eton

It was 18 October when George and I reached Winchester. Already a major settlement in Roman times, Winchester came into its own when the Anglo Saxons made it their capital, a status it was to retain under William the Conqueror. As late as the seventeenth century it was still important enough for Charles II to want to build a palace there, a fact Celia recorded in her journal.

> 'in the town is a new building begun by King Charles the Second for a Palace when he came to hunt, and for aire and diversions in the Country, I saw the Modell of it which was very fine, and so would it have been if finished, but there is only the outside shell is set up; there were designed fine apartments and two Chapples but its never like to be finished now.'

Nor was it. Despite the wave of expansion that was sweeping through the country at the end of the century, one senses from Celia's description at least that Winchester had been rather left behind. Her contempt for this old-fashioned straggler was barely concealed.

> 'Winchester is a large town was once the metropolis, there is a wall encompassing it with severall Gates, the streets are pretty good large and long, the buildings but low and old, only some few in the Close which are new built of the

Doctors houses by the Colledge and the Church . . . The Cathedrall at Winchester is one of the biggest in England and is to be admired for its largeness not its neatness or curiosity . . . the bones of the Kings of England . . . were buried there, for Winchester was the Regal Citty, which now it has lost as also a peculiar art of dying the best purples; in the Church there are no good Monuments worth notice; the Steeple lookes noble, but the Spire is not a neare so high as Salisbury'

That Winchester struck Celia as unworthy of the title 'metropolis' was all too clear. Three hundred years on it seemed still less like a capital city. We passed a Henry Moore statue here, a group of exotic-looking tourists there, but there was nothing really new, exciting or cosmopolitan about the place, and as I rode up the pedestrianised High Street with its twin-set shoppers and smart stores, I felt as if I had wandered into the very heart of the provinces.

The further east we travelled, the flatter the country became. There was little protection from the wind in this landscape of vast and sweeping ploughed fields, and I had taken to wearing two jumpers under my Barbour. I had also started wearing rubber boots as a protection against the rain. Their watertight airlessness had been unbearable in the warmer weather. Now it was a godsend. Each day brought with it a downpour of some kind and the evenings when we didn't finish drenched and dripping were rare. I scarcely noticed the countryside any more. Since Bodmin I had grown increasingly introspective, and hours might pass before the thud of a falling conker or the rasping call of a pheasant interrupted my reveries.

With just four days to go until the end of the ride, my feelings were far from clear-cut. So much had happened over the past five months – I had met so many people, seen so many places, renounced so many preconceived ideas – that I couldn't take any more in: I had reached saturation point. All I wanted now was to clear my mind. Only then would I be able to reflect on the impact of it all.

Quite apart from the drain on my emotions and my mind, I was feeling physically exhausted. I now slept for at least nine hours a night, yet each day I felt more tired and run-down. George was in the peak of condition, but I was sure that the quickening in his step had little to do with his physical well-being. He knew we were nearly home.

I too longed for 22 October, but I also dreaded it, for it signified not just the end of the journey, but a return to normality, to earning a living and to the constrictions of city life. Never again would I enjoy such freedom and mobility. Never again would I have the same access to England's landscape and its people.

I also dreaded 22 October because it would mark the end of my friendship with Catherine, George, Bleeper and Puppy. We had experienced so much together in the course of 1600 miles that I could scarcely remember what life was like without them. And yet, in four days' time it would be all over. Bleeper would have to be returned to his rightful owner, George would go back to pulling a dray around London and Catherine would move to the country with Puppy. No doubt I would see them all again, but it would never be the same.

As for me, I had no idea what the future held. Charles continued to occupy my thoughts, and not a week went by in which he didn't renew his proposal. If anything had kept me going through the journey it was him. Whether it was through his nightly telephone calls, his occasional visits, or simply the thought of his being there, his had been a constant presence. He could not have been more supportive, but the prospect of seeing him in London both excited and appalled me. During the past four and a half months our relationship had been defined by the constraints of the ride. After 22 October everything would be irrevocably changed. I would no longer have the excuses of an itinerary or a timetable to hide behind. I would have to come to a decision.

I wondered what thoughts had gone through Celia's mind as she rode these last few miles. Did she too have mixed feelings about the prospect of completing her journey, or was she merely relieved to escape the rains? Her terse account gave little indication:

'the next day I went to Alton, thence Farnum [Farnham],

this proved a very wet day; after an hours rideing in the morning it never ceased more or less to raine, which made me put in at Farnum and stay all the day after; I came in at noone but then it began to raine much faster and soe continued; thence next day I went over the Forrest in sight of Fairly [Farnham] Castle which is the Bishop of Winchesters Pallace, it lookes nobly on a hill; thence to Bagshott, thence to Winsor over the Forrest, this way most clay deep way, the worse by reason of the raines and full of sloughs.'

From Alton onwards, I knew we had left the countryside for good. What few bridleways there were seemed to skirt suburban gardens or to follow neat angular routes around factories and gasworks; but they were infinitely preferable to the roads. Elsewhere the motorists had treated us with surprising consideration. Now they sliced past, splashing us with water and forcing us into the curb. Even those on foot often exhibited an indifference that bordered on hostility. During our lunchtime stop at one pub, the landlord stormed out to tell us to move our lorry and George with it. 'I don't care if it is for charity. I've got my customers to think of and this thing takes up space.'

There were mercifully few people about at Sunningdale. High walls and fences, patrolled by guard dogs and electronic eyes, would offer occasional glimpses of enormous pre-war houses with wrought-iron verandas and forecourts deep in Rolls-Royces. Yet somehow it seemed unfriendly, and I was almost glad to get back to the noise and dirt of the main roads.

It was the afternoon of 20 October when we reached Windsor. We were two hours ahead of schedule, but as the day wore on I grew more and more despondent. By the time we reached Datchet I could bear it no longer. Seeing a small, wooded footpath leading off the main road, I took George down it and dismounted. Officially there were still another two days to go until the end of the journey, but for George and me it was already over. The next forty-eight hours would belong to START, to Whitbread and to the media. Even the route and timetable were no longer ours but the property of the mounted police, whose officers were to escort us all the way from Windsor to the Westminster Hospital and the very heart of London. This was the last time I would ever be alone with George, and I felt it was my final chance to say goodbye to him.

After all the places we had been together, it seemed ironic that our partnership should end up on a strip of footpath sandwiched between Datchet golf course and the B470. Empty crisp-packets, cans and bottles littered the ground and only a few dusty leaves separated us from the main road. But there was something about the way the sunlight dappled through the branches that was almost beautiful. Even the noise of the traffic seemed to fade beneath the comforting jangle of George's curb-chain and the occasional brittle rustling as he searched for grass amidst the dead foliage. Tearing a few fresh green twigs off a sapling I offered them to him and watched as he methodically chewed and swallowed them. A dead leaf had become caught in his forelock, and as he ate it trembled slightly. He seemed quite oblivious to it, but I carefully picked it off and brushed away the dust, thinking to myself as I did so that this would be my last opportunity to perform so small, but to me so precious, a service.

I had never felt any great tenderness towards horses in the past. Often I had found them graceful, occasionally beautiful, but certainly nothing to grow sentimental over. As far as I was concerned they were just another species of animal. And yet, as I stroked George, I knew that here was the exception, that here was a creature for which I would do almost anything and which would occupy a place in my heart for the rest of my life. Breathing in for the last time the bitter-sweet warmth of his coat, I hugged him and remounted. Windsor, London and the end of the journey awaited us. It was time to go.

Almost within putting distance of Datchet golf course was Windsor Castle. Throughout the afternoon its battlements had been visible in the distance, just as they would have been in 1698 when Celia rode by.

> 'Windsor Castle appeares standing on a hill much after the manner of Durham . . . the Castle . . . is the finest pallace the king has, especially now Whitehall is burnt but that was old buildings and unless it were the Banqueting House and

the apartment which our good Queen Mary beautifyed for herself, that was never soe well as Winsor'

Not only was the exterior magnificent, the interior of the castle was sumptuous enough to excite even Celia's admiration. Describing the Throne of State, she observed that:

'the cannopy was so rich and curled up and in some places soe full it looked very glorious and was newly made to give audience to the French Embassadour to shew the grandeur and magnificence of the British Monarch – some of these foolerys are requisite sometymes to create admiration and regard to keep up the state of a kingdom and nation.'

Judging from the number of sightseers in evidence, such fooleries were creating admiration even in 1988. But there was no time to linger, for we were expected at Eton.

Crossing the eighteenth-century pedestrianised bridge that spanned the Thames, we soon found ourselves in Eton's narrow High Street, a photogenic jumble of restaurants, antique shops and warming-pan tea rooms. Eton was every bit as overrun by tourists as Windsor. Although it was already late October, the sun had brought with it scores of Japanese, Germans, French and Americans, all drawn by the mystique of the famous school and all clearly making the most of finding themselves there during term-time. With cameras loaded they stalked anyone connected with the college, whether it was a gowned beak disappearing into an antiquarian bookshop or a stiff-collared schoolboy idling outside a newsagent's. Not even George distracted them from their quarry, and we continued up the High Street unnoticed.

Perhaps something of the same mystique existed in Celia's day. When she visited it, the school had already been in existence for nearly 260 years, having been founded by Henry VI for the worship of God and for the training of young men to the service of the Church and the State. Originally there were seventy scholars, all of whom were fed and educated free of charge. By 1698 that figure had swelled considerably.

'Eaton Colledge, a good stone building carved on the outside; its round a square, there is at the front a large schoole roome; 400 Schollars and 8 Fellows which have 400£ a piece yearely, the Master has 1000£, he payes all the ushers in number seven . . . The Chappel and Schoole room takes up two sides of the square, the two others is the Lodging for the Fellows and for the Schollars; then the middle there is an arch which leads to the Cloyster and soe into their kitchen and cellars which are very convenient and high but pretty old'

There were now some 1270 boys at the college, and the single schoolroom referred to by Celia had since been supplemented by a hundred more schoolrooms, laboratories, studios and libraries. There was even a silver workshop and a drawing office. Yet not all the old buildings had disappeared. In addition to the chapel, cloisters and Lower School, the kitchen still remained intact, its convenience and height clearly having enabled it to survive any plans for remodernisation.

How popular the kitchen was with the boys themselves I never found out, but I was to be more than impressed by its creations. We were guests that evening of the Head Master, Eric Anderson, and his wife, who had organised a seventeenth-century dinner in honour of our visit, prepared by the school chef. Had Celia tasted the fresh salmon, game pie and strawberries to which we were treated, I felt sure that she too would have been in favour of the preservation of one of Eton's oldest buildings.

Our conversation for much of the evening dwelt on Celia Fiennes and her bravery. To make any journey in seventeenth-century England, said Eric Anderson, must have required a great degree of courage, since travelling conditions at the time were so hazardous. I agreed, although my feeling was that her courage lay not simply in undertaking the journeys, but in the fact that she both recognised and was afraid of the hazards those journeys involved. In other words, fear was a prerequisite for bravery.

'And do you think yourself brave for having recreated the Great Journey?' asked the Head Master.

Definitely not, I replied. My decision to ride round England had been taken in a state of total ignorance. I had had no conception of the risks it entailed, and could therefore not be afraid of them. Once my awareness of the dangers had begun to sink in, it was much too late to withdraw. So many people had become involved that the shame of calling the project off would have been a thousand times worse than any accidents that might befall us en route. In that sense, then, my motive for recreating Celia's Great Journey had been quite the opposite of bravery: it had been cowardice. The Head Master of Eton College raised his eyebrows.

'I wouldn't say cowardice,' he said with a half smile. 'Foolhardiness, perhaps.'

We then discussed the concept of fear. My most frightening moment, I decided, had been the time I jeopardised George's life in the Lake District. What, I wondered, had been Eric Anderson's? Without the merest pause for reflection he replied, 'The day I accepted the Head Mastership of Eton.'

At 8.40 the following morning I felt I knew what he meant. Three months earlier I had accepted an invitation to address the School Hall Assembly. In the abstract it had seemed a small enough task: a fifteen-minute talk, accompanied by slides, to any senior boys who might be interested in the Great Journey. I had been told that attendance was not compulsory and so had expected no more than a handful of boys to turn up. It was only when I stepped into School Hall and found myself in a building with the dimensions of a cathedral, the acoustics of a station and the atmosphere of a mausoleum, that I realised how horribly wrong I had been. Few places could be more forbidding. Glowering marble busts guarded all the exits, dour portraits lined the walls and huge pillars rose up on all sides to support a stiffly ornate moulded ceiling. Most forbidding of all were the 550 empty chairs that occupied the centre of the hall.

'Surely you're not expecting to fill all these?' I asked the director of the School Hall Assembly, affecting as jocular a tone as I was able.

'Probably,' came the casual reply.

His prediction proved to be accurate. Five minutes later I found myself clutching Mr Boswell's lectern in quiet terror as 550 boys coughed and shuffled before me. The windows were shut, the doors were blocked and all eyes were upon me. Flight was impossible. Deciding to make the best of it, I took a deep breath and once the lights had dimmed began to speak. I had hoped to raise the odd smile here and there, but no one could have been more surprised than I when my first slide met with an eruption of laughter. Although I had built up quite a collection of slides during the course of the journey, I had never had a chance to view any of them on a proper screen. When I had held up this particular slide against a lamp the night before, it had seemed innocuous enough. Now, blown up onto a screen measuring ten feet by eight feet, it took on a whole new dimension. What I had intended as an introductory shot of George turned out to be the most uncompromising close-up of a horse's genitalia. The laughter didn't subside throughout the entire fifteen minutes, and continued until the last tail-coated figure had disappeared through the main doors. Once again George had come to my rescue.

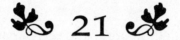

21

Eton to
Westminster

On Friday 21 October George and I set out towards Richmond. A thick, damp fog clung to the Thames Valley, so I felt rather relieved to hand over the responsibility for navigation to P.C. Dick Bird of the Metropolitan Police Mounted Division.

'We've got a right pea-souper here,' he observed wryly as he strapped fluorescent yellow leggings to his horse's legs. 'Still, you might be able to make out the odd landmark here and there, if you're lucky.'

It was to prove an optimistic forecast. Cooper's Hill was quite invisible, as were the Kennedy, Allied Forces and Magna Carta Memorials, while the Thames itself was engulfed in an impenetrable grey mass of water vapour. Yet somehow it didn't matter. Not even the fog could swallow up the objects that held the most meaning for me. I had spotted the first one at Runnymede, but as the day wore on we came across others with increasing regularity.

'What's that you're looking at? asked Dick as he caught me peering into the gloom for the twelfth time that morning.

'A black cab,' I replied.

He seemed puzzled, but I said no more for there was a lump in my throat. For the first time it really seemed as if we were almost home.

That night we stabled with the Mounted Police at Imber Court near Richmond. Catherine and I had often talked about what we would do once the ride was over. How strange it would be, we agreed, to sleep in our own beds, to eat our own food and to take a bath whenever we felt like it. How relaxing it would be to lie in when we wanted, and to spend whole days without talking to a soul. Even the prospect of falling ill every so often seemed to us an untold luxury. Then there were our friends. Throughout the ride our appointment diaries had lain dormant. How curious it would now be to take them up again after a five-month blank, to socialise, dress up, go to the cinema, eat out, to live again as normal people. We had passed many evenings in the box discussing what for us had taken on all the significance of an afterlife. Now, however, with just one day separating us from the end of the ride, that afterlife seemed oppressively close. In less than twenty-four hours the box would no longer be ours, and Catherine, George, Bleeper, Puppy and I would all go our separate ways. Words seemed inadequate to express the confusion of emotions that now preoccupied us, and Catherine and I spent the evening in virtual silence, soaping the sidesaddle and polishing the brasses in readiness for the next day's entry into London. Of the two of us Catherine had always been the less emotional, but I noticed that she held Bleeper even more tightly than usual that evening, and when she came back from giving George his final feed her eyes looked red and swollen.

I shared Catherine's sadness, but at the same time I felt that I had already made my farewells. My thoughts were no longer with the past, nor even with the present. What dominated my whole consciousness now was Charles. His proposals had become a daily part of our Vodafone conversations, and we had both grown used to my parrying them with a non-committal quip or some light-hearted banter. But the tone of our conversation that evening was different, and when he pressed me once more to give an answer, I made no jokes or fatuous comments. Instead I simply replied, 'I'll give you my answer tomorrow.'

I awoke the following morning feeling curiously divorced from my surroundings. Even my own body seemed strange to me, as if my movements were disconnected from any thought process. It struck me as odd, too, that I felt no apprehension about the next few hours. The night before I had felt so nervous that I had barely been able to sleep. Now all emotion seemed to have been drained from me. I had expected this sensation of numbness to pass once we set off from Richmond Park, but if anything it grew more intense. I could appreciate the burnished tones of the autumn trees and feel the hot sun on the back of my costume, but it was as if it were all happening to someone else. Even when I chatted with my police escort I felt like an eavesdropper, although we were the only two people there.

The numbness continued all the way to Putney Bridge, but now it no longer bothered me. Throughout the ride I had felt trammelled by the need to process each new experience. Every sight, sound, smell, taste and tactile sensation had to be analysed, catalogued and noted down. Now, suddenly, I felt as if I had been released. Unhampered by the burden of analysis I found myself noticing my surroundings more closely than ever before. Everything seemed more vivid and colourful, and as we stepped onto the bridge I realised how much I was enjoying it all.

I sensed a similar excitement in George. With nostrils dilated and ears pricked, his whole body seemed to be straining forward. There was a pride in his step as he picked his feet up high and brought them down again with a feathered flourish, and a haughty self-assurance in the way he held his head. It was only when he let out a long, loud neigh that I realised the reason for his excitement. Waiting at the midpoint of the bridge, their manes blowing and brasses glinting, were two more grey shires, harnessed to a Whitbread dray. George tossed his head with delight as they returned his call. Suddenly it was if he were quite oblivious to the crowds and double-decker buses, and it was all I could do to stop him cantering across all four traffic lanes to the two horses. A barrage of photographers had formed around the dray, and as we approached they cried:

'Smile, Alison!'

'Can you turn him the other way?'

'Migh-ty! Over here!'

But George wasn't listening. He was nuzzling up to his two friends, throwing back his head every now and then with a triumphant whinny. As far as he was concerned, he was already home.

I was beginning to share the same feeling. During the ride I had often caught glimpses of what I believed to be familiar faces. On closer inspection the resemblance had always turned out to be imaginary, and I would find myself staring at total strangers. Now as I looked at the faces of the people lining the bridge I could scarcely believe my eyes. Not only did they look like my friends, they *were* my friends. Charles didn't seem to be among them, but I recognised at least twenty-five people, all clapping and smiling. 'Toyboy' was among them and there was even a small contingent from the Rayne Riding Centre, the group which had escorted me across Essex all those months ago.

Many of them were wearing START T-shirts, and as George and I set off once more with our police escort, they followed us with collecting tins. The atmosphere was infectious. Donating money without even being asked, people in the street began to walk alongside us, so that by the time we reached the King's Road our small band had grown into a sizeable procession. From open-mouthed tourists to cynical punks the whole of Chelsea seemed to stop in its tracks. Pound coins and five-pound notes flowed in from every direction, and as we continued towards Sloane Square more collecting tins had to be sent for, to cope with the rapidly swelling donations.

All about me now were the buildings and streets I knew so well. If I had felt apprehensive about returning home, my doubts now evaporated as we made our way up Sloane Street to Knightsbridge and Hyde Park. Five months earlier Catherine, George and I had begun our journey from this very spot. We had set ourselves a challenge, we had met it, and now we were returning in victory. I felt all the pride and gratitude that Celia must have felt when she concluded her Great Journey:

> 'here ends my Long Journey this summer, in which I had but 3 dayes of wet except some refreshing showers some-tymes, and I thinke that was not above 4 in all the way; in all which way and tyme I desire with thankfullness to own the good providence of God protecting me from all hazard or dangerous accident.'

For at least an hour my facial muscles had been aching from so much smiling, but I couldn't help it. I was so happy I felt as if my heart would burst. Continually scanning the pavements for Charles, I barely noticed Hyde Park Corner, Constitution Hill and Buckingham Palace, so it came as a surprise suddenly to find myself in Parliament Square with the ormolued pomp of Big Ben rising high above me.

'What's all this abaht then?' asked a taxi driver drawing up alongside us at the traffic lights. 'Fancy dress parade, is it?'

I explained that it was for a charity.

''Ow far've you come?'

'Over 1600 miles,' I answered with pride.

'Where djew start out from?'

'London.'

'Blimey! You must 'ave got bleedin' lost!'

A quarter of a mile further and we reached Millbank. Westminster Hospital was in sight. In a few moments the Lord Mayor of Westminster would greet us and it would all be over. George was now so worked up that I could hardly restrain him, and it looked as if we would cover the final few yards in a matter of seconds. A group of people was waiting outside the hospital, and as we neared them I was gradually able to make out their faces. There was Catherine with Bleeper and Puppy, and next to them my brother and mother. I recognised several more faces, and was about to call out to them when I realised that they were looking not at me but at a shiny black limousine drawing up in front of them.

'It's the Lord Mayor,' someone cried, 'Look!'

My gaze, however, was directed in quite the opposite direction, towards the figure that had appeared as if from nowhere and was now making its way with arms outstretched towards me and George. I knew now that I had come home, and even before I heard the question I had answered 'Yes.'

The Lord Mayor and Lady Mayoress of Bristol, Mr and Mrs Derek Tedder; The Bristol and West Building Society; Doreen Britten; Naomi and Victoria Broadhurst; Barry Brooks; Raymond Brooks-Ward; Brother Office Equipment; Barbara Brouet; Broughton Post Office; Virginia Brown; Peveril Bruce; The Duke of Buccleuch; Jo Buckley; Anthony and Jill Bullen; Charlie and Sarah Bullen; Ceri Burgum; Staff Corporal Keith Burns; Butcher's Arms, Beccles; Brian Butler; Mike Butler; Caldene Clothing Company Ltd; Cambridgeshire County Fire Service; Hazel Cant; Capel-Cure Myers; The Earl and Countess of Carlisle; Mrs Carlo; John Carter; Miss Mary Cashmore; Robert Chalmers; Rosie Chapman; Ray Charlsworth; Charterhouse School; Mrs D. Charville; Viscount Chelsea; The Children's Channel; Kate Clarke; Mike Clarke; Tim Clifford; Davina Clift and family; Sylvia, Lady Clitheroe; Clyst Equestrian Products; Patrick Cobbold; Mrs Carol Cole; Claudia Cole; P.C. Liz Collishaw; Jonathan and Judy Coode; The Ernest Cook Trust; Min and Helen Cooper; Rosie Cope; Dr Peter Copeman; John Cornelius Reid; David Cornwell and family; John Costello; Nancy Costin; Andrew and Tessa Counsell; Countesthorpe Baptist Playgroup; Richard Coward; Mrs J. Cox; James Cox; Patrick Craig-McFeely; Michael Crammer; Peter and Dolores Craven; Mr and Mrs Eustace Crawley; Simon and Christine Crisp; Philippa Cropper; Mrs Marilyn Crowhurst; Chrissie Cullimore and family; Maggie Culver and the staff of Mount Edgcumbe; Cumbria County Fire Service; Pat Cummings; Gordon Dakin; Barbara Daly; The Lesley David Trust; P.C. Gillian Davies; Frances Dean; The Earl of Derby; Betty d'Erlanger and family; Lord Digby; Mr and Mrs C. Dive; Amanda Dixon; Chris Dlutsowski; Mary Dobson; Antoinette Doe; Dorset Police; Michael Dowding; Lieutenant Colonel and Mrs Christopher D'Oyly; Sylvia Drake; The Drapers' Company; Peter and Judy Duckworth; Jo Eckett; P.C. David Eden; The Edgcumbe Arms, Cremyll; Philippa and Peter Edwards; Tim Edwards; The Bishop of Ely and Mrs Jean Walker; Mr and Mrs Nick Embiricos; Liz and Mike Epsom; Eton College; Paul and Rosemary Exmouth; Richard Eyre, Dean of Exeter; Sian Facer; Mrs Joyce Farnham; Richard Fiennes; Diana Finan; Sam Foley; Ford Ltd; The Forestry Commission; Bill and Diana Foulkes; Mrs Kathleen Fowler; Johnny Francome; Dr Helga Frankland; Mr and Mrs Harry Fraser; Richard and Sue Froggatt; Richard and Caroline Fry; Lieutenant Patrick Furse; Mrs Betty Galyer; Julie Gammon; John Gardiner; Ian Gates and David Clark, Westminster Hospital Illustration Department; Dr John Gayner; Kate Gayson; Pat Gaywood; Robin Geldard; Chief Superintendent Gibbens, Metropolitan Mounted Police; Captain Ian Gibbs, The King's Own Scottish Borderers; Julian Gibbs; Tonie Gibson; Lieutenant Colonel Seymour Gilbart-Denham; Jeni Gilbert; Lady Penelope Gilbey; Mrs Madeleine Ginsberg, The Victoria and Albert Museum; Sir William Gladstone; Gloucestershire County Fire Service; Pam and Paula Gough; Richard Gowing; The Duke and Duchess of Grafton; Andrew and Virginia Grant; Mrs Jennie Graves; Denys Gray; Miss Grace Gray; Professor and Mrs Malcolm Greaves; Mrs Marjorie Green; Johnny Gunston; Mr and Mrs Adam Gurdon; Melanie Gurdon; Mr and Mrs Gwennap; Robin and Louella Hanbury-Tenison; Cathy Hancock; Mrs Liz Hancock; P. Handley and Sons, Blacksmiths, Market Drayton; Mike Hardy; Colonel and Mrs David Hargreaves; Charles and Janet Harker; Ian Harkness, Shire Inns; Chris Harrington; Roger Harrison; Harrogate Police Mounted Section; Harthill School; Debbie Hartill; Ken Hartill; Louis Hassett; Kay Hastilow; Alan Hawken; Miss Nancy Hay; Peter Hayden; Wensley Haydon-Baillie; Paul Haynes; Arthur and Laura Hazlerigg; Lord Hazlerigg; Mr and Mrs John Heathcote-Ball; Mike Heaton-Ellis; Margaret Hedley; Dr John Hemming, Royal Geographical Society; Lucy Hennessy; Paul Henry; Sue Henwood; Hereford and Worcester County Fire Service; Major James Hewitt and family; Judith Hill; Kathleen Hill; the inhabitants of Hilton; Jenni Hinkes; Helen Hodges; Mr and Mrs R. Hodgkiss; Mr and Mrs John Hodgson; Ruth Hodson; Dan Hogan; Jane Holderness-Roddam; Duncan Holloway; Mr Howard, Brookhouse Farm; Mr and Mrs John Howard; Philip Howard; Jackie Howells; Sheila and Bruce Howlett; Mrs Hudson; Andrew Hugh-Smith; Lesley Hunt; Clive Hurst; Jonathan Hustler; David A. Hutchinson and Cory Luxmore, Dorset County Council Transportation and Engineering Department; Betty Ikavinix; Ilketshall St Lawrence Primary School; Sir Thomas and Lady Ingilby; 'In Residence', Corbridge; Ipswich High School; John Irvine; Jeremy James; Maureen and Amanda James; Mrs Lindy Janson; Ruth Jarratt; Mr and Mrs R. N. Jarvis;

Richard Jeens; Audrey Johnson; Paul Johnson; Sally Johnson; Glynis Jones, St Mawgan Horse Show and Gymkhana Committee; Mr and Mrs Mervyn Jones; Mollie Jones; Miss Nesta Jones; Peter Jones; Mrs Mary Kaye; Thomas Kelly; Sally Kenyon; Penny King; John Kingsley and family; Mrs Pat Kingston; General Sir Frank and Lady Kitson; Graham Knight; Rosemary Knight; Knighton House School; Lord Knutsford; The Köchel Quartet; Professor Sir Hans Kornberg; The Lady Jockeys' Association of Great Britain; David Lambert; Land's End Ltd; Chris Langham; Professor Ariel Lant; John Lawless; Sir John and Lady Lawrence; Mrs Nicolette Lay and family; Mrs Ann Ledwidge; Leeds Police Mounted Section; Julia Lenkenaw; Leominster Round Table; Anna Leslie; Sir Thomas Lethbridge; Mrs Lesley Lewis; Liverpool Police Mounted Section; Mrs Florence Lloyd; The Members of Lloyd's and Lloyd's Brokers; Nicholas and Julia Longe; Mervyn Longhurst; The Earl and Countess of Lonsdale; Charles and Marie-Louisa Lowther; Tony Lyons; Miss Jean Lywood; Irving McBratney; Nancy MacDonald; Flora McDowall; P.C. Dave McKay; Captain Barry McKie, Riding Master, The Household Cavalry Regiment; Neil MacKy; Sandy McNabb; Captain Toby Maddison, Queen's Royal Irish Hussars; Gerald and June Maddox; Alexander and Margaret Maitland; Andrew Maitland; Captain the Honourable Gerald Maitland Carew; Sylvia Major; Mrs Judy Malleson; Kathy Manock; Karen Mansell; The Mare and Colt, Kidderminster; Hugh Marriott; Mr and Mrs Masterman; Mr and Mrs Richard Matson and family; Mrs Joanna Matthews; Phyllis Maurice; Chief Inspector Roger Mayne; Frances Mecklenberg; Kath Meikle; Janet Miller; The Honourable Mrs Susan Milln; Father Dominic Milroy; Peter Milton; Patrick Mitford Slade; Dick and Jean Monks; Mr and Mrs Andrew Moore; Mr and Mrs Charles Moore; T. R. W. Moore; Peter Moores; Christopher Morris; Lieutenant Colonel R. J. Morrisey Paine, Commanding Officer HCR; Mary Moss; Sir Monty Moss; Moss Bros Ltd; Jim Moulder, Colchester Garrison Saddle Club; Mabel Mudge; Mrs Shirley Muirie; Mr and Mrs Peter Murray-Smith; Min Murray Threipland; Charles and Caroline Musker; Musto Waterproofs; The National Trust; National Westminster Bank plc; Jim Needham; K. Newman; the inhabitants of Newton Toney; Janet Niepokojczycka; North Yorkshire County Fire Service; North Yorkshire Police; The Lord Mayor of Norwich; Norwich Union Insurance Group; Mrs Jean Nurse; Nick Nuttall; Ross Nye; Mrs Oakden, Wynless Beck Stables, Windermere; Mr and Mrs Bill Oakey; Stephen Oates; The Old Ship, Padstow; The Old Trooper Inn, Padstow; The Old White Beare, Norwood Green; Margaret O'Neill; Mrs Nadine Orchard; Ordnance Survey Ltd; Nick O'Sullivan; Mr and Mrs Bernard Owen; Mr and Mrs Noël Page-Turner; Gay Park; Ted and Madeleine Parker; Paul Patten; Mary Paul; Alfred Peacock; Roger and Margaret Peacock; Mrs Peake's Trust; Mr and Mrs Pearn; Donald Pearse; Clare Peckham; Lyn Peers; Mr and Mrs Richard Perkins; Anthony and Charlotte Perry; Chief Inspector Andrew Petter, Metropolitan Mounted Police; Barry and Diane Pewter, Rayne Riding Centre; Bob and Lin Phillips, Wyke Equestrian Centre; Sue Pipe; Porterfield Films; Paula Powell; Oliver Prenn; Colin Prescott; Tracey Price; Richard and Nicky Pridham; Selwyn Pryor and family; The Psoriasis Association; Martin and Sarah Pumphrey; Major and Mrs Tony Pyman; Racal Telecommunications Group Ltd; Robert and Julia Raffety; Margaret Rainford; Pippa and Arnold Rakusen; Andrew Ralli; Fiona Ramsay; Mr and Mrs Gordon Ramsay; Sarah Ramsden; Jude Ratcliff; John Redvers and family; Mrs P. Reid; Mrs Megan Rhys-Jones; Mrs T. A. Richard; Simon Richey; Major Rodney Riddell; David Robertson; Stuart Rock; Anita Roddick, The Body Shop; Susan Rogers; Mrs Lisa Roper; The Rose and Crown, Harnham; Rose Farm, Drift; Lieutenant Colonel and Mrs Malcolm Ross; Graham Ross-Russell; The Rotary Club of Plymouth; The Rotary Club of Warrington; Marion Rundle; Philip Ryder-Davies; Gill Sabath; The Saddlers' Company; St Anne's College, Oxford; St Peter's Roman Catholic Primary School; Josie Sandford; Lord and Lady Sandys; Peter de Savary; Henry Scatt; Delia Secker Walker and family; Sennen Cove Fish Bar; Jason Shaw; Miss Maria Sheiderer; Melissa Shendrigg; Sarah Sherwin; The Shire Horse Society; Mrs Amanda Short; Jane Sidnell; Jennifer and Tracey Simms; René Skule; Christopher Smith; David Smith; Fiona Smith; Julia Smith; Lindsay Smith; Rachel Smith; Victoria Smith; Mr and Mrs A. H. Sneesby; Derek Sonell; Ian Southall; Helen Speakman; Christopher and Joanna Spicer; Mrs Eileen Stamers-Smith; Mrs Maggie Stanton, Teignbridge District Council; Dr Richard Staughton; Debbie Stead and family; Adrian Steger;

Mrs Jennifer Steinbugler; Avril Stephens and family; Ashley Stephenson, Balliff, Royal Parks; Madeleine Stickels; James Street; Barry Swain; Swaine Adeney Brigg and Sons Ltd; Ernest and Valerie Swinburn; Jane Talbot Smith; Tamar Cruising Company; Alan Taylor; John Taylor; Sonja Taylor; Tesco Ltd; Thames Valley Police Mounted Section; Peter Thirlwell; Angus and Margaret Thomas; Kieren Thomas; Mr and Mrs William Thomas; Linda Thompson; Piers and Vicky Thompson; Neil Thorburn; Piers Throssell and family; Olivia Timbs; Tommy's Cabs; Sarah Touabi; Trago Mills plc; Tuffnell's Parcel Express, Andover; Anna Turner and family; Canon John Turner, Lichfield Cathedral; Ken Turner; Tutbury Castle; Twiggy; Mrs J. Tyler; Jill Tyler; Ulverscroft Large Print Books; Amanda Ursell; Carl Uttley; Sarah Utwin; Maurice Vaillancourt; Peter Veitch; Mr Vennell; Peter and Sarah Vey; Tony Voden; Mrs Charles Volkers; Nigel Wakeley; Catherine Walker; Victoria Walker Sloan; June Warner; Major and Mrs Tony Warre; Phil Webb; Richard Webb; Ken Wellam; West Yorkshire County Fire Service; The Duke of Westminster; the Lord Mayor of Westminster, Elizabeth Flach; Gerry Whent; Patrick Whitehead; Viscount Whitelaw; Mrs Whitfield, The Pigeons, Curload; Whitford Plastics Ltd; Robin Wight; Mrs Eve Wilkinson; Lucy Wilkinson; Bernice and Gwynn Williams; Gary and Louise Williams; Keith Williams; Rhian Williams; Robin and Caroline Williams; Mrs Valerie Williams; Brian and Anne Willder; Davey 'Wonka' Willis; Tony Wills; Alistair Wilson; Mrs Maxine Wingfield; Sister Nora Wipp; Sir Charles and Lady Wolseley; Henry Woolston; Andrew Worrall; Giles Worsley; Sir Marcus and Lady Worsley; Michael and Nancy Wright; Sarah Wyld; P.C. Dale Yates; Yorkshire Ladies' Side Saddle Costume Display Team; John and Henrietta Young; Mrs Tessa Young-Jamieson; Zetland Hunt Kennels.

I would also like to thank Imogen Parker, Rupert Lancaster and Robert Lacey for their editorial good sense.

Finally, my greatest debt is to Mighty, George, who for the five months of the trip was my constant companion and friend. On his return to London he was put out to grass after pulling the Lord Mayor's coach, and spent six happy months of retirement at the Whitbread hop farm in Kent. Early in 1989 he developed a cancerous growth in his throat. It proved inoperable, so to spare him any pain he was put down in May. If there is a heaven for shire horses, I'm sure he will be there now.

The photographs between pages 118 and 119 are by Emma-Louise Ogilvy, with the exception of: first page, top, Anthony Appleby; second page, top and bottom, Catherine Bullen; fifth page, top left, *Newcastle Chronicle and Journal*, top right, the author; sixth page, top; seventh page, top, Catherine Bullen; seventh page, bottom; eighth page, top left, the author.